Take A Moment

Nina Kaye is a contemporary romance author who writes warm, witty and uplifting reads with a deeper edge. She lives in Edinburgh with her husband and much adored side-kick, James. In addition to writing, Nina enjoys swimming, gin and karaoke (preferably all enjoyed together in a sunny, seaside destination). Nina has previously published *The Gin Lover's Guide to Dating* and has also been a contender for the RNA Joan Hessayson Award.

Take A Moment

NINA KAYE

CANELO

First published in the United Kingdom in 2021 by

Canelo
31 Helen Road
Oxford OX2 0DF
United Kingdom

A CIP catalogue record for this book is available from the British Library.

Print ISBN 978 1 80032 473 2
Ebook ISBN 978 1 80032 474 9

Look for more great books at www.canelo.co

Printed and bound in Great Britain by Clays Ltd, Elcograf S.p.A.

1

For James and my family, who supported me through the most difficult time of my life.

Chapter 1

'Give me a bite. *Stop it*. You're such a tease.'

'I'll give you a bite… if you give me a kiss.'

'I'd give you a kiss anyway, monkey. You're so damn cute.'

'And you're beautiful.'

The nausea-inducing kissy slurping noises flood my consciousness yet again, and my patience finally combusts. Abandoning the email I'm typing, I snap the cover over my iPad screen and hastily gather my stuff. Ignoring the giggling whispers of 'what's her problem' and 'bet she's not getting any', I stagger down the aisle of the moving train carriage, seeking a table that isn't occupied by the rail network's answer to *Romeo and Juliet*. The train is busy, so I'm forced to walk through two carriages before I find another spot.

As I awkwardly manoeuvre my way into another four-seater table, nodding politely at, but barely acknowledging, the man occupying the seat opposite, I lose my grip on my belongings. My iPad falls into the aisle with a loud thunk.

'Allow me.' The man slides over from his window seat, retrieves my iPad and places it on the table in front of me.

'Thanks.' I meet his gaze with an appreciative look. I'm slightly taken aback as my senses focus on him. He's rather attractive: athletic looking, around thirty, with deep chocolate-brown eyes, mid-brown hair and a close-cut beard.

'No problem. Issues with your table neighbours?'

'Sorry?'

'Your armful of belongings suggests you've cut and run.'

I survey my things, gracelessly dumped on the table in front of me, and break into an amused smile. 'Spot on. I can zone most things out, but a pair of loud lovestruck teenagers are beyond my limit.'

'I hear you.' The man grins at me, revealing a sexy smile and a cute dimple on his left cheek. 'I'll keep it down, I promise.'

'No need. Unless your super-delicious girl- or boyfriend is in the loo and about to return and eat your face off.'

'You're safe. I have no significant other on this train. Or at all for that matter.'

I hesitate briefly, unsure if that disclosure of availability was intentional, or just a conversation filler.

'That's good. Two days at a conference has done horrible things to my inbox.' I pick up my iPad and start to scroll down the sea of unread emails, searching for the highest priorities.

'I'll leave you in peace then.' The man seems mildly disappointed.

I immediately feel a stab of guilt, though I know I shouldn't. Shaking it off, I tap away at the screen and start quickly firing off one response after another, my mind fixed on getting back up to speed as quickly as possible. Having the project board quarterly review first thing after my conference isn't ideal, but I'll be on it. Most people dread the scrutiny; I welcome the challenge.

After about an hour immersed in my emails, I start to feel bleary-eyed: a clear sign I need a break. It was a full-on conference, so it's not really surprising. I snap the cover over my iPad again and sit back in my seat, closing my eyes momentarily. When I open them, I catch my tablemate stealing a glance at me. Offering him a genuine smile in return, I decide there's no harm in striking up a conversation to pass the final half-hour of the journey. After two days of seminars and professional networking, I'm craving a bit of 'crap chat'.

'Do you live in Glasgow?' I ask him.

'No,' he replies. I can't place his accent apart from it's English. 'I'm heading there for a stag weekend. Mate from uni.'

'A stag weekend in Glasgow? *Good luck.*'

'Thanks, think I'll need it. Will be a lively one: there might just be a leopard print mankini involved.' He gives me a wink.

'Ouch.' I wince in sympathy for the poor groom.

'Not my doing, I must add. His friends from school. They're a bit wild.'

'I hope you enjoyed knowing him.'

'That's been on my mind too.' He chuckles and I find my eyes drawn to that cheek dimple. 'I've been on a couple of nights out with them before, so I've an idea what he's in for. Are you from Glasgow yourself?'

'Yup. Can't you tell?'

'I didn't want to be presumptuous.' He takes a swig from his bottle of mineral water. 'Not that familiar with Scottish accents.'

There's a short silence between us. I fiddle with my phone, while the man thumbs the pages of the book in front of him. Not quite the flowing 'crap chat' I was hoping for. More like the tongue-tiedness of a first date.

'You said you were at a conference. Anything interesting?' he asks eventually.

'Interesting to me, but job-related. So maybe not interesting to you.'

'What does that mean? Do I gather you enjoy your job?'

'Possibly more so than the average person would consider healthy. Anyhow, if you're not from Glasgow, where are you from?'

'I'm a Brummie. From Birmingham, born and bred.'

I pick up my phone and google the term. 'Ah, I see. A colloquial name for Birmingham or the Birmingham dialect. It's also a Portuguese surname, according to Wikipedia. Did you know that?'

'I did not.' He raises an eyebrow at me. 'And I'm not sure I'm any better off now I do. Do you verify everything you're told through your phone? Or is it just to make sure total strangers don't feed you false info?'

I replace my phone on the table. 'I'd say it's more of a bad habit.'

There's another slightly awkward silence, then he asks, 'Was the conference in Birmingham, then?'

I nod.

'What did you think of it? Had you been before this trip?'

'Yes, but not for years. I liked it. It's really changed.'

The man nods. 'It has. Birmingham's never been seen as a place to visit, but I reckon the city centre regeneration is putting it on the map.'

'It certainly appealed to me. In some ways, I preferred it to Glasgow. Didn't see as much as I'd hoped, but I loved the openness of it, like the coloured fountains at that plaza near the conference centre.'

'Centenary Square.'

'That's it. The canals are awesome too. I had drinks by the waterside with a few of the conference delegates I met.'

'You do seem to have enjoyed it.'

'I did.' I pause reflectively. 'Think if I ever had to go south for work, I'd certainly consider moving there.'

Though we haven't even introduced ourselves, we continue to chat. By the time the train is pulling into the platform at Glasgow Central, we're fairly well acquainted; as we're alighting from the train, we're at the stage of having a proper 'goodbye'.

'It was nice chatting to you.' I gather my stuff and get to my feet.

'You too. Good luck with the career.'

'And good luck with the stag do. Hope the groom makes it down the aisle in one piece.'

'Me too.'

We step down onto the platform separately, which acts as a natural opportunity for us to go our separate ways. But as I make my way towards the ticket barriers, I feel a hand touch my shoulder lightly. I turn and find myself looking once again into his unsettlingly attractive dark eyes. My stomach swirls in response to this.

'Don't suppose you've time for a quick drink?' he asks uncertainly. 'I don't need to be anywhere til this evening.'

I'm caught off guard by this advance. 'Oh, I err... sorry. I'm... engaged.'

His face falls and his eyes flicker to my left hand. 'Right. Shit. Sorry, I didn't mean to—'

'Don't be sorry' – the fingers of my right hand instinctively go to my ring finger protectively – 'you weren't to know. I'm flattered, honestly.'

'And I'm embarrassed. Think I'll just… head.'

Before I can say anything more, he offers me a cringing smile and a half-wave and disappears into the moving crowd of travellers. I chuckle out loud and give myself a little shake as I try to digest what just happened: in particular, the notably inappropriate feeling of disappointment that's hanging around me. What the hell is that about? It's not like I'm never going to find other men attractive now I'm getting married. But I've got Dom – the most amazing man in the world – and I'm completely besotted with him. And I've missed him something rotten while I've been away at the conference.

Carrying on through the ticket barriers, I make my way outside and hurry across the road to the prearranged pickup point I agreed with Dom. I quickly throw my case in the car boot and jump into the passenger seat so he can take off before a traffic warden books him, but he seems more concerned with greeting me.

'Hi, kitten. How was your journey?' His piercing blue eyes search mine.

'Long but fine.'

'I know it was only two nights but I missed you.'

He pulls me into a tender kiss, which I melt into welcomingly, enjoying the familiar citrusy scent of his eau de toilette, and the minty taste from the gum he's been chewing. Then he puts the car into gear and pulls out into the road. I gaze out of the window, watching the citizens of Glasgow going about their business as we zoom past them.

'Guess what?' I say suddenly. 'I just got asked out by the guy sitting across from me on the train. How crazy is that?'

'You did? I trust you politely declined.' Dom chuckles.

'I considered his offer, but I think I'll stick with you.'

'*Cheeky*. Sooner we get that engagement ring back on your finger the better. Don't want some other bloke stealing you away from me.'

'Like that would happen. The jeweller called, by the way. It's ready for collection – and apparently, it's now a perfect size match to my wedding ring. Can't believe how close our big day is getting.'

'I know, Lex.' He reaches across and squeezes my hand affectionately. 'Just five months to go. I can't wait for you to become Mrs Dominic Lauder.'

'Me neither.' I gaze at him adoringly, the man from the train already forgotten, as I look forward to an evening relaxing with Dom.

Chapter 2

'Dom? Have you seen my keys? I'm going to be late for work.'

Dom's handsome bearded face appears round the edge of the bathroom door, having just emerged from the shower, his wet brown hair slicked back. 'When did you last have them?'

'Hmmm… don't know.' I try to persuade my sluggish Monday morning brain to recount my movements over the last twenty-four hours.

'What were you wearing yesterday? Think I unlocked the door when we got back from the supermarket.'

I have a thought, then rush to the wooden chair in the bedroom. Pouncing on my fleece, I let out a triumphant whoop as I hear the familiar jangle come from the pocket. 'Thanks, lover. You're the best. Don't know what I'd do without you.'

'You're welcome,' he yells from behind the now closed bathroom door. 'Have a good day, kitten.'

I blow a little kiss towards the bathroom, despite the fact I know Dom can't see me, then sprint out the door of our tenement apartment.

A few hours later, I'm hunched over, gasping for breath. My regular lunchtime run is not going to plan today.

'Are you OK?' My best friend, Sasha, doubles back and jogs on the spot in front of me, concern etched across her face. 'Maybe it wasn't such a good idea to skip lunch.'

'I'm fine. Think I may have a cold coming on. Been a bit off the last few days.' I'm panting like a tired dog, feeling the burn in my lungs, my muscles, and on my weatherbeaten cheeks.

'Maybe you should take a break from running?' Sasha suggests as she continues to bob up and down in front of me, Glasgow's Kelvingrove Park with its colourful explosion of spring flowers providing an appealing backdrop behind her. 'You shouldn't work out if you're sick. A week won't make a difference. Your wedding's still four and a half months away.'

As my breathing begins to settle, I straighten up, piercing Sasha with my well-practised *are-we-seriously-having-this-conversation* look: the one I generally save for my mother when she harps on about irrelevant or unnecessary stuff. 'Sasha, how long have you known me?'

'Oh, Lex, don't start—'

'If you don't want me to start, then why play surrogate mother? I already have a real one who melts my head every chance she gets.' I place my left hand on my hip to punctuate my remark, while allowing just the hint of a cheeky grin to sneak through.

'OK, I hear you. You've a lot going on right now. I'm just... *concerned*.'

'Well, don't be. I'm fine. I may have a lot on, but it's stuff that's really important to me: great career, great man

– soon to be my husband. I'm planning the wedding of my dreams, Sash. And I love running – plus it's good for me. That's all *good* stress. One little cold is hardly going to floor me.'

'I know. I get all that.' Sasha comes to a standstill. She chews her lip, uncertain whether to risk another ear-bashing or take the easy option and play ball. She opts for the former. 'I'm just saying planning a wedding is one of the most stressful things you can do, even if it is good stress as you say – and you're only a few months into your new job. If you're getting sick, it can all add up.'

I study my friend's concerned face and smile at her affectionately. Sash and Lex. Joined at the hip since ninety-three. Her, the hesitant worrier. Me, the impulsive go-getter. Such opposites. But together, a perfect harmony.

'Sash, I'm fine. I promise.' My tone is gentler than before. 'But that's reminded me, we need to talk wedding stuff. So, maybe we can walk the rest of the way back to the office.'

'Fabulous idea.'

Sasha zips up her hooded top to protect her from the chill of the spring breeze. She links arms with me and we start to amble along the tarmacked path, breathing in the delicate scent from the flowering cherry blossom trees.

'How's the entertainment side of things going, by the way?' she asks. 'Did Dom cave on the karaoke?'

'Of course he did.' I crack a sly smile. 'He knows what's good for him. Karaoke will be straight after the buffet – when everyone's loosened up enough to have a go. Then the band will finish off the night with the classics.'

'Is "Loch Lomond" going to be your big finale? I love that song so much.'

'Yup.'

'Oh, I can't wait! It will be totally amazing. And seeing you sing in your wedding dress, with that incredible voice. You're going to blow everyone away.' She starts to flap her free hand in front of her face as her eyes redden and the emotion threatens to spill over.

'Calm yourself. I'm hardly Leona Lewis.'

'I know that.' Sasha dabs at the corners of her eyes with her sleeves. 'But you're way better than you realise. What are you going to sing? Have you had any thoughts?'

'I've been plotting.' I grin mischievously. 'It's a surprise though.'

'Oh, come on. You can tell me.'

'Nope. This one is between me and the karaoke compère. You'll have to wait.'

'Bah humbug.' Sasha pouts at me, but I know she's grudgingly respecting my silence on this.

I decide a swift change of subject is needed. 'So, other stuff. We need some shoes to go with that stunning dress of yours.'

My diversion works a treat.

'I can't wait to try on my bridesmaid dress again. It's just *sooo* gorgeous,' Sasha gushes. 'What were you thinking? I wondered about strappy silver, bit of bling as a contrast to the teal?'

'And that's why I love you.' I pull her in for a sideways hug, trying to ignore the fact that my body feels like a lead weight. 'Exactly what I was thinking.'

–

Back at our Anderston-based office, after a quick shower and change we head in opposite directions, an afternoon of wedding shoe shopping synced in our smartphone calendars for the coming weekend.

As I hurry along the fourth-floor corridor to my project meeting, I pass a few colleagues from the marketing department where Sasha works, and offer polite greetings as I go. My legs feel heavy, my muscles still complaining, making me wonder if Sasha's right. Maybe I should take a short break from running – just for a week, til I'm over my cold. Don't want to risk putting myself out of the game even longer by being stubborn. That *would* get in the way of me reaching my goal weight for my big day.

I reach the meeting room and discover that my project team are already there.

'Hi, everyone.' I grin as I scan each face in the room. 'Great timing, as ever. You *really* do like to make me look bad.'

There's a collective chuckle in response.

'How are we all?' I half-glance at them as I haul my laptop and project documents out of my overfilled bag. As I do, my hand seems to slip, and my papers make a dramatic bid for escape, scattering across the carpeted floor.

'Dammit,' I curse, bending to pick them up. 'Sorry guys. Let me sort these and we'll get started.' Two members of my project team rush forward to help me.

'Afternoon, Alex.' An affable female voice comes from behind me. 'Good to see you in control as always.'

I stand up quickly, feeling the protest in my aching thigh muscles as I do, and turn to face my boss. 'Laura, hi. Didn't see you there. Are you joining us?'

'Thought I would today.' She smiles supportively at me. 'Get a feel for how things are coming along. That OK with you?'

'Of course.' I gesture to the only empty seat round the table. 'Make yourself comfortable. Some great progress we can share with you. The team have been at it hard, and the results are really showing.'

I beam round the room at my fifteen-strong project team, who are mirroring my gesture, appreciative of the good press in front of the big boss.

'Well, just carry on as normal. Pretend I'm not here.' Laura makes for the back of the room.

I kick off the meeting and start to run through the weekly actions, seeking input from the team on their various tasks. As I do, I become aware that my concentration is not as sharp as it usually is. I'm dealing with the short responses all right, but for some reason I'm struggling to follow the more in-depth explanations being offered.

'Sorry... so you're saying the system user testing is not covering all required areas?' I ask John, our business analyst on the project.

'That's not *exactly* what I'm saying, Alex.' John shakes his head. 'In theory, it is covering all areas. But I'm concerned about the level to which the testing is being done: the lack of detail in the test scripts, particularly for the new accounting processes.'

'Right.' I pause, giving my head a shake as if to throw off whatever is causing my brain to feel like cotton wool. 'So... what are we going to do about this?' I'm intentionally stalling to try to get my jumbled thoughts together.

'I was hoping you would tell me.' John cocks his head quizzically. 'As I said, I've exhausted all options. Perhaps this now needs to be escalated to the project board?'

'Right… yes, of course.' I surreptitiously pinch my leg under the desk to try to jolt myself out of this odd, fatigued state. 'I'll escalate it. OK, what's next?'

As the team member next to John starts sharing their update, I find I'm unable to take in a word they're saying. I am not just below par; my inability to function properly is starting to make me anxious. What's going on? Is it because Laura's here? No, it can't be. Laura and I get on great. She's joined meetings before. Then a thought hits me. Maybe it's my cold. Or worse, the flu. Please, I so don't have time for the flu.

'Alex? Do you agree?'

I snap back to the conversation. 'Oh… sorry. Eh… yes. Definitely, Sandra.'

'Really?' Laura suddenly pipes up from the back of the room, making it clear my fifty-fifty gamble hasn't paid off. 'I'm not sure I agree with that, Alex. And I'm surprised *you* do.' She's eyeing me curiously.

'I… eh… gosh, no, you're right, what am I thinking?' I grab the project update in front of me, desperate for a clue as to what this conversation is about, but the words are blurred, and I realise I'm seeing double.

'Alex, is everything OK?' Laura asks. 'You look a bit… hot and bothered. Maybe get some water from the cooler?'

I realise that must be it. I'm dehydrated from my run. And starving too. That on top of a cold isn't going to help me at all.

'Good idea. Just give me a moment.'

I get up and move quickly towards the meeting room door. As I do, the room swims in front of me, making it difficult to keep my balance. In an attempt to steady myself, I try to grab the door handle, but instead make contact with nothing but fresh air. This proves too much for my already struggling body and before I realise what's happening, I've slipped on something and I'm falling sideways. The last thing I'm aware of as I claw at the air, trying frantically to rescue myself, is a collective gasp from behind me, followed by a sudden sharp, shooting burst of pain in my head.

Chapter 3

'Alex? Lex, hon. Can you hear me?' Sasha's voice sounds distant, like it's emanating from another world.

'She's starting to come round.' Another faint voice enters my consciousness. 'Alex? Alex, can you hear me, sweetheart?'

I open my eyes slowly, unable to communicate as my disoriented senses attempt to comprehend my environment: intermittent beeping, flashing lights in front of my eyes, blurry heads bobbing above me with muddled voices, the smell of well-worn carpet. Then throbbing pain.

'Oh… oww…' I whimper. 'What's… my head… so sore…'

I'm so groggy and dizzy, I can barely get the words out. I try instead to sit up but feel an immediate resistance on my shoulder.

'Stay where you are, sweetheart,' a caring but commanding female voice – the owner of the hand gently pressing against my body – instructs me. 'Don't try and get up. You've hit your head and we're concerned about your neck because of the way you fell. You need to stay completely still until we put a neck brace on you and get you onto a spinal board. Just answer yes or no – do you understand what I'm telling you?'

'I… yes… am I… hospital? Smells… hospital.'

'You're still in your office, Alex,' the woman, who smells clinical, reassures me. 'I'm Jill. I'm a paramedic and I'm here to look after you.'

'Office… *paramedic*…' I repeat, confusion clouding my mind until it all starts to come back to me, and I begin to panic. 'Wait… oh, no… my team… the meeting… are they…'

'Sshhh… they're not here, Alex,' Jill soothes me. 'Forget about all that. It's just you, me, my colleague, Dennis, and your friend, Sasha, who's going to talk to you in just a second, OK?'

'OK.' Tears begin to track their way down my face, just below my temples: partly from the pain and shock, but also from a rising sense of humiliation that this has happened in my place of work.

'Alex, we're going to take you to hospital,' says Jill. 'Sasha's going to come with you and your fiancé's going to meet us there. Now, I just need to do some basic checks with you. Can you tell me what day it is?'

'Eh… Monday.' I blink at Jill, trying to take her in properly, but my brain doesn't seem to be able to connect the different parts of her. She's still more of a blur.

'That's great, Alex. And what city are you in?'

'Glasgow.'

'You're doing really well,' Jill continues to encourage me. 'Now, can you tell me how many fingers I'm holding up?'

Jill's hand appears in my sphere of vision. I try my best to focus on it, but my eyes refuse to cooperate; fingers seem to be swimming everywhere.

'Five?' I try.

'How about now?'

'Three?' My trickle of tears turns into a sob from being unable to do anything but guess.

'OK, sweetheart. That's enough for now.' Jill gives my hand a gentle squeeze. 'We're going to get you onto the spinal board in a moment. Sasha's going to keep you company while we get it sorted. Meantime – really important – I need you to tell me straight away if you start to feel sick, and I need you to keep talking to us, even if you feel sleepy. Can you do that?'

'Uh-huh,' I whisper through my tears.

'Good girl.' Jill strokes my hand before moving away towards her colleague. Then I hear her say, 'There's visual disturbance. We need to get her to the hospital asap.'

Before I have a chance to process this and react, I hear Sasha's voice, and a warm hand grasps mine.

'Lex, hon. Oh, I knew something wasn't right. I shouldn't have let you get back to work without having something to eat and drink.'

'No… Sash… not your fault.' I cling to her hand, trying to make out her fuzzy features. 'My stupid fault… should have listened. Did they see? My team. So… humiliated.'

She dabs at my teary face with a tissue. 'Don't worry about that. Everyone's just concerned. I was so worried when you didn't wake up at first. I'm still worried…' She tails off, realising that she's not helping to keep me calm.

'I'll be fine.' I smile weakly at her blurry profile. 'Just a silly fall, right? Serves me right… total bridezilla.'

'Aww, you're not. You've been great.' Sasha squeezes my hand, but her voice is choked with emotion.

'Is that a sense of humour sneaking through?' Jill the paramedic appears above me again, only recognisable by her voice. 'That's a good sign. Let's get you sorted and across to the hospital.'

Several hours later, I'm lying propped up on a trolley in a dreary cubicle within Glasgow Royal Infirmary's Accident and Emergency department. It's clinical in every way: the smell of disinfectant, lights that are uncomfortably bright, just a mobile monitor keeping an eye on my vitals and two black plastic chairs for company. The curtain protecting my privacy on three sides is a cold uninviting shade of arctic blue.

I've been poked and prodded, stuffed into machines and asked to repeat what happened several times over to different medical professionals. I'm exhausted and sore, with seriously wounded pride. I want nothing more than to go home to my meteor-sized sofa and cuddle up with Dom.

As I'm pondering my chances of getting home, wincing from the razor-sharp pain that intermittently shoots through the omnipresent ache in my head, the curtain to my cubicle is whisked open and Dom appears with an armful of goodies, looking mighty pleased with the bounty from his hunt.

'Got a couple of sandwiches from WHSmith.' He plonks his broad, masculine frame down onto one of the plastic chairs, which seems to sigh a little under his weight. 'Bought your two favourites: free-range egg and watercress, and chicken and avocado mayo. Also got some crisps – those pea sticks you like. Thought you might want some chocolate to cheer you up as well.'

I eye the assortment of confectionery bars on his lap. 'Thanks, lover. I'll take the chicken and avocado. And the pea sticks. No chocolate. Behaving like a lunatic bride-to-be and landing myself in hospital is no reason to abandon my pre-wedding diet altogether. Or to indulge in self-sympathy.'

'Don't you think you're being a little hard on yourself?' Dom dumps his offerings on the chair next to him, then hands me my chosen items. 'No one thinks you're a lunatic. But you said yourself you thought this happened because you *did* go too far with your diet. You need to eat to help yourself recover quickly – and you also need a little TLC.'

'I *am* eating.' I tear open the sandwich pack and take a bite as if to prove it. 'I just don't want to ruin my efforts unnecessarily. Especially as I've been told I won't be doing any running for a couple of weeks – at *least*.'

As the creaminess of the mayo hits my taste buds and the soft avocado squirms around my mouth, I feel a sudden gagging reflex in my gullet, followed by a wave of nausea. I fake a small cough to cover this up, all too aware that Dom noticing will lead him to the view that I need to stay in hospital overnight.

'OK, sure.' Dom regards me with some doubt. 'You know I love you for you. Right? Not for how you look.'

'Oh, stop it. I know that. I'm doing this for me, not you. I had you trapped a long time ago. You're not getting away.' I give him a mischievous wink, ignoring the unpleasant swirling feeling in my stomach.

'It's so good to see you smiling, kitten.' He hovers over me closely, giving me a waft of his delicious eau de toilette, and plants a firm, affectionate kiss on my lips. 'You worried us all there.'

'I'll be fine.' I continue to chew reluctantly. 'You must be hungry too. Eat the other sandwich. I'll be getting out of here later, so I won't need both.'

'Did they tell you that while I was away?'

'Nope. But there's no way I'm spending the night here.'

'Lex.' Dom takes my hand in his. 'I'm not sure it's a good idea for you to be coming home. And I'm not sure you should have unrealistic expectations. Only hours ago, you were lying unconscious on your office floor.'

'And I'm fine now. I can see properly again and everything.' As I offer him my most confident smile, my mouth unexpectedly begins to water and there's a sudden lurch in my abdomen. 'Oh, man… I'm going to— *sick bowl.*'

Dom demonstrates Olympic medal-winning reflexes as he grabs the bowler-hat-shaped sick bowl from the end of my trolley and whips it in front of me, just as my undigested sandwich makes a sudden and unpleasant reappearance. Holding my hair out of the way with his other hand, Dom tries to soothe me as I battle between trying to control the spasms in my oesophagus and coping with the searing pain in my head that explodes like fireworks with every fresh round of retching.

As I'm starting to regain some composure, the curtain is pulled back and the first doctor I saw when I arrived in A&E, Dr Amani, enters with a nurse. The nurse takes the sick bowl from Dom and leaves, while the doctor swooshes the curtain back over again to safeguard my privacy.

'How are you doing?' Dr Amani offers me an empathetic smile. 'Not so good, it seems.'

'I'm fine. I really am.' I try for upbeat, but the tremor in my voice and the spatters of puke down my hospital gown tell a different story.

'Alex, you have a moderate concussion.' He cocks his head slightly. 'You are a good way away from fine. And I am afraid that means you will need to stay in overnight, maybe even for a couple of nights.'

'But...' I look up at him helplessly.

'We need to monitor you. There is no spinal injury, but you do have some swelling on your brain and it is our responsibility to make sure you are totally fit to leave. The fact that you have just been sick tells me you most certainly are not.'

'Right.'

I feel Dom's hand clasp mine reassuringly.

'We are going to admit you to the neurology ward,' says Dr Amani. 'The consultant there will see you tomorrow morning. She is going to review your scan results, first thing.'

'And then I might get out tomorrow?'

'Why don't we take it one step at a time?' He picks up the chart at the end of my trolley and scribbles something down. 'We need to check on some possible anomalies in your scan. The additional MRI scan we did.'

'Anomalies?' Dom looks alarmed. 'What do you mean by anomalies?'

'There is nothing to be overly concerned about at this stage.' Dr Amani expertly placates him. 'It is due process to have an expert review the results. We just need to rule things out.'

'What do you need to rule out?' I'm mildly irritated by this unexpected diversion.

'As I said, one step at a time.' Dr Amani smiles kindly at me. 'Now try to rest and let that head of yours recover.'

He disappears from the cubicle with the swiftness of a magician, leaving Dom and me looking at each other blankly.

Chapter 4

I wake early the next morning from a fractured sleep: a combination of endless disturbance through the night from the desperately unwell patients in my shared room, the lack of familiarity of my surroundings, and the unrelenting thudding pain in my head, despite being dosed up with strong painkillers and anti-inflammatory drugs. The ward smells the same as the A&E department – cleaning products mixed with medical disinfectant and cotton wool. Although it doesn't feel like the best environment for rest and recovery – which seems ironic given that's part of the reason I'm here – I do now at least have a proper bed with crisp white linen and a more robust curtain to shut out the rest of the ward (though not the noise). There's also a wooden locker built into my bedside unit, housing my personal possessions. Thankfully this means I now have my precious iPad to distract myself.

Bleary-eyed, I thank the man who delivers my breakfast from his trolley, pulling across my tray table so that I can eat from my propped-up position. Having been admitted too late the previous evening to choose my own breakfast, I've ended up with the menu selection made by one of the ward's previous tenants. Someone lucky enough to have escaped this pseudo prison – although I sincerely hope it wasn't via the morgue.

I survey the contents of my tray: a glass of fresh orange juice, a bowl of cornflakes, two slices of white toast accompanied by individual portions of butter and jam, and a plate with a metal cover over it. I tentatively lift it and immediately regret doing so as I'm engulfed by the smell of cooked egg. This sends a fresh wave of nausea sweeping through my hypersensitised body. I slam the cover back down, pluck the orange juice from the tray and push the tray table as far away as I can.

At least there's one advantage to having a head that feels like an overworked church bell: if it lasts much longer, I'll meet my goal wedding weight well in advance of my self-imposed deadline. As this thought cheers me slightly, another moves across my consciousness, blocking out my little ray of sunshine. Dr Amani's words from the evening before: 'some possible anomalies in your scan'. What did he mean by that? It seemed to unsettle Dom, although a lot of things unsettle Dom. That probably means it isn't anything to concern me. It would be useful to know when I'll be seeing the consultant though, not least so that I can find out how much longer I'll have to endure these breakfasts.

'Excuse me?' I call to a passing nurse. 'Do you have any idea what time the doctor will be seeing me today?'

She approaches the end of my bed and takes a quick look at my chart.

'You've been assigned to Dr Harlow. She'll be doing her rounds late morning, so a few hours yet. Probably best you settle back and relax. Are you still feeling sick?' She surveys my untouched breakfast tray.

'Oh... a little.' I shrug. 'But not as bad as yesterday. At least my juice has stayed down this time.' I tap my glass of orange juice.

'That is a good sign.' The nurse smiles at me encouragingly, then walks away.

For a few moments, I just lie quietly, trying to persuade my body to surrender to the rest I keep being told I need. It doesn't work. As someone not used to doing nothing, I'm soon looking for something to occupy me. Reaching over, I pull my phone and iPad out of my bedside locker. It's early, but Dom will be up and getting ready for work by now. I tap out a WhatsApp message:

> Morning lover. Hope you got more sleep
> than I did. Been told the doctor will see me
> late morning. Fed up and bored. xx

While waiting for Dom to reply, I open the BBC News app and scroll through the top stories. I'm halfway through reading about the latest political drama at Westminster when a WhatsApp badge notification appears at the top of my screen, indicating that Dom has replied. I immediately click into it:

> Morning kitten. Sorry you didn't sleep well.
> I didn't either without you beside me. Want
> me there for support when the consultant
> comes round? My boss will be cool with
> that. Dx

I smile at Dom's message. That's exactly why I'm marrying him. He's my rock. Always there when I need him, whether I know it or not. The latter is certainly the more common occurrence and sometimes a source of contention due to my independent streak – I prefer to believe I only need myself to get by. But in this case, probably all I need is a set of discharge papers and a lift home. I'm sure if I was dying, they'd have mentioned this. It's probably just a smudge on the scan that's made it hard to read or something. I've had inconclusive smear tests, which have been fine when they redid them. Reassuring Dom that I'm fine, I wish him a good day at work and tell him I'll keep him posted on when I'm getting out.

I switch back to the news, but I'm restless and it's not long before I cast my phone aside in search of something more practically focused. Ignoring the persistent pounding in my head, I power up my iPad and spend some time browsing different sites for wedding shoes. It's unlikely Sasha and I will manage our planned shopping expedition this weekend, so some early research will help save time when we do eventually go out together. I may be restless but I'm not feeling that sharp. I manage to create a shortlist of shoes for both of us: mine focused around beautiful high-heeled, lace-detailed peep toes, while 'bit of bling' strappy silver sandals make up the top choices for Sasha.

While pondering what else on my wedding to-do list I could use this unexpected opportunity to address, I realise I'm actually quite beat. My head injury has clearly knocked me off par, perhaps helped along by the cold I'm developing – though I note that no respiratory symptoms have appeared. Deciding that maybe it's best to do as the nurse suggested and try to rest for a bit, I lie back and close my eyes.

–

It feels like ten minutes later when I wake with a start, groggy, a path of drool tracking its way down the side of my chin. I quickly grab a tissue from my bedside cabinet and wipe it away.

'How do you feel now?'

I look up and see the nurse I spoke to earlier standing at the end of my bed. 'OK, thanks. Think I manged to sleep for a few minutes.'

'You've been out for three hours.' The nurse points at the clock above the door on the ward. 'Will have done you good. I was about to wake you. Dr Harlow has started her rounds.'

'Oh, right.' I perk up slightly, hoping that means I'll be home by late afternoon.

'Expect she'll be with you soon…' The nurse turns away distractedly. 'Oh, Elizabeth, love, you need to keep your nightgown *on.*'

She makes a beeline for an elderly patient who is heading for the ward's main corridor starkers. I watch this scene unfold in front of me, feeling a tinge of sadness that poor Elizabeth is so unwell, she no longer possesses the shackling inhibitions that keep so many of us in check. But I also can't help chuckling a little as the nurse wrestles Elizabeth back to her bed and quickly pulls the curtain round just as an elderly male patient starts to wolf-whistle from the corridor. The cruel reality of ageing. Having a sense of humour must be an essential quality for the staff on this ward.

To pass the time until Dr Harlow visits my bedside, I switch my iPad back on. My finger is hovering over the Safari icon, ready to resume my wedding-related research, when I spot the app for my work emails. Unable to resist, I bring up my inbox and scroll through the unopened messages from the afternoon before. Most of them are business as usual, but there's also a thread titled 'Re:

Contingency for Finance Systems Project'. Curious, I tap on the latest reply and scroll to the bottom so I can read from the beginning. As I take in the words before me, I feel a sense of anger rising.

'No. NO. *Definitely not*,' I say out loud. 'Laura, what are you doing?'

They're putting plans in place for a temporary project lead to take over in my absence. What *is* Laura doing? She has no idea how long I'm going to be off. Neither do I yet. But one thing's clear. It will be for as little time as possible. Hell, I'll be back next week if I get the all clear by then. It's only Tuesday. There's plenty of recovery time between now and Monday.

I send an email to Laura to this effect and impatiently tap the side of my iPad with my fingers while I wait for her reply. It arrives quickly and her message is clear. I'm off sick, which means I've to stay away from my work emails or anything work-related. Full stop. It's a message that's padded out with supportive words, concern and querying how I'm doing, but all I can focus on is the line that says Alan Davies, my deputy project lead, is about to take control of my project plan, my team and my board reports.

As I'm working myself up into a well-pulverised stew, I initially miss the approach of people to my bedside, looking up only when someone starts hauling the curtain noisily open.

'Oh, hello.' I force a smile, wrenching myself away from my work-related crisis, wondering why I have so many visitors.

'Alexandra. Good morning.' The oldest of three doctors, a very tall, thin greying woman, who smells a bit like my late grandmother's wardrobe and sounds like she's swallowed a broken harmonica, addresses me. 'I am

Dr Harlow. I understand you had quite a bump to the head yesterday.'

'I did, yes.' I hit the button to lock my iPad and give her my full attention. 'Please, call me Alex.'

'Of course.' She nods stiffly, then gestures to her companions. 'I am accompanied by two medical students this morning. They are here only to observe and further their learning. Are you comfortable to continue the conversation with them in attendance, Alexandra?'

I glance at the two students hanging at the back, one male, one female, peering at me like I'm some newly discovered species. Although Dr Harlow is asking my permission – and she's doing it very politely – I don't really feel I have a choice. It reminds me of when I was a child and got a telling-off for asking my mother if Sasha could stay overnight, when Sasha was standing right there. I did it on purpose because it meant my mother couldn't say no. Karma. Serves me right.

'OK… sure.' I half-smile at the two students, who immediately shuffle forward to get a better look at me.

'Thank you, Alexandra.' Dr Harlow attempts an amiable smile but it's so forced it makes her look constipated.

'It's Alex.' I bristle slightly, not used to hearing my full name, and not particularly liking it.

'Of course.' Dr Harlow purses her badly liplined lips. 'Shall we get on then? Firstly, I know you have been through this a few times, but would you mind awfully telling me what happened to you yesterday?'

Really? Why does no one write this stuff down? I sigh inwardly to hide my frustration.

'Yes, I can do that,' I reply. 'I was out for a run yesterday lunchtime, something I've been doing regularly for the last few months…'

I reluctantly take Dr Harlow through my well-worn story from beginning to end. She doesn't ask any questions, just listens intently, giving absolutely nothing away, while her protégés watch on, totally mesmerised.

'So, tell me, how are you feeling today?' she asks once I'm done. 'Any more nausea? Double vision? How are you feeling generally?'

I do a quick self-check. 'I'm OK. Felt a bit nauseous at breakfast time, but I kept down my orange juice, so that's good. No more double vision.' I hold up my index finger in front of my eyes to confirm this. 'I only had that before the fall. Afterwards, everything was just really blurred, but that only lasted a few hours. Generally, I'm all right, other than a sore head, some fatigue and difficultly concentrating. Probably just be a cold coming on.'

'I see.' Dr Harlow nods, while the two students seem to lean in even further. 'And these symptoms: the double vision, the fatigue. Have you had them before, Alexandra?'

Seriously? She can get a medical degree, but she can't remember what name to call me by? I furrow my brow but refrain from pointing this out. Probably best I keep her on side if I want to get home today.

'Not that I can remember.' I try to recount any similar episodes, but nothing comes to mind. 'I've been fatigued like this before, but that's just been my body fighting off some kind of cold or viral infection that's doing the rounds at work. I don't get properly ill that often. Lucky that way. My fiancé says if I wasn't so damn clumsy, I'd be the perfect package.'

'Have you always been clumsy?' Dr Harlow asks.

I mull this over. 'Eh… no, actually. It's pretty much just been the last few years. It's because I'm so busy with work and other stuff. Always having to do everything on fast-forward.'

My eyes dart to the male student, who's had some kind of spontaneous reaction to this statement as if what I've said excites him. The moment he clocks my curious glance, his expression turns to one of fright, then stone.

'Tell me more about that, Alexandra.' Dr Harlow zones in on me. 'In what way are you clumsy?'

'Oh, you know, just walking into things, I'm not great at catching. Nothing out of the ordinary.'

A sound like air escaping from a balloon erupts from the male student's mouth. He immediately turns a stunning shade of scarlet.

'Roderick, perhaps you need some water for that throat?' Dr Harlow's voice is steely.

Roderick looks crestfallen as he scuttles off.

'Thank you, Alexandra,' says Dr Harlow. 'Would you mind awfully if I did a few simple tests with you?'

'No, that's fine,' I say. 'Are these to check on my concussion?'

'They are to check your nervous system response.'

'Right.' I rub my pounding head, unsure what that means.

Dr Harlow proceeds to perform some kind of sorcery as she carries out a number of bizarre visual and physical checks. She has me touch my nose, then her finger, repeatedly, asks me to resist as she pushes her hand against my arms and legs, and gets me to stand on the spot with my eyes closed and then to walk in a straight line, heel to toe. Finally, she asks me to sit on the edge of the bed while she taps at my knees with a small hammer. All the time this theatre is taking place, the remaining student peers at me from behind Dr Harlow, like an inquisitive meerkat.

Once she's finished her checks, Dr Harlow invites me to lie back on the bed. By this point I'm relieved to be able to do so, wondering how on earth I'm going to make it back to work on Monday if I'm this exhausted from a physical examination. My balance is also off, probably from the concussion.

'I realise I'm not in the best form.' I'm still panting a little as I say this. 'But is there any chance I'm going to get home today?'

'Definitely not today,' Dr Harlow confirms. 'But perhaps in a day or two.'

OK, that I can live with. Monday could still be on the radar, as long as this fatigue lifts.

'So, my concussion isn't too bad?' I ask.

'Alexandra.' Dr Harlow peers at me over her tortoiseshell-rimmed glasses. 'Did Dr Amani mention to you yesterday that there were some anomalies in your MRI scan?'

'He did, yes. Said you were going to review them?'

'I've reviewed the results.' Dr Harlow fixes me with her clinical gaze. 'Alexandra, there's no easy way to tell you this. Dr Amani was correct in what he thought he had seen on the scan yesterday.'

'Which was?' I suddenly feel uncomfortable with where this conversation is heading.

'I shall explain so you understand the full picture. Normally we would not do an MRI scan for a concussion. Only a CT scan. Dr Amani was concerned by your account of your fall, notably your double vision. He thought it important to complete an MRI scan and spotted a couple of irregularities – some damage to your brain. We call them lesions.'

'Some what? What does that mean? Are you telling me I've got a brain tumour or something?'

'No. You do not have cancer, Alexandra—'

'Well, thank the shining stars for that.' I let out a premature sigh of relief.

'What you do have…' Dr Harlow continues. '…is an autoimmune condition called multiple sclerosis. Or MS, as you may know it.'

Chapter 5

'Sorry… what?' Suddenly, I feel like I'm trapped in a bad dream. 'I'm in hospital for a concussion. I just had a stupid fall.'

'I realise this is a lot to take in,' says Dr Harlow. 'In particular, as you had no awareness of your condition. It is generally not diagnosed in this way.'

'Hang on.' I stare at her in disbelief. 'I'm still stuck at… *what*?'

'Would you like me to explain some more about what MS is, Alexandra?'

'*No*. I want you to make sense. And I want you to call me Alex. Is that really so hard?'

'Of course. My apologies.' Dr Harlow seems totally unperturbed by my reaction.

'This can't be right.' I shake my head. 'I know what MS is and I don't have it. I'm healthy – well, not right now obviously because I have a cold and a concussion. But normally, I'm busy and active and successful. I have a really good career. I'm planning my wedding. I'm on top of *everything*. How could I do all that if I have MS?'

'As I said, I realise this is a lot to take in.'

Dr Harlow removes her glasses and sits down on one of the chairs beside me. Her shadow – aka the medical student – immediately follows suit.

'It's not a lot to take in.' I exhale loudly in frustration. 'You've just got it wrong.'

'I wish we did, believe me. Medical professionals always want to be wrong when it comes to the diagnosis of life-limiting illness. But I am confident of this diagnosis. It is my responsibility to communicate this to you, as well as provide you with the treatment and support you need.'

'MS is a death sentence. If you're right, my life is basically over. I can't afford for you to be right.'

'That is not actually correct. Your life expectancy is not directly reduced by MS, although secondary complications can be a problem – particularly when the disease is well progressed. It is primarily your quality of life that will be impacted. There is no known cure for MS, but there are some effective treatments available to you. It appears to be in its early stages, and though it is hard to be sure at this point, early indications suggest it to be the relapsing-remitting type.'

'Right.' I stare at the blanket covering my legs, unable to deal with any more of this.

'We will do some further tests to check there is no damage to your spinal cord,' Dr Harlow continues, oblivious to my need to terminate this conversation right now. 'And we can only rule out the progressive type once we have monitored your disease pattern for some time—'

'OK, well thanks.' I cut her off. 'I think I'd like to rest now. I'm very tired.'

'Of course.' Dr Harlow finally seems to get the message. She and her mini-me stand and move towards the curtain. 'I understand that you need some time to digest this. I would like to talk to you some more about the treatment and support available to you, but we can do that later. Perhaps with your fiancé there for support?'

'Thanks,' I mumble as she pulls back the curtain. The two of them disappear.

I sit in silence for a moment, paralysed into inaction, while my usually pragmatic mind tries unsuccessfully to reboot itself. What the hell was she talking about? How can I possibly have MS? These people around me, they're sick. Really sick. But I'm not like them. She's got it wrong. The scan results must have been mixed up or something. I don't need to understand about treatment and support options. What I *need* is a second opinion.

–

'Hi, kitten. How are you feeling?'

I look up from my iPad to see a huge colourful bouquet of flowers with a body and legs approaching my bed.

'Hey, lover.' I grin at him. 'How was work? Am I glad to see you, this place is driving me insane.'

'Are you being a bad patient?' Dom hands me the flowers, which are actually artificial ones, and sweeps in for a long, lingering kiss. 'I've missed you.'

'I've missed you more.' I rest my forehead against his, breathing in his familiar scent.

'How are you feeling?' He pulls back and scrutinises my face.

Not keen to start off on the topic of my health, I try a diversion.

'I'm fine. Thank you for these. They're beautiful. Peonies are my absolute fave.' I stick my nose in the bouquet as if expecting them to have a fragrance.

'I remembered they don't allow real flowers in most hospitals anymore for hygiene reasons. Probably for the best though. I'm sure I remember bringing you home lilies once upon a time and getting an ear-bashing for it.'

'It wasn't an ear-bashing. I'm allergic to lilies. It was a choice between asking you to chuck them or respiratory arrest.'

'Slight exaggeration.' Dom takes the flowers from me and dumps them on my bedside cabinet. 'But I wouldn't have wanted to go to my work's black-tie dinner that evening with a wheezing, hive-ridden date on my arm.'

'Touché.' I smile. 'Maybe ask the nurse for an empty water jug to sit them in?'

'I'll do that in a bit.' Dom plonks himself down on one of the chairs beside my bed. 'I'm more interested in how my beautiful fiancée is doing. That OK?'

Not really, I think to myself. Because that means you're going to ask questions I don't want to answer.

'So, how are you?' he prompts me.

'I'm fine. Told you that already. I've not been sick at all today. Still fatigued, but that will pass. Looks like I'll be out tomorrow or the day after.'

'Great. And the consultant? What was the chat this morning about the anomalies on the scan?'

'Oh, that. It's nothing. Just some weirdo doctor who doesn't know what she's talking about. So, I was looking at table centrepieces for the wedding today, and I really like the idea of—'

'Lex, what are you not telling me?' Dom interjects, his suspicion evident. 'I know you well enough to know you're glossing over something because you don't want to discuss it. What's going on?'

I consider trying to change the subject again, but I know that won't work. Instead I opt for the only remaining avoidance strategy: a full-on character assassination of Dr Harlow.

'Oh, look, it's nothing. The consultant was on another planet. She sees a couple of smudges on a scan and jumps to conclusions. I mean, she couldn't even get my name right. What's that all about? I've asked for a second opinion.'

'That doesn't sound like nothing.' Dom's brow furrows in concern. 'This woman is a fully trained consultant, surely?'

'She was a proper neurologist. But she just wasn't on it. Didn't you hear me? She couldn't even get my name right.'

'Well, if that's the case, maybe you do need a second opinion. And perhaps you should raise your concerns about her.'

'That's probably not necessary.' I shut down that route quickly. 'I just need to speak to someone I can trust and communicate with properly.'

'Sounds fair enough.' Dom rubs his forehead, a dead giveaway that he's exhausted.

'Long day?'

'*Tough* day. A number of client cock-ups I had to bail my team out of. I should only be getting involved in the most complex issues, but we have so many new staff, I keep getting pulled into the detail.'

'That's rough.' I beckon for his hand and he slips it into mine. 'Maybe you should just get off home. I'm fine here. Bored and fidgety, but fine.'

'No, I'll stay for a bit.' He squeezes my hand. 'Want some time with my gorgeous wife-to-be before I head home to an empty apartment. It feels *really* empty without you.'

'Hey, lover, it's not like we haven't had nights apart before. What's this all about?'

Dom's face has an undecipherable look on it. I'm used to being able to read him like a book, so this unsettles me slightly.

'I don't know.' He smooths his palm against the side of his head as he does when he's uncomfortable talking about something. 'I just... when I got that call yesterday, I was terrified in case—'

'It was just a stupid fall.' I find myself wondering why I keep having to justify that to everyone. 'Look at me. Do I look like you're going to lose me?'

'Well, no.' Dom meets my gaze and I can tell he's been really spooked by this. 'You look a bit tired, but otherwise, just like the woman I proposed to.'

'There you go, see. You can stop being silly now.'

'OK, boss. How about I sort out that water jug then?'

'Good thinking.'

He heads out of the room and makes his way down the corridor towards the nurses' station. I lie quietly for a moment waiting for him to return, and as I do an unwelcome thought insinuates itself into my head: what if Dr Harlow isn't mistaken? What if I do have MS?

Annoyed at myself for even allowing these ideas through, I snatch my iPad from the bedside cabinet and resume scrolling through my wedding-related boards on Pinterest. I've just got too much time on my hands. I'm a doer. I live life through action and achievement. My job is something I enjoy and I am successful at it. Being stuck here, it's like caging a bird. I need my freedom back.

I look up expectantly as someone enters the room, but it's not Dom, it's another consultant. A man this time. He's a bit younger than Dr Harlow, not by much, but he seems more human. He nods and smiles at the other patients as he makes his way through the room.

'Alex?' He addresses me as he approaches my bed. 'I gather that is what you prefer to be called?'

'That's right.' I cringe a little, realising that the naming issue has obviously been discussed with Dr Harlow. 'Are you my second opinion?'

I glance uncertainly at the door, hoping Dom will remain on his quest long enough for me to get the information I need, or to be able to put this guy off until later.

'That is correct,' he confirms. 'My name is Dr Salessi. I am a consultant neurologist here in the hospital. I have been here for twenty years, diagnosing and working with patients with a range of neurological diseases.'

Why is he practically regurgitating his CV? I'm not interviewing him for a job. He must be making sure I know that he's experienced and that I can trust his judgement – or, to put it another way, that I shouldn't question his judgement. This irks me slightly but I force a smile as he pulls the curtain round my bed.

'The nurse said your fiancé is here?'

'He is. But he's gone to find a water jug. No need to wait, you must be very busy.'

'Sure. Just let me double-check something in your notes first.' Dr Salessi seems to be stalling for time.

'Knock, knock.' Dom's head appears round the curtain. 'All right to join you?'

'Ah, you must be Alex's fiancé. I am Dr Salessi. And you are…?'

'Dominic.' Dom shakes his hand briskly.

'Alex, are you happy to have Dominic join us?' Dr Salessi asks. 'Or would you prefer to speak to me alone? It is your decision.'

Karma has come back for a second bite of revenge. It's Dom that's looking at me expectantly this time. There's no way I can say no.

'Obviously, it's fine.' I wave Dom inside.

Dom enters the makeshift cubicle with an empty plastic water jug, sets it down on my bedside cabinet and stuffs the bouquet of flowers into it.

'What have I missed?' He takes a seat.

'Nothing. We were just at the stage of introductions,' says Dr Salessi. 'I was just telling Alex that I have been a consultant neurologist here in the hospital for twenty years, diagnosing and working with patients with a range of neurological diseases.'

'Right…' Dom looks understandably confused. 'I may be behind the curve on this one, but is a concussion classified as a neurological disease?'

He looks to me to check if I am confused as well. I pretend there's something causing me discomfort in my bed and start to overzealously rearrange my covers. I only need to stall long enough for Dr Salessi to confirm there's been an error in the diagnosis.

'You are not "behind the curve",' Dr Salessi clarifies. 'We do not classify concussion as a neurological disease. I am not here to discuss Alex's concussion.'

'Ah, you must be the second opinion Alex asked for?'

'I am indeed here to provide that. Alex was visited by my colleague, Dr Harlow, earlier this morning. Dr Harlow explained to Alex that the anomalies on her MRI scan were in fact what we call lesions – that is damage to the nerves in the brain. It is caused by an autoimmune condition called multiple sclerosis or MS.'

Dom's face immediately drains of colour. 'I'm sorry. Did you just say—'

'It's fine, Dom,' I interrupt. 'It's a misdiagnosis. There's no way I have MS. I mean, look at the way I live my life. If I was ill, do you think I'd manage all that?'

'Alex, I know this is very difficult for you,' says Dr Salessi. 'But I have reviewed the scans, as well as Dr Harlow's notes, and I very much support her diagnosis. I will of course perform the same neurological examination but the scan itself provides enough evidence of the disease. It also explains your fatigue, the clumsiness you describe, and why you experienced double vision before your fall.'

I look at Dom, who's staring straight ahead, completely bewildered, then focus my attention on Dr Salessi.

'I'm sorry, I just can't accept what you're telling me. The anomalies must be related to my concussion. I need another opinion – from a different hospital altogether. What do I need to do to arrange this?'

'Alex, you are in shock, which is a normal reaction.' Dr Salessi's tone is kind and empathetic. 'You can request other opinions. We can even redo the scan once your concussion has subsided. Unfortunately, it is not going to change the outcome.'

'But I need—'

'Lex, *please stop*.' Dom suddenly comes back to life. 'You're not helping yourself. I completely understand your wish for this to go away. I want it to go away. But it's not going to, no matter how hard you push. It's clear that the doctor knows what he's talking about, and two people can't be wrong.'

He grabs my hand and squeezes it, his eyes slightly pink round the edges from the emotion he's trying to suppress.

'You've got MS, Lex, and the sooner you accept the diagnosis, the sooner we can get you the support you need. I'm so sorry, kitten. I'm so *bloody sorry*.'

I look into Dom's big blue eyes, which are now filling with tears, and I can't speak. I can't think. I'm completely lost.

'I will give you a few minutes alone.' Dr Salessi discreetly moves away and disappears behind the curtain out of sight.

'Dom?' I whisper. 'Is this really happening?'

He leaps up from his seat and envelops me in his big strong arms. 'It is. I'm so sorry. I really am.'

A lump of emotion forms in my throat; it's so intense that it hurts trying to hold it at bay. 'What did I do wrong, Dom? What? Tell me.'

He pulls me closer. 'You didn't do anything wrong, Lex. Don't ever, ever think that. Life is just so damn cruel sometimes.'

'But I just… I can't even…'

I cling to him as I try to process this information. I'm ill. Really ill. And the only way is downhill. I'm going to lose my physical abilities, my independence, perhaps even my confidence and self-esteem as my body breaks down bit by bit. What does this mean for my career, my future? Our future. Normally when I have a problem, I solve it. Or Dom helps me solve it. We're the ultimate pragmatists, perfectly matched in every way.

Except that's just changed. Because I'm not going to be able to keep up. And I don't want to hold Dom back. I don't want him to have to become… my carer. I can't bear the thought of being a burden on him. Will he even want to marry me now? Why would he? We can't have the future we were so looking forward to together. I'm broken and no one can fix me.

This uncharacteristic whirlwind of thoughts becomes too much for me and I finally break down in tears: huge, heartbreaking sobs, causing Dom to pull me in tighter.

'It's OK, kitten. Just cry.' He soothes me. 'We'll get through this together. It doesn't change anything. It's you and me against it all, I promise.'

As I listen to his words, it has the opposite effect of what he intended. I don't feel safe or secure. I feel vulnerable and exposed. Because as much as he says that this doesn't change a thing, it already has. The balance in our relationship has shifted for ever. The only question that remains is – will it survive?

Chapter 6

'You OK?' Dom slams the driver's door of our double-parked BMW 3 Series and canters round to the passenger side to help me out of the car.

'I'm fine.' I pull my hand away from his. 'I can manage.'

I haul myself out of the car, trying to hide how much this simple action is taking out of me. My muscles feel like dead weights and I'm panting heavily; way too much for what should be very light exertion.

Dom hovers in front of me looking helpless. I can see how much he wants to step in and help. 'I'll need to park the car properly. Will you be OK getting up the stairs?'

'Yes. Go.' I usher him away, relieved he won't be around to witness my sorry ascent to our third-floor tenement apartment.

He hesitates for a moment, then makes his way back to the driver's side of the car and speeds away, keen to get parked and back to me as quickly as possible.

By the time I've climbed the five steps to the main door, I'm out of breath again, so I lean against the metal railing, noticing for the first time what a beautiful day it is – the sky is the bluest of blue, not a single cloud in sight. It's the kind of day that would normally have me itching to pound the tarmac with my Nikes, then laze the afternoon away with Dom or Sasha in a beer garden on Ashton Lane. Instead, I'm facing a day on the sofa, watching my way through a box set on Netflix.

Flattening my palm against the red sandstone facade of our West End tenement building, I enjoy the warmth it's soaked up from the morning sun: a feeling I've always loved, and partly why I had my heart set on one of these apartments. Will that now have to change? It would be gut-wrenching to have to give up our place after it took so long to find, all because there's no lift. But I also don't want to be housebound for weeks on end every time I have one of these relapses.

Feeling suddenly weighed down by these life-altering thoughts, I shift my focus back to something more pragmatic: how the hell am I going to get up these stairs? As much as it pains me to give in, I need to swallow the bloody great lump of pride I'm stubbornly chewing on and accept that I can't cope on my own – just until my symptoms remit.

'Hey... kitten. Are you all right?' Dom appears out of nowhere, jogging up the path behind me.

'I'm admitting defeat just this once.'

'I did wonder if you'd manage.' He unlocks the door, then scoops me up into his arms.

'Hey, that's not what I meant!' I waggle inelegantly in his arms.

'I know.' He pulls me towards him and kisses my nose. 'But I like the idea of being your handsome prince. You're so independent. Let me have my moment.'

I take in his gorgeous, smiling face. His bluest of blue twinkling eyes and cheeky grin. A personality that can light up any room.

'Fine. You can play the hero today – as long as I get to be me the rest of the time.'

'Deal.' Dom grins at me. 'It's a bit soon to be carrying you over the threshold, but this might be the only chance I get.'

—

A few hours later, I'm camped out on my enormous sofa watching an episode of *Big Little Lies* when the apartment buzzer sounds.

'I'll let her in,' Dom calls from the bedroom, where he's tidying up. 'Just you stay where you are.'

Having decided the less physical effort I have to put into anything right now, the better, I don't argue. Staying still means I don't have the constant, conscious reminder that my body has embarked on a bewildering and relentless pursuit of self-destruction.

'Lex. Oh hon, how are you?' Sasha bursts through the living room door and launches herself on me with a massive hug.

'I'm OK.' I hug her back, feeling her squeeze even harder in response.

'I cana-buluf-ahapae-naufa,' she wails into the sleeve of my hooded sweater.

'What was that?' I attempt to pry her off me, but my arm muscles burn in protest. 'Sash, I've no idea what you're saying.'

'You weren't really supposed to.' She sits up and dabs at her eyes. 'I just feel so angry for you and so hurt and powerless. It's not fair.'

'Life isn't fair. But we'll get through this together, right?'

'We will. I can't change that you're ill, but I can make sure I'm there when you need help, support, carried up the stairs, anything.'

'There's no way you could carry me up the stairs.' I chuckle. 'Even Dom struggled earlier. Not that he'd admit it, the silly sod.'

'I'll pretend I didn't hear that.' Dom enters the room with his jacket on.

I blow him a little kiss. 'Is that you off to the supermarket?'

'Yeah. Got your list. Though I note there's a glaring lack of chocolate on it. Can I really not tempt you into a little treat after everything you've been through?'

'Definitely not.' I shake my head.

'Can you get me some?' Sasha asks.

I catch her giving him a little wink, clearly meant as a message of once-I'm-eating-it-she'll-have-some-too. I don't know why, but this irritates me.

'Sure,' Dom replies with a warm smile. 'OK, see you ladies in a bit. Have fun.'

He disappears back out of the living room and seconds later the apartment door slams.

'So, how are you really?' Sasha pulls off her ankle boots and makes herself comfortable on the sofa beside me. 'I'm sorry I didn't make it to the hospital.'

'Don't worry at all.' I shift over to give her more room. 'I was only in for a couple of days, and I know you've a lot going on with your mum.'

'Yeah, but I should have been there. You were going through...' She tails off as her eyes start to well up again.

'Hey, stop it.' I grab a tissue from the box on the coffee table. 'How can you be there for me if you dissolve into tears every few minutes? Anyway, the two hundred-odd WhatsApp messages you sent were more than enough to show you care.'

'Oh, Lex, I'm so sorry. You're *actually* going through this. And I'm falling apart. What kind of idiot friend does that make me?'

'A great one. You'd make a rubbish nurse though.'

'For sure.' Sasha blows her nose. 'I'll try again. Are you coping OK? You don't need to act all brave in front of me.'

'I'm honestly OK, Sash. I mean it's a shock, for sure. I had some moments in hospital where I felt as if my whole future had been thrown up in the air like a pack of cards. I questioned everything: my career, the wedding, me and Dom. I cried to the point that my nose was so raw it burned. And I asked the universe why this has happened to me – it didn't answer, in case you're wondering – but I came up with nothing productive. So, I decided I have to face it the same way I face everything else in my life. I'm going to take it head on and work through it.'

'You're amazing, Lex. I'm not sure why I expected anything else. You *live* life, you don't let it happen to you. Why would that be different now?'

'Exactly. Either that, or it really hasn't sunk in, and I'm days shy of throwing myself out of the living room window.' I grin at her.

'I can tell you're definitely not about to do that.' Sasha giggles.

'Couldn't if I tried – not in my state. One thing that is bothering me, though, is how Dom and my mother and sister are behaving. I may have questioned the wedding in my head during a moment of irrational despair, but they talked seriously about postponing it – and like I wasn't even there.'

Sasha ponders this for a second. 'Would that be such a bad thing?'

'*Yes.* We've been planning it for two years. It's still four months away and I'll be back on my feet in weeks.'

'So did they back down?'

I let out a long sigh. 'They did, but now they've taken over the wedding planning. All I'm getting to do is plan my outfit, hair and make-up and turn up for things that I'm needed for.'

'Oh dear.' Sasha winces, feeling my pain. 'Though maybe it is what's needed for the next while, until you're back on your feet.'

'It won't be that though, Sash. My mum's already taken it upon herself to mess with the colour scheme and she and Dom have reduced the guest list because they don't think I'll be able to cope with so many people being there on the day. It's like I've lost control of my own wedding.'

'I get that you're frustrated, Lex, but you've been through quite an ordeal. We all just want to take care of you.'

This comment sends a ripple of frustration through me. Not Sasha as well. She's meant to take my side on everything. To avoid an argument – which Sasha would undoubtedly run a mile from – I change the subject.

'Hey, you want to see something? I was bored in hospital so I ended up writing a song.'

'A song?'

'Yeah, the inspiration came from seeing so many really sick people on the ward – much worse than me – and then it kind of evolved from there. Head was foggy, so it was a bit of a struggle, but a welcome distraction.'

I hand Sasha my phone with the notepad app open. She quietly reads through my rough lyrics, then looks at me in awe.

'It's amazing. Comes straight from the heart. How does it go?'

I start to hum a melody and she joins in, singing the words on the screen.

We grow up unassuming, we grow up unaware
We live in a world where too many people, they don't care
Take a look around you, tell me what you see
Illness, conflict, suffering, too much poverty…

'It needs a bit of work.' I stop our duet abruptly. 'But it's not like I don't have time on my hands.'

'I think it's brill. I've no doubt you'll turn it into something amazing.' She hands me back my phone. 'So, other than the wedding planning, how's this all affecting you and Dom?'

'It's been mixed.' I reach across to the coffee table and take a sip from my glass of water. 'When they first gave me the news, I was in total denial and he was just so solid. He was like: it's you and me, and we do this together, no matter what. It really helped me come to terms with things.'

'That's good. I've always wished I could meet someone like Dom. He's such a great guy.'

'Yeah, he is. His heart is definitely in the right place. It's just… difficult adjusting, you know? Particularly when his head's so wrapped up in my illness and when and how it might strike again. He's treating me like an invalid, though I've just made it clear that he needs to let me be me, so I'm hoping that'll change.'

'Did you ask your doctor about how to handle it?'

'We did.' I nod. 'We spoke to the consultant. He said I can help myself by living healthily, which I'm trying to do anyway. But in terms of relapses, it's like trying to predict the lottery numbers, so there's no point in putting so much focus on it.'

'I suppose.' Sasha chews her lip for a second, showing me that she's not totally convinced by this. 'And what about work?'

'Same strategy.' I grimace. 'It's killing me that Alan's been put in charge of the project while I'm off. He's a good guy and capable, but he's not quite there yet. I really hope Laura's giving him the support he needs, otherwise I could go back to a complete car crash.'

'That's the last thing you'll need on your return. Hopefully you won't be off long enough for him to cause too much damage.'

'I really hope not, Sash. Not least, because I don't have the patience to be stuck like this for too long.'

Chapter 7

'This just doesn't feel right,' I complain, as I slowly extricate myself from the front passenger seat of the car. 'I shouldn't be out doing our menu tasting while I'm signed off work. What if someone sees me?'

'No one's going to see you.' Dom closes the car door behind me and locks the car. 'We're going straight into the hotel and straight back home again, and your mum explained how important it is to test the food well in advance to allow for changes.'

'Yeah, and she's right about everything,' I mutter, earning myself a look.

The gusty wind whips playfully around me, lifting my skirt and plastering my hair to my Candy Kiss lip butter. This is Scottish weather in its full glory. After a rare two weeks of uninterrupted sunshine and warm spring days, a stormy weather front has brought a never-ending dusk and teeth-chattering highs of seven degrees Centigrade.

In front of us, the Eastwood Hotel, a beautifully renovated Victorian building, looms ominously in the half-light, surrounded by thick, rolling dark clouds like a scene from *Ghostbusters*. It's such a contrast to how it looked on the day we first visited, if I were superstitious, I'd think this were a sign.

'There they are.' A haughty voice carries towards us.

I look round and see my mother and stepdad, John, battling their way through the wind.

'Come on, let's get you inside.' Dom puts his hand on the small of my back and gently urges me forward. 'They can catch us up.'

'I'm fine here.' I stubbornly resist his instruction. 'We used to go out running in this, remember?'

'Right.' Dom purses his lips and removes his hand from my back. 'So, are you going to give me a manual then?'

'What?' I look at him searchingly.

'You know. So I know when I'm allowed to be caring and when you want me to back the hell off.'

'Dom, don't be like that,' I say through gritted teeth, trying my best not to lose my patience with him. 'I'm just… I'm OK here.'

'Alex, dear, you shouldn't be out in the cold.' My mother rushes towards me, my stepdad trailing behind. 'Dominic, get her inside. She'll catch her death.'

'Hasn't that already happened?' I plant a sarcastic look on my face and greet them both with a hug and a kiss on the cheek.

'You doing all right, love?' John asks me, his kind features almost glowing in the half-light.

'Improving every day.' I smile brightly at him. 'Shall we go inside?'

'Yes, please.' My mother grabs her scarlet chiffon scarf before it shoots off across the car park.

Making our way towards the hotel entrance, I deliberately take my time, so no one can see me struggle when I hit the invisible wall that's materialised in my stamina. It wasn't a lie that I'm improving, but it's going a damn sight more slowly than I'd hoped.

As we approach the hotel reception, our wedding coordinator, Jasmine, appears from the direction of the bar and spots us.

'Alex. Dominic. *Lovely* to see you both,' she gushes, in her very wedding coordinator-esque way, her tonged blond hair bouncing energetically around her shoulders. 'Alex, you are looking *so* much better than I expected. I was *ever* so upset for you when your mother told me, but don't you worry about a thing. My team will make sure all your needs are accommodated.'

'Err, thanks.' I shift uncomfortably on the spot, wishing she wouldn't be quite so theatrical and public about it. I'm also willing her to take us somewhere else, as my listless body nags at me for a seat. 'Where are we tonight?'

'We'll be in Whitecraigs, our AA Rosette restaurant, for the tasting.' She seems to suddenly think of something. 'Oh now, I meant to call you… I contacted JLP Karaoke to ask about AV requirements and they said you'd cancelled them. I wasn't aware.'

'What?' I assume a puzzled expression. 'I didn't cancel them.'

'That was me.' My mother pitches in. 'You won't have the energy for karaoke, Alex, and it's a little… *cheap*.' She says this as if it's a dirty word.

My hackles immediately rise. 'It's not "cheap". It's called fun, Mother. You should try it some time.'

My mother's look borders on acidic. She's happy to hand out the shit, but if anyone dares challenge her, they've caused a scene and embarrassed her.

'Maybe the karaoke is too much now, Lex,' says Dom. 'I mean, we don't even know if you'll be up to enjoying it.'

I lock eyes with him. 'The karaoke stays. End of.'

Dom assumes a resigned expression and takes a step back to disengage from the conversation. My mother simply shakes her head in disapproval.

'Let's get you seated then.' Jasmine's eyes dart back and forth curiously between us, aware that something's not quite right.

We trail behind her into the restaurant, where she takes our drinks order as we take off our coats and settle ourselves. Although I could murder a gin and tonic – to numb my senses enough to ignore my mother's inevitable judgemental comments – I refrain and opt for a tomato juice.

'How are you feeling, Alex?' my mother asks the moment Jasmine is out of earshot, our earlier confrontation already buried deep. 'You're looking a little peaky.'

'I'm fine.' I offer her the same bright smile I gave John outside, trying put her off.

'Is that true?' She looks straight past me to Dom. 'I never know when I'm getting the truth out of this one.'

I attempt to bring her focus back to me. 'Mother, that's not—'

'I'm asking Dominic, dear.'

I flinch in response to her flippantness. Though I don't know why. This is exactly how she's always been with me, so untrusting of my ability to know what's best for me. Normally I can hold my own with her though.

'Alex is doing great,' Dom replies. 'She's been taking it easy and has stopped constantly checking her work emails – though I practically had to pry the laptop from her.'

'Good.' My mother looks at him pointedly over her wire-rimmed spectacles. 'She's incapable of taking advice from those who know better. It's like talking to a steam engine.'

As I listen to this exchange, I feel completely patronised. Dom's talking about me like I'm a toddler who made it through her first day at nursery, while my mother, who always behaves with a grandiose air, is putting on an enhanced performance. They continue their competing assessments of my progress and general existence. I'm particularly irritated by my mother's ill-informed diatribe about MS and how it will affect me – information she's clearly just googled and is now pretending to be an expert on. Eventually, I decide I've heard enough.

'Eh… *hello*? In case you haven't noticed, I'm right here, and perfectly capable of speaking for myself. You don't need to discuss me like some case study.'

I glance at John, who has actually (and thankfully) been a calming influence on my mother – until now, it seems. He leans forward and pats my mum's knee.

'Isabel. How about we change the subject?' he gently encourages her. 'Alex is living with this every day. I'm sure she'd appreciate a night off.'

My mother looks at him, then laughs, almost sheepishly. 'Of course. Let's have a relaxing drink – then we can talk about Alex's treatment plan over dinner.'

I'm about to protest that her proposal doesn't just fail to meet the definition of a night off, it's completely inappropriate and intrusive, when Jasmine reappears at our table with our drinks.

'*Here* we are.' She plonks them down in front of us theatrically and beams at us like an overenthusiastic street-light. 'Your starters won't be long. Oh, and Alex, you *must* tell me if any of your dietary requirements have changed following your diagnosis.'

I'm left telling her disappearing backside that a diagnosis of MS most definitely doesn't mean a change to the menu for our big day. As well as wondering how the hell I'm going to get through this evening on soft drinks.

–

'*How* is the food?' Jasmine has skirted across the oval-shaped restaurant to our table like a heat-seeking missile. 'I *do* hope it is meeting your expectations – and more.'

'It's wonderful.' My mother doesn't look up from devouring her *cuit rosé* saddle of lamb with redcurrant and rosemary jus. 'The dauphinoise potatoes are to die for.'

'*Super.*' Jasmine claps her hands in delight. 'I am *so* pleased you are enjoying it. And the beef?'

Feeling her eyes on me, I rush to swallow my half-chewed mouthful so I can answer. I glug at my mineral water to help it along, but this causes me to choke and I start coughing and spluttering in an undignified way.

'Oh, my *word.*' Jasmine looks shocked.

I wave my hand to signal I'm fine, but Dom overreacts and slaps me on the back vigorously, making things worse.

'Stop. Stop!' I splutter as soon as I have enough breath to do so. 'I just need a moment.'

All eyes round the table are on me as I compose myself.

'The beef is really good too,' I eventually manage to tell Jasmine.

Instead of her usual over-the-top response, Jasmine just nods and smiles sympathetically, then excuses herself. Confused by this, I look round at my table companions and notice they're sat stock still.

'What's with the mannequin challenge, people?' I raise an enquiring eyebrow. 'Should I join in?'

My attempt at humour is returned with awkward expressions and an equally awkward silence.

'Alex, dear,' says my mum. 'I think we all just got a bit of a shock there.'

'Because I choked?' I laugh in disbelief. 'I'm fine. Hardly a butt-clenching moment.'

My mother flinches at my use of language. 'It wasn't because you choked. It was *why* you choked. You do realise that MS can cause issues with swallowing.'

This statement flattens me like a ten-ton truck. That's what this is about? I take in the screamingly uncomfortable body language of John and Dom. They're all thinking the same thing. Is this how it's going to be? Now I have a 'disability', perfectly plausible explanations like 'I didn't chew my meat properly' are no longer viable? No, I can't allow this.

'Hold on a minute.' I flatten my palms on the tabletop to channel my frustration. 'What happened there was *nothing* to do with my diagnosis.'

I stare accusingly at my mum, then Dom and John, who at least have the grace to look ashamed.

My mother shifts in her seat and purses her lips. 'Alex, darling, you don't need to hide it. We're all here for you and we're going to manage this together.' She puts her hand on mine and I immediately pull it away in annoyance.

I almost can't bear to listen to any more of this. I take a deep, slow breath to keep my temper from boiling over.

'I'm not hiding anything. If you'd bothered to read up on it properly, you'd know that people with MS don't experience every possible symptom listed, and it could also be years before I need proper care.'

'Oh, I know that, darling.' She tuts at me and returns her attention to her food. 'We can talk about it another day, when you're feeling a bit calmer.'

This final comment infuriates me, but I'm too aware of our surroundings to let this show. Instead, in a gesture of protest, I clatter my knife and fork into the six o'clock position on my plate and push it away, leaving my food unfinished.

This was meant to be a pleasant experience, an exciting adventure for a dizzy bride-to-be. Instead, all I feel is anger and dread. I had thought the worst part of being diagnosed with MS was going to be my physical symptoms and limitations. Now I'm starting to wonder – is that going to be outdone by the behaviours of those who supposedly love me most?

Chapter 8

A few weeks later – and for the first time in two months – I'm crammed into the pokey clementine-coloured subway carriage on my way to work. As I cling to the hand-rail, jerking from side to side, the windows of the train's automatic doors within licking distance, I feel a mix of emotions. A big part of me is excited to get back to work and resume normal life; the independence that's driven me all my life is still well intact. It will also helpfully show Dom that I don't need him breathing down my neck and questioning almost every move I make – this being a continuing and rather significant bone of contention between us. But there's also an unpleasant swirling in my stomach, which, alongside the vibration and shaking of the carriage, makes me feel a little nauseous.

I recognise the unpleasant swirling as nerves: the kind you get when starting a new job. This is annoying because I'm returning to a place where I've enjoyed working for several years, but the longer I've been away, the more detached from it I've felt. Add to that the question of how my colleagues will behave with me, knowing I've been away so long. I asked Laura for complete discretion, and I know she'll honour this without question; however, there are other ways people could have heard. Glasgow may be a city of nearly six hundred thousand, but in the corporate sector it feels more like a village.

On top of the nerves, there's something else going on that I can't quite grasp. It's more unsettling, more of a nagging feeling, like something's just not quite right.

The subway train whooshes into my station, coming to an abrupt and destabilising halt. As the doors fly open, I alight from the carriage and move along the platform, carried by the momentum of the commuters around me. I'm relieved to be getting closer to work, where I won't have to move around much for the rest of the day – because while the fatigue has lifted enough for me to cope with the demands of everyday life, I'm still far from where I was before my relapse.

Emerging from the underground station into the bright morning sunshine, I find myself more aware of my surroundings than I ever was. Instead of hurrying along the road, face planted in my emails, I make my way along Buchanan Street at about half the speed I might have done previously (not by choice, of course).

I take in the buzz of my surroundings: revving car engines, the whoosh from the brakes of the double-decker buses, the vibrations coming from the subway below, the strum of a guitar from an early-bird busker trying in vain to attract the attention of the passing worker bees. And people all around me. For the first time, it dawns on me how people seem to sleepwalk through their lives, locked on autopilot as they pound the endless hamster wheel of life. Like an early scene from an apocalyptic movie – but in this one, the threat to humanity is that people live their whole lives without looking up from their gadgets, then discover they've missed so much of what life has offered them.

As I continue along the pavement, passing by one smombie after another, I'm suddenly inspired to make a change to the lyrics of the song I wrote. I stop moment-arily to punch it into my notepad app, then quietly sing back the words I've written, ensuring no one can hear me.

'*Just take a moment, open up your eyes, look beyond your gadgets, lift your disguise.*'

It's a pleasant distraction from the nervous churning in my stomach and the awareness that, whenever I try to up my pace, my body resists these instructions like a stubborn mule.

Eventually I reach my office and climb the steps towards the main entrance, my legs feeling like lead, providing an unwelcome reminder that I'm about to face the unknown. Is that the nagging feeling I'm having? No, that's not it. It will be tough getting back into the game, but I'm determined, and I've got a medical opinion that supports my ability to do so.

'Alex. So good to see you back.' My manager, Laura, gives me an unexpected but not unwelcome hug when I reach my desk. 'We've missed you.'

'That's good to know.' I hug her back, then turn to dump my bag under my desk. 'Oh, looks like someone's sitting here. Was there a desk move while I was away?'

I look around and note that all my other colleagues seem to be sitting in their usual places.

'Sorry, I should have said.' Laura's face is apologetic. 'Alan's sitting there. Didn't make sense us having to shout across the desks to each other all the time.'

'Right.' I try not to show that this has bothered me. 'So, I guess he can move back now then.'

'Why don't you put your stuff over at Alan's desk? We've got a catch-up in the diary anyway.'

'We have?'

This is news to me. I checked my calendar on my work phone before leaving my apartment and there were no meeting requests pending.

'Yes, I thought we'd go for a coffee and a chat.'

'Sure, sounds good.'

I'm pleased that Laura's prioritising me. This is exactly what I need – to throw myself into things, take the focus off my medical situation and more importantly, get Alan packed back off to assistant project manager-land.

'Shall we?' Laura grabs her purse from her handbag and gestures in the direction of the lifts.

We engage in light-hearted chit-chat about the latest Netflix box sets we've gotten hooked on as we make our way down to the brightly lit office cafe. Then, drinks in hand, we find a table at the furthest corner by the floor-to-ceiling windows to allow us some privacy.

'How are you feeling?' Laura ditches a sachet of sugar into her coffee and gives it a good stir.

'I'm fine.' I sip at my own drink. 'Just so pleased to be back.'

'I bet you are. You must have been going stir crazy stuck at home, especially with the active lifestyle you normally lead.'

'It *was* frustrating, but it's in the past now – thankfully. What's the latest on the project? I assume Alan knows I'm back today. It must have been a lot of pressure on him having to step up like that.'

Laura hesitates mid-sip, like she's weighing up how to answer.

'What's up?' I ask. 'You can tell me about Alan. I need to know what's been going on so I can help him develop.'

'Alex.' Laura places her coffee on the table. 'Alan has done just fine. He's had some moments of uncertainty and has inevitably made mistakes, but he and I have gotten to a good place. A lot like the way you and I did when you were learning.'

An air raid siren starts blaring in my head. What's with the speech? And the reminder of my humble professional roots? What should be most relevant here is that I have a wealth of experience that Laura can draw on with confidence that I'll be on it, whatever 'it' is. Why do I have a looming feeling that I'm about to hear something I really won't like?

Laura picks up on the ticking in my brain and takes the conversation in a different direction.

'Alex, I don't want us to move on to work too quickly. As your manager, I have a duty of care to you. It's important we discuss your wellbeing, so I can support you in the best way possible. Let's have a chat about how you're doing.'

'What? Oh, come on, Laura. This is you and me. We've worked together for ages. Surely we don't have to go through that stuff.'

'Actually, we do. You've been off for a significant period with a not insignificant health issue that, although you say it's in the past, is not a one-off event. You also had an accident at work related to your condition—'

'I slipped on a piece of paper.'

'Because of symptoms related to your condition.' Laura cocks her head in an attempt to make me understand this. 'Alex, I have a *legal* obligation under the Equality Act to look at reasonable adjustments to your role that will make it easier for you to attend work regularly.'

The air raid siren is joined by mini explosions in my brain as Laura drops these bombs on me. Equality Act? Reasonable adjustments so I can attend work regularly?

This all sounds so alien to me. Between the endless blazing arguments with Dom at home, my mum, sister and even Sasha mollycoddling me, and now this, I'm starting to wonder if I'm stuck in one long nightmare.

'Sorry, Laura. I need a moment to process this.' I rest my elbows on the table and massage my temples. 'I wasn't expecting this kind of conversation this morning.'

'Take your time,' Laura encourages me, and sits back to give me space.

After about twenty seconds of silence, which includes an inner pep talk to keep myself calm, I mirror her position.

'OK, let's get this out of the way. What do you want to know?'

'Alex, this isn't an interrogation.' Laura laughs. 'I'm here to support you.'

'Well, why does it seem like one then? All I want is to get on with things and not focus on my situation.'

'Why don't you start by telling me how you've been feeling?' she suggests.

'OK… sure.' I attempt a smile, but feel too exposed. 'I've been feeling all right. Still a bit fatigued, but that's reducing gradually.'

'And how did you feel about coming back today?'

'Good.'

Good until I got here and this conversation started.

'I'm glad.' Laura stirs her coffee absently. 'Alex, it's absolutely your right to keep your condition confidential, but it might be worth considering whether to tell your teammates. So they can offer you support and understand what's going on next time you have a period of absence like this, which seems likely. They've been worried about you.'

As Laura says this, there's an uncomfortable jolt in my abdomen and the nagging feeling from this morning returns with a vengeance. I suddenly realise what it is. It's fear. Fear of being seen differently. Fear of being *treated* differently and of being seen as unreliable. Because as much as I can pretend nothing's happening to me, it's not like I can persuade my body to play along.

This realisation spooks me and almost derails my thoughts entirely, but as I see Laura looking back at me expectantly, I know I have to hold it together. She can't be allowed to see this uncharacteristic sense of vulnerability that has emerged. I straighten myself up in my chair to give myself a mental boost.

'Look, Laura, I hear what you're saying, but I think I'd rather keep this to myself. I'm just getting my own head around things and the last thing I need is lots of questions and sympathetic looks.'

'That's fair.' She nods. 'I hadn't thought about it that way.'

'And if you don't mind, can we do this whole "reasonable adjustments" thing later? I'd rather focus on getting back into things, then I'll be able to tell you what support I think I need.'

Laura studies me for a moment. It's clear she doesn't want to let this conversation go, but she's also smart enough to realise it will be more productive when I'm ready to deal with it.

'OK, fine,' she concedes reluctantly. 'But there are a couple of things I want to cover before you head off.'

'What's that?'

She hesitates again. 'I'd like you to work shorter days this week, to avoid you getting too tired. Coming back to work after a long period of absence can be tough.'

'OK… I suppose that makes sense.'

'Also, I'm going to keep Alan on as project manager on the implementation. It's a challenging role with a tight timeline and a lot of pressure attached to it. Pressure I don't think you need, given the circumstances.'

As she says these words, a feeling of hurt mixed with anger starts to simmer inside me. This isn't about looking after me. If it was, she'd be asking me what I need, not causing me stress by taking away something that's so important to me. She doesn't trust that I can do the job any more and unfortunately there's nothing I can do about it – she can assign me to any project she wants me on.

'Right. So if you're taking me off that project, what are you reassigning me to?' I force the words through my tensed jaw.

'There's a new piece of work being set up to look at some issues with our time and attendance system. It's something we've been needing to address for some time. I thought you'd be perfect to lead that and fortunately it doesn't have a hard deadline against it.'

This winds me up even further. A project to address a longstanding problem with no set timeline? Translation: something unimportant that nobody really cares about. I'm being handed a made-up project so they can keep me out the way.

I take a deep breath to make sure I don't blurt out how I'm really feeling. 'Laura, this feels a bit like you're demoting me.'

'Not at all, Alex. But it is important that we don't push you beyond what you can cope with, and we must have that conversation about your wellbeing – not least because the company is strict about absence levels. I need to make sure we've done everything we can to ensure future absences are minimised, otherwise we'll have another problem on our hands.'

I feel a sharp sting as these words sink in. Not only does she no longer trust me to lead a business-critical project, she's hanging formal absence management procedures over my head. It doesn't matter that I've been a consistently strong performer – that label I worked so hard to earn for myself has been replaced by a bloody great flashing badge that declares 'problem employee'. The loyalty I've shown Laura, shown the organisation, counts for nothing. Suddenly my feeling of vulnerability grows hugely as the realisation hits me: I'm no longer in control of my own professional destiny.

'Right.' I can no longer look at Laura. I'm so disappointed to find her following this predictable managerial path, without even attempting to fight for me. 'Well, I'll get back to my desk. Sorry… Alan's desk.'

'Alex, please don't be like this.'

Laura tries to make eye contact, but I continue to avoid her gaze. Then as we get up to head back to our floor, I'm unable keep my frustration at bay.

'You know, Laura. I might have been diagnosed with a horrible illness. But I don't feel like I'm the one that's changed.'

–

'Hi, kitten,' Dom hollers as he enters our apartment, slamming the door behind him.

'Hi,' I respond with the enthusiasm of a caged rhinoceros.

I'm lying on our bed with my eyes closed, having not moved since arriving home and discarding my coat, bag and shoes on the floor beside me, two hours earlier. Unable to sleep, but too exhausted to get up and do anything, I've spent most of that time staring at the ceiling, replaying the events of the day.

Dom pushes open the half-closed bedroom door and surveys me and the pile by my bedside. 'Tough first day back?'

I reluctantly open my eyes and look at him. 'That's an understatement.'

'Sorry to hear that.' He gives me a sympathetic smile and a kiss on the lips, then moves round to his side of the bed, where he changes out of his suit. 'It was always going to be tough going back.'

'I didn't realise how tough.' I rub at my tired eyes. 'Like that I was going to be robbed of my work. Did you get my text?'

'Yeah, I did, sorry. Barely had a chance to read it. You said something about Laura treating you like you're incapable, and Alan's stolen your project?'

'That pretty much sums it up. Oh, and about three hundred people either asked me how I'm "keeping" or walked straight past, pretending not to see to me. People I know well, who'd normally crack a bit of banter with me. It's clearly gotten round the office about my MS. Even Sasha was doing my head in at lunchtime, wittering on about vitamin supplements and telling me to pace myself.'

'That's rough, kitten.' Dom joins me on the bed, stretching himself out, putting his arms behind his head. 'But with your role, it's doesn't sound totally unreasonable to suggest you take it easy for a while. You are still recovering and if it were any of my team members, I'd do the same.'

A switch suddenly flicks in my consciousness, irritation bubbling inside me. Here we go again. Why, when I just need a bit of moral support, does Dom have to put his manager hat on? He already treats me like an invalid. Why can't he be my fiancé first?

'And I suppose you'd threaten your newly returned team member with formal absence management as well?' I demand.

'*Whoa.*' Dom turns his head towards me. 'Where did that come from? I'm just saying that supporting you is a good thing. If they'd chucked you back into the shit straight away, *that* would have been unfair, irresponsible – and a risk to your wellbeing.'

My irritation develops into full-blown exasperation. 'There's that *bloody* word again. Everything's about my *wellbeing* now. It has never been used in my presence before all this, and now it's haunting me like the sodding ghosts from that Christmas film. I am the ghost of workplace future. Your career will spontaneously combust at the chime of midnight, unless you look after your wellbeing and never go off sick again...'

'Lex, what's gotten into you?'

'What's gotten into me is that this is all bullshit. I haven't changed, Dom. I'm still the same person, but for some reason I'm being treated like some kind of lesser being.'

'Hey, come on. That's not true.' He tries to stroke my hair, but I flick his hand away.

'*Really?* Were you there?' I eyeball him accusingly. 'Because I'm pretty sure you have no idea. You waltz through life without a care in the world, with your perfect health and your perfect job. You have no idea what this is like. Being constantly poked and prodded, the gruelling physio, the disease-modifying drugs, then on top of all that, people treating me like I'm incapable.'

I pull myself up from the bed, my whole body screaming at me in protest.

'Is that what you think?' Dom sits up as well, hurt and resentment clouding his face, his voice rising. 'You think all this is a stroll in the park for me? I may not be experiencing the physical side of this, Lex, but it's sure as hell not easy for me either.'

'Oh, *come on*. There's no comparison. Try being me for a day, then you'll realise how easy you've got it.'

Dom looks at me in disbelief. 'Are you *kidding*? I've been doing the cooking, the cleaning, the laundry… I've had to take on all the wedding-related stuff.'

'Don't give me that. You and my mother took over the wedding planning without even consulting me.'

'And you could have handled it, could you?' Dom locks eyes with me, his temper hot like lava. 'You couldn't do anything for yourself for weeks. I've been waiting on you hand and foot ever since—'

'Well, no one's asking you to,' I spit back. 'I never wanted to be treated like a patient. *You* turned me into one.'

'That may be the case to a certain extent, but things *have* changed, Lex. You need to wake up and start accepting this situation because I'm not sure I've got the energy to take much more.'

This statement takes me to boiling point. '*Accept it?* Oh, I've *bloody* accepted it, Dom. I've got no sodding choice. What I can't accept is being treated like I might fall over if there's a slight breeze outside. I can look after myself.'

'But that's the thing, Lex,' Dom roars back at me, his face contorted with rage. 'You can't. Not when you're like you've been the last few months. If I'm going to look after you at these times – yes, I know that's hard to hear, but it's the reality – I suggest you learn to accept the help more gracefully, because otherwise—'

'*Otherwise what?*' I stare him out defiantly as his gaze drops to the floor and he wrestles with his thoughts, clearly trying to stop his temper from exploding again.

After a few moments, he looks me straight in the eye.

'You know what, Alex?' His tone is ominously calm and even. 'I didn't sign up for this.'

This blow is so hard because it's not been thrown at me in a blind hot rage. He's had this thought more than once.

Without another word he gets up and stalks out of the room. I hear him angrily grab his car keys, then the main door of the apartment opens and slams so hard it shakes the apartment – and me – to the core; and he's gone.

Chapter 9

Two months later, I'm sat in a hipster-style cafe in the West End opposite Sasha, while torrential rain lashes the pavement unforgivingly outside. Tears track her cheeks as she watches the passers-by hurrying past, trying to dodge the streams of water rushing around their feet.

'Sash, you understand why I have to do this, don't you?' My eyes seek out hers, but her gaze remains where it is. 'Sash, please?'

She finally looks at me, eyes red-rimmed and slightly bloodshot. I feel a stab to my heart as I see what I'm doing to her, but there's no room for guilt here. This is about having a future I can bear; perhaps even look forward to.

'Of course, I understand, Lex. I know you better than anyone, but it doesn't mean I like it or that I won't worry about you.' Her glassy eyes probe mine. 'It's like you're rejecting everyone who loves you when you need them the most: your mum, John, your sister, me… Dom.'

'Please don't bring him up. Dom made it perfectly clear how he felt; it wasn't what he signed up for.' There's a slight wobble to my voice and I realise I need to change the subject quickly. 'All I'm doing, Sash, is making sure I can live my life on my terms. I can't do that here. My colleagues treat me like I'll crumble to dust at the slightest thing, and my mother and Carol are suffocating the life out of me.'

Within this outpouring, I omit the fact that Sasha herself, with her well-cultivated worry farm, has also not helped the situation.

She sighs and shrugs helplessly, unable to refute my case. I reach out and take her hand as a bolt of lightning pierces the sky outside, followed by an ominous cracking and deep rumble of thunder.

'What about when you have a relapse?' she asks. 'What will you do?'

'You know they have the NHS in Birmingham too, right? It's not like I'm emigrating to the US without health insurance.'

'I mean, if you're struggling...' Sasha chews her lip anxiously. 'Who's going to do your shopping? And what about work – you really think they manage sickness absence differently south of the border?'

'Don't worry, I've thought all that through. Soon as I hear back about this job, you'll be the first to know. Just trust me.'

We sit silently for a moment. Sasha looks deeply hurt. This doesn't surprise me, given I haven't shared any of this plan with her until today, but that's how I've discovered I must now operate. Everyone's so quick to tell me what I cannot, must not, should not do, so I now share information on a need-to-know basis. I'm only telling Sasha now because it's almost signed and sealed, and I need her on side when I take the dreaded step of sharing it with my mother and Carol.

'I'm not just worried about your health situation.' Sasha breaks the silence between us. 'I'm going to miss you so much.'

Feeling unexpectedly overwhelmed by emotion, I take a deep breath to steady myself. As much as Sasha's recent worrying and overprotectiveness has frustrated me, she's still my best friend in the world.

'I know, Sash.' I stare into my empty coffee cup and try to compose myself. 'But I can't live like this. I'll lose my head if I have to endure—'

I'm silenced as my iPhone bursts into life. I look down and see a Birmingham number illuminated on the screen.

'Sorry, just give me a moment.' I answer the call. 'Hello, this is Alex speaking.'

'Hi, Alex. It's Jim from New Horizons,' says the caller.

'Hi, Jim. I hope you're calling with good news?'

I wince as Sasha resumes staring out of the window miserably.

'I certainly am,' Jim's upbeat voice confirms in my ear. 'Your relocation package has been approved and we've found you a small one-bedroom apartment to rent near the city centre. I'll email you some photos. They'd like you to start next month.'

'I'm sure that can be arranged, Jim. I'll put my notice in tomorrow. Thanks again.'

I terminate the call and take a moment to digest its full meaning. It's all sorted. I'm moving to Birmingham in a few weeks' time. My stomach churns with a mix of excitement, nervous anticipation and melancholy: for the second chance I've gained, and the life I loved so much, that I've lost. I turn back to Sasha.

'It's all confirmed. Are you ready to hear the details?'

-

By the next morning, I've managed to get Sasha on side. I also may have let her think she can come with me if she can find a job in Birmingham. Something I'm not particularly proud of, but it serves two purposes: perking Sasha up by thinking she'll be with me 'every step of the way', as she put it; and I've realised I can use the idea of her moving with me to call off the wolves aka my mother and sister.

By the time Sasha realises that uprooting her whole life for me is ridiculous and totally impractical (her mum is also unwell with long-term heart problems and having suffered a recent heart attack), I'll be home and dry, so to speak, in my new-build rental apartment. Sasha's too much of a home bird to leave Glasgow anyway.

We've arranged to meet my mother, John and Carol for Sunday lunch at the Art Lover's Cafe out at Bellahouston Park, my intention being to prevent them kicking off Glasgow-style when I break my news.

Sasha and I park the car at the back of the house and amble through the well-manicured gardens towards the beautiful iconic white building, designed by the late Charles Rennie Mackintosh. It's one of my favourite places to visit, with its lavishly detailed interior design. So much so that Dom and I had actually considered it as a wedding venue, until the wedding coordinator told us they couldn't cater for our numbers.

As this memory develops in full technicolour in my mind, my body reacts with an emotionally charged lump in my throat and an anguished tug at my heart, a feeling I've become too familiar with since our split. I place a hand on my chest, take a deep shaky breath to calm the swelling feeling of loss, and draw my focus back to what today is about.

'You OK, Lex?'

I feel Sasha's concerned eyes on me. 'Yes, fine. I just love this place. Always gets me, you know?'

'I do.' Sasha appears convinced by my answer, her eyes following my gaze towards the building. 'It really is one of Glasgow's special places.'

The thunderstorms of the previous day have freshened the air, and the late July sunshine sporadically peeks through from behind light wispy clouds. Despite a drop in temperature, we're still comfortable in our short sleeves and cropped trousers, so with ten minutes to spare, we grab a seat on a bench to enjoy the warmth on our faces.

'Thanks again for this, Sash. I know I've put you in a bit of a position on this one.'

'It's fine.' She looks at me from behind her green-rimmed oversized sunglasses. Her flaming red hair looks almost alight from the way the sun is catching it. 'I may not like it, but I kind of get it.'

'I appreciate that.' I suddenly feel a bit guilty for having gotten so irritated by Sasha's overbearing support over the last few months.

'Anyway, I've already started looking for jobs in Birmingham and there are tons of options. Maybe this is what we both need. I've always wondered what it would be like to pack up and move somewhere else, but I've been too scared. Doing it together makes it seem easier.'

'That's good,' I say automatically.

The guilt immediately dissipates. Despite me knowing Sasha won't follow through on this, I realise it could become exhausting, very quickly. Probably more so because I know it will all be for nothing and she'll eventually find a reason to back out (her mum being an obvious and quite genuine one).

We sit quietly for a few more minutes, enjoying the sun, until our zen is obliterated by the arrival of my mother and sister with John in tow.

'There they are. Hey, wee sis!' Carol's high-pitched voice carries right across the gardens from the car park.

I can see my mother waving at us theatrically from afar. They trot along the path towards us, John trailing behind them at a slower pace.

'Alex, dear, how are you?' My mother reaches me and inspects me at arm's length. Her wire-framed spectacles have darkened in the sun. 'You look not bad. Have you been following that eating plan I sent you?'

'No, I haven't.' I sigh.

'Why ever not?'

'She's just being Alex, Mother.' My sister perches her lipstick-pink sunglasses on her head and rolls her eyes dramatically. 'Has to rebel against anything we say or do.'

I observe my mother and her familial shadow and decide this is not going to be how today is going to go. I invited *them* here, so I'm going to take the lead from the off.

'Yup, I sure do. But can you blame me?' I greet John with a warm hug and lead them towards the entrance to the house at a reasonable pace, my fatigue thankfully now more manageable than it was.

We enter the Art Lover's Cafe via the gift shop. It's a bright, open space with fairy lights strung across the ceiling, square pillars perforating the room and tastefully art-bedecked white walls. We're shown to our seats, where I strategically place myself between Sasha and John for reinforcement.

'So, how are you doing, Alex?' John asks me, while my mother and Carol debate the fat content of the duck liver parfait on the menu, and whether that would be good for me *in my condition*. 'I mean generally, not in relation to your health.'

'I'm fine, John.' I smile at him warmly. 'Getting on with things.'

'Good for you. Just you keep doing that.'

'I intend to.' A thought pops into my head and I lower my voice. 'In fact, perhaps I should give you some advance warning. I'm about to give those two some news they're not going to like – for which I apologise in advance.'

'Whatever it is, I'll cope.' He gives me a little wink.

The waiter appears and is subjected to a painful ordering session, during which Carol interrogates him on the ingredients of almost every dish on the menu.

My idea to bring Sasha along works better than I thought. She keeps my mother and sister talking until our starters arrive, which she knows is when I'm going to share my news and the proverbial will hit the fan. If my plan works out, that will play out in a very restrained way, perhaps even allowing some sensible discussion to sneak through.

I allow us to get started on our food, then give Sasha the nod. She signals her understanding and expertly disengages herself from her conversation. I clear my throat in preparation to speak, then immediately regret doing so as this sets off my mother and sister's annoyingly hypersensitised off-target MS radars.

'OK, Alex?' Carol cocks her head to one side and regards me like she would a crying puppy, a behavioural trait I'm sure she's only acquired since my diagnosis.

'Fine, thanks.' I keep my tone bright. 'Actually, I've been feeling a lot better recently.'

I'm deliberately paving the way for the message that I'm reclaiming my independence guerrilla-style.

'You do seem so much better.' Sasha delivers her supportive narrative. 'It's almost as if your relapse never happened.'

'I think so too.' I nod thoughtfully, with an air of gosh-we've-both-come-to-the-same-conclusion-so-it-must-be-true.

'It happened all right.' Carol readjusts her sunglasses and bleached-blond top knot. 'Visits me in my nightmares, that day. My little sister, taken so young – nature can be so cruel.'

'I'm not dead, Carol. If you're going to milk this one, how about not doing it with the person who went through it? You were nothing more than an irritating spectator.'

'Alex, don't speak to your sister like that,' my mother hisses quietly at me. 'Carol's gone out of her way to support you these last few months. The least you can do is be a bit grateful.'

I'm about to suggest that Carol's support is about as welcome as a battered turd in a haggis supper, when I realise I need to stay focused on my original goal for today.

'Sure, whatever. Sorry, Carol. Thank you for being there for me when I was unwell.' I flash her a semi-sincere smile, which Carol seems a little too satisfied with.

'The main thing is that you're doing so much better.' Sasha prompts me back on track. 'Which we're all so pleased about.'

'Exactly. It's almost—'

'As if it never happened.' My mother cuts me off. 'Yes, we heard that, Alex. Now, are you going to share whatever it is you've brought us here for today?'

I quickly take a mouthful of my smoked mackerel salad, knowing I won't get a chance to enjoy my food once I've stepped across enemy lines. 'Right, yes. How do I put this… Probably best to be frank. I've got a new job and I'm moving to Birmingham.'

'That'll do it, all right,' I hear John mutter under his breath as my mother's fork clatters onto her side plate.

I stifle an involuntary snigger as Carol's head snaps towards me so fast her sunglasses escape their perch and land in her duck liver parfait.

'What a way to deliver a message like that,' she sneers, and turns to my mother, who's now an interesting shade of Tippex and uncharacteristically silent. 'Mum, are you OK? Don't listen to Alex. She's not serious, it's just her way of digesting this change in her life. Once everything settles down—'

'Oh, I'm serious, Carol. I'm moving to Birmingham – in a month.'

My mother finally comes to, but she's clearly dazed. 'In a month? Alex, what are you talking about? You're—'

'I'm what?' I stare at her defiantly. 'Broken? Damaged goods? An *invalid*?'

'Darling, please don't be so melodramatic.' My mother tuts at me, her usual air of superiority returning, along with the colour to her cheeks. 'You're none of those things. But you do need *support*.'

'Yeah, you need us, little sis.' Carol joins in the lecturing. 'We're in this together – for the long haul.'

She gazes at me with a demeanour to rival Mother Teresa and I feel myself gag a little. I can think of nothing worse than a life at the mercy of my mother and sister: my own personal eternal hell. But I was ready for this overprotective and patronising behaviour. Glancing across at Sasha, who gives me an encouraging smile, I take a deep breath to ensure I respond in a calm and composed manner.

'Mother, Carol, I understand you have concerns. That is natural. You've been a great support to me and I do appreciate that very much. But you have your lives to live, and I have mine—'

'Alex, you're talking as if you've sprained your ankle,' my mother interrupts. 'This is MS we're talking about, a degenerative autoimmune disease that will slowly destroy your body, bit by bit.'

'I'm aware of that. Though I'm not sure you need to be quite so graphic.'

'But it's the reality of this, Alex,' Carol pitches in. 'Mum, it's OK, I can see what's going on here. This is textbook denial and exactly the kind of behaviour we can expect.'

My mother's face blooms with realisation and relief. 'Oh, you are quite right, Carol, which means why didn't we think of this before… we need to—'

'Get Alex a counsellor to help her work through this.'

As I watch them wind each other up, I suddenly feel exhausted. Though I expected this kind of ridiculous behaviour, I felt more prepared for it in my head. Now, here, in the brightly lit restaurant, with the waiting staff bustling around me, I feel my composure start to slip. I steal a look towards Sasha and instantly regret doing so – she's reflecting back similar concern. I take a moment to arrange my thoughts, then straighten up in my chair and push my plate away from me.

'Mother, Carol, once again, I appreciate your concern. But I've considered this very carefully, and it's something I'm going to do, I'm afraid to say: whether you like it or—'

'But it's totally absurd, Alex.' My mother's tone is dismissive. 'If you can't see that then you're obviously—'

John places a calming hand on my mother's shoulder, silencing her. 'Isabel, how about you let Alex explain?'

My mother flinches, clearly unhappy at the suggestion, but she stays quiet. Carol looks like she's ready to let loose again, but she respects John's request.

'Thank you.' I give them all an appreciative smile. 'Before my diagnosis, I was flying high. I was acing my career, getting married, everything was amazing...'

I suddenly feel a swell of emotion in my throat and I swallow aggressively to avoid showing any weakness that could be misconstrued.

'Now, all that's changed,' I continue. 'Because of a stupid diagnosis. If you both know me as well as you think you do, then you'll understand that I can't and won't be defined by my MS. I'm ill, not ninety. I need my independence back and the only way to do that is to start afresh, somewhere I won't be mollycoddled by generally well-meaning but overbearing, overprotective and highly risk-averse people.'

As I finish my well-practised speech, I look round the table at the abandoned starters, realising it wasn't such a good idea to do this over lunch. A waste of food and money. Then I look up into the dumbstruck faces of my mother and sister and see my message has well and truly hit home.

'Look, I'm sorry to sound harsh but this is happening,' I say to them. 'I'm a grown woman and it's my decision. I'd rather do it with your support, but if it comes to it, I'll do it without it.'

'Right, well.' My mother snatches up her bag, yanks on her camel cashmere cardigan and gets to her feet.

'Where are you going?' I look at her incredulously.

'I'm leaving, Alex. Just like you. I assume you don't expect to be part of my decision, given I wasn't involved in your.'

This I was not expecting. Neither was John, apparently. He reaches for my mother's hand, but she flicks him away.

'But… hang on, this is ridiculous,' I protest. 'We haven't even had our main course yet.'

'No. Shame really.' She looks genuinely disappointed by this. 'I was quite looking forward to the sea trout. They do it so well here.'

'Isabel, please?' John appeals to my mother in a last-ditch attempt to get her to stay.

'No, John.' Her voice is almost a whisper but her message is strong. 'Not this time. My daughter has carefully planned this event to keep me out of her life. I would *never* have done the same to her. You can tell her she can get in touch once she wakes up from this silly fantasy and is ready to discuss a realistic plan for her future.'

I'm shocked to the core as I watch my mother exit the restaurant, careful to remain composed while there's the possibility of eyes on her. As I watch her go, Carol scrambles to her feet. She looks at me with venom.

'Well done, brat. You've always been so blinkin' selfish.'

Less bothered about making a scene, she gallops off after my mother, as the restaurant comes to a standstill and forty pairs of eyes land on our table.

'Well, that went well.' John chuckles, more out of discomfort than amusement. 'Perhaps I'd better go as well. I've got the car keys.'

'I'm so sorry about that, John.' I chew my lip in discomfort. 'I genuinely thought coming here would allow for a calmer, more constructive conversation.'

'She'll calm down. Just give her some time. Can I pay towards the bill?'

'Definitely not.' I shake my head firmly. 'This is my mess. I'll clear it up.'

'If you're sure.' John gives me a hug and a fatherly kiss on the cheek, then heads out of the restaurant.

As I watch yet another member of my family vacate the restaurant, I feel a reassuring hand on my arm.

'Sorry that's how it turned out.' Sasha gazes at me sadly with her big blue eyes.

'It was never going to go well.' I shrug. 'She doesn't understand my position at all. It shows me that I was absolutely right to exclude her from this decision. Well intended but false promises would be all I'd get from her.'

'So, what next?'

'No idea. But we should probably get out of here.' I reach up and signal to the perplexed waiter.

Chapter 10

One month later, I'm wandering around my empty Glasgow apartment, doing my final checks, my footsteps echoing loudly through the empty high-ceilinged rooms. The home I shared with Dom, once so warm and inviting, now cold and vacant; reminiscent of how my life here has become.

'That's us ready to go, love,' one of the removals men calls out to me.

'OK, thanks.' I join him in the hallway. 'You have the key for my new place, right?'

'Sure do.' He jangles a set of keys in his pocket.

'Great. And thanks again for agreeing to set up the furniture for me, it'll be good to be able to move straight in tomorrow.'

'No problem. All the best now.'

I see him out, then finish my checks before locking up for the final time and heading into the city centre for my train.

On entering the concourse of Glasgow Central Station, my senses are immediately engulfed by garbled train announcements, guards whistling, the smell of diesel, and people rushing to catch their trains. For some, this is an essential passage from A to B. For me, it oozes vibrancy and opportunity. Not just because of my brand-new start, but because this is the type of living I love: bustling, active, energetic.

Making my way across to the huge departure boards, I zone in on the illuminated timetable declaring the final destination of Birmingham, and I'm pleased to see that my train is on time. I feed my ticket into the machine and the paddle-shaped barriers snap open, allowing me onto the platform.

On locating my train and carriage, I'm about to board when an unexpected wave of emotion rushes over me. All of a sudden, my chest feels like it's filled with cement, and my breathing becomes shallow as I fight the lump in my throat. Reaching up, I dab at the corners of my eyes, realising there are tears forming. Tears that I refuse to let come. What the hell is wrong with me? This is something I want to do, that I'm looking forward to.

But is it? A voice creeps into my head. The same one that visited me briefly in hospital. I only 'want' to do this because I've been left with no other choice. What I really wanted to do was get married, be Dom's life partner in crime, continue my kickass career – and maybe have a couple of mischievous but amazing kids. Am I actually kidding myself? Is this the textbook denial my sister described?

'You getting on board, love?' The train guard shocks me out of my self-doubt. 'The train's about to go.'

Time to decide. Is this really the future I want and need? Can I really do this alone? Or am I doing it for no reason other than being fiercely independent and stubborn? Perhaps more like my mother – who, along with my sister, has refused to have anything to do with me since I told her I was moving – than I thought.

I tune back in to the buzz of the station, to everything that it represents for me, and my answer is clear. This is not me – I don't ruminate and second-guess myself. I find solutions and I get things done. It might not be the future I would have chosen, but it's the best one for me now – and I'm going to damn well make the most of it. Decision made, I push the button to open the carriage door and climb on board.

By the time I've settled into my spacious first-class seat (a little indulgent perhaps, but it's not like I up and move hundreds of miles away every day) and engrossed myself in a gritty crime novel, my floundering on the platform back at Glasgow Central is long forgotten. The beautiful Scottish countryside flashes past me outside the window, accentuated by the early autumn sunshine. The contrast between the racing images of the outdoors and the quiet calm of the carriage adds an extra layer of relaxation to my experience.

I've chosen a two-seater table so I can enjoy a real sense of comfort, which is enhanced by the seat opposite me not being reserved until Oxenholme in the Lake District. Checking the journey on my phone, I'm pleased to note that I have nearly two hours of not having to share the space with a stranger.

About twenty minutes into my journey, the train crew begin serving food and refreshments. They gradually make their way up the carriage towards me.

'Tea or coffee?' a man with a Yorkshire accent, armed with two large metal jugs, asks me.

'Coffee, please.'

'Right you are.' He serves me at record speed, then moves to the next table.

I add milk to my drink and give it a stir, before enjoying a satisfying slurp. It's not the best coffee I've had, but it tastes good because of what it represents: my return to freedom, independence and a fulfilling career. I return to my reading but within minutes I'm interrupted again as my lunch is served and the drinks cart arrives at my spot. The woman in charge of it is very cheery, with a thick accent from somewhere in Europe. I smile warmly at her as she jokes animatedly with the people across the aisle from me.

Having an advance nosey at what's available, I see a range of soft and alcoholic drinks on her trolley. My eyes land on the miniature spirits, conjuring up memories of many enjoyable holidays (with both Dom and Sasha), where these Lilliputian bottles have been a symbol of celebration on board our outbound flights. A clear marker for the beginning of endless sunshine, exotic landscapes and architectural delights.

Though I'm following quite a committed 'healthy living' plan, I can sense a longing for that celebratory feeling. It feels quite fitting right now. I'm certainly viewing this move as an achievement and a new adventure. My neurology consultant didn't expressly forbid alcohol either. He suggested I limit my intake and apply common sense, particularly when I experience symptoms like balance issues that might be made worse by alcohol. I decide that one drink isn't going to do me any harm.

Once she's finished with the other passengers, the jolly woman turns towards me. 'Anything to drink, madam?'

'Yes, please. Could I have a gin and tonic? Actually, can I be cheeky and ask for two cans of tonic so it's not as strong?'

'Of course. Good choice, gin.' She dumps some ice and lemon in a plastic tumbler and places it in front of me on a paper coaster. 'You go home or away?'

'Sorry?' I blink at her. I'm certainly not going to be opting for takeaway.

'Home or away? Holiday, business or go home?'

'Oh… I'm…' I realise I don't know how to answer. 'I don't know. I've just left home. But I'm moving to Birmingham today, so I guess I'm going to my new home.'

'You have two home. Like me. I have home in Hungary, but also now here in UK. Enjoy.'

She places a miniature bottle of gin and two cans of tonic water in front of me, along with an equally miniature packet of crisps. Then she releases the brake on her drinks cart and moves along the carriage to the next table.

Alone once more, I pour my drink and just sit for a moment, watching the bubbles dance in the plastic cup. Two homes? I never really considered the question of 'home' in my decision to move. But one thing is clear: home is where you feel comfortable and safe. At the moment neither Glasgow nor Birmingham can tick both those boxes. I've just got to hope that Birmingham will – and right now I feel positive about that.

By the time we're approaching Oxenholme station, I'm tentatively anticipating the arrival of my tablemate and sincerely hoping they won't be incredibly annoying. I've also had an enjoyable lunch of a chicken and chorizo flatbread, paired with my 'long' gin and tonic, and I'm feeling quite chipper. My drink has very much added the air of celebration I was seeking to my trip. But it has also depleted my attention span, causing me to cast aside my book in search of something more interactive.

I pick up my phone and start scrolling through Twitter. I'm in the process of commenting on someone's rather unfortunate encounter with an overzealous sheep at a petting zoo, grinning to myself as I do, when a voice comes from above me.

'You look like you're enjoying yourself.'

I half-glance up to see that my tablemate has arrived. He appears to be squeezing a hiker's style backpack into the luggage rack overhead.

'Oh, hello,' I greet him briefly, unable to drag myself away from my Twitter discussions.

I continue to dip in and out of various discussion threads, some funny, some political, some involving more emotive and important issues like mental health. As I do, I become aware that my now seated tablemate is watching me. I look up from typing a tweet in support of an environmental activist group, and my breath catches in my throat. It's the Brummie man from the train all those months ago.

'We meet again.' He smiles warmly at me and my senses feel like they've taken a dive into a cake mixer.

I remember him being quite attractive. He's not. He's absolutely bloody gorgeous. His well-manicured beard gives him a look not dissimilar to Dom's, but those dark chocolate eyes paired with his chestnut hair and that bone structure take him to a whole other level. He's also wearing trendy outdoorsy gear that makes him look like Bear Grylls. It certainly explains the athletic physique: about right for someone who evidently hikes in the Lake District.

I set my phone down on the table in front of me and try to breathe normally. 'We do indeed.'

'How are you? How's the career going?'

It's an obvious conversation starter, given where we left off before, but with my changing circumstances, I'm not keen to chat about myself.

'It's… fine. I'm fine. And you? You've been hiking, I assume?'

'Sure have. Three days, three peaks. Just ticked Scafell Pike, Helvellyn and Old Man of Coniston off my list.'

'Right… I've heard of Scafell Pike. But not the others.'

'They're the three highest peaks in the Lake District.'

'Gosh, you're keen.'

'Can't get enough of the outdoors.' He gazes longingly out the window at the hills and woods scooting past. 'I'd live in a tent on a mountainside if it weren't so impractical.'

'The commute would certainly be a bit of a bitch.' I smile at him and he chuckles in amusement. 'I've never done the full-on hiking thing.'

'You should try it. Once you get a taste, you'll never go back. Promise you.'

'Not sure I'm a stay-in-a-tent-with-no-running-water-and-pee-outside-in-the-middle-of-the-night kind of girl.'

'What kind of girl are you then? A married one by now, I'm guessing.'

I hesitate. 'Actually, no. I split from my fiancé a few months ago.'

His face immediately falls. 'Shit. I'm really sorry. Got a habit of asking the wrong questions, haven't I?'

'It's OK. You weren't to know – either time. My ring was getting resized, by the way, I'm not one of those women who removes it to get attention.'

'Right. Still haven't covered myself in glory though, have I?'

'You're fine. How about we change the subject? What was it you were asking me?'

He rubs his beard thoughtfully. 'Ah, yes… what do you like if tents aren't your thing?'

I consider how to answer this question, given what I enjoy doing and what I can actually do don't always match up any more.

'I've always enjoyed park runs, crime novels, and I'm quite partial to a bit of karaoke.'

'You're a singer?'

'No, doing karaoke and being a singer are two very different things. I can just about hold a tune.'

'That's better than most.' He shrugs. 'So, back to hiking, there are such things as hotels and hostels, you know. You don't have to do the tent thing. Or you could just do a day's hike in the mountains.'

'Maybe I should try it sometime then.' I'm saying this more out of politeness than anything else.

'You do mountains as part of big change?' The cheery woman with the food and drinks trolley has reappeared and decided to join our conversation. 'Good change to life. Good for heart and head. Drink for you, sir?'

The man scopes out her offerings. 'Why not? As I'm in Scottish company, I'll have a whisky and Coke, please.' He glances back towards me. 'Join me?'

I hesitate at first, unsure whether it's a good idea to have another drink. But, caught up as I am in the moment, and enjoying another chance encounter with the god of the countryside, my better judgement appears to be on ice for now.

'Sure, if it's on you,' I joke, then turn to the woman serving us. 'Gin and tonic again, please.'

'Two cans of tonic?'

'That would be great, thanks.'

She serves our drinks, chatting merrily about the time she visited London and how it has no mountains, and then moves on to the next row, swaying a little as the train whooshes round one of the tighter bends.

'You've made a friend, it seems,' the man comments as he pours his drink.

'She's just really friendly.'

'I'm Matt, by the way. We never got properly acquainted last time, and if we're going to drink together, we should at least be on first-name terms. Unless you have some kind of title, which I'm more than happy to use.'

'Hmm…' I tap my jaw reflectively. 'Shall I go with Lady or Dame? Which makes me sound cooler?'

'Dame, definitely. Then you can be known as "that damn fine dame".'

'I like that. I'm Alex. No title, but just as fine.'

'Perfectly put.' He gives me a little salute.

'Cheers.' I hold out my drink. 'Good to see you again.'

'Cheers, Alex.' He takes a mouthful of his drink and makes a pained face that's a dead giveaway he's not a regular whisky drinker. 'So, where are you off to this time? Another conference?'

His dark eyes penetrate mine searchingly. Though his gaze is intense, it's not in a creepy way. More just keen interest. I decide that, as much as we've met before and my inhibitions are currently on a minibreak, I mustn't give too much away. After all, the 'Belfast Strangler' was utterly gorgeous – and a serial killer. And though I know that was a fictional storyline, there's a remarkable physical resemblance between the two of them.

I take a sip from my drink, enjoying the alcoholic heat of the gin and the bubbles teasing my lips. 'I'm actually moving to Birmingham for a new job.'

'You are?' He seems surprised and – if my instincts aren't totally off – pleased to hear this. 'What's the new job?'

I purse my lips thoughtfully as I consider this question. 'I want to say big important television producer for the BBC...'

'But...?'

'I'm a project manager.'

'I see your problem. They are worlds apart.'

'It gets worse. I'm an IT project manager.'

He puts on a repulsed face. 'I'm with you. Can't get much worse than that.'

'What about the fact that I love it?' I cringe.

'OK, that does it. Excuse me, could I move seats, please?' he jokes to a passing member of the train crew, who seems unsure whether to stop or keep walking.

I laugh and shake my head, giving the poor staff member a signal that it's fine to walk on.

'And your wholly superior job is...?' I prompt him.

'Superhero?'

'Come on. I shared my shame. It's your turn.'

'I'm a manufacturing engineer.'

'Ha, that sounds even worse,' I hoot triumphantly.

'I'd say that's debatable. Shall we ask your friend with the drinks cart to take the deciding vote?'

'Not sure she'd be with either of us. So, what does a manufacturing engineer actually do?'

Rather than waiting for an answer, I pick up my phone and look up the term.

'Still got the same bad habit of validating everything through Google then.'

I look up from my phone and laugh. 'You got me. Very guilty of that, as well as being a notorious "smombie". Trying to get on top of these things.'

Matt looks amused. 'I'd say by my observations so far you're not doing so well at either. It took you long enough to notice me.'

'Yeah, well, who made you chief phone-use observer?'

As we continue our flirty banter, I realise that for the first time in months, I actually feel like my old self. Like a woman. A strong, desirable woman who can flirt and be flirted with. Not someone's patient. Not someone who needs care or looking after. It reminds me of the way Dom and I used to bounce off each other, the chemistry between us still electric, despite being several years into our relationship. Where did it go? I didn't even notice it disappearing until it was gone. All because of the cruelty of nature and the inability of the people in my life to continue to see me as the person I was – as the person I *still am*.

Would this guy behave the same way towards me if he knew I had MS? Or if I were sat here in a wheelchair? It's sad, but based on my experience so far, I do doubt it. I feel an unexpected smarting inside me: frustration at the injustice of it all.

'You OK?' Matt breaks through my thoughts. 'Think I lost you there.'

'Sorry, yeah. Totally zoned out.' I pick up my drink and knock the last of it back.

'Hope it was over something good.'

'It was… something I need to think about less.'

'Fair enough. So, do you have friends in Birmingham?'

'No.' I shake my head and pour myself a refill. 'Don't know anyone who lives there.'

'Right then.' He looks a bit bemused. 'Must be a damn good job if you're up for starting over by yourself. Hats off to you. Though I do remember the last time we chatted, you said you liked it there.'

We continue to laugh and chat all the way to Birmingham New Street Station. The two-and-a-half-hour journey has seemed to pass in a flash and, when the conductor's voice comes over the intercom, announcing our imminent arrival and reminding us to take all our belongings as we alight from the train, I can't help feeling a little disappointed that the journey is over so quickly. I've enjoyed my bit of escapism with gorgeous Matt.

'Do you know where you're going all right?' he asks me, as we descend the steps from the train and find ourselves standing opposite each other on the busy platform.

'Yeah, I remember a bit from when I was last here, and I've pretty much got the image from Google Maps stored in my head. I'll find my way just fine.'

He nods his understanding but shows no sign of moving.

'It was nice to see you again.' I feel the need to fill the silence. 'Thanks for the company.'

'You too.' He looks at me, almost shyly this time.

I realise that, knowing I'm single again, he now wants to ask for my number but is perhaps wondering if it's a good idea so soon after my break-up. As much as I'm attracted to him, I'm not sure I want him to. It's only been a matter of weeks since Dom and I went our separate ways, and I'm still a bit battered and bruised from that experience. I decide I should be the one to move away, so as not to give the wrong impression.

'OK, see you then.' I turn and start to walk off.

'Wait.' Matt steps forward and gently places his hand on my arm to stop me.

I curse myself for not shutting this down sooner and slowly turn towards him. 'What's up?'

'Uh… you don't happen to need a tour guide, do you? I could show you around. Point out the good places to eat, bars, etc.'

My stomach flutters. He looks so vulnerable, standing there waiting for my response. There's something appealing about a man who gets nervous when asking a woman out – it shows a human side that speaks volumes over laddish bravado. There's no doubt I'm attracted to him, but something just doesn't feel right, which must surely be because I've just ended my engagement. But as he stands there, I can't bear to let him down.

'Sure,' I hear myself say automatically. 'How about you give me your number and I'll give you a call once I'm settled?'

'Great.' His face immediately lights up.

He relays the number and I type it into my phone.

'Thanks, Matt.' I smile at him. 'I guess I'll speak to you soon then. Now off you go before I change my mind.'

'Right you are.' He gives me a final grin, this time more confident, and strides off along the platform.

As I watch him go, I wonder if maybe I was too quick to rule out a date. It doesn't mean it has to go anywhere, and I do need to meet people to build my life here. I've just been handed my first Birmingham connection on a silver service plate. What's wrong with enjoying the company of a gorgeous and genuinely nice guy? I definitely shouldn't be ruling anything out at this stage in my new life.

As I make my way along the platform, I notice the escalators to the main station concourse are out of order. There's a lift nearby, but a queue is forming outside it, mostly elderly people and travellers with big cases, so I head for the stairs.

I don't think twice as I make my way up the first few steps, but by the time I reach the halfway point I'm out of breath, my muscles burning in protest. It's a stark reminder that as much as I can feel quite normal when not doing anything too taxing, my body still isn't coping well with more challenging physical activities – especially stairs.

I pause and stand to the side by the handrail, allowing the other passengers to pass me while I get my breath back. Then I start to climb the second half of the long steep flight. By the time I reach the top, I'm really wishing I'd waited and taken the lift. Panting heavily, my legs now weak and heavy as lead, I find a seat in one of the waiting areas and allow myself time to recover: something I've had to get used to. As I'm resting and indulging in a bit of people-watching, my mind starts to tick once again – and not in a helpful way.

It's not such a good start, feeling like this, only minutes into arriving alone in the city that is to be my new home. I haven't even made it out of the station yet. It's so easy to forget that I'm ill when I'm just sitting having a laugh, like I was doing on the train. But here, now, too fatigued to make it to the shop across the walkway for a bottle of water, I'm almost starting to question my sanity. I've decided to move three hundred miles away from everyone who loves me, everyone who was willing to support me with my condition. I've snubbed the lot of them.

My only connection in this huge city is a man I've met twice on a train, who probably wouldn't look twice at me if he knew the truth. Because really, as Dom so eloquently put it, who would willingly 'sign up' for that? Certainly not someone who scales mountains for fun. What was I even thinking, taking his number?

Frustrated, I pull out my phone, look up Matt's number and hit delete. Sure, he'll be disappointed. He might wonder what he did wrong, perhaps even think I'm just some tease who led him on. But I'll be doing him a favour in the long run – he just won't know it.

Chapter 11

Once I've recovered enough to get going, I seek out a taxi to take me to my new place. As the cab rattles along the busy Birmingham roads, past the huge high-rise buildings that would dwarf most of those in Glasgow, I look out the window curiously at the passers-by. It's a far more diverse city population than that of Glasgow, something I noticed last time I was here too. A city that attracts all types of people – hopefully that will mean I can blend in here quite nicely.

The cab eventually pulls up alongside the residential development that houses my new apartment at the edge of the city centre. It looks just as it did in the pictures: a large modern building, with two floor-to-ceiling windows, allowing me a peek at the sparkling grey marble floor and white walls of the foyer inside.

I pay the driver and get out of the taxi, noting how fresh the air is in the middle of the UK's second largest city. Digging out my keys, I flash my key fob in front of the door sensor and the excitement at the thought of walking across the threshold of my new place finally returns. This is more like it.

Once inside, I cross the foyer and get into the waiting lift. As it ascends, I inspect my appearance in the mirror, noting that I look a bit off colour. Not surprising really, given the way I felt before in the station. Perhaps I shouldn't have had that second gin and tonic after all. Nor so much fun on the train.

As I tune in to my inner voice chiding me – something it never used to do – I stop and take a reality check. What's the real situation here? Stairs were never my best friend. Now they're my worst enemy, alcohol or no alcohol. And if I can't have a bit of fun occasionally, then what's the point in anything?

The lift arrives at the fifth floor and the doors spring open, bringing me back to the moment. I find my apartment and unlock the door, which opens into a tiny hallway. Closing the door behind me, I dump my bag on the floor, keen to explore my new habitat. It's more compact than my apartment in Glasgow, but it does have a small balcony to enjoy the warmer weather the West Midlands enjoys over Glasgow.

My furniture and boxes greet me in the kitchen-living room and the bedroom, giving the place a welcome sense of familiarity. It's just as I'd hoped. Aside from unpacking my things, which I can do gradually, I'm already moved in.

While exploring the kitchen, I find there's a surprise waiting for me. The fridge is filled with some basic essentials, including milk, butter, bread and a block of cheese. Confused, I look around me. There's washing-up liquid and a sponge beside the sink, and a pack of teabags on the counter.

'Where did all this come from?' I ask the empty room.

Then I spot an envelope propped up against the wall near the kitchen's electrical sockets. Ripping it open, I find that it's a 'new home' card from the removals company.

'Dear Ms Morton,' I read aloud. 'Thanks for using Bridgeton Removals. We hope you had a smooth journey. Thought you'd appreciate not having to visit the supermarket as soon as you arrive. All the best for the future.'

In perfect synchrony, my stomach emits a hungry grumble. I cross the room and place the card proudly on my round glass dining table.

'How nice is that?' I continue my conversation with the empty room. 'Probably the only card I'll get.'

Digging a plate, a mug and some cutlery out of the brown cardboard box marked 'kitchen crockery', I give them a quick wash and make myself a cheese sandwich, which I hungrily wolf down with a cup of tea. Then I look around at the brown packing boxes and feel immediately exhausted. There's no way I'm dealing with them now. Instead, I go through to my bedroom, make up my bed and switch on my small flat-screen TV, which the removals men have helpfully tuned for me. Lying back, I start watching a film that's just begun, but it's not long before my eyelids start to feel heavy, so admitting defeat, I climb under the covers and allow myself to drift off.

–

Having arranged not to start at my new job until midweek, I spend the next few days unpacking and familiarising myself with my new surroundings. This includes basics such as finding the closest supermarket and testing out the walk to my new office, as well as the essential task of signing up with a GP – something my neurologist suggested I do immediately, so I can access help quickly should I need it.

Being a high-calibre example of life's 'doers', my natural instinct is to rush around like a hummingbird seeking nectar, getting everything done as quickly as possible. But, aware of my limitations and the potential to set myself back, I force myself to work at a reduced pace. This doesn't come easily, and on several occasions, I find myself starting to flag the way I did at the station. While I'm becoming more attuned to the warning signs, it seems that only when I'm hanging by my fingernails do I take proper notice. It will take practice to learn to hit the brakes sooner, but at least I'm no longer soaring off the cliff edge Thelma and Louise style.

–

By the time my first day at my new job comes round, I'm properly settled and ready to get going with my new career challenge. As I stand in front of my full-length mirror, assessing the suitability of my 'day one' outfit, I'm a jangle of nerves and anticipation. This is where my brand-new start really begins. No more awkward conversations and pitying looks. No more being kept away from tasks considered too challenging for me while my boss tries to dress the alternative up as a 'development opportunity'. I will just be Alex, the experienced project manager who's moved down from Glasgow. Full stop.

The only downside to this experience is that I have no one to share it with. My previous firsts were something I did with Dom by my side. He was my biggest supporter, as I was his. It makes me wonder whether he's felt it too. Or if he's already moved on, relieved at the second chance he's been given by walking out of my life. As this thought buzzes around my head, attempting to hijack my positivity, I mentally swat it away. That's part of my old life now. It's locked away in a box and I've hurled the key so far into the sea of forgotten experiences, it can't be opened again.

Back on track, and happy that I look the part, I grab my bag and head out of my apartment. When I emerge into the still morning air, I can't help thinking that the spectacular sun for my first day is a good sign.

As I reach Sheepcote Street, the strip of road that separates the quiet of my residential area from the urban buzz, I receive my first reminder that I'm in a large city. The huge modern commercial buildings of Brindley Place stand regally, like huge chess pieces, and heavy traffic signals that the morning rush is very much in progress.

I cross the road and make my way to the main plaza of Brindley Place, experiencing the same bubbly, energised feeling I've had each time I've walked through it over the last few days. The design of the space, the splashing of the fountains and the cafe situated in the centre all give it a bit of a European feel. Just beyond the water features, there's a cluster of bars and eateries, housed in more traditional, red-brick buildings. And beyond that, an entry point to Birmingham's canal network with its fascinating reminders of the city's industrial heritage: the old cranes used to unload narrowboats, the charming cast-iron bridges, and the renovated canal house, now a pub, but with its beautiful original features retained. An open-air warren of pathways just itching to be explored. It's an area that's already stolen my heart. I just know I'm going to love living here.

For a moment, I just stand and take in the large office block that is home to my new employer. It's about eight storeys high, with a glass-fronted facade made up of individual floor-to-ceiling windows that allow passers-by to see the workers at their desks. Taking a final deep breath to ground myself, I walk inside and approach the reception desk.

'Good morning, madam. May I help you?' an attractive blond woman wearing a headset greets me.

I give her my most confident smile. 'Hello, yes, please. My name is Alex Morton. It's my first day at Fletcher & Co. I've to ask for Emmanuel Akintola.'

The woman types something into her computer at lightning speed.

'Perfect. Just give me a second and I'll call her.' She punches a number into her desk phone and waits for an answer. 'Ms Akintola? Hello, it's Lara from reception. I have Alex Morton here waiting for you… OK, great, thank you.' She disconnects the call and returns her attention to me. 'Just take a seat. Ms Akintola will be down shortly.'

'Thank you.' I give her an appreciative nod and make my way to the seating area, perching myself on the edge of one of the charcoal-grey armchair-style seats. A few minutes later, my new manager appears out of the lift and enthusiastically click-clacks her way across the tiled floor towards me. She's about ten years older than me, with beautifully braided dark hair tied up in a ponytail, make-up that looks like it's been applied by a professional, and a very stylish dress sense; she's wearing a figure-hugging caramel-coloured faux leather pencil skirt and a cream asymmetric sweater.

'Alex, hi. It's so great to finally meet you in person.' She extends her hand and I get to my feet and shake it vigorously.

'It's great to meet you too.' I smile at her. 'I've never done the whole interview process by phone before. It's a different experience.'

'It is that. But no point in dragging you all the way down here with the technology we have available to us these days.'

I'm expecting us to head for the lifts, but Emmanuel gestures instead to the main entrance.

'How about we go for a coffee first? Get to know each other properly. Then you can meet the rest of the team. We can sort your staff pass on the way back.'

'Great.'

We make our way outside and across the plaza to an Italian cafe-restaurant called Conti's, nestled right in the centre of the cluster of bars and eateries that overlook the canal and the International Conference Centre.

'This all right?' Emmanuel asks me. 'They do great coffee and delicious toasted panettone.'

'Sounds wonderful.'

We enter the warmly lit cafe. It's certainly very inviting, with its shelves of authentic Italian produce, and wide selection of Italian-style cakes and pastries arranged beautifully in the glass counter by the bar. Emmanuel leads me to a small table in the far corner, away from the smattering of customers further towards the front, and we get ourselves settled.

'Let's get our order in and then we can chat properly.' Emmanuel hands me a menu. 'I'm going to have coffee and panettone. Have whatever you like. This is on me.'

'Oh, there's no need for that,' I protest lightly. 'I can get it.'

'Absolutely not.' She holds up an instructive finger, which seems a little at odds with her kind and bubbly demeanour. 'This is my way of welcoming you to the team.'

As this is my first proper encounter with my new manager, I decide it's best not to get into an unnecessary bickering match over the bill.

'OK, if you're sure. Thank you, that's very kind. I'll just have a small skinny cappuccino, thanks.'

'And to eat?'

'Nothing for me, thanks.'

'Now, Alex, I hope you're not declining out of politeness.' She cocks her head a little.

'I'm not. I promise. I'm just trying to live a bit more healthily these days.'

'All right then. That I can understand, even if I don't abide by it myself.' She chuckles at her own joke and I follow suit, already won over by her easygoing demeanour.

The waiter appears to take our order, which Emmanuel delivers on our behalf. He then disappears behind the bar to make our coffees.

'So, tell me, how was your trip down?' she asks me. 'Are you all settled into your new apartment?'

'Yes, that's me sorted. Give or take a couple of boxes of stuff I'm wondering why I kept.'

'That's always the way. My husband accuses me of being a hoarder but I don't see him complaining when I magically produce something he needs in the moment. Selective grumbling, I call it.'

'Sounds very apt.' I laugh, pleased that my new boss is so open and friendly.

'Are you all settled in your new place? Finding your way around all right?'

'Yes and yes. The city centre is nice and compact, which makes it easy to navigate.'

'That's good. And your move went well?'

'Very smooth. The removal people even left me some food so I didn't have to go straight out to the shops when I arrived.'

'That was kind of them. What a lovely touch.'

We pause our conversation as the waiter delivers our drinks and Emmanuel's panettone. I immediately regret not ordering some myself. The sweet, bready aroma wafts into my nostrils and my stomach grumbles in annoyance at having only been fed fresh fruit for breakfast.

'Would you like some?' Emmanuel spots my look of longing.

'Oh, no. Sorry, it's just the smell. It's wonderful.' I can tell I'm not fooling her one bit.

'Here.' She plonks one of her three slices onto her unused napkin and places it beside my coffee cup. 'One piece won't do you any harm. You'll need the energy. First week of a new job is always tiring.'

I realise she's spot on. I should have thought of that myself and allowed myself a little more breakfast fuel. There's healthy living and there's practically starving myself, like I was doing in the run-up to the wedding (I've now admitted to myself), and I'm not sure I've found the right balance yet.

'OK, thanks. You're right. I feel bad taking yours, though.'

'Not at all.' She sips at her coffee 'You've done me a favour. I always feel guilty after the third slice.'

'Sounds a bit like a win-win then.'

'It definitely is. So, shall we get on to some work stuff then?'

'Yes, please.' I sit forward enthusiastically as I take a bite of panettone, which tastes like fluffy, buttery heaven. 'I'm looking forward to getting stuck in.'

'Great. The team are looking forward to meeting you. Most of them are in meetings all morning, but I've arranged for us to go for lunch today as a bit of a welcome. Hope that's all right with you?' She involuntarily glances at the panettone on the napkin in front of me.

'That's absolutely fine. Honestly, I'm not obsessed with healthy eating. Or if I am, I've just realised I need to stop it. Right now.'

Emmanuel laughs at my self-deprecation. 'That's great. We thought we'd go for Thai.'

'Perfect. I love Thai food. Thanks for doing this.'

'All part of helping you settle in. Building relationships and feeling part of the team is just as important as understanding the organisation and the work.'

I beam like a lighthouse as Emmanuel takes me through the company background, structure and where my role fits in. Despite knowing about my MS, she hasn't led with that. She has treated me like any other new employee: someone with great potential, who simply needs the knowledge and tools to do the job. We talk about everything but my medical situation, to the point that I wonder if it's even going to come up.

'One last thing before we head over and meet the team…' Emmanuel wipes some rogue panettone crumbs from her chin. '…let's have a very quick chat about your medical situation – if you don't mind?'

Despite all the reassurances I've received, I stiffen slightly. Not because I don't trust Emmanuel – I've seen no reason not to so far – but because I've become so hypersensitised to being treated differently, this reaction is now automatic. Although I try to hide it by taking a mouthful of my cappuccino, Emmanuel picks up on it immediately.

'If you'd rather not talk about it just now, that's absolutely fine, Alex. We can do it whenever you're ready.'

I silently curse myself for allowing this weakness to show through. I used to think I'd be a great poker player because of how easily I could let things bounce off me. Now, I realise, I'd be fleeced for every penny in the first game.

'No, it's fine, honestly.' I attempt as genuine a smile as possible. 'Let's cover it off now.'

'All right then…' Emmanuel seems to consider her words very carefully. 'Alex, I want to start with some reassurance. We recruit through New Horizons for a reason – and that reason is that we believe a truly great workplace only comes from having a diverse workforce. Ethical standards and seeing people as people are at the very heart of our operation. As you know, New Horizons specialises in finding the right fit for experienced professionals who have a long-term illness or disability that doesn't affect their ability to do a great job – they just need a more flexible and supportive environment in which to do it.'

'They're really great.' I nod. 'I never once felt there was a focus on my medical situation.'

'Which means they're doing their job just as they should. And we will do ours. All I want to do today is review the arrangements we agreed when we were discussing your contract, and check that you haven't thought of anything else we should consider. That's it. Everything else will be managed as normal.'

'OK, sure. Sounds good.' I feel genuine relief on hearing this.

'Great. Now, you're working five days a week – two from home, and you'll also work from home on an ad hoc basis where you feel you need to. Regarding sickness absence, we understand the relapsing-remitting nature of your condition may mean you have more regular periods of absence, and some that may be a bit extended. We accept that and we will arrange cover as required.'

'This almost seems too good to be true.'

Emmanuel looks at me sincerely. 'Sadly, in some ways it is, if you think about the UK workplace as a whole. But slowly, we are becoming less of an exception.'

'I think your approach is amazing. The one thing it doesn't help me with, though, is me.' I chuckle briefly, then turn serious as the memories flood back. 'I experienced a lot of guilt and frustration when I was off previously. I'm really driven, and not being able to do my job was like someone had tied my hands behind my back.'

'It must be very difficult for you having to face physical limitations in a way you never have before; I could see from your CV that you're a go-getter. Let's just keep talking, and when the time comes, I'll help you in any way I can.'

I flinch a little at the use of the term 'when the time comes'. It's a frank and certain statement – too much so for my liking. But I'd be kidding myself if I used the word 'if' – it's inevitable I'll have another relapse; I just have no idea when it will be. On top of that, it's been explained to me how my more permanent symptoms can worsen under some circumstances, such as from colds and viral infections, or extreme stress and pressure.

'Is that all right with you, Alex?' Emmanuel prompts me.

I drag my mind back to the moment. 'Sorry, yes. That works for me.'

'Good. Just one final thing. As per your request, no one but myself, Sally, the HR consultant who also interviewed you, and the occupational health doctor is aware of your situation. It is completely confidential, and that situation will only change should you wish it to.'

'That's really important to me.' I look her straight in the eye to accentuate this point. 'So, thank you.'

'I know it is. Now, shall we head back to the office?'

Chapter 12

Back in the main reception of my new office, Emmanuel signs for my staff pass, which is there waiting for me, then we head for the office. As the lift doors ping open on the ninth floor, we're met by a long bright corridor with opaque glass walls separating us from the workspaces on the other side. Emmanuel leads me to an office suite with the company's name and logo proudly displayed at the door.

I follow Emmanuel across the office space where there are about a hundred and fifty desks in total and a sea of people looking very busy.

'This is your desk.' She stops at a bank of six desks and pats the back of one of the chairs, right beside the window, overlooking Brindley Place. 'And this is your laptop.' She picks up a smart-looking HP laptop and hands it to me.

'Great.' I take a few steps forward so I can see out the window, down to the plaza below. 'Nice view. I'll enjoy sitting here.'

'Bagged yourself a window seat.' A female voice comes from behind me. 'Who did you have to pay to get that?'

I turn and find myself face to face with a woman about my age. She has honey-blond hair that cascades down to her elbows and piercing blue eyes that look almost feline. She's very pretty in a sharp way. Even though her comment was obviously intended as a joke, there's something a bit cold and icy about her; like there's just a hint of resentment.

I decide the safest approach is to engage with the joke. 'It wasn't too expensive. I'll still afford my groceries this month.'

'That's funny,' she says in a voice that suggests it's nothing of the sort. 'I'm Danielle. I'm on the project team. You must be Alex?'

'That's right.' I extend my hand. 'Nice to meet you, Danielle.'

'Likewise.' She shakes my hand, smiling brightly, but her eyes fail to join the party, leaving me in no doubt as to the insincerity of the gesture.

I've come across people like Danielle over recent years, so I know that I can trust my instincts screaming at me. What I need to work out next is, can I win her over enough to have a productive working relationship, or is she just going to be bloody hard work?

'I'm off to get a coffee, Emmanuel,' she chirrups in a voice that's sweeter than syrup. 'Want anything?'

'I'm fine for now, thanks,' Emmanuel replies.

'No probs.'

Danielle stalks off in her skyscraper-heeled shoes, making sure everyone sees her as she goes.

Emmanuel says to me in a low voice, 'Confidentially, it may be helpful for you to know that Danielle went for your job when it was first advertised internally. She was unsuccessful and hasn't taken it very well. Her father is a friend of the chief exec, but the chief exec doesn't make the hiring decisions at this level.'

'Thanks so much for the heads-up. That will make it easier for me to manage the situation – though I do have some empathy. It's never nice to not be successful for a job. But nobody should have a sense of entitlement, just because of who they know.'

'Agreed.' Emmanuel nods solemnly. 'I think you and I are going to get along very well, Alex.'

'Me too.' I grin at her. 'And don't worry about me and Danielle, I've dealt with similar behaviours quite successfully before.'

'I have absolutely no doubt about that.'

-

By the time lunchtime comes round, I'm bleary-eyed from reading the company intranet pages and working my way through the mandatory (and extraordinarily boring) e-learning modules.

'Are you ready for a break?' Emmanuel gets up from her seat.

'Am I ever.' I blink several times to adjust my focus from the blocks of text swimming in front of my eyes to the wider office environment again.

'Is that lunchtime already?' Danielle lifts her head from the screeds of data she's been poring over on her screen. 'I've barely had a moment to breathe this morning.'

Apart from the twenty-minute coffee stop and the extensive (and surprisingly loud) bitchfest with another colleague over by the printer, I think to myself.

'You're obviously being very productive.' I smile at her, still willing to make an effort to build a relationship nonetheless. 'I'm glad to have such a dedicated project analyst on the team.'

'I'm a *senior* analyst,' she corrects me in her sweet but poisonous tone.

'Right, of course. My apologies. Not yet fully familiar with the project structure.'

'Shall we?' Emmanuel gestures towards the lifts, giving me a subtle 'don't worry about it at all' look.

The three of us take the lift down to the ground floor, then wander across the plaza in the sunshine. It's remarkably warm for September but I'm unsure whether this is normal now I'm living that bit further south.

'I love these water features,' I comment, as we make our way along the landscaped path between them. 'Reminds me of holidays spent in France when I was young.'

'You like France?' Danielle's ears prick up. 'Me too. My family spent most of our summers there.'

'Really? We stayed on the campsites. Keycamp, Eurocamp, that kind of thing. We visited so many different parts of France. It was amazing freedom as a kid. Did you do the same?'

Danielle raises an eyebrow. 'No. We stayed in a villa.'

'Ah, right.' I nod, understanding. 'My family considered hiring a gîte one year, but we just loved the outdoor lifestyle of the campsites too much.'

As I say this, a memory of happier times spent with my family pops into my head. A time when my parents were still together. Before my mother became so bitter and judgemental following the death of her brother and drove my dad to divorce – and then a stroke ripped him from our lives altogether.

'Yeah… we didn't hire villas, we owned one.' Danielle tries to sound nonchalant but her face is leaking an unapologetic air of superiority. 'In St Tropez. We went twice a year.'

I let out an impressed whistle, keen to keep Danielle talking to understand more about her. 'Gosh, lucky you. That pales my holidays into complete insignificance.

Rubbing shoulders with celebrities, were you?' This last statement is intended as a joke.

'There were a few around that my pops knew.' She shrugs. 'So, are you a French speaker then, Alex? *Parlez-vous français?*'

She's challenging me. But I'm not going to engage in a game of one-upping. I'm happy for the mine-is-bigger-than-yours behaviour to remain entirely one-sided.

'Oh… no. My French is terrible.'

Danielle seems satisfied with my response. I can tell that, in her head, it's now one–nil to her.

We reach Thai Paradise, a culinary sanctuary of peace and tranquillity with its babbling water feature just inside the entrance, Thai-inspired interior decoration, and zen-like woodwind tones floating down from the wall-mounted speakers. Danielle struts ahead of us, keen to join her teammates at the table, and quite possibly to see if she can assemble the front line her way ahead of my arrival. Emmanuel hangs back and gives me a curious look.

'That was an interesting conversation. I'm sure I remember languages featuring on your CV, and in particular your semi-fluency in French. Thought it would come in handy in dealing with the Paris office.'

'Is that right? Must have slipped my mind.'

Emmanuel smiles at me. 'You're right not to get into all that. It's only day one and you're impressing me already, Alex.'

I'm pleased with this early feedback, but decide there's no need to say anything. I simply return her smile and approach the table and its occupants, at whom Danielle is already talking animatedly. I'm relieved to see that none of the others look too heavily engaged with her.

'Everyone, this is Alex,' Emmanuel announces as we reach the table.

'Hi.' I give them a friendly wave, which is immediately mirrored by all, except Danielle.

As I look around at the Birmingham-based part of my new project team, I feel quite encouraged. There's five of them, including Danielle: two men who look around my age or slightly younger and two who look like they're in their late forties or early fifties.

'I'll do the introductions,' says Emmanuel. 'This is Felix, Dhruv, John and Aadesh.'

I nod round the table at each of my new colleagues, knowing I'll never remember their names straight off.

'It's so great to meet you all.' I smile my most warm and open smile at them.

'Felix is the change manager on the project,' says Emmanuel. 'He'll be working closely with you to make sure people are ready for the new ways of working. Isn't that right, Felix?'

'It is, yes,' he confirms with a strong Germanic accent. 'I am looking forward to working with you, Alex.'

'Me too.' I meet his kind eyes and already feel like we'll get along. 'Where are you from, if you don't mind me asking?'

'I am from the north of Germany. From Hamburg.'

'Well, that will certainly help with communications with the Frankfurt office.' I notice Danielle out of the corner of my eye. 'And Danielle is our French-speaking champion, I gather.'

Danielle looks immediately smug, which I note with interest sparks some subtle negative reactions round the table.

'All we need now is a resident Spanish speaker and we've got a full house. Anyone?' I look round the table jovially. 'No? Oh well, I'm sure Google Translate will come in handy there.'

'Dhruv and I can speak Punjabi,' Aadesh offers. 'If there is ever the need.'

'In this connected world, it's good to have as many bases covered as possible.' I grin at Aadesh, mentally filing away that piece of information.

'Everyone pretty much speaks English anyway.' Danielle divebombs the conversation and, seemingly without realising it, her own usefulness as a French speaker. 'It's people in the UK who are ignorant and don't bother learning other languages. I, for one, have made it my personal mission to speak at least three languages fluently.'

She's dying for me to ask which ones, but I can see that she's deflating the positive and collaborative ambience at the table, so I decide to move things on.

'Good for you.' I give Danielle an acknowledging nod and sit myself down at the table. 'Now, I hear the food at this place is great. What do you all recommend?'

'Well handled,' I hear Emmanuel whisper, as she takes her seat next to me.

Chapter 13

By the time I get back to my apartment that evening, I'm beyond exhausted. I kick off my trainers (which I wear to and from the office), dump my bag, and collapse onto my bed.

It's not the same exhaustion I felt after returning to work from my sickness absence. My low-level MS symptoms are playing a part, as they now do every single day, but the overriding feeling is one of information overload. So many new names, new faces, new structures, processes and procedures. Overall, it seems like it will be a great place to work and I'm just desperate to get stuck in. I always hate having to be shown the ropes and getting up to speed; my natural instincts are to be in control and moving things forward. But it shouldn't be more than a few days before I can take the project reins and get us off and running.

My relationship with Danielle, however, is going to be a different story. She spent much of lunch and the rest of the afternoon emitting her laser beam of superiority: her knowledge of the company, her apparent closeness to the chief executive, and her understanding of the project from the data analysis she's completed so far. She's going to be a royal pain in the arse. Nothing I can't handle, but it is going to require careful managing, which has the capacity to zap my energy pretty quickly. I'm just so relieved she doesn't know about my medical situation: a weapon I suspect she would use and abuse.

This is something I would ordinarily have discussed with Dom, keen to get his take on things and sharing that feeling of camaraderie. I feel a wave of sadness wash over me as the familiar Dom-shaped hole in my life opens up once again, and I realise that I have nobody to chew the Danielle issue over with. How isolated that makes me feel.

Unwilling to engage with this concept, and determined to think that I'm made of stronger stuff, I push the emptiness aside. Danielle is not going to take over my evening as well, so I turn on the TV to the six o'clock news headlines. I lie there for about twenty minutes, not really taking anything in but unable to muster the energy to do anything else. After a while, my mind starts to wander and lands on the memory of Matt from the train. He was so fun and charming, not to mention absolutely gorgeous. Did I overreact by binning his number? I clearly liked him, and we did have a connection. But our lives couldn't have been further apart – he scales hills for fun while I can barely manage a flight of stairs. No. It was a non-starter.

Eventually I tear my thoughts away from Matt and drag myself off the bed and into the kitchen to make some food. Just as I'm preparing a tofu salad my phone starts to ring in my bag, so I pad through to the hallway and dig out my phone to see that the caller is Sasha. My first instinct is to let it go to voicemail. I'm just too tired to engage in any more conversation today. But there's something inside me that just won't let me do that. Instead I hit the answer button.

'Sash, how you doing? Everything OK?'

Sasha's bouncy yet anxious voice echoes in my ear canal. 'Hiya, Lex. Everything's fine. I just wanted to know how your first day went?'

'It was fine.' I rub my forehead exhaustedly, an automatic response to the high energy of Sasha's side of the interaction.

'Just fine?'

'No, sorry, it was good. Really good.'

'Tell me more. What were the people like?'

I return to my bedroom and lie back on the bed as I currently don't have the stamina to stand and talk at the same time. I recap the day for Sasha, telling her Emmanuel and I are on the same wavelength and the rest of the team seem nice and capable. I also mention Danielle and the trouble she's already causing.

'Oh, Lex, that's not good. You don't need that with your...' She trails off.

'With my what?' I instinctively challenge her.

There's a silence, then a smaller voice comes down the line. 'Nothing. Sorry, just ignore me.'

'I'll be fine, Sash. I get why you're concerned, but you know me. I'm good at dealing with difficult people. Maybe not as exceptionally good as I was, but I'm still right up there. Way better than you,' I add to punctuate the point, then immediately feel a pinch of shame at my meanness.

'That's not hard.' The vibrancy returns to her voice and she giggles, taking no offence whatsoever. 'Not sure there's anyone who runs faster from conflict than me.'

'Aww, you're not *that* bad.'

'Bad enough that I'm too scared to broach the whole Birmingham thing with my mum.'

I grimace, wondering why Sasha still isn't showing any sign of shutting this move thing down. 'That's different. Your mum's ill. It will really affect her if you move.' I pause and consider whether to go on. 'Look, Sash, it's lovely that you want to come and join me, but I'm not sure I should be your first priority. Your mum needs you much more than I do.'

There's another silence at the end of the phone.

'Sash?'

'I know you don't need me,' she says eventually. 'I was really worried about you before, but I've seen that you can look after yourself. At least, you can when your symptoms aren't too troublesome.'

'So, what's going on?'

She exhales sharply. 'I don't know. I guess… seeing you go off and make a new life for yourself, it's made me think about my own. I'm worried I'm going to get forty years down the road and regret never having properly lived – all because I'm too scared to take any risks.'

'But it's not just about risks, it's about your mum too. You have very strong family values. You'd feel so guilty if you left her. How would she even cope?'

'I don't… my mum doesn't need… oh, what's the point in covering this up? I think she'd manage just fine, Lex.'

'Sorry, what?' I wonder if I've heard correctly. 'Sash, what are you talking about?'

'I caught her out.'

'What do you mean you caught her out? You're not making any sense.'

'What I mean is, I was really fed up at work the other day, so I asked if I could take a half-day. On my way home, I decided to stop by my mum's place to check on her and I caught her…' Sasha's voice wobbles as she trails off, sounding ashamed.

'You caught her what?'

The silence resumes once again.

'Sasha? Spit it out.'

'I caught her having sex with a man.'

'WHAT?' I'm so shocked, I sit bolt upright on my bed. 'Wait, how? No, sorry that's a stupid question. I thought she was way too ill for that. She has to walk with a frame. She can hardly breathe. And… I mean, does she even have a bloke?'

'These were all questions I asked myself, believe me.' Sasha now sounds quite miserable.

'Well, what did she say when you caught her?'

'Nothing. She doesn't know. She was… in the moment.'

'Eww!' I wail. 'That's so gross.'

'It is. I can't get the image out of my head. She wasn't the mum I've known these recent years. She was so… energetic.'

'Stop it, please. I can't take any more.' I start to laugh and then clamp my hand over my mouth as I realise this is no joke to Sasha. 'So, are you going to have it out with her?'

'I am,' she says quietly. 'At least, I want to. But I'm really crap at these things, as you well know. I wanted to get my facts straight, so when she was having a bath one evening, I went through her cupboards and found her medical letters.'

'And?'

'And the night she went into hospital with a heart attack, it turns out it was just a panic attack.'

'Huh? Why would she tell you she had a heart—'

'Hang on, there's more.' Sasha uncharacteristically silences me. 'There's absolutely nothing relating to a long-term heart condition in any of her paperwork either. Her official diagnosis is ME.'

'ME? But that's a serious condition as well.' I'm back to rubbing my forehead exhaustedly, but this time from trying to follow the complexity and complete absurdity of this story. 'Why would she lie to you about that?'

'I wondered that myself. And then I figured it out. It's because she's faking it. ME can be faked because it's so difficult to confirm it. But my mum obviously thought it would sound more convincing if she told me she had a heart condition – and it's not like I could go and ask the doctors, due to the whole patient confidentiality thing. Lex, I think my mum's a benefits cheat.'

My jaw drops as I put it all together. She's right. What else could it all mean?

'Shit, Sash. I'm so sorry. All these years and she's been at it the whole time. You're going to face up to her about it, right?'

'I really want to.' Sasha sounds despondent. 'I just don't know how.'

As she says this, I feel genuinely saddened. Sasha's spent the last seven or so years putting her life on hold to look after her mum – all for nothing. She's the most genuine, caring person I've ever met and she's been completely taken advantage of. And for what? So her mum could live a lazy, selfish life, and keep her daughter from moving on and living her own.

With these thoughts swimming round my mind, I realise I've been a bit selfish too. I've been so focused on restarting my life on my terms, I've forgotten my best friend needs me. My support is everything to her, as much as her being able to support me. A two-way relationship – as it should be. I also realise that I really miss Sasha. She's the only person I can truly rely on, and I want her back in my life properly, just like before.

'You know what?' I say to her suddenly. 'You can work up to having it out with her. Take it one step at a time. First thing you need to do is come down and visit – in the next few weeks. Leave her on her own for a weekend and let her fend for herself. We can catch up, make a weekend of it, and you can see if you actually like it here before you make any kind of decision.'

'Oh, Lex, really?' Sasha sounds encouraged at this suggestion. 'Are you sure? You might find it too tiring so soon into your new job. Not because you have MS, but because everyone gets exhausted in a new job,' she rushes to add.

'I'm sure. I'll be settled properly in a few weeks. And while you're down we can work out how you're going to handle your mum.'

'That would be amazing. Thanks, Lex.'

I'm pleased to hear Sasha's spirits lift. 'OK, great. Plan sorted – can't wait. Now go and book your tickets, and let me get my dinner before I keel over from day-one exhaustion.'

Chapter 14

By the end of my second week at Fletcher & Co, I'm getting my bearings and the real work has started. We're finishing up our final meeting of the day: a virtual meeting with our German, French and Spanish project teammates, with whom we've been completing a full walkthrough of the project plan.

'OK, everyone,' I address my teammates in the room, as well as those who have joined via the video call system, 'I think that's everything for today. Thanks for all your input. We're making good progress. Have a great weekend and I'll talk to you again next week.'

There's a chorus of thanks and goodbyes, some of them expressed in their own languages. I end the video call and turn to my colleagues.

'I think that went well for a first walkthrough. What do you think?'

'It was good,' says Felix. 'I am seeing now how I can align the change plan to your project plan.'

'I'm much clearer too.' Dhruv nods agreement.

'Great.' I smile at them. 'That's what I was hoping to hear.'

'Actually, I think there are some key tasks missing from the plan,' Danielle pipes up in her syrupy voice.

My senses go into high alert at this suggestion. 'Really? I thought we covered everything at the workshop earlier this week.'

'You haven't included some of the key reporting elements in the plan.' Danielle purses her lips in a way that tells me she's withheld this information on purpose.

I study her for a moment. 'Right. And did we cover them at the workshop?'

'I did mention them. But I'm not sure you were listening.'

I pause for a moment to stop myself having an immediate (and probably unhelpful) reaction to this statement. Even if Danielle did bring up these points – which I'm certain she did not – she had every opportunity to cover them during the call we just had. She's trying to undermine me again to weaken my credibility. I can tell she's looking for a reaction, but there's no way I'm giving her the satisfaction. Instead, I calmly type a reminder into my laptop, then close it down.

'OK, thanks for flagging that, Danielle. I've set a reminder for Monday. We can sit down and ensure that everything is included.'

'No problem. Happy to help.' Danielle flashes me one of her 'sincere' smiles that I can see through better than a freshly cleaned window.

'So, are we hitting the pub?' Dhruv asks, just as Emmanuel appears through the meeting room door.

'We are indeed.' She grins broadly at us all. 'You lot definitely deserve to let your hair down after such a productive week. I'm amazed you've almost got the project plan nailed down already.'

'Credit for that has to go to Alex.' Dhruv aims finger guns at me. 'She's quite the machine – in a good way, I mean.'

From his face, I can tell he's just realised the possible connotations of his remark.

'I can see the compliment in that, don't worry,' I reassure him. 'And it's been a team effort, all right? There would *be* no plan if it weren't for the hard work you all put in.'

My team members all beam as I say this, pleased to have their efforts recognised. That is, all of them except Danielle, who I catch subtly rolling her eyes. I'm not the only one to clock this; Emmanuel does too.

'Well done to you all.' She looks at each of us meaningfully in turn. 'But especially well done to Alex, who hasn't just grabbed the bull by the horns, she's hurled it right in the direction we need to land.'

Somewhat uncomfortable receiving this level of praise in front of my team, I quickly change the subject. 'Right, I'm pretty sure someone said the word pub. What are we waiting for? Let's go.'

We finish packing up our things and make our way out of the building. Although I'm feeling exuberant about the great progress we've made, as well as excited to be having my first ever Friday drinks session with my new workmates, I feel myself flagging a little. The newness of the job is still taking its toll. But once we're outside, I breathe in the warmish September air, absorbing the buzz that Friday has injected into the workers of Brindley Place, and I'm determined to push through.

How much my life has changed in just a few weeks. From the claustrophobic, limited state it had reached back in Glasgow, to the complete reinvention of myself here in Birmingham. Nobody here knows of my illness and I can plan for every situation, adapting the way I go about my life to fit with my medical needs without interference from my family or Sasha. I have, in preparation for this evening (and in true project manager style), already thought through how I'll handle it.

We make our way across the plaza, chatting in that adrenaline-fuelled 'Friday feeling' kind of way. Aware that I'm still the newbie and careful not to step on any toes, I stick firmly to the role of participant, rather than driving the banter. Dhruv, it turns out, is resident joker on the team. We're laughing helplessly at his re-enactment of a recent interaction with his mother – who doesn't speak much English – when suddenly it's like my foot seems to malfunction and I fall heavily onto the steps by the plaza's fountain. I go down hard and a shooting pain rushes through me as my knee collides with the sharp edge of the step. It takes everything I have not to cry out in agony.

'Alex. Shit. Are you OK?' Dhruv doubles back and rushes to my aid, closely followed by Emmanuel.

'I'm… yeah… oh, that was sore.' I'm now sitting on the step, holding my injured knee, my face burning with embarrassment.

'It is bad? You think you can walk? I can give you a piggy-back if you like.'

Thankfully, this kind-but-ridiculous suggestion has the effect of distracting me from my pain and my wounded pride.

'That won't be necessary.' I laugh weakly. 'I'm OK. Plus, I don't think we're quite there yet, do you?'

'Didn't know there were qualifying criteria for that. Seriously, Alex. I know people fall about laughing because of my incredible sense of humour, but I think you took it too far.'

'Not sure that's so helpful right now, Dhruv.' Emmanuel swoops in from behind him. 'Alex, are you really all right?'

'I'm fine,' I assure her. 'Really. It was one of those falls where it's far more painful in the moment.'

Helped up by Dhruv and Emmanuel, I dust myself down and spot Danielle standing with Felix and Aadesh. To say she is enjoying my unfortunate accident would be an understatement. Thankfully, the guys are not wearing similar expressions; they look as concerned as Dhruv and Emmanuel, but they've clearly decided I'm in good hands.

'Can you walk all right?' Emmanuel asks.

I put weight on my leg and automatically flinch as my injured knee protests about the movement. But there's no way this is ruining my evening – especially as I'm painfully aware of why it happened in the first place. This time there's no disputing it's an unfortunate by-product of my MS. Every now and again, I seem to misjudge things spatially or my body doesn't quite do what I expect it to. Not badly, but enough to bump my leg on a cabinet or have a minor trip of some kind. Normally I can cover it up, and no one notices. Today's unfortunate incident obviously doesn't fall into that category; this time I've gone down in style and I'm going to have a hell of a bruise to remind me of it. It's a stark and grim reminder of my illness. However, I'm determined to rescue whatever pride I can from this situation.

'I'm fine. Honestly.' I bend and straighten my knee a few times to loosen it up. 'Now let's go before they give our table away.'

I don't need to tell Emmanuel twice. She instinctively trusts me to handle this situation myself. If this had happened back home, my mother-slash-sister-slash-colleagues would be carting me off home in a taxi faster than Usain Bolt could reach the hundred-metre finish line.

We amble across the remainder of the plaza into the cluster of food and drink establishments on the canal-side of Brindley Place. Reaching the team's regular drinking haunt, I quickly forget my hot, throbbing knee and soak up the 'gateway to the weekend' celebrations.

–

An hour later, we're sat at a picnic-style table in the outdoor section of a trendy hipster cocktail bar, bathing in the remnants of the warmth from the day. The sun has sneaked behind the roof of the restaurant opposite, leaving us in no doubt that we'll be heading indoors before long.

It turns out my colleagues are a lively bunch and quite different to how they are in the office. Either that or they've been on their best behaviour with me, and now they're letting their true personalities filter through. Dhruv is very much the leader in this social context, using his humour to bring everyone together. Emmanuel is a solid figure within the group whom everyone clearly respects (even Danielle to a certain extent). She joins in the banter, giving the team space to enjoy themselves and forget they're in the presence of their manager. Felix and Aadesh are less dominant characters, but they still get involved in the jokes and the laughter. It's a really pleasant social dynamic and I find myself grinning like a new moon, happy to have found such positivity in my new life already.

'I'll get the next round in,' Emmanuel announces. 'Same again?'

We nod or confirm verbally as she gets up from her seat, her braided hair swishing around her shoulders, having been released from her 'work bun' as soon as we left the office.

'Alex, are you going to have a proper drink this time?' Dhruv teases me in a friendly manner. 'We need to get you drunk so you don't remember what we get up to this evening.'

'I'd remember it regardless.' I flash him a mischievous smirk. 'Alcohol doesn't affect my memory. I've got loads of drunken escapade collateral saved up over the years, ready to be wheeled out at any time – big birthdays, weddings, *leaving speeches...*'

He considers this with a glint of humour in his eyes. 'Looks like you're one to watch out for.'

'Don't worry. I only do it to people I don't like.'

'So, if you ever "red-neck" me publicly, I'll know it's because you secretly want to off me.'

'Not at all. If I want to off you, no one will find you. You know I'm from Glasgow, right?' I give him a cheeky wink as his face turns to one of white shock, then amusement.

'You're *good*.' He hoots. 'I know you're just joking, but now I'm wondering if that's a double bluff. I'll be careful not to get on the wrong side of you.'

I start to laugh myself, then glance across at Danielle, who looks less than happy that I'm engaging in such easy banter with Dhruv.

'I'll go and help Emmanuel with the drinks.' I climb out of my seat and head for the bar.

As I walk inside, I'm engulfed by upbeat music, loud voices and the sweaty humidity from a bar packed with people who've been stuck in the office all day. I carefully pick my way across to where Emmanuel is patiently waiting to be served. It's so busy, the queue is three people deep and she's still at the back. I touch her on the arm and she turns and gives me a little wave.

'I thought I'd come and give you a hand.' I have to raise my voice to be heard over the noise.

'Thanks.' She does the same in return. 'This might take a while.'

'In that case, I'll just nip to the loo. Back soon.'

Emmanuel signals her understanding as I turn in the direction of the ladies' toilets. Weaving my way across the busy bar, I feel a tap on my own shoulder. Assuming I've inadvertently stood on someone or knocked their drink, I turn round ready to apologise. But instead of an angry punter, I find myself face to face with Matt from the train. Gorgeous Matt, who, despite being someone I can't date, gives me a heartstopping moment the second we make eye contact.

'Oh… hi.' I smile at him awkwardly. 'Fancy meeting you here. Wouldn't have thought this would be your regular after-work haunt.'

'It's not.' His dark chocolate eyes feel like they're boring through to my soul, searching for answers as to why I didn't get in touch. 'But my factory's local is full of old men talking about horse racing and playing card games. Not really my scene. We – the younger crowd – prefer to come into the city centre. Plenty of good places around.'

'Fair enough.'

He watches me for a moment. 'You never called.'

'No, I didn't, did I.' I cringe a little.

'Find yourself another tour guide?'

He looks a mixture of curious and slightly hurt. I'm unsure whether this is just a joke, or whether he's asking if I've met someone else. He's certainly a bit more forthcoming today than he was on the train platform. I eye the pint in his hand, wondering how many he's had.

'I… err… no. Just found my own way around.' I look around me uncomfortably. 'It's been a busy few weeks with getting settled, you know how it is.'

'I guess I do.' He seems to read an unintentional hidden message in my response. 'Well, I won't keep you.'

'OK, sure. See you around.'

I feel guilty but also mildly relieved that I can continue on my way. I glance at him as I move away. He simply shrugs, a defeated look on his face, and turns back to his workmates. By the time I reach the toilets, I feel a bit flustered. How did that even happen? I'd assumed I'd never see Matt again – Birmingham is supposed to be enormous, after all.

I lean on the sink, gazing at my reflection in the mirror, as I try to calm myself. So I bumped into a guy I dissed. So what? It's not like that hasn't happened before. What's wrong with me? Actually, I know what's wrong with me. If this had been before I got ill, I would have called him. We would've gone out on a date and who knows what might have happened next. What's wrong with me is that I didn't call Matt, not because I didn't like him or because of my recent break-up, but because of my MS. Because it would have ended badly. Again. If he knew the truth, he'd be glad of that fact. My fall outside earlier is proof of that. Much as it tears me in pieces to admit it, my body just can't keep up with my aspirations and desires. I may have found a good enough compromise with my career, but men and dating, that's a different playing field altogether.

I stare at my reflection for a few moments longer, as if challenging it to disagree with me, then I let out an exasperated cry at the injustice of it all and head for one of the cubicles.

Returning to the main bar, I weave my way back through the groups of punters, this time taking a different route so I don't bump into Matt again. Reaching Emmanuel, I can see that she's now being served, so I excuse myself to the other people queueing as I slide my way through towards her.

'Can you grab these?' She hands me my drink and two bottles of beer, which I take by their necks in my other hand.

As we manoeuvre our way back out from the bar, I involuntarily stop and glance over to where Matt and his workmates are standing, immediately picking him out from the group. Sensing my eyes on him, he looks over and his eyes lock on mine, causing my stomach to perform a double backflip.

'Is that someone you know?' Emmanuel's eyes follow my gaze. 'He's very handsome.'

'Oh... err, yeah. Sort of.' I drag my eyes away from Matt and focus my attention on her. 'Just someone I met on the train.'

'He looks like someone I'd be more than happy to meet on a train. Or any form of public transport, though don't tell my husband I said that. Are you going to meet him again in any *other* circumstances?'

'No. I don't think that's a good idea.'

'All right... sure. That's your prerogative.'

Emmanuel's eyes narrow slightly and it's clear she's trying to read what's really going on. Uncomfortable about taking the conversation any further, I look away and start making my way through the crowded bar again.

Chapter 15

The next couple of weeks pass uneventfully. In my new world of living with a life-changing illness, this is definitely a good thing. I get into a nice rhythm at work and my social life is quiet – it turns out my team only go out once a month, straight after payday – so I have plenty of downtime to rest and recuperate in the evenings and at weekends. This takes a bit of getting used to, my natural preference being to burn the candle pretty much anywhere it will burn.

So that I don't expire from boredom or become a semi-permanent sofa accessory, I take up a membership at a leisure club just a ten-minute walk from my apartment. I'm still not able to pound the treadmill, so I start with some gentle swimming, having read online that it can be a good way of reducing MS-related fatigue. I also do some more exploring, so I'm knowledgeable enough as to what Birmingham has to offer in time for Sasha's visit.

On the day of her arrival, I walk to work with what could almost be described as a spring in my step – or as close as I can get given that whenever I attempt a gradient beyond the pace of a tortoise, my body feels like it's been hijacked by a ten-ton weight. The silver lining to that being, in the well-loved fable, the tortoise did eventually beat the hare. This appeals to my go-getter instinct.

It turns out to be a long day. For the first time since my day-one experience with the excruciatingly boring introductory e-learning modules, I find myself watching the clock. Because having realised that Sasha is still as important a part of my life as she always was, I've also realised how much I miss her. As the clock hits five past five, I decide it's safe to make my bid for freedom, so I shut down my laptop and pack up my stuff.

'That you off to meet your friend?' Emmanuel looks up at me from the desk opposite.

'Yeah, her train gets in just after half past.' I throw the last of my things in my handbag, then lock my laptop, notebook and papers in my desk pedestal.

'I hope you have a lovely long weekend together.'

'Thanks, Emmanuel. And thanks for giving me tomorrow off at late notice. It won't be a big weekend. More just a nice quiet catch-up.'

As I say this, I feel a twinge of annoyance at myself. With Emmanuel, I've gotten into the habit of permeating all conversations relating to my social life with the message that I'm behaving sensibly – just in case I end up off unwell at some point. Though Emmanuel never says anything directly, she has quickly become attuned to this.

'Go have fun.' She gives me a pointed look that I read as I-know-you're-far-from-irresponsible-and-you-need-to-have-a-life-without-constantly-looking-over-your-shoulder.

'OK, thanks.' I nod my understanding, then say my goodbyes to everyone.

Heading for the lifts, I see Danielle flouncing in my direction, her laptop tucked under her arm. She makes eye contact with me, and I immediately know she's going to make some kind of unwelcome remark.

'Heading home already?' Her tone is breezy, deliberately so: the cruise missile within her statement a stealth one.

Having just found myself justifying my social life to Emmanuel, it hits its intended target square on: exploding in my gut, irritation rushing through me like shrapnel. Even more so because this is the first time I've left the office before 5:45 p.m. – and Danielle regularly disappears off home before me. She really is a piece of work, but I refuse to show any weakness.

'First time for everything, I guess.' I mirror her false smile to see if she even picks up on it, which she doesn't.

Once outside, I leave Brindley Place via the canal bridge, walk through the ICC, and pass the leaping fountains of Centenary Square, enjoying the fresh autumnal breeze that's whipping around me as I go. As I make my way through Victoria Square, past the magnificent columns of the town hall and the late nineteenth century Council House, standing proud and full of grandeur, I feel a swell of excitement: not just for my weekend with Sasha, but also for how at home I already feel here. Halfway down New Street, I'm drawn to a busker singing a tuneful and energetic rendition of 'Here Comes the Sun' by the Beatles. His enthusiasm is contagious, and I'm quickly sucked into his music and singing along.

After a couple of minutes of musical escapism I realise I'm going to be late for Sasha, so I throw some money into his hat and continue on my way to the station.

Minutes after I arrive, I see Sasha wheeling her purple weekend case along the busy rush hour concourse. She looks unsure, navigating her way towards the exit barriers, commuters whizzing past and dodging in front of her, keen to get home as quickly as possible. It doesn't help that she hasn't got her ticket ready and inadvertently causes a jam in front of the automatic barriers, earning a few looks of irritation. I smile at her affectionately, wondering if this experience alone will be enough to put her off living here, but now hoping that won't be the case.

Sasha hesitantly makes her way through the barrier, almost getting her case caught as she wrestles with it and her hand luggage. She continues to look exasperated and overwhelmed as I step forward to greet her, then she spots me and her face lights up like the Edinburgh sky at Hogmanay.

'Lex. Oh, my goodness, I'm so happy to see you.' She ditches her case and dives into my arms.

'Is that because you're having a total mare navigating your way round this station?' I joke.

'No. Obviously not. But this place is bonkers.'

'It's great to see you too.' I give her a big squeezy hug in return.

She pulls back and looks at me properly. 'If I may say, you look *really* well, Lex.'

'You may indeed.' I reach out and grab the handle of her case, pulling it towards us as someone almost falls over it.

Sasha's eyes pass over my face searchingly. 'This place is obviously working for you.'

'It really is, Sash. I love it here already. I feel so anonymous and free.'

'Well, here's hoping I fall in love with it too, eh?' She grins at me.

For a moment all I see is fourteen-year-old Sasha, with her long tumbling red waves, train-track braces and a face full of innocence and hope for the future. Excitement bubbles inside of me at the thought of showing my best friend in the world my new home – and exploring it properly together.

'Absolutely. Are you hungry?'

'I'm starving. Was so paranoid about someone stealing my stuff, I didn't leave my seat at all.'

'You're a numpty, Sash.' I laugh. 'I'm sure your case would have been fine.'

We take the escalator up to Grand Central, bickering good-naturedly about where to eat before deciding on a Vietnamese restaurant that I've been keen to try. Once we've ordered, we settle properly into catching up.

'So, how are things with your mum?' I'm keen to get this out in the open quickly, so we can chip away at it gradually over the weekend.

Sasha's face tells me this might not have been such a good idea. Practical, yes. But not necessarily a relaxing start to her weekend away.

'Sorry, Sash. That's the last thing I should have led with. You know me, always the problem solver.'

'No, it's fine. As much as it's the most mortifying thing that's ever happened to me, and I feel utterly betrayed by my own mother, I want to talk about it. Means I can get it off my chest and just enjoy myself.'

We're interrupted momentarily by the waiter bringing our drinks. We thank him, then continue our conversation.

'So how are things then?' I repeat my original question.

'They're… weird. She has no idea I saw her. She's just acting the same, but now I know she's putting it on, I'm starting to see that she's a blinking good actress. She could have gotten a role on *River City*.'

'It's all a bit ironic really. She's putting an incredible amount of effort into making sure she doesn't have to do anything.'

'Exactly. Now every time I'm in her flat, I'm getting flashbacks to that day. I want to have it out with her, but every time I get close to forming the words, my legs turn to jelly and it's like I'm going to hyperventilate.'

Sasha looks so morose about this, I feel a burst of anger at her mum that I have to swallow down. 'You're anxious about it, I understand that, Sash. Your whole world has been chucked up in the air. I tell you, your mum's lucky I'm not living in Glasgow any more because I'd have been round there by now.'

'I know you would have.' She plays absently with her straw. 'I kind of wish you would…'

'I'll do it over the phone if you want?'

Sasha shakes her head miserably. 'No, Lex. Thank you. What I was about to say was that I kind of wish you would, but this is my problem to solve. I just need your help to do it.'

'Well you've got it.' I take her hand across the table and give it a squeeze. 'I'll help you figure out how to deal with this – in a way that won't leave you racked with guilt, because I know what you're like.'

Our food arrives and we dig into our steaming, aromatic dishes. Mine, a portion of delicious deep-fried pork and prawn spring rolls, and a large bowl of pho noodle soup. Sasha has ordered fresh, herby prawn summer rolls and a chicken noodle curry dish, from which wafts of coconut and lemongrass keep teasing my nostrils.

'You're settling in well then?' Sasha's not so much asking as prompting me to tell her more.

'Yeah, I'm loving it here, Sash. Not just because I can be me again – that's obviously a massive part of it – but also because it's just *so me*. It's fast-paced, busy, lively. And diverse. I feel like I could never not fit in here, if that makes any sense?'

Sasha wrinkles her nose. 'Not yet. Hopefully by the end of the weekend though.'

'I hope so too.' I pause as a thought comes to me. 'Actually, Sash, I want to apologise to you.'

'What for?' She looks up from her curry and I sigh, the weight of what I'm about to admit pressing down on me.

'For pushing you away in the way that I did. When I was diagnosed and my family were breathing down my neck like a bunch of wildebeests and everything was going to shit with work and Dom' – I swallow as emotion threatens to clog my throat – 'all I could see were people getting in my way and treating me differently. I felt so… suffocated.'

'I know that, Lex.' Sasha leans forward earnestly. 'You don't need to apologise for feeling trapped and over-whelmed. You dealt with it the way you had to.'

I hang my head slightly. 'That's fair to a certain extent. But I was so fed up with it all, I was ready to keep everyone who was suffocating me at arm's length permanently – including you. I let you think you could move down here with me because it made my life easier at the time.'

I hear the air expelling itself from Sasha's lungs as she digests this blow.

'Obviously, I was being ridiculously self-indulgent,' I rush to explain properly. 'I realise that now and want you to know how sorry I am… and that I do *really* want you to move down. I've had to come clean because… you mean so much to me.'

I look up and see Sasha's eyes are red-rimmed and brimming with tears. She's quite rightly taking this personally.

'It's OK,' she whispers. 'Not a big deal.'

'I don't believe that for a second. You won't tell me what a crap friend I've been, so I'll do it myself. I've been a crap friend. All you were trying to be was the loyal and bloody marvellous rock I actually truly need in my life.'

Sasha's tears are receding, which tells me I'm on the right track, so to add some humour, I get out of my seat and kneel down beside her theatrically. 'Sash, will you forgive me for being a selfish cow and let me be your bestie for life?'

Sasha looks down at me and starts to giggle. 'Of course I will, silly.'

I get up and hug her, and raucous applause breaks out across the restaurant. Startled, we both turn round to discover it's being directed at us: all the customers and staff are grinning broadly at us, a few of them even looking quite emotional.

'Congratulations!' a woman two tables down from us shouts, setting off the applause once again.

Sasha and I look at each other and blanch.

'Do they…' Sasha is wide-eyed with shock.

'Umm… I think so.'

'Right… and now?'

'We have to just go with it.' I straighten up and give a feeble wave of thanks, then sit back down in my seat as we try desperately to stifle the giggles that have overcome us. 'Sash, get that down you fast. We need to get out of here before someone asks us when the wedding's going to be.'

Back at my apartment, we get comfy on my enormous sofa, which (like most of my furniture) I was fortunate enough to hold onto following my split from Dom.

'That food was amazing.' Sasha rubs her stomach contentedly at the memory. 'How is it though that I'm really full, but I still have a hankering for something sweet? Got any dessert in that fridge?'

I screw up my face as I try to visualise whether there's anything in my kitchen that might semi-resemble dessert. 'I'm afraid the best I can do is dried fruit and mixed unsalted nuts.'

'Yeah, that's not going to cut it. Ooh, I know… I have some chocolate in my bag.'

She pads through to my bedroom, then reappears in the doorway waving a bag of mini Toblerones in front of her.

'They're basically just chocolate-coated nuts.' She gives me a devilish look.

'Chuck it across.'

Sasha launches the bag in my direction and I brace myself to catch it. But I misjudge the trajectory, and my clumsy attempt to save the situation results in an empty mug being knocked off the coffee table and breaking into pieces.

'Shit.' I tentatively pick up the bits. 'Forgot I can't catch any more.'

Sasha starts to laugh, then, realising I'm referring to my lack of coordination caused by my MS, she bites her lip guiltily to cover it up.

I glance up at her and smile. 'It's OK to laugh. It *was* funny. We need to find some humour in this nonsense.'

Expecting this to relax Sasha, I'm shocked when she suddenly bursts into tears.

'Hey…' I cross the room and put my arms round her. 'What's going on? Please don't get upset. I told you, we need to laugh – otherwise this happens.'

'Ama-no-crian-coz-a-tha,' Sasha mumbles miserably into my shoulder.

'Sorry, what? I can't make out a word you're saying.'

'It's… not… that.' She lets out a half-shudder-half-hiccup as I release her and hold her at arm's length. 'I'm just… it upsets me so much that you're getting on with things, accepting no help. When my mum… she's selfishly taking the kind of support people who are ill like you need and deserve, and there's not a damn thing wrong with her.'

I take in my best friend's face, reading the hurt she's feeling from what she considers to be the ultimate injustice.

'Aww, Sash.' I pull her back in for another hug as she dissolves into tears once more. 'I totally get why you feel that way, but life isn't fair. I don't need the kind of help your mum's taking, and I don't want it. I intend to stay independent for as long as I bloody well can. Be angry at your mum for how she's hurt you, not how you think she's hurting me, because she's not. Yeah?'

'Ah-sapo-sat-mahks-shens.'

'I'm going to take that as you accept and agree with what I say.' I chuckle, patting her on the back affection-ately.

Sasha wipes her eyes with a tissue I hand her and I notice that her expression has turned thoughtful.

'Lex… if I ask you a question, will you be honest with me?'

'Depends what the question is—' I give myself a mental kick up the arse. 'Sorry, sorry. Yes, I'll be honest.'

'Thank you.' Sasha chooses her words carefully as she unwraps a mini Toblerone. 'I want to understand how things are with you. If you don't tell me, I make it up myself, then I get it wrong and annoy you.'

I realise Sasha's right. Trying to pretend nothing's wrong leaves her in an impossible situation.

'What I want to know,' she continues, 'is how your MS is affecting you now; and what support you need. I want to help you.'

I take a moment to digest her question. 'I suppose it's natural for you to want to support me, but only if that "support" doesn't start to take over or smother me.'

'Lex, you only seem to see two polar opposites: totally able-bodied or totally disabled.'

I flinch as she says this.

'Sorry.' She picks up on my discomfort. 'What I mean is, you're neither. There are so many shades of grey along that scale. Let's work out your current "Lex status" and work with that. You need an approach that's tailored perfectly for you – then I can support you with that.'

Sasha's words erupt inside me like a volcano of comprehension. She's exactly right. I've been avoiding things I might actually be able to do, and covering things up when I'm struggling. I need to find the right balance. This is something I can work with. It's a problem to solve and I can do that without it having to be an emotional thing.

'You know, I could kiss you, Sash.'

'Maybe best not, given recent events.' She giggles.

'Hmm… yeah, good point.' I waggle my eyebrows at her faux-lecherously. 'But seriously, you've just made so much sense. I'll grab a pen and we can work through it.'

Padding through to the small desk in my bedroom, I retrieve some stationery, then return to the sofa.

'OK, let's do this.' Sasha dabs at the remaining dampness round her eyes with a tissue. 'How do you want to start?'

'I think I'll answer your questions, then we can use that information to start to build a framework and approach.'

'Said like a true project manager. I'll be note-taker.'

'Deal.' I hand her the notebook and pen. 'OK... how my MS is affecting me... it's not nearly as bad as when I had my relapse. Back then, I struggled to get out of bed in the morning. It took me two hours just to get ready for a hospital appointment because I kept having to stop and rest. I had to sit down in the shower. It was hellish.'

'And now?' Sasha scribbles away on the notepad.

I take a moment to really tune in to how things have been recently. 'Now... it's like a perma-exhaustion. A bit like walking around with weights strapped to my body. Nothing is as easy as it used to be – stairs and hills are my nemesis.'

'Anything else?'

'I get this tingling in my hands and feet. Turns out that's a symptom – I just thought I had poor circulation. My balance, coordination, spatial judgement... they're all off, and I actually fell in front of my colleagues a few weeks back when my foot malfunctioned. That was pretty humiliating.'

'Oh, Lex, you never said.' Sasha looks gutted for me.

'Didn't seem much point.' I shrug. 'Wasn't like you could do anything to change it.'

'Maybe not, but this is what I'm talking about. It's not just about you being physically capable, you also need emotional support. Sharing that with me at the time might have helped you process how you felt about it.'

'I suppose.' I know she's right because I gave myself a bit of a hard time in the days following that incident, but I'm not going to offer that up too willingly. 'So that's mainly it. There are moments when I struggle with my concentration, but I generally have a clearer head. It's not like the "cog-fog" I experienced before. That's a positive thing because that made it very hard to concentrate at work.'

'That's great. So what support do you need? How do I get you to be a bit kinder to yourself? How do we have fun together without going overboard? Or, on the flip side, how do I make sure I don't become the "fun police"? And what about alcohol? Do you drink? Not drink? If you don't, should I not either? Or will that annoy you?'

'Whoa! Slow down,' I tease her in an attempt to hide the fact that I'm now the one feeling overwhelmed.

'All valid questions though, right?'

'Yeah, they're valid, but can we tackle them one at a time?'

An hour later, we've chatted it all through and agreed a plan for the weekend. It includes regular coffee stops, some downtime before going out in the evenings, and Sasha being allowed to say if she thinks I'm looking tired – but if I say I'm not, she's not allowed to keep asking. We also agree that I'll stick to my two-drink limit and Sasha will behave as she normally would – though I draw the line at having to carry her home.

It doesn't quite produce the plan for managing my life I'd hoped for, but it provides some good starting blocks, and I can treat this weekend as a bit of an experiment. I'll certainly be testing my limits just with Sasha being here, and all the things we're planning to do together.

Chapter 16

The next morning, after breakfast, we get showered and dressed and take a taxi to the Jewellery Quarter.

'I can't wait to see this.' Sasha's face is one of an excited toddler as she hops out of the cab on Vyse Street and makes a beeline for the first shop window she sees. 'Look, Lex, their stuff is gorgeous.'

I join her and we gaze longingly at the stunning array of diamonds winking back at us.

'Come on.' I give her a nudge. 'There's plenty more shops like this to nosey at. According to what I read online, the Jewellery Quarter is "Europe's largest concentration of jewellery businesses" and it's become known as "the golden heart of Britain". It's an area steeped in history too. I think you're going to enjoy what's further down the road.'

'You sound like a tour guide,' Sasha giggles. 'Obviously been doing your homework.'

'You know me. Google's my best friend.'

We slowly make our way along the street, which in itself is also appealing with its Victorian charm, lined with quaint cast-iron lampposts and cute red-brick terraced buildings.

'Which one would you choose if you could have any of these?' I ask Sasha, as we peer at yet another display of engagement rings.

'I'd love one like that.' She points to a platinum one-carat round-cut diamond ring, with smaller glittering stones embedded round the band. 'It's stunning.'

'And expensive. Though I gather you save money if you buy from here rather than the high street.'

'Useful to know, but it's not like I'm even close to getting some bling like that on my finger.'

I put my arm round her shoulder. 'The online dating isn't going well then?'

Sasha makes a face. 'Put it this way, of the last three guys I've been on dates with, one turned out to be twice my age, one conveniently discovered his wallet had been "stolen" when the bill arrived, and the other spent the whole evening talking about his ex-wife.'

'They sound like a bunch of charmers. And you never heard back from the one you did sort of like from a couple of months ago?'

'Nope. Totally ghosted me. Was probably married or something.'

'Aww, Sash. You will meet someone good one day.'

'I sincerely hope so.' She sighs loudly. 'Otherwise I'm going through this ridiculous torture for nothing.'

We turn away from the window display and continue down the street until we reach the Museum of the Jewellery Quarter.

'Ooh, this looks interesting,' says Sasha.

'I think you'll like it. It used to be a jewellery factory.'

We enter the museum and pay the cashier, who invites us to make our way through the two galleries before joining the workshop tour.

'So, how about you? Have you heard from Dom?' Sasha asks, as we wander round the bright airy gallery, taking in the exhibits.

'No, and I don't expect to. Dom's not the kind of guy to ruminate. Once that decision was made, it was final. We only "talked business" after we broke up – to get the flat sold and divide our things. There was no sentimentality whatsoever.'

'Did you not find that hard? You were together for a long time. I would have been devastated if a guy I'd been engaged to just switched off from me like that.'

'Oh, I was hurt – badly. I thought he was so cold. Wondered even if he had ever really loved me. But I guess he was doing what he had to do to cope. Dom does feel things, he takes them quite personally, he just doesn't know how to process those feelings, so he pretends they're not there.'

'Sounds a bit like you.' Sasha's eyes widen in horror and she puts a hand to her mouth. 'Sorry, I didn't mean that how it sounded.'

I pause in front of a glass cabinet containing an intriguing range of gold and silver samples that the factory workshop used to make. 'Don't be sorry. It's probably true. Dom and I worked well because we never dwelled on anything. We considered ourselves quite resilient. It seems naïve now, because as much as it's not healthy to wallow, it's equally unhealthy to never face up to issues. As soon as things got a bit tough, we crumbled.'

'I'm sorry. I really liked Dom. I'm also sorry I suggested a few months ago that you drove him away. That was unfair. I just didn't want you to leave.'

'I know that, Sash. No need to apologise. I've admitted that I didn't face up to things. So in a way, you were right. I did drive him away.'

I look at the floor, expecting the familiar sadness and empty Dom-shaped hole I've been holding together with metaphorical sticky tape to burst open again. But the tape stays intact. Surprised by this, I do a self-check. Am I over Dom? No, I can't be. Not fully. Not yet. But something has changed. As this thought works its way through my brain, it's chased closely by another. The man from the train. Matt. With his gorgeous penetrating brown eyes, his endearing inquisitive nature. And his defeated look in the bar just a few weeks ago.

'What is it?' Sasha asks. 'Something's bothering you, I can tell.'

I look at her blankly, then come to. 'It's… nothing. Nothing at all.'

I move on to another exhibit, pretending to be fascinated by its contents.

'Lex, come on. I've known you almost all our lives. Have you… met someone?'

A hot flush creeps up my neck. 'No. Why would you say that?'

'Because the look on your face there was *exactly* the one I've seen every time you've met a guy you like – Dom included.'

'No, it wasn't.'

'Yes. It was. Who is he?' She bounces up and down impatiently.

I roll my eyes at her overenthusiasm, aware that she'll be very disappointed by the anticlimax I'm about to deliver.

'Sash, there's nothing to get excited about. I met a guy on the train. Twice actually. He was sitting opposite me and we got talking. He then asked me out and I said no. End of.'

She scrutinises me intensely. 'Why did you say no if you clearly like him?'

'I don't...' I realise I can't fool her. 'OK, look, I took his number but I didn't call him. Just didn't think it was a good idea, being so soon after Dom and I split up. I was still a bit broken from that.'

This, of course, is a half-truth. It was about Dom at first, but then it was about my MS. After the stairs up from the platform half-killed me.

'Fair enough. And?'

'And nothing. That's it, story over. Told you there's nothing to get excited about.'

'Nah, that's not it. There's something else you're not telling me.' Sasha manoeuvres herself between me and the exhibit, forcing me to make eye contact with her.

I let out an exasperated laugh, realising there's no way I can put the blinkers on her.

'I might have bumped into him in a bar after work.'

'And?'

'And he asked me why I didn't call...' I tail off as the memory starts chasing round my brain again.

'AND?' Sasha looks like she's about to take off. 'Lex. Will you just give me the whole story without me having to force every last bit out of you?'

I groan in surrender. 'I met him again in a bar when I was out with my workmates. He asked why I didn't call, and I said I'd been busy.'

'But why reject him again if you obviously like him? The first time I understand, but you were a few weeks into things here. As you said yourself, you don't dwell on the past. So why not have one date? See if the spark was real.'

I pick at a loose thread on my cuff, not wanting to admit the truth. Or say it out loud. I could try to maintain it was about Dom, but what would be the point? Sasha would see right through that facade.

'Lex?'

I exhale theatrically, eyes to the ceiling. 'I did it because it was for the best. I did him a favour, Sash.'

'How was that doing him a favour?'

'Because who would willingly take on someone in my situation? Dom verbalised what everyone else must think. Why would anyone knowingly sign up for a relationship with someone who's already broken – at this age? And for whom they would eventually have to become the main carer. Who, Sash? Tell me who.' I can feel my eyes start to sting with emotion, so I look away quickly to hide it.

Sasha seems genuinely troubled by my monologue. It's clear that she wants to tell me that I'm wrong, and that it doesn't merit a second thought. But the thing about Sasha is that she *really* can't lie. And I've got her in a headlock (metaphorically speaking).

'So, there you go.' I shrug and return to picking at the thread on my top. 'I did him a favour. He's an active guy. Second time I met him, he got on the train at the Lake District after completing a three-peak challenge – that's a thing, in case you didn't know.'

'I've heard the term before.'

'Someone like Matt needs a woman who'll join him on that kind of adventure, not hold him back.'

'Matt. That's a nice name.' Sasha links arms with me and guides me towards a large wall-mounted infographic.

'It is. And?'

'I don't know. It's a name that makes me think of a kind, genuine person. Someone who'd care more for others than himself. Who'd perhaps be a bit hurt if he knew why you gave him the cold shoulder.'

'Are you trying to guilt me on this?'

'*No,*' she replies in a tone that makes it clear to me that's exactly her aim. 'Just giving poor Matt the benefit of the doubt. You're right, Lex. A lot of people wouldn't take on the situation you described. But *people* are different. Perhaps some *people* wouldn't see it like that at all. Matt might be one of them.'

I snort with laughter. 'Think you've gotten a bit wrapped up in the romance of that film we watched last night.'

'No, I haven't. I've already agreed with you that most men wouldn't take your situation on. But you don't want most men, Lex. You want one that's amazing. What are you going to do otherwise? Spend the rest of your life alone? Never date again?'

'That was kind of the plan.' I give her a sheepish look.

'Well it's a daft plan. Sorry. But it is.'

'If it were you, what would you do?'

She considers my question. 'I obviously can't say for sure, but I'd like to think I'd give Matt the benefit of the doubt. Maybe go on a few dates and see what he's like before sharing my situation. Then if he ditched me because I'm not a perfect specimen, I'd be hurt, but I'd know he wasn't the right one.'

'When did you start talking so much sense?'

Sasha nudges me playfully. 'Since I dated half of the men in my local area and realised that most of them are totally self-absorbed or a complete waste of space. If I met someone that had even the slightest bit of potential, I'd be on his trail like a sniffer dog.'

'You realise that makes you sound like a crazy stalker?'

'Ha ha. You know what I mean. I'm just saying, Lex. What if you wake up from this understandable but illogical viewpoint several months from now and the only guy who might have fit the bill isn't available any more – because some other sensible woman has snapped him up?'

'Appealing to my competitive side now, are you?' I chuckle.

'Did it work?'

'A little bit. OK, say I agree to follow your play on things. What if I don't bump into him again?'

'You said he was part of the Friday night after-work crowd. It's Friday today. Let's go back to the same bar. Start there.'

'What are the chances he'll be there?' I give her a doubtful look.

'If he's not, then you'll have to hope you see him again when you're out with your workmates. But it's worth a try. I could do with a night out. See if I can meet a nice Brummie lad for myself. That is, if you're up to it?'

'I'm up to it. OK, let's do it. But to be clear, this is just about me being more open-minded, nothing more.'

'Great.' Sasha looks super pleased with herself for bringing me round. 'Shall we head to the guided tour?'

Chapter 17

Several hours later, as we're returning from our trip to the Jewellery Quarter, I feel myself flagging, which triggers doubts about how I'll manage a night out as well. Other than a couple of reasonably short Friday after-work drinks sessions with my team, this is the first time I've tried to be active through the day and also well into the evening. And it's the first weekend since starting my new job that I'm not going to have a significant rest period. It plays on my mind: particularly how I'll be on Monday after it all. This annoys me. What was it Emmanuel said? Just go have fun.

As we reach my apartment and let ourselves in, I feel my eyelids drooping.

'Don't know about you, but I'm quite beat,' Sasha declares. 'Shall we have a siesta?'

I'm unsure whether she's picked up on how I'm feeling, whether she's just playing it safe, or whether she really is tired herself. At this point I really don't care. I need to lie down, before I fall down.

–

By 7:30 p.m., Sasha and I are glammed up and waiting to be served in the bar in which I bumped into Matt. It's just as busy as last time, full of workers in corporate outfits, but thankfully I'm feeling much fresher after my ninety-minute not-so-power-nap.

'What are you having?' Sasha raises her voice over the music and the lively after-work chat in the bar.

'Gin and Fevertree, please. And a glass of tap water.'

'Sure thing. So… is he here?'

'We've just got here. Give me a chance.' I shake my head at her overzealousness. 'Anyway, that's a side task for this evening. If I bump into him then I'll say hello. I'm not committing to anything else.'

'But you agreed.'

'I agreed to be more open-minded. And not rule out dating for the rest of my existence. That's all.'

'That's as good as agreeing to go out with him.'

'Not sure where you get that logic from.' I gesture towards a woman in too-high heels tentatively leaving the bar, trying not to spill the four champagne cocktails on the tray she's holding. 'Quick, claim your space.'

Sasha expertly dodges into the eighteen-inch opening that's appeared at the bar. As I stand behind her waiting for her to be served, my eyes roam around the room. I try to convince myself I'm just soaking up the atmosphere, but I'm kidding myself. Much as I'm resisting Sasha's puppy-like excitement, she's made me consider things from a different perspective and see that my application of my 'new life' rules has been inconsistent. It *is* totally unrealistic to think I can happily trot along through life in full celibacy. I was getting married before my body committed the ultimate betrayal and I still want that – with the right guy. I'm adamant that I'm going to live as normal a life as possible. So why did that vision not include a relationship, possibly even marriage?

This realisation has ignited something in me. I want that date with Matt. It doesn't need to mean anything at this stage. I can just have some fun and use it as an opportunity to get back into the dating scene.

As I scan the room, it becomes clear that Matt's not here. It's now chucking down domestic pets outside, so it's not likely he's in the outdoor seating area either. I feel a twinge of disappointment. What if it was complete coincidence that I ran into him before? What if I never do so again? My problem-solving brain immediately steps in to answer this: in that case you'll move on and meet someone else.

I decide I'm not satisfied with this answer and refocus my attention on Sasha, who's now being served. She passes my drink back to me and we make our way across the bar to see if we can find a seat. Luckily there's a group just leaving, so we're able to commandeer one end of their table.

'Is he here?' Sasha asks me again.

'No, he's not,' I confirm, instead of trying to deny I was even looking. 'Not that I can see anyway.'

'That's a shame. Maybe he'll still turn up.'

'Doubt it. It's a bit late to come from work. He might not be out at all tonight. Or is somewhere else.'

'Hey, how about we play detective and try and track him down?' she suggests.

'You mean stalker-style?' I raise a judgemental eyebrow.

'What? No. But you want to run into him again, don't you?'

I let out a small groan as I sip at my drink. 'Fine. You win.' I relay some details while she taps them into her notepad app and stares at them thoughtfully.

'OK, Sherlock. What do you deduce from the information I've given you?'

Sasha looks thoughtful. 'Well... the most obvious lead to follow is his job. Let's see if we can find him on LinkedIn.'

She opens up her mobile web browser and types 'Matt Manufacturing Engineer Birmingham' into Google. The search quickly returns a list of results.

'Look, Lex. There's quite a few.' She clicks into the first one. 'Is that him?'

'Does that look like the kind of man I would be interested in? Think thirty years younger and one hundred per cent less grey hair.'

'Right. But I need more info. What *am* I looking for?'

I conjure up an image of Matt. As I do, the memory of his easy smile immediately morphs into his defeated acceptance as I shamelessly palmed him off with my lame excuses. It makes me wish I had the flexibility of a contortionist, so I could give myself a good kick up the arse for being such a stubborn idiot.

'You OK, Lex?' Sasha gives me an odd look.

'Eh... yeah. Just thinking. He's tall and athletic, mid-brown hair, dark chocolate eyes and... a close-cropped beard that defines his jawline perfectly, a kind of Jamie Dornan look about him... and when he laughed, his eyes glinted with just the slightest air of mischief...' I trail off dreamily.

'Oh wow, you've got it bad, Lex.' Sasha giggles. 'Not sure I ever heard you describe Dom in that way.'

'What? No, I haven't...' I redden as my mind plays back the physical description of Matt I've just unwittingly verbalised. 'Oh, stop it, Sash. All you need to know is:

athletic, brown hair and eyes, beard. Probably much like a lot of men around here.'

'OK, OK. Is he any of these guys?' She clicks in and out of another three LinkedIn profiles.

'Nope. Who would have thought there would be so many people called Matt or Matthew who were manufacturing engineers in Birmingham?'

Unwilling to give in, Sasha searches Facebook and Instagram as well, but to no avail.

'Sash, this is hopeless,' I say. 'Let's just enjoy our night.'

Reluctantly giving in, she puts her phone away as I try to ignore how disappointed I feel knowing I might have missed my opportunity with Matt.

–

By the time it hits ten p.m., we've enjoyed a delicious Thai meal in the restaurant I went to with my team on my first day, and we're now contemplating our next move.

'What do *you* want to do?' I ask Sasha. 'This is your weekend.'

'I'm quite full and the food coma may be clouding my judgement. I'd like to go to a bar and see a bit more of the Birmingham nightlife, but I could just as easily go back to yours and veg on the couch. Also...' She glances at me and hesitates.

'You're wondering whether I'm feeling up to going somewhere else.'

'Well, yeah.'

'I'm OK, Sash. Actually, I'm feeling quite good. Makes me wonder if I've actually made my fatigue worse by not being active enough.'

'You're sure?'

'What did we agree?' I raise a reproving eyebrow at her. 'You're allowed to ask, but you have to accept my answer.'

'We did agree that. OK then, I can battle through the food coma. Where are we going?'

I consider this. 'I've no idea. Bars-wise, I haven't ventured further than Brindley Place yet.'

'Broad Street is the main nightlife strip, isn't it?' Sasha asks. 'Someone at work told me that.'

'Yeah it is. And it's right near here. Shall we start there?'

'Sounds like a plan.'

We pay our bill and venture into the distinctly wet and chilly late evening air. The rain splashes into growing puddles that mirror the inviting lights of Brindley Place, making us glad we thought to bring an umbrella. As we approach Broad Street, we're greeted by a sea of well-oiled, boisterous people, whose behaviour as a collective is not miles away from the troop of chimpanzees I watched in a nature documentary recently. There's certainly a lot of screeching and alpha male behaviour on show, watched over by the local police, and a couple of ambulances standing by.

'What is this?' Sasha looks genuinely intimidated. 'I thought Glasgow was lively on a Friday night. This is more like Magaluf.'

'Perhaps it's not for us?' I suggest. 'Especially as I've already hit my two-drink limit. I'd need to be a good bit merrier to even consider joining that lot.'

'Maybe we could walk on a bit and see what we find?'

'Good thinking.'

We quickly continue along the street, but not without being propositioned by a couple of men and a woman. There's a man throwing up in a bin, and another taking a pee just round the corner of one of the bars. He keeps poking his head round the corner to check the police haven't clocked him, which makes me wonder why he doesn't just go to the men's toilet inside – and whether his shoes are still dry.

As we pass a side street, my attention is drawn down it to a hub of activity. It's another bar, but the punters standing around smoking outside appear a bit more sober.

'What about there, Sash?'

'Seems all right.' She peers along the street, trying to get a better feel for it. 'Saves us walking any further, at least.'

'Let's take a look.'

We make our way towards the bar, nodding at the punters outside as we enter. It's closer to a pub, with more traditional decor and upholstered furnishings that, while a bit tatty and worn, further add to the charm of the place.

'It's my round,' Sasha informs me. 'What would you like?'

'I'll just have a Coke, thanks. You have a proper drink though – if you want one.'

She nods her understanding and makes her way to the bar, while I make a beeline for the only vacant table in the place. I sit myself down on the fixed bench-style seating, facing into the room. It's packed out with high-spirited Friday night revellers, giving it a warm and welcoming feel. The energetic dance track pumping through the ceiling-mounted speakers doesn't quite match the decor.

It's very much a bar that attracts all types. I'm just sizing the place up as a potential Friday after-work drinks venue for my team at work when a booming voice comes over the PA.

'Right, then. Who's up next? It's… *Shanice*. Shanice, up you come.'

As the room breaks into whooping applause, my karaoke radar goes into overdrive. I crane my neck to get a better view of the other side of the room. There, I spot the owner of the booming voice, as well as a television screen emitting full 'karaoke blue'. A beautiful woman in her twenties, jet black hair piled high on her head and wearing a figure-hugging gold dress, makes her way across the room. She plucks the microphone being offered to her from the karaoke compère and poises herself, ready to sing.

I watch with interest as the opening bars of a well-known upbeat Whitney Houston song begin to play. No one generally attempts a Whitney Houston number unless they have some level of vocal competence. I'm not disappointed. The second she starts to sing, it's clear that Shanice was born for this. Her pitch is flawless, the strength in her voice evident but perfectly controlled, her breathing well measured. She moves seamlessly through the first verse and chorus, making it appear completely effortless.

'It's karaoke,' Sasha excitedly states the obvious as she plonks our drinks down on the table. She shimmies her way round to sit beside me, keen to watch the action as well. 'Are you going to sing? You *have* to sing.'

Sasha's merely verbalising the thought swimming round my mind since the compère called Shanice up. Karaoke is my thing. For me, there's nothing more energising than a mic in my hand. It makes me feel alive – almost invincible. As I continue to watch Shanice, I feel the familiar uncontrollable urge rising inside me. Sasha's right. I *have* to sing.

'OK, but what shall I sing?' I ask her. 'That woman is amazing. Maybe wait a bit before I put my request up.'

'Rubbish. You're as good as her. You just sing a different style of music. Ooh, wouldn't it be cool if you could sing your own song – the one you wrote when you were recovering from your relapse – at karaoke one day?'

'Ha, yeah. That's never going to happen. It's doomed to a life of concealment within my notepad app.' I suddenly realise something. 'Shit, Sash, I've never sung in public without plenty of drink in me. Not sure how I feel about doing it almost stone-cold, here, in front of all these people.'

I tune back in to Shanice's singing; half the bar has now merrily joined in. Shanice herself is busting some serious moves as the song comes to its climax.

'She should be on a stage, not doing karaoke in a city centre bar.' I swallow thickly, now feeling quite intimidated. 'What if they're all like that in here?'

'You talking yourself out of it? If it's too scary without a drink for extra courage, don't do it. No one's forcing you.'

'You're doing that reverse psychology thing again.'

'And?' She chews her lip in anticipation.

'And it worked. As usual.' I give her a little wink. 'Back in a sec.'

I get up and make my way across to the karaoke compère, propelled by Sasha's triumphant hoot from behind me. He nods a greeting, while simultaneously managing the changeover from Whitney Houston to a current chart hit I recognise but can't name. Shanice hands back the mic, before making her way back through her adoring crowd.

'Evening, bab,' he says to me. 'Not seen you in here before. What you singing?'

I make my request, which is acknowledged with two thumbs up, then return to our table.

'What did you put up for?' Sasha asks before my backside has hit the seat.

'You'll have to wait and see,' I reply, and she puts on a pouty face. 'Might be a while. There's a lot of people here.'

We sing along to the track that's playing until it fades out and the karaoke compère's voice booms through the mic once again.

'*Isaac.* Come on up.'

Sasha and I look eagerly around for the next singer but no one seems to have claimed the identity of Isaac.

'Come on, Isaac,' he tries again. 'Don't be shy. Friendly bunch, we are.'

Finally a man makes his way across the room, earning himself a smatter of applause for what's perceived to be his bravery. He briefly engages in conversation with the karaoke compère, then walks off again.

'OK then. Turns out Isaac's a little worse for wear.' The compère chuckles through the mic, triggering a collective 'boo' from the punters. 'Change of plan. Let's have... *Alex.*'

I blanch. Surely not yet. I haven't yet warmed up to the idea of singing in almost full sobriety.

'It's you,' Sasha squeals.

'Hang on. It might not be me.' This is blind optimism on my part. 'It could be another Alex – a guy or a woman.'

'That's true.'

We sit back and wait for someone else to make their way to the mic, but no one appears.

'Not again.' The karaoke compère sounds perplexed. 'I'll try once more. Alex – the young lady who just requested the Killers – up you come.'

'Shit, that is me.' I feel an instant sense of panic.

'Oh, I love it when you do that song. *Go, quick.* Before you miss your turn.'

I hesitate a moment longer, then autopilot kicks in, overriding my instinct to sink into my seat and pull an Isaac. I get up and cross the room. As I do, the karaoke compère spots me and expresses his relief publicly.

'So great you can join us, Alex. Give her a show of appreciation, everyone.'

The bar erupts into raucous applause, making me want to walk straight past the makeshift stage and out the main door. Of course, I don't. Because as much as I've been called too soon and I haven't had enough to drink to settle my rather overexcitable nerves, I still *really* want to sing. It's been so long. Back in Glasgow, karaoke was a regular thing. Dom was never a fan, but I didn't need him to be. A private karaoke room was a staple activity on a work night out or for a leaving do, and there were regular trips with Sasha to our old local. A few G&Ts and they'd have to pry the mic out of my hands.

I'm just feet away from the mic handover when my thigh unexpectedly and violently collides with the corner of a table I'm passing. A white hot, shooting pain surges through my leg, causing me to yelp out loud, clutching my injured limb. There's a collective 'oooh' from the punters around me as they feel my pain – both physically and psychologically. Face burning, leg throbbing, I plaster on a brave face and continue on towards the mic.

'You all right, bab?' The karaoke compère looks genuinely concerned. 'That was quite a knock.'

'I'm OK.' I force a smile.

'Still want to sing?'

'Don't think this lot can be let down a second time.'

'That's the spirit.' He gives me an encouraging nod and speaks into the mic. 'All right, everyone. Think Alex needs some extra support after that bash. Might have had one too many as well, but at least she's made it up here.'

The bar erupts into yet more cheers, with some cat calls of 'go Alex' as the karaoke compère hands me the mic.

'Off you go, bab. Sing the pain away.'

Thanking him, I turn towards the blue screen as the title of the song appears in stark white letters. I can feel myself trembling slightly, my breathing laboured, as I wait for the on-screen lyrics to count me in. What a difference it makes to have the reassuring hug of a couple of gin and tonics. It almost makes me wish I'd breached my two-drink limit in preparation.

'*Amazing song choice*,' someone shouts from across the bar, which eases my nerves ever so slightly.

I flash a grateful smile in the direction of the voice as the room falls silent in anticipation. The light, emotive intro plays and I start to sing the opening lines. There's very little by way of instrumental accompaniment, which always make me think I'm off tune at first. But as the track builds to its full volume and tempo, and the punters in the bar clap to the beat encouragingly, I begin to relax. I power my way through the first verse and chorus, feeling less exposed, the music and emotion consuming me like a tidal wave.

I dare a glance around the room and find myself spurred on by approving grins and whoops. This fuels me to take it up a level, which seems to please my audience even more, and I become so lost in the song, it's almost over before I've had a chance to really experience it. The whole bar sings with me as I reach the song's climax, in an explosion of power and intensity. Then as I complete the soulful lyrics, the music fades out and I'm left standing, alone and exposed, once again. But not for long. The bar erupts into a swarm of cheers, of applause and foot-stamping. My audience is clearly happy with my performance – which is an enormous relief.

I give an awkward bow, thrust the mic back into the karaoke compère's hand and rush back to my seat, eyes to the ground, nodding thanks to the positive comments being directed at me as I go. I reach our table and slide into my seat, my face hot and flustered from all the attention.

'That was incredible.' Sasha grabs me into a vice-like hug. 'You totally nailed it. See, you don't need alcohol. You're a complete natural.'

'Am I?' I screw up my face. 'Pretty sure I was visibly shaking at the start.'

'Didn't look like that at all. You seemed so confident. No one will have picked up on it. How's your leg though? I really felt for you there.'

'My leg?' I'm momentarily confused. 'Oh, my thigh. It's… gosh, I'd almost forgotten about that. It's still throbbing, but you know, I didn't feel any pain at all while I was singing. Don't know if it was the adrenaline, or just that I was so into the song. Must be a natural painkiller.'

I hitch up my skirt to inspect my leg and despite the low lighting, I can see a large swollen, purpling area about two thirds of the way up my thigh.

'Ooh, *shit*,' Sasha gasps. 'That looks sore. Want me to get you some ice?'

'Nah.' I pull my skirt back down again. 'Don't want to give the people in here an eyeful.'

My eyes scan the room, taking in the lively atmosphere: people making the most of their night, enjoying each other's company. Men, women, older, younger, a whole range of ethnicities, all packed in together, joined in the sense of community that comes with karaoke. Then to my astonishment, a familiar face jumps out of the crowd, sending my senses into a spin.

It's Matt. He's here.

Chapter 18

I fumble to grab Sasha's hand. 'Sash, that's him.'

'That's who?'

'Matt. He's here. In this bar.'

'Where?' She's immediately alert. 'Point him out.'

'I'm not going to point in case he looks over. See the guy with the bright orange top? Matt's the one talking to him.'

'In the grey shirt?'

'Yeah, that's him.'

'He's *gorgeous*, Lex.'

'He is a bit, isn't he?' I crinkle my nose in appreciation.

'Well, what are you waiting for?' Sasha gives me a little nudge. 'Go and speak to him – before you miss your chance again.'

The nerves from my 'onstage appearance' immediately resurface. I want to go and speak to Matt, to get that date that we missed out on. I was so ready to do it earlier. Now, here, in a bar full of uninhibited Friday night revellers while almost totally sober myself, I feel less sure of myself.

'Right, yeah.' I pick up my handbag. 'I'll just nip to the loo first. Check my make-up.'

'What? No.' Sasha looks at me in alarm. 'You look gorgeous. What if he's not there when you get back? You need to do it now.'

I glance across at Matt. His companion is clearly in the middle of telling a story and Matt and another bloke are listening intently, laughing along with him. As I watch him, the urge to go and speak to him overwhelms me. I want that kind of banter with him, to have him that interested in what I've got to say.

'OK. Wish me luck.' I start to get up from my seat.

'Wait, stop.' Sasha grabs my arm. 'Who's that?'

I slowly sit back down and watch as a stunning blonde, with teeth so white I can see them from here, joins the conversation. She drapes herself across Matt, whispering something in his ear. He laughs, then affectionately puts his arm round her waist. It's a level of intimacy that makes it clear they haven't just met. I feel like I've been punched in the stomach.

'Well, she's certainly not one of the staff.'

'Bugger,' Sasha huffs on my behalf. 'I guess he did move on quickly.'

'Shit happens.' I shrug, trying for nonchalance, but I actually feel quite flat. 'How about we call it a night? Not sure I want to watch those two lovebirds fawning over each other. Best not to overdo things as well.'

'I think that's a good plan. Just let me run to the ladies' first. That gin has gone right through me.'

As Sasha heads for the toilets, I try not to look in Matt's direction, but I'm like a piece of metal trying to evade a magnet. I keep catching myself glancing in his direction, then have to quickly look away. I'm at the point of physically manhandling my chin to keep myself facing the other direction when Matt happens to look over and makes eye contact with me. My first instinct is to look away, but his gaze is so mesmerising I find myself unable to break the connection. Instead I give a little wave, which he returns. Then, to my surprise, he unravels himself from the blonde, excuses himself from the conversation and makes his way across the bar towards me.

'Hi,' he greets me as he reaches my table. 'Nice to see you again. I hope you're not here on your own?'

'My friend's just in the ladies',' I reply automatically.

'I remember you said on the train you liked a bit of karaoke but I didn't realise you were a pro. You played that one down.'

His eyes search mine. My pulse quickens, and I feel like every coherent thought has fallen out of my head.

'You saw? I… err… guess I can hold a tune.'

'That was quite obvious. You have an impressive voice.'

'Oh… thanks.'

'How are you? Are you still settling in all right?'

'Yeah, I'm loving it actually.' I finally get myself together. 'My best friend from Glasgow is down this weekend, so we're making the most of it.'

'Good stuff.' He nods in approval, smiling.

There's a momentary silence between us, during which I mentally kick myself up the arse ten times over for letting the ridiculously attractive blonde have this man.

'I'm glad I've bumped into you,' says Matt eventually. 'I actually wanted to apologise.'

'For what?'

'I may have been a bit stand-offish last time we spoke. Probably a male pride thing.' He cringes a little.

He's apologising to me? After my behaviour? Allowing this man to slip through my fingers has been a far greater mistake than I even realised.

'Matt, no. No way. I was the one that was off. I was… dealing with some stuff.'

'I'm sorry to hear that. Is everything all right now?'

'It is.'

'That's good.' His gorgeous, melty-dark eyes are searching mine again.

I realise I can't bear it. If I no longer have a chance with him, I need to get rid of him.

'Think your girlfriend's looking for you.' I tilt my head towards the blonde, who's looking right at us, her face – naturally – curious.

Matt turns and signals to her that he'll be right there. 'That's my sister. Nosey one, she is.'

His sister? Matt's words and what I saw don't seem to match. I glance across at the blonde again. She's still standing with the two guys Matt was chatting to before, but now she's teasing the one in the orange T-shirt, arms round his neck – in a very non-sibling way. Which means: Matt may still be single.

'Your sister?' I purse my lips in anticipation. 'Huh.'

'Baby sister,' Matt clarifies, as though this is important.

'Any actual girlfriend here tonight I should know about?'

'Not a one.'

'Or back at home? At her apartment? Getting legless with the rest of Broad Street?'

'No. No. And no.' He grins, having now cottoned on to my game. 'There's no girlfriend or significant other. Period.'

'*Ri-gh-t.*' I digest this rather glorious information. 'And you don't hold grudges, it seems.'

'Life's too short for that nonsense.'

I bite my lip coyly. 'Then in that case... how would you like me to show you round Birmingham?'

Matt throws back his head and laughs loudly. 'That would be great.'

'Excellent. Err, I might need your number again.'

'I can't believe you deleted it. That's harsh.'

'I'm sorry, I was—'

'I'm kidding.' He gives me a flirty nudge, which sends a tingling sensation right through my body. 'Got your phone handy?'

I pull out my phone and we exchange numbers.

'Right then,' says Matt. 'I'll wait to hear from you. Hopefully go better than last time.'

I flush with embarrassment. I can't blame him for wondering if I'll actually follow through this time. Even though he's joking, I feel the need to reassure him. 'I'll be in touch after the weekend. I mean it this time.'

He fixes me with his spellbinding gaze once more. 'I look forward to hearing from you, Alex.'

My stomach responds by melting into a little puddle. Matt walks off and returns to his companions. He says something in response to their questioning looks, then his sister looks across and gives me a friendly smile, which I tentatively return.

'Oh my goodness, what just happened?' Sasha suddenly rushes across to me. 'I've been waiting over there because I didn't want to interrupt and risk ruining things for you.'

I give her a mischievous smile. 'The basic run-down: that's his sister, he's still single and we're going on a date.'

'A-ma-zing.' Sasha bounces on her toes and claps her hands excitedly. 'Let's get one more drink and you can tell me *everything*.'

Chapter 19

By the time Monday rolls round, I'm shattered and almost dragging myself to work. I've used Sasha's visit as an experiment, and now have results, which are that I really need some rest at the weekends. The up-side, though, is that I coped much better than I expected. I can feel reasonably confident about having a life again, as long as I don't go at it like I do in the office. And that's fine. I can settle for 'work hard, play moderately'.

Sasha and I certainly made the most of our time together. As a follow-on from Friday night, we spent Saturday morning wandering round the impressive interior of the Birmingham Museum and Art Gallery, with its ornamental ironwork, eye-catching high ceilings and colourful mosaicked floors. We then made a pit stop at the museum's Edwardian Tearooms for a scrumptious afternoon tea, before going shopping at the Bullring – which included an inordinate amount of time spent in Selfridges. The evening was spent on the couch in front of an edge-of-your-seat psychological thriller. On Sunday, we checked out the stylish new library at Centenary Square, before taking a trip to Cadbury World (an obvious choice for the mature adults that we are). Then I saw Sasha onto her six o'clock train back to Glasgow.

It was an emotional goodbye this time, quite the opposite to my stoic departure from Glasgow all those weeks before. Needless to say, there were tears on Sasha's part, but even I found myself having to swallow a bit too hard as I waved her off.

By the time she left, Sasha was ready to face her mum. I'd made sure of that. And the best outcome of the weekend by far was that she loved Birmingham. My fingers remained firmly crossed that she'd follow through on this one and join me here soon.

'Good morning, Alex.' Emmanuel greets me with a broad smile as I dump my bag under my desk, pull out my chair and log on to my computer. 'How was your weekend? I hope you had a lovely time with your friend.'

'I did, thanks.' I return her smile, making sure I don't let any sign of my exhaustion leak through. 'It was so great to see her. Thanks again for the time off at such late notice.'

'Not at all. It's your holiday time to use as you wish. I fully trust you to manage your own workload.'

'Well, it was appreciated all the same.'

'Speaking of your work… I'd like to have a catch-up with you this afternoon, if you have time?'

'Sure.' I quickly check my calendar. 'I've nothing in my diary from three p.m. Does that suit?'

'That's perfect. We can go out for a coffee.'

As I add the meeting to my calendar and ping an invite across to Emmanuel, curiosity takes over. We had our fortnightly catch-up on Thursday last week. What could she want to talk to me about so soon after? My mind starts to tick over my project plan, wondering if there's something I've missed. I really hope not. I've been meticulous in making sure that all bases are covered. Unless… My gaze moves across to Danielle's desk, where she's diligently poring through some data on an Excel spreadsheet. She senses my eyes on her, looks across and smiles in her false, expressionless way.

'Everything OK, Alex?' she asks.

Is it just me, or was there a bit of gloating mixed in with her usual sugar-coated acidity?

'Everything's great,' I reply. 'Did you have a good weekend?'

'I did. Visited my parents in London – a weekend of shopping and shows. Funny actually, turns out John was in London too. We all ended up having afternoon tea together at my parents' house in Kensington.'

'How lovely. Who's John? Is that your boyfriend?'

Danielle smirks, eyes returning to her screen. 'Hardly. I mean John Chambers. Our chief exec.'

'Right. How… lovely.' I turn back to my own computer screen and start scrolling through my unread emails.

Danielle's telling me this for a reason. It's no secret that she likes to one-up me at every opportunity, but what if… No, surely not. I glance across at Emmanuel, who's immersed in her own work. What if Danielle's still not given me the full picture of the data for the project, and she's sown a few seeds with the chief exec to suggest I'm not on it? Is she *that* vindictive? I want to answer my own question with 'absolutely not – don't be paranoid'. But I can't. My reading of Danielle is that she'll do anything, and take out anyone she needs to, in order to get what she wants.

I decide there's no point in mulling this over too much. I'll have my answer this afternoon. Instead, I throw myself into my work, ensuring I'm on top of everything.

By lunchtime I'm feeling quite confident that Danielle has nothing on me, but I'm annoyed that she's managed to rattle me in a way I've never experienced before. I've never doubted myself because of someone else. Either Danielle's a level above anyone else I've met, or – and I don't even want to admit this to myself – my medical situation has knocked my confidence and self-esteem more than I've realised.

Irritated by this thought, I decide I need some air, so I quickly grab my things and head out of the office. Despite being late autumn, it's an unseasonable fourteen degrees with only a light breeze. So even though I'm exhausted, I decide to take a walk by the canal to clear my head. As I wander along the canal bank, watching the Canada geese dabbling in the water, I take some deep refreshing breaths.

So what if Danielle has set me up? I can handle her. I *will* handle her – like the professional that I am. I need to focus on my strengths, not my weaknesses – and one of them is dealing with people like her. With this narrative running through my mind, I feel cheered and more in control.

Spotting a bench, I sit down and start to eat my quinoa salad while checking my personal emails on my phone. As I do, a flicker of a memory from Friday night flashes in my mind: my brief conversation with Matt. A smile spreads across my face.

I open up my messages app and tap out a new text message.

> Hi Matt. Hope you enjoyed the rest of your weekend. Mine was too busy. Exhausted today. When are you free to be wowed on your own private tour of this fine city? Alex.

My thumb hovers over the end of the message. Should I add my signature double kisses? We are going on a date... but I hardly know the guy. I suddenly feel like I'm fifteen again. Guided by my hesitation, I decide to leave off the kisses and hit send. Then I put my phone on my lap and continue to eat my lunch.

My thighs are getting a bit chilled from the bench but it doesn't bother me. I'm enjoying the peace that this inner city waterway provides. It's like a little sanctuary away from the vibrancy of Brindley Place – something I wouldn't naturally seek out, but with my energy levels not being what they were, I've learned to appreciate the odd bit of peace and quiet.

To my surprise, my phone lights up in my lap with a very quick response from Matt. I pick it up and read it.

> Hi Alex. Good to hear from you. Spent all weekend biting my nails, wondering if you'd actually get in touch this time. Sorry, just kidding – that's the last time, I promise. This weekend's wide open. How about I spare you the research and take you out for a drink on Friday instead? x

I laugh as I read his response. He's got a cheeky side to him, all right. I like that.

As I have no plans for this coming weekend (other than recovering from Sasha's visit and a busy week at work), I accept Matt's offer of drinks and arrange a time and place with him. I can get my rest on Saturday and Sunday. We message back and forth, his fun side really starting to show through, and I find myself getting sucked into the banter.

So much so, I only remember I'm due back in the office for a project-related meeting with ten minutes to spare.

I quickly pack away my empty plastic box and hurry back along the canal path at a more intense pace. I can feel the fringes of my fatigue starting to nag at me: that low-level, weighted-down feeling that intermittently kicks in when I push myself physically. Then, on climbing the steps of the bridge that crosses the canal from the International Conference Centre to Brindley Place, my body goes into full-blown protest. Between my busy weekend and now this, I've pushed myself beyond my limits.

I reach the top of the steps, respiring so heavily that I have to stop to regain my composure. My muscles are burning from the exertion. It's like someone has poured hot lava through my body. As I'm leaning on the side of the bridge, trying to regulate my breathing, a voice comes from behind me.

'Alex? Is that you?'

I look round, still panting, and my heart sinks. It's Danielle. She's with a woman I've never seen before.

'Oh, hi.' I try my best to sound relaxed. 'Yeah, I'm good. I was just… taking a lunchtime run. Overdone it a bit.' I feel the heat in my face, aware that I'm flushed from the overexertion. I'm hoping she'll buy it.

Danielle raises a sceptical eyebrow. 'Might be wise to wear running gear next time. You've probably overheated in those clothes.'

Her companion smirks, her expression one of cruel judgement, and I look down and realise my spontaneous excuse might not have been the most convincing. Though I changed into my trainers for the walk, I'm still wearing my grey trouser suit and black tie-neck blouse.

'Yeah, you're probably right.' I laugh, my composure thankfully returning. 'What was I thinking? Should have abandoned the run after I discovered I'd forgotten my running gear.'

'Sure.' Danielle's smile is so false, she's not even trying to hide it. 'You know, I like running. We should go out together one lunchtime.'

I take in Danielle's smug face, not believing for a second that she's a runner, and decide to play her at her own game.

'Absolutely. Let's sort that out.'

With a flick of her hair, she struts off with her companion, the two of them whispering and giggling as they go. That's all I need.

-

By three o'clock, I'm beyond exhausted and feeling somewhere around one-prod-and-I-may-actually-hit-the-deck.

'Ready to go?' Emmanuel pops her head over the divider between our desks.

I grit my teeth. 'Yes, definitely.'

Locking my computer, I grab my notepad and purse and wait at the end of the bank of desks. As I'm standing there, Felix returns to his desk with a freshly made coffee and gives me a friendly smile.

'That was a good meeting earlier, Alex. You under-stand change very well. I am surprised. Most project managers, especially IT project managers, see only the technical side.'

I return his smile, the positive and unexpected feedback giving me a boost I very much needed. 'Thanks Felix. We're definitely on the same page.'

'You're full of surprises, Alex.' Dhruv leans back in his desk chair and folds his arms. 'I reckon you're actually a spy – James Bond-style. Admit it, this job is just a cover.'

'You got me.' I hold up my hands in mock surrender. 'Seriously though? If all it took to be James Bond was project *and* change management skills, those films would be pretty dull.'

'That's true.' Dhruv puts on a movie trailer voice. '*Project management super-spy saves the world, one change impact analysis at a time.*'

We laugh in response.

'There's no hidden superpowers.' I smile at him. 'I'm just a regular IT project manager.'

'That's what Clark Kent said.' He eyes me suspiciously and I shake my head despairingly at him.

'Right, sorry, Alex.' Emmanuel finally joins me at the end of the desks. 'What a day it's been. If every Monday was like this, I'd burn out in no time.'

I offer her a sympathetic look.

We make our way out of the building and across the plaza to the same Italian cafe-restaurant she took me to on my first day. Once we're seated she orders cappuccinos and toasted panettone, this time not allowing me the opportunity to decline. I wonder if this is to soften the blow of whatever message or feedback she's about to deliver.

'How's your day been?' she asks. 'Less hectic than mine, I hope.'

'I'd say so. I even managed a walk along the canal at lunch.'

'That's good. You need to make sure you take breaks.' She reaches up and fiddles with the huge bun her braids have been pulled up into. 'I've noticed you working through your lunch most days.'

Emmanuel purses her lips, like she's preparing to say something.

Here it comes. What bomb has Danielle dropped in an attempt to unseat me from my position?

Before Emmanuel can share her thinking, the waiter arrives at our table with our food and drinks. We thank him, then busy ourselves for a moment stirring our coffees and savouring our first bites of panettone.

'So, what did you want to catch up about?' I ask to move things along.

'Right, yes.' Emmanuel sips at her cappuccino. 'Now I know you haven't been here long, Alex. But the feedback I've received strongly suggests a need for some kind of intervention.'

'Feedback?'

This does not sound good.

'Yes, I've been gathering feedback from a range of sources, and I'm confident this is the right time for this conversation, even at this early stage.'

A *range* of sources? I thought Danielle was the only one. 'This conversation being…?'

'Oh, sorry, Alex. I'm talking in riddles. Didn't manage to get lunch. Think my blood sugar is low.'

She takes another bite of her panettone, leaving me with the agony of having to wait until she has swallowed before I know what's going on. I watch her intently, willing her to chew faster so I can hear the case against me and prepare my defence.

'All right,' she says finally. 'I'll get to the point. Alex, I know you've only been with us for a few months, but what I see in you is a level of potential I've seen in very few people. I'd like to nominate you for the Future Leaders talent programme. That is, if you're interested?'

What? This isn't the showdown I was expecting. Far from it. I was convinced that Danielle had finally made some progress in her bid to oust me. Realising this not to be the case, I feel a bit guilty for jumping to conclusions. Then I remember how Danielle has behaved towards me since I joined and the guilt evaporates faster than a puddle in a hot desert.

I break into a huge smile. 'Of course I'm interested, Emmanuel. Thank you so much. But are you sure about this? As you say, I've only been here a couple of months. Also, what about...' I can't bear to finish my sentence.

'I've taken all that into consideration. We *need* greater diversity at senior levels within the company. I realise that one day you may no longer be able to take on such a challenge, but why shouldn't you have the opportunity to do so while you can? With your potential, and the right development, I can see you taking on a role at my level within a year. And I expect that within three to five years I'll be reporting to you.'

I'm stunned by Emmanuel's candour. She's talking about me succeeding and climbing the career ladder beyond her, and she's not just accepting it, she's encouraging it.

'Emmanuel, wow. I don't know what to say. Thank you for having such confidence in me.'

'You made it easy, Alex.' She smiles at me, almost affectionately. 'Now, eat up and I'll run you through the programme, what the expectations are, etc. Just to be sure this is for you.'

I take a satisfying bite of my panettone as Emmanuel starts to share the details. While she talks, I find myself getting more and more excited. Me? One of the company's future top leaders? I've read about the programme; only a handful of employees get put through it every year. I was doing well in my previous job, but the talent scheme there was like the holy grail. So many people pursuing it, but never seeming to get the tap on the shoulder. I came to Birmingham to claim back my life and, boy, have I managed that.

I had nothing to worry about. Danielle is a dissatisfied, spiteful person. But she's not really a threat. I won't let her get to me again. This is the confidence boost I needed to make sure of that.

Chapter 20

Emmanuel's vote of confidence carries me through the week, pushing my nagging exhaustion to one side. Things seem to happen very quickly: I receive my programme information by email, then a date is set for an induction day that I'll attend alongside some other company colleagues. Between this and the flirty, stomach-swirling messages torpedoing back and forth between me and Matt, I keep thinking this is all too good to be true. Even Danielle doesn't rattle me, though she keeps popping up, armed with some snarky comment or other.

Friday is no exception to this. As we're parked in our usual meeting room, having our weekly project meeting with colleagues from our international offices joining through Zoom, Danielle decides to throw in yet another of her grenades.

'Sorry for keeping you a couple of minutes late – especially on a Friday.' I start to wrap things up. 'That was really useful to work through the specific stakeholder issues we're experiencing. Before we sign off, does anyone have any final questions or concerns about what we've discussed and agreed today?'

There's a collective 'no' in response.

'I'm just concerned it's 4:32 p.m. on a Friday and I'm not in the pub yet,' Dhruv jokes.

'Shall I add that to the issue log?' I throw back.

There's a smattering of laughter in response to our regular double act. I'm about to wish everyone a good weekend when Danielle pipes up.

'Actually, I have a question.'

'Sure, Danielle.' I smile easily at her, but I'm wondering why she feels the need to hold everyone up even longer and what kind of shit she's about to try to stir up. 'What's on your mind?'

'I was just *wondering*… if you're going to have less time to manage the project now, have you put plans in place to cover some of your responsibilities?'

'Sorry, Danielle. I'm not sure what you're referring to?'

'Oh, you know, because you're on the Future Leaders programme now. That will take up quite a bit of your time. Congratulations, by the way.'

I blanch internally, but ensure I keep my face poker-straight. How the hell does she know about that? Emmanuel and I were keeping that between us until next week, when she was going to announce it at the quarterly departmental meeting. Emmanuel has already warned me that this kind of internal success can cause resentment among colleagues who have not been successful – Felix, our change manager, being one who didn't quite make the cut – which is why the announcement was to be carefully managed.

I take a moment to consider my response, so I can ensure that I keep things as smooth as possible.

'Thank you, Danielle. Everyone, this news was supposed to be shared next week. I haven't yet had the chance to digest it myself.'

'So, will you be delegating some of your responsibilities?' Danielle asks, before anyone else can get a word in.

'We're still working things through, Danielle. I expect I'll keep the majority of my workload, but I may need support with some of the project governance activities.'

I actually do know this answer to this – Emmanuel's arranging for me to have a project assistant – but it's not appropriate to share this now.

'Now that Danielle's ruined your big news…' Dhruv throws a look in her direction. '…may we offer our congratulations as well?'

I look around my project team, trying to gauge their reactions. My eyes linger on Felix for a fraction of a second longer, but he shows no obvious negative reaction.

'I… eh… sure, why not.'

There's an immediate flurry of congratulatory messages.

'Well done, mate.' Dhruv gives me a slapping hand-shake. 'Fantastic news. Good to know we're learning from one of the best in the company.'

'This is very good news, Alex,' Felix chips in, and to my relief, sounds genuinely pleased for me. 'In Germany, we say *Herzliche Glückwünsche*. This means… heartfelt wishes of luck.'

The others follow with their support in quick succession, including those on the Zoom call, and I'm quite overwhelmed by the collective sincere and supportive reactions. Danielle aside, they really are a great bunch.

'Thank you, all of you. It's my hope that I can bring what I learn back to this room and be the best, most supportive leader I can be.'

'Hear hear,' Dhruv calls out. 'Now let's get out of here. My pint isn't going to pour itself.'

We laugh as we say our goodbyes to our international colleagues and head out of the meeting room. As we walk along the corridor to the lifts, I notice Danielle looking a bit smug, despite the fact I received such a positive response from the team. I up my pace slightly so that I can catch her up.

'So, Danielle, how did you come across that particular piece of information?' I keep my tone deliberately casual.

'Oh, you know. It was doing the rounds. Can't remember where it came from.' She looks me straight in the eye, but I can tell she's lying through her teeth.

'Right. Seems funny though, if it was getting around, that it was such a surprise to the rest of the team, doesn't it?'

'Guess they must have missed it somehow,' she says, then struts off ahead of me.

Yeah, and I'm the Queen of Sheba. All too aware that Danielle's behaviour may be escalating, and needs to be nipped in the bud, I decide to schedule some time with Emmanuel to discuss how to do just that. Emmanuel will be very unhappy that this has leaked. But where did it come from? Suddenly, I get a flash of memory, back to bumping into Danielle that Monday lunchtime. She was with someone. Another member of her coven, it seems. I wonder who that person is, and where she works.

I'm beyond shattered by the time I'm unlocking the door to my apartment. A heavy week was not what I needed after Sasha's visit, but I'm still in high spirits, despite Danielle's attempt to steal my sunshine. I push her and her nonsense firmly to the back of my mind.

As I'm not meeting Matt until 7:30 p.m., I have a quick catnap and when I wake to my alarm forty-five minutes later, I feel groggy, as if I've been asleep for hours. I'm also less refreshed than expected. Padding lethargically around my apartment, I get ready to go out, while throwing something resembling a meal down my throat – all the time wondering why I didn't ask Matt if we could do Saturday instead. That would have given me a bit of recuperation time. But by the time I'm walking out the main door of my apartment block, I've perked up, and the adrenaline and excitement of finally spending some proper time in Matt's company have kicked in. Along with some stomach-churning nerves.

I look up where I'm meeting him on Google Maps and start walking in that direction. Something I've realised I love about living on the fringe of the city centre is that everywhere I want to go is within easy reach. I cross the plaza at Brindley Place, descend the arc-shaped steps and amble along the canal bank, scrolling through Twitter on my phone. Although it's dark, I feel quite comfortable doing this alone. It's a well-lit path and there's plenty of people around, meandering between the handful of eating and drinking establishments that line the waterway.

I reach the Tetris-like exterior of the Cube, tentatively enter the foyer, locate the lift and take it to the twenty-fifth floor. My stomach feels like it's going through a forty-degree wash. Between the feeling of ascension, my giddy nervousness and my underlying exhaustion, I'm ever so slightly nauseous. It's a feeling I've never quite experienced. Not even on my first date with Dom.

Several seconds later, the lift stops and the doors ping open. I step out into a much smaller foyer as the second lift dings and out steps Matt, nearly colliding with me as he does.

'Hi there.' His gorgeous features break into a grin. 'Seems we both have good timing.'

'So we do.' I smile back at him, my nerves having now kicked into spin-cycle mode.

He leans across, touching me lightly on my upper arm as he greets me with a kiss on the cheek. It's hardly off the scale in terms of physical contact, but this, along with his fresh, citrusy eau de toilette wafting into my nostrils, sets off a symphony of fireworks in my body. He's even more delicious than I remember. His beard is perfectly groomed, hair just the right balance of styled with a hint of 'just out of bed'. And those eyes: like melted chocolate. They make me want to dive right in.

'How was your day?' he asks a little too forcefully, his Birmingham accent thicker than I remember.

I can tell he's trying to break the ice quickly, his initial confidence wavering. That's all we need. The two of us turning into a pair of gibbering idiots who can't manage a coherent conversation.

'It was fine. Busy.'

'Mine too.' He nods.

For a few moments we stand silently, muted by our first date nerves, and I have to force down a giggle threatening to rise in my throat. It's a bit awkward, but not like previous experiences, where I've been planning my escape the from moment I clapped eyes on my date. There's an added layer of intrigue and chemistry that's overwhelming the two of us.

'Shall we get a drink?' I suggest.

'Of course.' Matt seems to come to. 'It's this way.'

He leads me into the chic surroundings of Magenta: a rooftop bar with low lighting, contemporary decor and floor-to-ceiling windows that provide a panoramic view of Birmingham's skyline by night. The silhouettes of the historical landmarks nestled among the more imposing modern structures create a breathtakingly majestic cityscape, made all the more alluring by the twinkling lights that look like static fireflies in the sky.

'Oh, wow.' I'm immediately impressed. 'This place is incredible.'

'It's good, isn't it? One of my favourite places in Birmingham. You can see right across the city.'

'I'd love to see it in the light as well.'

'We can always come back.'

I glance at him and bite my lip. 'Planning our second date already?'

'No.'

He shakes his head a little too determinedly, eyes still on the view outside, and I feel disappointed. Then he looks back at me, a hint of a smile sneaking through.

'I've already got something else planned for that.'

As he says this, another symphony erupts in my abdomen. We've barely said two words but he already wants to see me again? I'm so elated, I feel like I could float above the Birmingham skyline myself, on a white fluffy cloud.

'Where would you like to sit?' asks Matt.

'How about over there by the other set of windows?'

We make our way across to the table I've chosen, where a waiter materialises almost immediately with the drinks list.

'They do great cocktails in here,' says Matt. 'Have anything you like. My shout.'

I read down the list and then wish I hadn't. As the gin cocktails jump off the page at me, I realise just one would have me at my two-drink limit – which I've set in units of alcohol, not actual drinks. I decide to stick with a gin and tonic, but I make it an interesting one.

'Good choice, madam,' says the waiter. 'Would you like a double or a single measure?'

'Single please.'

'You sure?' Matt obviously thinks I'm just being polite.

'I'm sure.'

'All right then. I'll have the same.' He hands the drinks list back to the waiter.

'*You* could have had a double.'

'I've been a bit slow to this gin thing. I take my lead from others.'

I watch him for a second, unsure what to make of this comment, then decide that it must be his way of making me feel comfortable.

Another silence develops between us, again more electrically charged than awkward. I study Matt's handsome features, feeling myself blush a little as I wonder what it would be like to kiss him.

'How's the world of manufacturing engineering?' I ask, mainly to divert the blood from my face to my brain.

He rubs his beard thoughtfully. 'I'd say… as boring as IT project management.'

'Hey, I love my job.'

'I know. That did make me wonder if I'd had a narrow escape before.'

I laugh. 'You're a bit of a cheeky one, aren't you?'

'Think I do that to cover up that I'm nervous.'

I expect this comment to be paired with a mischievous grin, but his face is neutral, which makes me warm to him even more. He's so open, just says it as it is. Such a refreshing quality.

'So, you're nervous?' I tease him.

'And you're not?'

'You know when a washing machine goes on spin cycle?'

'No. My mum does all my washing.'

As he says this alarm bells clang in my head. He's a mummy's boy? I knew this was too good to be true.

Matt gives a little wave to bring my attention back. 'Probably the time to tell you I'm joking, right? By the look on your face, you're about thirty seconds from the "I've just had a family emergency" call.'

I burst into relief-fuelled laughter. '*Seriously?* I thought that was real. Might be an idea to tone it down a bit. At least til I've got the basic facts.'

'Sorry. I'll try and reel it in.'

The waiter returns with our drinks and a small jar of what looks like seasoned corn kernels. We thank him and as he walks away, Matt lifts his drink and looks me straight in the eye.

'Cheers, Alex. Nice to finally have a drink with you again.'

I raise my own glass, clinking it against his. 'It sure is.'

We sip at our drinks while admiring the view, then simultaneously reach for the nibbles, causing our fingers to collide. I snatch my hand away as he does exactly the same, then we look at each other and start to laugh.

'You go,' he prompts me, grinning.

'Thanks.'

I take a few pieces of corn, then he does the same.

'I know you've been here a few months now, but how are you settling in?'

'Fine.' I nod, cringing a little as I crunch loudly on the corn.

'Don't worry. I can barely hear you over my own horse-like munching.'

'They're really good, but not sure they're first date snacks.'

'Unless you're a horse,' he points out.

I accidentally snort – horse-like – in amusement and then redden at Matt's resulting laugh. 'I'm settling really well,' I say, keen to move us along. 'I love working on Brindley Place. It's got a great buzz, and it's such a treat to be able to take a lunchtime walk along the canal – on the days I actually manage a lunch break.'

'I know the feeling.' Matt grimaces. 'A bad habit working through lunch, but for me it's a choice between that and working late every day.'

'Totally.' I abandon the corn and sip at my drink instead, enjoying the warmth from the alcohol, complemented by the spicy botanicals and the bitterness of the tonic.

'My best option for a scenic lunch is the industrial estate car park.'

'That's not going to suit someone who loves the hills and countryside as much as you do.'

'Correct.' He sits forward and leans on the table, hand propping up his chin, dark eyes glinting in the half-light. 'There's something about being on the peak of a mountain that's so liberating, you almost think you could leap off it and fly.'

'I suggest you don't try that.'

'No, obviously not. But you understand what I mean. When I saw you up singing last weekend, I could see that it did the same for you. You were so lost in the music. It was quite something to watch.'

My flush returns in response to the compliment; that and the feeling that Matt's eyes are almost scanning my soul, seeking out our compatibility.

'I do enjoy it.'

'And you're amazing.'

'Mmm…' I bob my head from side to side in a non-committal way. '…I'm not sure I'd go that far.'

'Modest too.' He raises an eyebrow. 'Is there no limit to your good qualities?'

How about a deteriorating central nervous system? Or a possible future in a wheelchair? As this flicker of negativity flits through my mind, I'm so shocked I have to catch my breath.

'You OK?' Matt looks concerned. 'Not choking on the animal feed?'

'Oh… no, I'm fine. Just a twinge of pain. Overdid the running, I think. Seem to have injured my knee.'

'Sorry to hear that. I wondered if you were trying to distract me from giving you compliments.' He pauses thoughtfully. 'It might be too soon to mention this, but one of my mates at the bar with me the other night is in a band. It's a semi-professional set-up. They play decent-sized weekend gigs, make all right money on the side, rehearse in a proper studio. They're looking for a lead vocalist – someone who can sing the likes of the Killers, in fact. He wanted to know if you'd be interested in auditioning?'

I purse my lips, aware that yet another commitment is not what I need when I'm trying to keep my health stable. Being far from ready to share my circumstances with Matt (which would undoubtedly send him scarpering for his beloved hills), I attempt to divert the conversation by mirroring his humour.

'You're right, it is too soon.'

'OK, sure.' Matt half-shrugs.

I immediately feel guilty as hell. 'I'm only joking. Just playing you at your own game – and realising that was a stupid thing to do.'

Matt chuckles and shakes his head. 'Shall we start again?'

'That would be good.'

'I'm Matt. Great to meet you.' He sticks out his hand and I burst out laughing, then shake it.

'Alex. It's a pleasure.'

'So. The band?' he prompts. 'Or should I go back to pleasantries?'

'No, please don't go there. Who knows where we'll end up.'

We slug at our drinks and it feels like the awkwardness is finally starting to lift.

'I think…' I look out the window at the twinkling city lights, wondering how to politely decline '…it sounds amazing. But being perfectly honest, I'm not sure I'm good enough and I get stage fright. I probably couldn't make the commitment right now anyway.'

'The commitment issue I can't help with. But having seen you, you'd get over the nerves quickly, and you need to dispel any doubts as to your talent. When I said my mate wondered if you fancied auditioning, what he actually said was "Matt, if you know her, you need to get her to my rehearsal studio – whatever it takes".'

'That would be a lovely compliment if it didn't sound a little sinister.'

'Yeah, maybe I shouldn't have shared it verbatim.' Matt swirls the ice round in his drink. 'But you weren't responding to the diluted version.'

'True. Well, thank you, that is high praise. But as much as that would be like my younger self's dream come true, I'm just not sure I can. My job is full on. I've just been nominated for their leadership talent development scheme, which is going to be all-consuming.'

'Wow. I really am in the presence of a superstar. I thought you had to drink two pints of blood, sacrifice a llama and master an impossible handshake to get on corporate schemes like that.'

I snigger with amusement. I love Matt's quick-witted responses and how he keeps me on my toes with his slick banter (when he's not getting all tongue-tied like me).

'That may be the case in some places but the company I work for is actually really great. So is my manager. Can't believe how lucky I've been.'

'I'm sure luck is only a small part of it.'

'It's not, believe me. Back in Glasgow, I would have had to develop superhuman abilities to have made it on their talent programme. Though I did have a challenging role and other development opportunities, until…' I trail off, realising I'm about to stray into difficult territory.

This has the effect of reminding me that while Matt has taken the 'play no games' oath, I'm not being completely up front with him. I don't think I can be – not yet anyway. I chew my lip and stare out the window distractedly.

'Hey, where did you go?' Matt reaches over and places his hand on my forearm gently.

'Sorry.' I come back to the moment, my skin tingling in response to his touch. 'Caught up in a weird memory there.'

'Didn't seem like a particularly pleasant one.'

'It's nothing. Office politics. You know how it is. Or maybe you don't.'

'Why would that be?' He gives me a curious look.

'Because you don't work in a corporate environment.'

'But I do work with *people*. *Lots* of people. With all sorts of different motivations and behaviours.'

'Point taken.' I lift my drink to my lips and drain the glass.

'Another?'

I agree and Matt signals for the waiter. As he relays the order, I chase away the buzzy interference in my mind. When I talked this through with Sasha, it was so clear – it's just dating, it doesn't need to go anywhere. And if it seems like it will, that's when I consider how I want to deal with it. If Matt's the right man for me, he'll understand why I held it back and he'll see me instead of my illness. Surely?

Chapter 21

Three hours later, the awkwardness is long gone even after I moved on to soft drinks, citing my need for a clear head the next day to do my leadership programme pre-work.

Matt and I have vacated the bar and are wandering casually along the canal-side together, chatting animatedly and flirting shamelessly. It's a still, clear night with a sky full of winking stars that add to the sense of romance. The temperature has also dropped several degrees. The closer we get to Brindley Place, where we'll likely part ways, the slower and smaller our footsteps become (which is useful for me when it comes to climbing the steps from the canal-side). When we reach the top we come to a complete standstill, our bodies just inches apart, and gaze out across the stillness of the water.

'So, I assume you'll head in the direction of Broad Street for a taxi?' I reluctantly ask, not yet ready for the night to end.

'That would normally be my route, yes.' He turns towards me, his breath billowing in clouds from the cold. 'I wonder though if you'd let me walk you home. It's only a small detour.'

'That would be nice.'

His dark eyes crinkle as he smiles back at me, and I'm taken by surprise as he takes my hand and intertwines his fingers between mine.

'All right?'

'Yeah.' I nod, biting my lip like a bashful schoolgirl.

We amble along the quiet residential streets until we reach my apartment block, where we come to a halt once more. I'm almost jangling with anticipation, while also wondering whether I should invite Matt in for a coffee – but obviously not in the clichéd sense. Is that what he's expecting? Or will it send out the wrong signals? I look up at him, his face partially illuminated by the streetlight, creating shadowy contours on his face that make him look very sexy indeed. This makes me even more conflicted. A big part of me wants more than coffee: for him to wrap his strong arms round me and stay there all night. But I barely know him. We've done nothing more than hold hands and I'm keen not to accelerate this beyond what I'm ready for, given my circumstances.

As if reading my mind, Matt takes the lead on drawing our evening together to a close.

'I've really enjoyed your company tonight, Alex. I hope we can do this again.' He squeezes my hand affectionately.

'I hope so too.'

We stand for a moment, paralysed by nerves. The chemistry between us is almost at overload. A kiss if it came now would be explosive. But we've faltered again. Feeling the moment passing from our inaction, Matt lets my hand go and takes a step back. I feel immediately disappointed and irritated at myself for not making the first move – nothing has ever stopped me in the past, so why now?

'Do you have plans for Sunday?' Matt asks.

'No. What did you have in mind?'

'Oh… I'm watching the football with my mates. I was just making conversation.'

Heat creeps up my neck as I realise I've been presumptuous. 'Right… shit… of course… sorry, I'm…'

'No, I'm sorry.' His hand goes to his mouth to conceal a guilty smile. 'I've done it again. I *was* asking you out, I just couldn't help myself. What is *wrong* with me?'

'Seriously? If it weren't for the fact that I malfunction around you as much as you do around me, I might have been offended.'

'But you're not…?'

'No, I'm not. But you'll have to ask again. Properly.'

'Right. Of course.' He clears his throat, humour glinting in his eyes. 'Can I see you again on Sunday?'

Lips twitching, I repeat my original question. 'What did you have in mind?'

'I thought we could go for a nice walk somewhere.'

'Up a hill?' I ask, sincerely hoping not.

'No. There's a nice, relaxed forest walk I know and a great gastropub we could grab some lunch at after.'

'That sounds lovely.' I beam at him, my insides doing cartwheels at the thought of seeing him again so soon. It definitely makes up for the absence of a kiss.

'Great, I'll pick you up at ten. Good night, Alex.'

'Night, Matt. See you Sunday.'

Without looking back, I make my way inside my apartment building, feeling like the cat that cleared out the entire stock of the local dairy.

–

'What do you mean you haven't kissed him yet?' Sasha almost squeals down the phone. I quickly switch to speakerphone so she doesn't perforate my eardrum. 'I was going to ask if he'd stayed over and done the walk of shame this morning.'

It's eleven a.m. the next day and as I've not responded to her three WhatsApp messages asking about my date, Sasha has run out of patience and called me.

'Sorry to disappoint you.' I chuckle lightly and lie back on my bed. 'It just didn't happen that way.'

'Was there no spark? Sometimes it's just not there. Was he boring? Or self-obsessed? They're a total turn-off, no matter how good-looking a man is.'

'If you'll let me get a word in edgeways, I might tell you.'

'Right, sorry. You go.'

Allowing the memory of the night before to wash over me, I take a deep, satisfied breath. 'It's actually the opposite. There's so much chemistry between us, we can't function normally around each other. Every time we brush hands or the conversation flows in the direction of anything more than flirty banter, I feel like I'm about to short-circuit. And he seems to be the same. We kept having these ridiculous moments where one of us said or did something stupid and it's all down to nerves. He's a confident guy, but he's got this kind of shyness that kicks in at points, and I seem to be the same.'

'That doesn't sound like you at all. When you first laid eyes on Dom, you were like, "mine", and that was it.'

'I know.' I roll over on my side and look out of my bedroom window at the lashing rain, crossing my fingers for a better day tomorrow. 'That's what's so weird about this. I was disappointed that he didn't kiss me, but I was even more baffled as to why I didn't just take the lead.'

'You must really like him. I'm so jealous. I had a Tinder date during the week—'

'You never said! How was it?'

'He spent the whole evening talking about bridges, then asked me if he could smell my armpit.'

'WHAT?' I let out an involuntary snort of laughter.

Sash sighs loudly. 'I'm paraphrasing. Obviously. But he did talk about bridges *a lot* – did you know that the Millau Viaduct in France is so high it sometimes sticks out above the clouds?'

I quickly do a Google Image search on my phone. 'Wow. That's actually quite cool. Have you seen it?'

'What? No. Is that really the focus here, Lex?'

'Sorry. So, bridges. What else did you learn?'

'That's not funny.' Sasha sounds exasperated but also amused. 'He honestly managed to link every conversation to some kind of bridge trivia. Holidays, interests, work. Even the nostalgia route resulted in him telling me about the bridge cake his mum made for his birthday one year.'

'That's not so bad. We all had novelty cakes when we were kids.'

'It was for his twenty-first,' she wails. 'And it was apparently a two-foot-high imitation of the Chang-yon Bridge in China.'

'It's actually the Chengyang Bridge,' I correct her, scanning the information on the Wikipedia search result.

'Seriously, Lex?'

'Shit. Sorry.' I press the home button on my phone and focus my attention on Sasha. 'That's a bit obsessive. So, where did the armpit request come in?'

'I was so desperate to get off the subject of ruddy bridges, I started yakking on about what I had been doing that day. Mentioned that I'd been to Boots – and listed everything I bought there, including a new antiperspirant.'

'And then he asked if he could smell your armpit?'

'Well, no. He wasn't saying *anything*. I'd finally found a topic he couldn't link to bridges – so I rambled on about my new antiperspirant having a lovely fragrance, and how I kept getting wafts of it as I was talking to him.'

'And then he asked if he could smell it?'

'Yes. What a weirdo, right?'

I bite my lip to hold back the laughter. 'Err... Sash. I think he was just being polite. He probably didn't know how to respond to the crazy lady describing her shopping in detail.'

The line goes silent.

'Sash?'

'Oh, man. *I'm a weirdo too.*' The wailing returns, having jumped an octave. 'I've had so many bad dates, I've turned into a bad date. This is it, Lex – the point of no return. I'm going to be alone for ever.'

I have to stifle a laugh. Sash and Lex. Joined at the hip since ninety-three. Her, a serial dater with a dismal track record. Me, there to pick her up after another bad date.

'No, you're not,' I reassure her. 'When you meet someone you properly connect with, you'll talk about good stuff. There may still be awkward silences – I can testify to that – but no more armpit or bridge chat, unless your dream man has a fetish you're willing to entertain.'

'Eugh, stop it!' Sasha complains, but I can tell she finds it funny. 'OK, that's enough date chat. What else is happening?'

'Not much really. I've started my leadership programme pre-work, and Danielle-the-devil-incarnate is still trying to oust me from my position. All is fine. Good, actually.'

'And your health?'

I hesitate briefly. 'No change really. I'm OK as long as I don't push myself too hard and get a bit of rest. How about the situation with your mum?' I'm keen to change the subject.

'I'm working up to it. She knows something isn't right. Keeps asking why I'm only calling rather than going round.'

'Right.' I get up from the bed and start to pace. 'And do you feel able to do it, Sash? You're stronger than you think, you know.'

'I know.' She says this in a small voice that suggests exactly the opposite.

'You are. It's going to be horrible, but remember our chat. Once you've done it, you can move on with your life and join me here. I'm sure that dreamy man you're looking for is right here in this city, just waiting for you.'

'You're right. Putting it off is making it harder. I need to do it.'

'You do. And you can. I'm here, as soon as you need me.'

'Thanks, Lex. You're the best. Oh, I almost forgot… I bumped into your sister the other day.'

'I'm sorry to hear that,' I joke, but I feel a smidgen of hope. 'And?'

'She asked how you were doing. I told her you were great and how well you were doing in your job. She was her usual judgemental self, made some comment about how that won't last long and how they'll soon have to bail you out of the hole you've dug for yourself.'

'No surprise there then. She just parrots everything that comes out of my mother's mouth. Sad that she can't develop her own world views.' I keep my tone blasé, but I'm a little deflated by this.

'Sorry, Lex.'

'Don't be. It is what it is. We've both been let down, but we have each other.'

'We so do.' Sasha's tone becomes resolute. 'I'm going to sort it – this weekend. And I'm going to apply for jobs in Birmingham as soon as I've done it.'

'Good for you. You can sleep on my sofa bed if you need to for interviews, and while you find your own place.'

'Thanks, Lex. Once again, you're the best.'

'You too.' I smile affectionately at the phone. 'Now go and pump yourself full of self-love and confidence. Good luck.'

A few hours later I'm camped out in front of the TV, laughing my way through back-to-back episodes of *Friends*. I've nothing but my duvet and some apple slices with peanut butter for company. And I'm completely content. Just months earlier I'd have wrinkled my nose in distaste at the idea of lounging around like this, and pulled on my running shoes. But having gotten used to the slower pace of life imposed upon me, I'm starting to appreciate that a bit of downtime is good for the soul. Especially when the rain outside is almost horizontal – and I have a date with a gorgeous man to look forward to (and be fit for) the next day.

Just as I'm checking tomorrow's forecast on the BBC Weather app for the third time, my apartment buzzer sounds, making me jump. Assuming it's a delivery person trying random apartment numbers to get access to the building, I ignore it. Someone else will let them in.

But moments later the buzzer sounds again. I reluctantly get up and pad across to my apartment door, lifting the receiver for the door entry system.

'Hello?'

There's no response.

'Anyone there?'

Still nothing.

Emitting an exasperated sigh, I return to the sofa, make myself comfortable again and hit play on the remote. The well-loved characters of Ross and Rachel immediately spring to life, playing out one of their many hilarious but flawed romantic encounters. I'm just settling into the episode again when there's a knock at my apartment door. I quickly grab the remote and pause the episode, joining Ross and Rachel in a real-life freeze frame. I'm not expecting anyone. Not even a delivery. Deciding they must have the wrong apartment, I maintain my statue-like pose, listening for the sound of departing footsteps. But there's no movement, and seconds later there's another rap at my door.

Irritated by this intrusion and the fact that I'm having to get up again for no reason, I walk to the door, unlock it and yank it open.

'I think you've got the wrong...' I tail off in shock as I take in the masculine form standing in front of me. '*Dom?* What are you doing here?'

Chapter 22

'Surprise.' Dom grins sheepishly at me, his dark hair soaked from the storm outside, beads of rainwater running down his face.

I stare back at him, utterly bewildered. 'I'm not sure that's the appropriate… whatever… Dom, what are you doing here? How do you even know where I live?'

'Can I tell you inside?'

'Eh… yeah, I guess so.' I step back and let him in.

Dom tentatively enters my postage stamp of a hallway and I close the door. The lack of space – and him clearly not wanting to presume that he's going to be invited in properly – means we end up standing uncomfortably close, to the point that I can feel his breath on my neck as I turn away from the door.

'Go on through.' I usher him towards to my kitchen-living room.

'This is nice.' He strides into the room more confid-ently, like an estate agent sizing up the potential for sales commission. 'It's compact but has a nice aspect, and a balcony too. You've done well for yourself, kitten.'

I flinch at the use of my old pet name.

Realisation dawns on his face. 'Shit. Sorry. Old habits and all.'

'It's fine. Do you want a cup of tea? And a towel?'

'I'd love a brew, thanks, Lex. Can I at least call you Lex?'

'Whatever.' I shrug, this being far from the main thing on my mind.

I bring Dom a towel from my storage cupboard and busy myself making the tea as he lingers by the French windows, inspecting the shared garden beyond.

'You not feeling so great today?' He shoots me a sympathetic look.

'Why do you say that?'

'The human-sized dog basket?'

I smile at his humour. 'I'm fine. Just having a lazy day.'

'Now I know you're not right. You don't *choose* to have lazy days. You're as restless as a cat on a hot tin roof.'

'Here, get that down you.' I hand him a mug of tea.

'Don't suppose you've any biscuits?'

'Sorry. Apple and peanut butter?'

'Not ditched the obsession with healthy eating, I see. Surely a couple of biscuits on a Saturday isn't the worst thing.'

I shrug and put my own mug on the coffee table, then clear my duvet to one side so we can both take a seat.

'So, you're doing OK? You're coping all right down here?' Dom ventures into the subject of my health once again, which irks me a little.

'I'm doing fine, Dom. You don't need to keep asking. Is it so strange to think that I've changed? That I might now enjoy a bit of R&R? We haven't seen each other in months and a lot has happened since then.'

Dom looks like he's been kneed in the balls. 'Sorry. Just trying to be supportive.'

'There's no need. I'm doing fine by myself. What would be helpful is if you'd tell me what the hell you're doing here.' My words come out a little more aggressively than I'd intended. 'Sorry, didn't mean it like that. But this is a pretty big shock, and for some reason you're the one asking the questions.'

'I was being friendly... trying to chat. You know, like humans do.'

'Don't even try that management bullshit on me, Dom. Putting me at ease and strengthening the rapport between us before approaching a more challenging subject. It's me you're talking to, not one of your team.'

'Right, sure.' Dom shifts uncomfortably in his seat. 'As you're in no mood for the niceties, I'll get to the point.'

'Please do.'

'Were you always this brutal?'

'I've always been focused and to the point, you know that.'

'Sure.' He nods uncertainly, as if trying to flick through his brain's memory bank to fact-check this. 'Well, to answer your question about how I know where you live, I'll fess up. I got in touch with your sister.'

'You must have been desperate.'

'She was OK actually. Seemed happy enough to pass the info on.'

'That doesn't sound like my sister. We haven't spoken since I told them I was moving here. Did she mention that?'

'No, actually. I know you've never been the best of pals. Did you have a falling-out?'

I roll my eyes at that understatement. 'She and my mother didn't agree with my decision to move here. They made it clear they wanted nothing to do with "such ridiculousness". Told me to get in touch when I came to my senses, or when I had my next relapse and needed to move back – whichever came first. Proper *Little House on the Prairie* family love.' I lift my tea and sip from it.

'Shit, Lex. I had no idea. I'm so sorry. Your mum and sister can be difficult, I know, but that's way harsh. If I'd known that I'd—'

'You'd what? Go back in time and change what you said? Decide you did want to sign up for a life with a disabled woman after all?'

I regret these words the moment they've left my lips but Dom just turning up like this isn't just an irritation, it's reopening old wounds. Stirring up feelings for him I didn't know were still there.

Dom visibly recoils. 'Lex, please. Don't be like that. That was something I said in the moment. Stupid, yes. But true? No.'

'It *was* true. You just wish you hadn't said it out loud.'

'No. I reacted. Just as you reacted to everything that was going on at work. To any offer of help from me, from your family—'

'So you're saying it was my fault?'

'What? No. I'm saying… although it was you who had something life-changing thrown at you, it affected us as well. We were all trying to process it and do what we thought was best, but things got out of control, and our relationship took the brunt of it.' Dom looks quite cut up as he says this.

My defensiveness wavers a little. I'd never really considered it that way before. I was so consumed by anger and denial that all I could think about was how everyone was getting on my nerves. They were trying to do what they thought was best – no matter how misguided that was. None of us got a manual on how to deal with a degenerative disease. We had to make it up as we went along.

'I thought you were relieved.' My voice is close to a whisper, eyes fixed on the floor. 'It was a get-out-of-jail-free card. Who wouldn't take that in your situation?'

'You make it sound so transactional, Lex. You accuse *me* of going into work mode.'

'Fair enough. So why are you telling me all this now, Dom? You never said any of this back when it mattered. I haven't heard from you for ages. Why are you here?'

Dom swallows thickly and fixes his piercing blue eyes on mine. 'I'm here, Lex, because since we finished, nothing's been right. It's like I've lost a part of me. I think about you all the time and I want you back. I don't care what your MS means for our future. We can face it together. I want to be your rock and I want to take care of you. And I still love you – more than you could ever know.'

I feel like the breath's been sucked out of me. The room blurs as unwanted tears brim. What do I do with this? I've been getting on great; created a whole new life for myself. But here, now, with Dom beside me, it's clear to me that I'm still in love with him too. How could I not be? We were getting married. Our relationship didn't fizzle out, we just hit a Ben Nevis-sized bump in the road. One that catapulted us in different directions, and now Dom's found his way back from that. But where am I?

'Shit, Dom.' I grab a cushion and clock him with it. 'What the hell am I meant to do with that?'

'Say you want to be with me too?' His handsome features are filled with puppy-dog-like hope.

'I can't just… I've only…'

Matt's face suddenly materialises in my mind, para-lysing me into silence.

'Are you still in love with me, Lex?'

'I'm… yes. Of course I am.' I look him square in the face. 'It's not that simple though. I have a new life here and I actually really love this city.'

'I'll move down. I can get a job here, no problem. Birmingham has a big financial district.'

'I can't ask you to do that.'

'You didn't. I offered.' He gives me a playful nudge.

'That is true.' I shake my head, trying to clear away the jumbled thoughts that have gathered like seagulls to a chip wrapper.

'Look, I know I've turned up out of nowhere and landed this on you. You've had no time to digest it. How about I leave you to think about things overnight? I'm staying along by the Mailbox. I could take you for brunch in the morning and we could talk things through a bit more.'

'The morning… oh, I…' My head goes into a spin as I remember that's when Matt and I have our date. 'What about the evening? Maybe give me a bit more time? Unless you're flying home before then…?'

Dom's disappointed but I can see he's trying to hide it. 'I'm here til Monday. Took a day off in the hope we could spend tomorrow together. But if you need that time, that's fine.'

I swallow guiltily. 'OK, thanks, I appreciate it. Let's meet later tomorrow then.'

We get up from the sofa and walk to my tiny hallway in silence, both consumed by our own thoughts. I can tell Dom is troubled by me putting him off. I'm certainly feeling guilty enough for doing it, despite him being the one to have turned up unannounced. As I reach for the handle of my apartment door, Dom surprises me by taking my hand. His touch is different to Matt's: familiar, warm and reassuring. Like a cosy blanket I want to dive under. It sparks something in me and I feel the need to be totally honest with him.

'Dom, the real reason I asked if we can meet later in the day is because I have a date tomorrow.'

I brace myself for his response.

'A date?' He seems genuinely surprised and equally disappointed. 'Have you known the guy long?'

'No. We bumped into each other a few times' – I decide it's best to leave out the fact that Sasha and I were like a heat-seeking missile trying to track Matt down – 'and we've been on one date. Tomorrow's our second.'

'Sure.' Dom's face has become unreadable. 'I suppose I shouldn't have expected you not to move on. I've had a few dates myself. But they just showed me all the more that you were the one.'

He smiles down at me and strokes my hand affectionately with his thumb. My senses respond with the urge to move closer to him, but as I battle to resist doing so, I miss Dom's advance, and before I know it, he's lifting my chin with his forefinger and drawing me in for a kiss. We lock together passionately, my body filled with longing for him. It's just like we used to be – before a big bloody elephant wedged itself between us. I let him wrap his arms round me and pull me into him. Then as suddenly as he kissed me, he pulls away.

'Oh, I err...' I stumble backwards, feeling myself colouring a little.

'I've wanted to do that since the moment I walked through the door.' Dom looks at me and smiles, his feelings on show like merchandise in a shop window.

'I was a little behind you. But I have to admit, that was nice.'

'Just nice?'

'Don't push your luck.' I give him a look and open my apartment door.

'Sorry. Couldn't resist.'

We do an awkward dance-like movement in the tiny space as we manoeuvre ourselves around the door for him to leave.

'I'll see you tomorrow then,' he says, then pauses thoughtfully. 'This guy you've met. Does he know?'

'Know what?'

'About your situation?'

I purse my lips, not keen to get into a conversation about Matt. 'No, it hasn't come up yet.'

'Right. Just wondered. See you tomorrow, kitten.' He gives me his sexy signature wink – the one he only ever used with me – which I can't help but respond to with a 'teenage' grin.

'Bye, Dom.'

I give a little wave as I close the door, then, after throwing the lock, I let my body slide down the door until I'm sat on the floor with my back against it. What happened? My new life was going so well. It was uncomplicated – as much as it could be. Now Dom's driven a bloody great train through all that. Him turning up was the last thing I expected and as much as I want to say it doesn't change a thing, it clearly does. Because – newsflash – I'm still completely in love with him. It was so much easier when I thought he didn't want me any more. I didn't think I had a choice. Now he's willing for me to keep my new life in Birmingham – with him as part of the package.

But what about Matt? Gorgeous Matt, who leaves me almost unable to form a coherent sentence. I haven't so much as kissed him. I know so little about him. And now I have to decide whether to pick up where I left off with the man I believed to be my soulmate, or gamble everything for what I currently know to be no more than an oxytocin-inducing, heady crush.

Normally I'm a great problem solver. But how can I make that kind of decision in just over twenty-four hours?

Chapter 23

After an agonising Saturday afternoon and evening spent trying to make sense of what's just happened, I predictably have an unsettled night. This leaves me feeling less than refreshed for my date with Matt the next morning. The good news, however, is that the weather has settled into a nice calm, sunny-but-chill day. While I wait for my buzzer to announce his arrival, my mind resumes whirring over my dilemma like an overworked CPU.

This would be an impossible predicament in any normal set of circumstances: choosing between going back to something that made me so happy pre-diagnosis, and something new and exciting but very much uncharted territory. The outcome of either is impossible to predict. I then have the added uncertainty of my MS.

Dom asked if Matt knew, and throughout the previous day I pondered his motives for this. Was it to give him the upper hand? To knock me off my perch, so I'd see him as the only realistic option? As soon as I think it, I brush these questions aside; that's not Dom's style, he wins by putting in the hard work. And his question is a fair one: one I've already allowed to get in the way, which Sasha then helped me see beyond. But Sasha's a romantic. Dom's more pragmatically minded, like me – though I've been wondering recently whether I'm losing my touch. Am I kidding myself thinking this thing with Matt could have any kind of happy ever after?

The buzzer sounds, signalling Matt's arrival, and I stop dead. Should I make an excuse? This initial instinct matches the logic, no matter what way I look at it. Then my conversation with Sasha floats into my mind: it's just dating; it doesn't need to go anywhere.

'For goodness sake,' I cry out loud. 'When did I become this overthinking, indecisive idiot? Just go on the date and don't think a moment beyond it.'

I grab my bag from the sofa and march out of my apartment, letting Matt know I'm on my way as I do.

'How are you?' I greet him as I emerge into the cold air, wrapped up in my grey puffer jacket, scarf and gloves.

He's leaning casually on the roof of his VW Golf, dressed in similar outdoorsy gear to what he was wearing on the train when we first met. It makes him look so strong and handsome. I feel an immediate flutter in my stomach.

'I'm great. You?' He walks round the car and gives me the same electric-shock-inducing greeting as on Friday night – a lingering kiss on the cheek, hand gently touching my upper arm.

'Bit tired. But otherwise good.'

'Bad night?'

I immediately regret admitting to this. 'Didn't sleep as well as usual. Nothing to bother about.'

'The fresh air will sort you out. I've been on a few walking holidays with the boys and while open campfires and cosy pubs are perfect for beers and banter, you never feel quite as clever the next day. The outdoors clears the thickest of heads.'

He grins at me and opens the passenger door for me. I climb inside and put on my seatbelt.

'Ready?' he asks as he gets into the driving seat and starts the car.

'Let's go.'

We drive through Birmingham's suburbs and out into the countryside, fields and woods whizzing past us as we go. An hour later, Matt is perched on the open boot of the car checking the weather on his phone and I'm marvelling at my surroundings, rotating on the spot as I take in the natural landscape around me.

'This place is fabulous. It's so quiet and peaceful, and the air is so fresh… the smell from the trees and vegetation… it's so invigorating.'

'What did I tell you?'

'They should bottle that smell and pump it into our workplaces. We'd surely all get more done.'

Matt chuckles. 'I'm glad you're so enthusiastic. Not everyone's as into the outdoors.'

'I genuinely don't know why I don't do this stuff more. I'm not just saying that. It really feels good for the soul.'

'You certainly seem less tired. Told you it would work. Just didn't expect it to be so quick.'

I fail to mention that it was the exhilarating hour-long drive with his gorgeous self, chatting about everything and nothing, that had the most invigorating effect.

'So, this is Wyre Forest. It's one of my favourite places.'

'You come here a lot?'

'Since I was a little boy. It's probably what started my obsession with the outdoors.' He glances at me. 'It probably sounds cheesy but it's had such a great effect on me. I hope to be able to pass on the same experience to my kids when I have them. You know, keep the active lifestyle in the family: wife, kids, dogs, starting out small and building up as they get older, eventually climbing the Munros together.'

For a second, I'm overwhelmed by him laying out his cards like this, until I realise it's with no agenda. This is just the kind of guy he is: an open book. It's certainly refreshing, but unfortunately, he's already given the ending to his story away – and I can't see how I would fit into it. There's definitely no room for a wife with seriously reduced mobility in that equation. Annoyed at myself for jumping ahead, I shake my head to scatter these thoughts and remind myself that this is just dating. Period.

He points to a path leading into the woodland. 'We're going to do the Buzzard trail – a five-kilometre walk. Should take us about an hour and a half, then a nice pub lunch. Sound OK?'

'Sounds wonderful.' I force myself to focus on the moment and begin to rotate on the spot again, gazing up at the tall, bare trees.

'Before we go though, there's something I need to sort.'

'What's that?'

I finish my three-sixty turn and find myself face to face with Matt. My breath catches in my throat as he steps forward, slips his arms round my waist and gently pulls me towards him, checking I'm comfortable with the gesture before drawing me in for the most delicious first kiss. His touch is firm but gentle and this on top of the incredible surroundings sends my senses into overdrive. I pull him towards me hungrily, and he responds by mirroring my body language.

'Wow,' is all I can manage when we eventually pull apart breathlessly. 'Forget putting forest air in our work-places. We'd all be randy as—'

Matt erupts with laughter. 'There was me thinking it was me that had that effect on you.'

'It was. But there's no doubt our surroundings made it that bit more enjoyable.'

He steps forward and pulls me in again, this time planting three solid but sensual kisses on my lips before taking my hand and intertwining his fingers between mine.

'Now we've got that bit out of the way… shall we?' he asks.

'Absolutely.'

We head off along the trail, lost in each other as we engage in affectionate banter, stealing kisses and keeping our bodies as close as possible. The invisible boundaries between us are now well and truly lowered, and all thoughts of Dom's proposition are banished from my mind.

As we walk, I'm relieved to find it's fairly easy terrain, with a gentle downward slope. However, not long into our walk, the realisation dawns that what goes down must come up as I spot a less forgiving upward incline emerging ahead of us.

'Do you have family in Glasgow?' Matt asks me.

'Yes, just my mother and sister. My dad passed away a while back.'

'I'm sorry to hear that.'

'It's fine.' I shrug, trying to ignore the fact that we're now starting to climb. 'I still really miss him, but I'm used to it now. My parents were divorced and he had moved down south, so I didn't see him that much any more anyway. It was like I was being prepared for losing him altogether.'

'That's rough. Your mum and sister must miss you now there's a similar geographical split between you.'

I'm ready to gloss over the messed-up relationship I have with them, but there's something about Matt that makes me want to open up to him. He's such a good listener.

'I actually haven't spoken to either of them since I moved away. They didn't agree with me leaving.'

'Gosh. Sorry to hear that. Why were they so against it?'

Shit. I haven't thought this through. As much as I'm happy to open up around most things, I'm most definitely not ready to tell him about my medical situation. My breathing starts to strain and I realise it's not just because I want to avoid the truth. My body – as if cruelly forcing me to share my deepest, darkest secret – is going into full protest. My muscles burn in response to the invisible force that seems to be pushing against me, and we're only halfway up the incline at best.

'I, err… they're both just…'

'You don't need to tell me if it's too difficult.'

'No, it's not… that. They're…'

Matt stops and places a gentle hand on my shoulder to halt me. 'Hey, are you OK? You're struggling, and you're sweating.'

'Not a good look, then?' I attempt a joke to avoid the scrutiny.

'You're still gorgeous. Obviously. But I'm concerned. It's not your knee, is it? I forgot you'd had a running injury.'

Relief at being handed a ready-made excuse floods me like a burst dam. 'Yeah, sorry, that's it. Thought I'd be all right, but the hill's obviously aggravating it.'

'Right. Well, there's only one solution for this.'

Before I know it, Matt has scooped me up and set off up the hill again. This immediately transports me back several months to the time Dom did the same in the stairwell to our apartments. Back when I was so reluctant to take any help at all – ever. But here, now, in Matt's arms, with my fabricated injury, I feel much more comfortable.

'OK?' he asks, as I cling to his neck.

'Shouldn't it be me asking you? You're the one engaged in some kind of Iron Man contest while I dangle gracefully – I hope – in front of you. Sorry about this.'

'I'm pretty fit. I can handle it.'

'I can see that. Do you hire yourself out? I could get used to this.'

'I'm happy to carry you around anytime.' Matt grins at me, then gently lowers my feet to the ground. I realise we've reached the top. 'There's another incline a bit further round the trail but it's much more gradual and my service will be readily available – for a cost.'

'What's that?' I raise an eyebrow.

'Another kiss.'

'That makes me feel slightly pimped out, but happy to oblige.' I reach up, put my arms round his neck and plant a sensual kiss on his lips.

'So… coffee?' he asks as we pull apart.

'Amazing. Oh, and there's a nice clearing here we can sit in.' I pat the ground with my foot. 'It's dry enough. Must not have had the same rain we had yesterday.'

Matt pulls a blanket from his rucksack and gestures for me to sit on it as he pours coffee from a flask into two picnic cups. I watch him, feeling a nagging guilt that I've just lied to him. He's so open and trusting. It's already as if I've known him for much longer. How long can I really pretend for? Or is that a premature concern? If I decide to get back together with Dom, then it won't matter anyway.

Chapter 24

Matt drops me back at my apartment later that afternoon. As I unlock my front door and step inside, I'm dizzy with teenage hormones and utter exhaustion. I take off my trainers and jacket and go straight to my bedroom, where I climb under the covers and allow myself a little indulgence as I relive my date with Matt – and those incredible kisses. Those eyes, his strength in carrying me up that hill, the playful banter that came so easily. We were drawn to each other like Instagrammers to a selfie hotspot.

But it doesn't take long for reality to come knocking. Matt's as addictive as salt and vinegar crisps. No question. But what about Dom? I'm due to meet him in a few hours and I've no idea what I'm going to say. The two situations couldn't be more different. Dom and I are comfortable, familiar, warming; like bread and butter pudding. With Matt, it's more electric, exciting; exotic fruit salad. They're both delicious in their own way. On the face of it, comfortable and familiar gets trumped by excitement, but that initial rush never lasts. What kind of relationship would Matt and I settle into, if we even lasted long enough to find out? Then there's my health. Dom knows about it and still wants me. Would Matt be the same?

As I'm running these thoughts through my head, I can feel myself drifting off to sleep and I don't even try to fight it.

—

By 6:30 p.m., after waking up groggy and woolly-headed, I'm showered and changed, and feeling more refreshed. But the nagging feeling of not knowing what to say to Dom is still hanging over me – a slightly sick feeling in my gut. Just as I'm zipping my lipstick and eyeliner into the inside pocket of my handbag, there's a knock at my door. I pad through to the hallway, peer through the peephole and unlock the door.

'You're really not for using the buzzer, are you?' I say to Dom in place of a greeting.

'Someone let me in again.' He shrugs.

'I'm going to guess that you don't like feeling like a visitor.'

'You know me too well. We did used to live together, so it doesn't feel right. You look beautiful, by the way.'

He steps forward and gives me what initially seems to be a lingering kiss, then pulls back as suddenly as before. It's a smart tactic and leaves me wanting more. I touch my lips gently, feeling guilty about how good it felt when I was doing the same with Matt just hours earlier.

'I've got a taxi waiting outside,' he says, before I can say anything. 'Ready?'

'Oh, are we going far?'

'Nope. But I thought it would be better to conserve your energy.'

As much as another walk is the last thing I feel like after this afternoon, I can't help feeling a bit irked that Dom hasn't let me decide what I think is best for me.

We head downstairs and get into the waiting cab. It meanders its way through the residential streets, joining the main road just before the Five Ways roundabout, and I realise I have no idea where we're going.

'What restaurant have you booked?'

'You'll see.' Dom has a glint in his eye that tells me he's up to something. 'Just sit back and relax.'

Minutes later, the taxi pulls into a wide driveway and comes to a stop outside an impressive white Georgian-style building with bay windows, and what looks like beautifully landscaped gardens (though it's hard to see in the dark).

'This looks posh.' I raise an eyebrow at Dom.

'It's a long time since I took you for dinner. Figured I owe you a good one.'

He pays the driver and we head inside, where we're greeted by solid dark wooden floors, white walls and tastefully art-bedecked walls. The lighting is low, creating a romantic feel, and there's an autumnal scent that smells a bit like fig and sandalwood in the air. The super-polite hostess immediately welcomes us with a broad smile and invites us to take a seat in the lounge for an aperitif. We're shown to one of the tables in the bay window, where we make ourselves comfortable.

'What would you like to drink?' Dom asks me.

I look around for a drinks menu but there doesn't seem to be one.

'Gin and tonic?'

'Um… sure. So you still drink alcohol—'

'Yes, Dom. It's not going to kill me. I've set myself a two-drink limit, which I live by.'

He looks at me uncertainly for a moment, then turns to the hostess. 'One of your best local gins with Fevertree, and I'll take a Campari and orange. Oh, and can we look at the menu now?'

'Of course, sir.' The hostess backs away and disappears from the room.

'What's this place called?' I ask.

'Addington's.'

'Haven't heard of it.' I take out my phone and google it. '*Dom*. This is a Michelin starred restaurant. What are you doing? It'll cost a fortune.'

'Sshh.' He chuckles. 'Here come our drinks.'

I quickly put my phone away and thank the waiter as he serves our drinks and hands us a menu each, then melts into the background as quickly as the hostess.

'Cheers.' Dom holds out his glass and I clink it.

'Cheers. This place is incredible. You shouldn't have done this.'

I glance up from my menu and catch him gazing at me adoringly. It's a look I was so used to until a few months ago – and that I missed so badly when he disappeared from my life.

'Stop it,' I complain. 'You're making me uncomfortable.'

'Am I?' He reaches across and takes my hand, stroking it affectionately.

'OK, not really. But it's just a bit weird having no contact for ages, and now this.'

'Sorry, you're right.' His expression neutralises but he keeps hold of my hand, squeezing it gently. 'I've just really missed you, kitten. You don't mind me calling you that, do you? What's a few months apart when we had six amazing years before that?'

'I guess… I don't know. Maybe I need to get used to you again. You know, sniff you like a dog.'

'And that's why I love you. Your ability to ruin a moment with an image of us sniffing each other's arses.'

I stifle a snigger. 'That's not what I meant. I meant like when you hold your hand out to a dog to let it get used to you before you pat it.'

'I know. I just like to see you squirm.'

'You bugger.'

'How was your date earlier?'

'Oh, err… it was… fine.'

'Just fine?'

'Dom, please.'

'I'm just keen to understand the competition. Because he *is* competition. I can tell by the way you're acting.'

'It's not… I can't… now you've really got me squirming in my seat. Did you bring me here to do this?'

'No. Definitely not. But we both know you went on a date earlier. Just talk to me. We're both adults. You know I dated during our time apart. A couple of dates started well and I thought I saw some kind of potential. But as I got to know them, I realised they weren't right for me. And that you are.'

I take a sip from my drink and swallow uncomfortably. 'OK. We went for a nice walk in a forest—'

'Romantic.' Dom nods approval. 'He's a smooth one. Tell me more about him.'

'OK. His name is Matt. He's… outdoorsy, has a sense of humour… I'm not sure what else to say.'

'Did you kiss him?'

I redden. 'Yes.'

'Hey, it's OK, kitten.' Dom squeezes my hand. 'I can't expect you to drop your new life the moment I turn up. Obviously, I'd prefer you weren't seeing someone else, but that's how it is.'

'And you're hoping I've chosen you.'

'I think that's clear.'

'You certainly seem to be the Dom I always knew. So confident, laid back; a grafter but always able to make everything look so easy. What happened to us?'

Dom shrugs and I see the slightest twinge of emotion in his face. 'You had a life-changing diagnosis and I didn't handle it well. Seems that I'm not entirely unshakeable after all.'

'That makes two of us. I was so stubborn, I've realised that now. It's still hard, feels unnatural, but I know that I have to let people support me.' I catch his eye. 'It just needs to be *appropriate* support.'

'Of course.' He nods automatically and I can tell that he hasn't really taken in what I've said. 'Does that mean having your mum and sister back in your life?'

'They know they can be in my life if they accept me being here. They've chosen not to. In their heads that's their way of showing they care but it also shows how much they want to control my life and choices, and I'm not up for that.'

'I hear you. Hopefully they'll chill out after a bit, especially if they know I'm down here looking after you.'

My breath stutters in my throat. Though it wasn't quite an assumption, the language jars with me: like Dom is my saviour and the solution to all my problems. I've made this change in my life myself and it's worked out so far. My mother and my sister are only part of the picture.

Realising I'm being oversensitive, and sorely aware of my track record in this area, I cast this thought aside and make an effort to continue the conversation without judgement.

'Sir, madam, are you ready to go to your table?' Yet another member of staff has materialised out of nowhere.

We drain our drinks, get up from our seats and follow him through to the restaurant.

–

Our meal is outstanding. The immaculate and colourful presentation of the food wows us, while the array of textures and flavours sends our taste buds into orbit. It's not just the different dishes we choose, but all the little extras: the freshly home-baked breads with artisan butter, the *amuse-bouche*, the pre-dessert. It's such an indulgent experience, I'm not even bothered by having to stick to my two-drink limit. I feel well and truly spoiled by the experience, and Dom is the perfect gentleman, showering me with affection and compliments. It's just like we were, but with the extra excitement of spending time together after so long apart. I can feel a longing inside of me to spend the night together, to be physically close to him as well as connecting again emotionally. Yet I'm also aware that something's still not quite right. Under different circumstances, I'd have no reason not to give Dom and me as a couple another go. Sasha and my family would certainly approve. The problem is: I can't get Matt out of my head.

'Madam, your dessert.' The waiter expertly places a beautifully presented dish in front of me. 'This is the dark chocolate and chestnut tartlet, with pomegranate coulis, pistachio meringue shards and sweet pumpkin foam.'

'It looks delicious.' I turn the plate to get a proper look.

'Sir, for you, the artisan cheese plate with charcoal crackers and our signature chutneys made with ingredients from our own allotment.' The waiter explains Dom's selection of cheeses and chutneys in the same way the sommelier described the wine options to him earlier.

'So, have you enjoyed this?' Dom asks me once the waiter has left our table.

'I'm still enjoying it. This tartlet is off the scale. I've never tasted anything so scrumptious.'

'I'm glad. And what about us? Where are we?'

I stop mid-chew. We've been having such a nice time catching up and just enjoying each other's company, I'd almost forgotten this dinner comes with a big fat obligation.

'Gosh, you just threw that one out there, didn't you?'

'Did I? I thought we were clear that this was what tonight was about.'

'Well, yeah, obviously. But I thought the big chat would come after dinner.'

'I'm not sure I can wait that long for your answer.'

I feel a rush of empathy for him, quickly followed by a tidal wave of guilt. 'Right, that's fair. I guess... well, I've had such a lovely evening with you. It's almost like we've never had that time apart...'

'I think so too.' Dom nods.

'...and I still have feelings for you...'

'But are you still in love with me? That's the biggest question.' He tilts his head to one side in a puppy dog-like way, making me laugh.

'How could I not be?'

As I say this, an overwhelming feeling of nausea passes through me. I instinctively get to my feet and Dom does the same.

'Are you OK, kitten?'

'I'm... err... sorry, can you just excuse me for a moment, I'm feeling a little odd.'

'You're not seeing double or anything, are you?'

I realise he's referring to my MS. 'Oh, no. Nothing like that. Probably just eaten too much.'

I give him an apologetic look and head for the ladies' toilets. Inside I'm temporarily distracted by how plush they are, then as my mind slinks back to what's just happened, that nausea washes over me again. What's going on? Is it my MS after all? Or am I really just too full from all the food? I run the tap and put my wrists under the flow of the cold water to ground myself and figure out what's going on. What *did* just happen? I was enjoying my dessert. Dom was asking about us. About our future. Without warning, my stomach flips uncomfortably. There it is again. It happens every time I think about Dom's question: where are we?

But why? I'm still in love with him. He made me so happy before. Why not now?

Because I've changed, a voice in my head informs me. I've gone through hell this year and emerged with a new life and a new outlook. I just don't know if that change means I should be with Dom or with Matt. I need more time. As this realisation hits me, I stare back at my reflection and swallow thickly. This is not going to be an easy conversation. Who wants to be asked: 'Would you mind if I keep seeing this other guy for a bit? Just in case he's actually the one and you're not?'

Unable to put off the inevitable any longer, I return to our table and sit myself back down.

'Are you all right, kitten?' Dom reaches across the table and gives my hand a reassuring squeeze. 'We can go back to your apartment now if you're tired.'

'No, no. I'm fine. Think I'm just a bit full.'

'If you're sure?'

'I'm sure.'

'OK, then.' He signals something to one of the waiting staff, then focuses his attention on me. 'You still eating that?'

'I am. But I'm not sure I can finish it. Want a taste?'

'Thought you'd never ask.' He leans over and takes a forkful of my dessert. 'Wow, that's chocolatey. The chestnut complements it really well. Ah, here we are…'

He acknowledges the arrival of two waiting staff at our table: one who places a flute of champagne in front of each of us; the other, a plate of home-made confectionery with the words 'Will you marry me? (2.0)' piped onto it with chocolate. Before I can even register what's going on, the waiting staff have disappeared, and Dom's out of his seat and on one knee on the floor.

'Kitten, I'm so happy you're still in love with me, because I can't imagine how crushed I would have been if you'd said you weren't. We were set the ultimate test this year. It did break us temporarily, but now I feel we'll wind up stronger together. All I want in my future is you: in sickness and health, til death do us part. Will you marry me?'

It's my turn to respond and I'm so dumbstruck by what's just happened, I have no idea how to reply. Dom's beaming up at me lovingly, arms extended, holding an open ring box, which I note with interest doesn't contain the same ring I returned to him earlier this year – the diamond is about twice the size.

'So, Lex, what do you say?' Dom prompts me. 'Can we resume our future together?'

I take a deep shaky breath and glance around me anxiously. Thankfully, as our table is situated in a narrow alcove of the conservatory-style dining room, and the table along from us has been vacated, there's no one within hearing distance.

'I… err… gosh, Dom, this is a bit out of nowhere.'

His smile wavers slightly. 'I know it's a surprise, and I wondered myself whether I should do this so soon. But I figured as we were engaged before, we should pick up where we left off. I so badly want to marry you, kitten.'

I bite my bottom lip nervously, my eyes starting to sting from the horribly conflicting mix of emotions at play. 'I get it, Dom. I really do. This is all so lovely, and that ring is incredible. It's just that… we haven't actually discussed any of the issues that broke us up. Sure, we've both had time to take in my diagnosis and settle our emotions over it, but does that mean we'll be able to pick up where we left off before all that?'

'Why would we not be able to?'

Dom's starting to look hurt and I can't really blame him. He gets up from the floor, closes the ring box and sits back in his seat. I think carefully about my next words.

'One of the things I realised after we broke up was that we always avoided the hard stuff, and that was without my diagnosis in the mix. I honestly don't think it's as simple as picking up where we left off. Plus…' I shift uncomfortably in my seat and Dom spots this straight away.

'You want to keep dating this other guy. Shit, I don't believe this. I'm too late, aren't I? Two months ago and it would have been a totally different situation.'

'Perhaps.' I reach across and put a reassuring hand on his arm. 'I'm not saying never, Dom. It's just that my life has been a blinking rollercoaster these last months. When we broke up, you just had to deal with our break-up. I had to deal with that and losing my sense of identity. That's something you can never fully understand until it happens to you.'

Dom takes a deep breath and exhales loudly. 'I never thought about it like that. Sorry, kitten, I thought I was doing the right thing. I really meant every word.'

'I know you did. And I particularly appreciated the "in sickness and health" part. Though perhaps the wedding vows were a little premature.' I let out an awkward chuckle. 'I just need some time to wrap my head around all of this—'

'And to figure out whether it's me or this other guy.'

I grimace. 'Don't. Please. You make it sound so grubby. Just give me some time, yeah?'

Dom shrugs defeatedly. 'I don't like it, but it's only fair. All I can do is hope this bloke is someone you need to get out your system, like I did with the women I dated.'

'Thank you. I realise that's a difficult request to agree to.' I smile appreciatively, then raise a suspicious eyebrow. 'Just how many women were there?'

'Three. But not one of them a patch on you. Don't keep me waiting too long, yeah?'

I take his hand and squeeze it. 'I won't. I promise. I have far too much respect for you.'

Chapter 25

Monday morning arrives and despite my being emotionally and physically exhausted from the events of the weekend, it's a welcome distraction going back to work. Today is the start of my leadership programme – three intense days of workshops – something my career-focused mind has been looking forward to. Before heading to the conference room where the welcome session is taking place, I swing by my desk to grab my completed pre-work.

'Good weekend?' Emmanuel's head peers over the PC screen opposite as I perch on my chair and unlock my desk drawer.

'Yes, thanks. Not as relaxing as I'd hoped though. How was yours?'

Emmanuel eyes me for a moment. It's clear she's tuned in to the slightly forced tone in my voice, but she sticks to answering my question. 'I had a lovely weekend, thank you. My sister flew in from the US – she emigrated there a long time ago – and we had a great catch-up over wine and sushi. Haven't seen her in three years.'

'Sounds like it was well overdue.'

'It really was. Anyway, Alex, there's something I need to tell you before—'

She's interrupted by Danielle, who sweeps into the office and plonks her stuff on her desk noisily.

'Urgh. Morning all. Don't you just hate being guilted by homeless people all the time? I passed three of them on my way here. *Three.* All of them asking me for money. I work hard for my salary. They should try doing the same.'

Danielle's words rattle through me like a pinball and I shoot Emmanuel a look that loosely translates as 'she is so out of order'. Emmanuel nods in silent confirmation.

'Do they have so many people on the streets in Glasgow, Alex?' Danielle asks me. 'I feel like we're awash.'

I grit my teeth to be sure I give a measured response. 'Homelessness is a problem all over the UK, Danielle. And it's not an issue caused by laziness. You're smart enough to realise that.'

'Huh, sure.' She sniffs, not accepting my view at all.

Grabbing my pre-work and my bag, I excuse myself from the conversation so I can get to my session on time.

'Are you heading to the conference room now, Alex?' Danielle asks. 'Wait for me, I'll chum you.'

I stop dead. Danielle's coming to the leadership event? Surely not. I slowly turn, catching Emmanuel's eye as I do. She mouths 'I'll explain later', face full of apology. Taking a deep breath, I offer Danielle as genuine a smile as I can muster.

'Sure. I didn't know you were on the programme.'

'It's not really been public knowledge.' Danielle joins me and we walk out of the office together. 'I didn't want to boast about being one of the company's future leaders. You know how it is.'

'I sure do.' But you most definitely don't, I think to myself. So, what's really going on here?

The morning passes quickly and despite Danielle being irritatingly domineering in the group conversations, I find I'm able to filter her out and focus on the quality conversations with the other like-minded colleagues in the room. That is, with the exception of the introductions stage, when we're sharing a bit about ourselves, including our hobbies. This is where Danielle decides to tell the group that she and I are both avid runners, and suggests we all go for a run at lunchtime the next day to help us gel as a group. As the responses of 'why not' and 'sounds fun' reverberate around the group, I have to resurrect my fantasy injury as an excuse, which unfortunately allows Danielle to sit back smugly with a look of 'I knew it' plastered across her face.

When we break for lunch, I make sure I shake off Danielle before returning to the office to seek out Emmanuel.

'How did Danielle end up on the course?' I whisper to her, hunkered down at her desk.

'Let's take a walk.' Emmanuel gets up and ushers me out of the office.

We walk along the corridor of the main floor until we find an empty meeting room and duck inside. Emmanuel closes the door behind us.

'I am so sorry, Alex. This is not my doing, I *promise* you.'

'So, who's "doing" is it?' I'm unable to hide my frustration.

'I was told this morning. I shouldn't be telling you this, but I trust you and I think it's important you understand what's going on. It seems her father has finally succeeded in bending the ear of the chief exec. I'm not happy about it. It undermines my role as a leader and this is not what this company is meant to be about.'

My blood feels like it's at boiling point and I want to scream with frustration. 'She doesn't demonstrate any of the key behaviours in the leadership framework. Also, I thought the programme was only open to staff at my level and above. She's a grade below.'

'I agree, and it is. But strings have been pulled here. The one saving grace is that, because she's at a more junior grade, the chief exec has been clear that she's only to benefit from the development at this stage. She won't be up for consideration for any of the leadership positions on offer at the end of it.'

'I suppose that's something. But it's still unfair to everyone else who works their backsides off. Sorry, I know I'm probably overstepping things here, but it's just not right.'

'Do not apologise.' Emmanuel takes a seat opposite me and looks me square in the eye. 'You have every right to feel this way, Alex, and you're not the only one who does. As you know, Felix was really keen to get on the programme. You can imagine how he's feeling this morning.'

'Of course, yeah. Perhaps I should shut up then. At least I'm on it. He deserves it a hundred times more than she does.'

'You don't need to "shut up". The fact that you care so deeply about this shows me – even more – that you're exactly the right person to be on the programme. My advice: forget she's there and take everything you can from it. Do not let Danielle get in the way of your career opportunities.'

'Don't worry. I don't intend to.'

'That's the spirit.' Emmanuel gives me a supportive pat on the arm. 'Now, have you time for a spot of lunch?'

By the time the day is over, my mind is jangling with business jargon, strategic challenges and snippets of leadership theory. I can tell it's going to be a great programme – even with Danielle attempting to hog the limelight and show how amazing she is at every possible opportunity. The rest of the group have cottoned on to her pretty fast, and her suggested team-bonding run has already fallen by the wayside. They didn't want to leave anyone out: me and one of the others, who declared that the words 'running' and 'fun' should never feature in the same sentence. So we're going for lunch together instead.

As I'm walking home, I pull my phone out of my coat pocket and see to my delight that I've received a message from Matt.

> How was your Monday? Already feels like days since I've seen you. Can you cope with a midweek date? Or is your leadership thing too full on this week? x

My immediate instinct is to put him off. I'm overtired and that leaves me vulnerable. But I'm already dying to see him again too. The fizzy, whirly feeling in my stomach every time I think about him is like a withdrawal. I need my Matt fix – and I can't wait until Friday to get it.

I make myself wait until I've arrived at my apartment before I text him back. Then as I flop onto my bed, I tap out a reply.

> My Monday was good, thanks. The programme seems like it will be really interesting. How was yours? Reckon I can cope with a midweek date. xx

I lie back and close my eyes, but his reply is almost instant.

> Wednesday work for you? I have something in mind. You can leave the rest to me. x

He has something in mind? Not only does this have me immediately intrigued, I'm impressed by his proactivity. Then the nervousness that he'll choose something active and I won't be able to keep up kicks in. I just have to hope my phantom injury will deter him from that.

> Wednesday's great. Any hints as to what you have in mind? xx

He replies with a simple 'wait and see' and a winky face. Chuckling to myself, I toss my phone across the bed out of reach, banish the guilty thoughts of Dom that are trying to hijack my mind and close my eyes again.

After a brief, reinvigorating catnap, I make myself a quinoa salad with feta and pomegranate seeds, then stick the TV on. I'm about to put on a new drama that everyone's been raving about on Twitter when my phone lights up beside me, signalling a call from Sasha.

'Hi you,' I greet her as I hit the answer button. 'Boy, have I got something to tell you.'

'Can iv ait.' A loud sob comes down the line. I switch off the TV to give her my full attention.

'Sash? What's up?' Realisation hits me. 'You've done it, haven't you?'

There's a deafening honk and I can't decide whether it's Sasha blowing her nose or an attempt at a response.

'Sash? Talk to me.'

Another goose-like honk blares through my eardrum and this time it's clear that it's actually her trying to speak.

'OK, let's get you calmed down. Take some deep breaths. In through your nose and out through your mouth. Do it with me. In… and out.'

It takes several attempts and more bird-like tones, but Sasha does eventually manage to compose herself enough to give me a few fractured sentences.

'Was going to… the weekend… chickened out… she called me… why avoiding… her.'

'So, you had it out with her over the phone?'

'No… after work… tried to deny it… lied to my face… stormed out.'

I massage my forehead in consternation. It was bad enough for Sasha having to do this, but the fact that her mum didn't respect her enough to be honest or show any level of remorse is another thing altogether.

'Sash, that's really shit. I'm so sorry. But you know what, there is a positive here.'

'What's that?'

'If she'd been full of apologies and saying she'd change, begging for your forgiveness and all, you'd be torn, wouldn't you? You'd feel a responsibility to support her as she got back on the right track. Then she'd probably just let you down again. Am I right?'

There's a trumpeting noise at the other end of the phone as Sasha blows her nose. 'I suppose.'

'I'm right, Sash. Because sorry to say it but that's how people who cheat behave. It might be too early for you to hear this, but if that's how she's going to be, you're absolutely better off with her out of your life.'

'But she's my mum, Lex.'

'I know. But even parents can let us down.' Didn't I just know it.

'I guess. You're right, Lex. You're always right.' Sasha lets out a shuddering sigh.

'I'm not always right. I get things wrong just like the next person, especially when it comes to my own life. But I'm pragmatic and I see a huge opportunity for you in this. It's time for you to be a bit selfish and follow your dreams – whatever they might be.'

There's a sniffle from the other end of the phone. 'Actually, I kind of already am… I have an interview for a job in Birmingham.'

'What?' I'm elated to hear this. 'I thought you were going to start applying after you spoke to your mum.'

'I was. But I set up a job feed a few weeks ago and something suitable came through it within a few days. I figured I had nothing to lose by putting my CV across to them.'

'Sash, that's amazing. Well done, you. That's the first step. When is it? You can stay with me.'

'Next Tuesday. It's actually a videophone interview. They were keen that I didn't have to face any unnecessary costs.'

'Even better. That's how mine worked too. Oh, good luck. I'm totally rooting for you.'

'Thanks.' Sasha doesn't sound half as enthusiastic as I am, but how could I expect her to right now?

'You'll be all right, Sash. I promise. It will be hard but time and eventually distance will make things easier. I'll look after you, just like you've done for me.'

'You've no idea how much that means to me, Lex.' Her voice starts to wobble, so I quickly deploy a distraction technique to stop her losing her composure again.

'Want to hear something ridiculous?'

'Always. What's your news?'

Stretching out on my sofa, I quickly fill her in on the events of the weekend.

'Lex, what the hell?' she cries once I'm done. 'What are you going to do? Can't believe Dom just turned up like that.'

'Me neither.'

'He's such a great guy. Solid husband material. But Matt's totally delicious too.'

I moan in despair. 'See my problem?'

'Wish the only problem I had was two amazing guys fighting over me.'

I wince at this but decide not to indulge Sasha's negativity to keep her in the better frame of mind she's managed to get to.

'Technically it's a one-sided fight. Only Dom knows he has competition. Kind of thinking Matt doesn't need to know anything right now, it's such early days. Is that wrong?'

'No, I don't think so. Though I wouldn't take it too much further without being up front. If you end up with Matt, you don't want this lurking in the background, growing big wiry horns.'

'That's sound advice. Thanks, Sash.' I expel a troubled sigh. 'That means I potentially have two unpleasant things I'll have to reveal to him at some point. Maybe I should cut my losses now and just get back with Dom...'

'No, don't. I love Dom to bits, but I want you to choose the man that's right for you. You helped me see that I had to do something difficult to get to the right outcome. Now it's time for you to do the same.'

'I guess you're right. I should heed my own advice.'

We chat a bit longer, keeping the focus on the possibilities for Sasha's new life here in Birmingham, and then say good night. I'm about to switch the TV back on when I realise I haven't heard anything from Dom. He's probably giving me space, but I feel the need to check in with him, especially as he came all the way down here. I compose and send a quick WhatsApp message.

> That you home now? Hope your journey was OK. Thanks again for the lovely dinner. I'll be in touch soon, I promise. xx

I can see that he reads it immediately. He types a response.

> Hi kitten. Yes, home and settled. Missing your beautiful face already. Dx

I smile at his message, then feel a pang of sadness as my mind flicks through happy memories of our relationship – our first date, the moment he told me he loved me, the day he proposed on the Rialto Bridge during our trip to Venice. It all seemed so perfect until everything changed.

I miss you too, Dom. I didn't think I did but I really do. So why is that not enough for me to sign up to a future together right now?

Chapter 26

The week flies in as expected and by the time my Wednesday evening date with Matt comes round, I'm filled with heady excitement and anticipation for where he's taking me. All I know is he's picking me up outside at 6:30 p.m. – and thankfully, he hasn't suggested I wear any active gear.

'Where are we off to?' I ask, as I slide into the passenger seat of his car.

'Patient one, you are.' He chuckles. 'Hi to you too.'

'Sorry. I'm just intrigued. Hi.' I lean over and meet him halfway for a slow, sensual kiss. He puts his hand on the back of my neck and pulls me towards him longingly.

'Any clues at all?' I ask again as we pull apart.

'Let's just say it'll be a lively evening. You did have something to eat, didn't you?'

'Just as you instructed me to.'

'Good.'

He puts the car into gear and pulls away. We drive for about ten minutes, but not being that familiar with Birmingham's roads, I have little sense of where we're going. My best guess would be that we appear to be skirting round the perimeter of the city centre. Matt eventually pulls into a space in a multistorey car park and turns to me.

'It's about a five-minute walk from here.'

'And *it* is…?'

'So close now, you may as well wait and find out.'

I exhale impatiently. 'I'm not good with surprises.'

'Clearly. It will be worth it. Promise.'

We get out of the car and head out of the car park onto a street-lit road.

'This is the Newtown area of the city,' he explains. 'You're unlikely to have been over this way.'

I look around me. It seems to be a more industry-focused area of the city, with red-brick factory-style buildings and grey steel shutters covering garage door-ways, sporting the words 'no parking' in white spray paint. We walk hand in hand, silently, mirroring the calmness of the empty dark streets.

'Gosh, this is a bit creepy,' I joke. 'Maybe I should have vetted you before agreeing to this. You could be some psycho and I'm merrily trotting along beside you to my untimely death.'

'Crime drama fan, per chance?' He gives me an amused sideways look.

'That's me. Think I prefer the fictional stuff though. True crime is a bit morbid, knowing it's really happened. Makes me feel like a voyeuristic weirdo at a crime scene.'

'I know what you mean. Ah, here we are.'

Matt stops outside a nondescript building and presses the buzzer by the doorway.

'Hello?' A crackling voice comes through the intercom.

'Hi, it's Matt. Sammy would have mentioned I'm coming along tonight.'

'Come on in, mate.'

The door unlocks and we step inside.

'What is this place?' I ask, as live band music starts to filter along the corridor. 'Is this one of these underground bars with a "members only" policy?'

'You'll see.'

Matt leads me along the corridor until we're right outside the room the music's coming from. It's very loud and I can't help wondering how small this bar is; it sounds like the band's right behind the door. Matt pulls me in for a quick and intoxicating lip-smacking kiss, then opens it and beckons for me to follow him inside. As we enter, I realise it's not a bar at all, but some kind of rehearsal studio. We move across to the other side of the room and take a seat at a small table.

'Is this your friend's band?' I have to shout to be heard over the punchy rock music.

'It sure is. Like them?'

'They're brilliant.'

I tap my foot to the beat until the song finishes and when they wrap up, we give them a mini round of applause. The lead guitarist turns and bounds across to us, giving Matt a blokey handshake and an affectionate slap on the shoulder. He has a friendly face and hair like Bob Marley.

'Matt, mate, good to see you. Didn't notice you sneak in just then.' He turns to me. 'And I remember you from the karaoke bar. How could I not?'

'I thought you looked familiar,' I reply. 'Great to meet you.'

'You too. And these guys here are Simms, Carter and Andy.'

I give a friendly wave to the other members of the band, and they wave back casually.

'Are you here to "audition"?' He gives me a hopeful wink.

'Not that I'm aware of. Although now you mention it… Matt, why are we here?'

A guilty look spreads across Matt's face. 'I know you said you've got too much going on, but as your childhood dream was to be a singer, I didn't see the harm in letting you have a taste of the magic.'

My stomach immediately does a somersault and I can't tell whether it's because I'm touched by Matt's incredibly thoughtful gesture, or if it's a premature dose of stage fright.

'No pressure, eh? I've never been in a rehearsal studio before. Closest I've got to singing with a band is "bandaoke", but even then, I had the words in front of me.'

'We've got lyrics sheets.' Sammy points to the drummer (Carter, if I've got it right), who holds up a folder. 'How about you listen to a couple more tracks, warm your voice up by singing along, then you can see how you feel? Want a beer?'

'Oh, no, thanks, I'm fine. I guess that sounds OK.' I look to Matt for reassurance and he gives me an encouraging nod.

As Sammy rejoins the band, Matt leans across the table and grabs my hand. 'You OK with this? You don't have to sing if you don't want to. But you're so good, it would be a shame to waste the opportunity.'

'Why do I get the feeling you're up to something?' I narrow my eyes at him playfully.

'I'm not. I just genuinely want you to have an experience.'

I keep my suspicious eye on him a moment longer, then turn towards the band as they launch into a perfect rendition of 'Sex on Fire' by the Kings of Leon. The buzz of the music is contagious and before I know it, I'm enthusiastically singing along. One song rolls into another, with T-Rex, Arctic Monkeys and Pulp featuring on the playlist. Eventually they wrap up once again and Sammy bounds back across to us.

'What do you think, Alex?'

'I think you guys are amazing! Do you do your own stuff too?'

'We do. We mix covers into our sets with some of our own stuff. Tends to go down well.' He shoots me a grin. 'Ready for a shot? We've got the Killers lined up for you.'

The stomach flip returns. I look to Matt, who nods again.

'OK, then. Suppose now I'm here I can't pass up the opportunity.'

I get up from my seat and follow Sammy across to the microphone. He hoists his guitar strap back over his head and turns to me.

'We'll stick as close to the original as we can. You're on straight after the second note, remember.'

I nod mutely, tap the microphone a couple of times to get a sense of its volume, and take a deep breath to calm my now trembling body.

A piano-like, haunting pling comes from the keyboard, and I start to sing the opening lines, which, with almost no instrumental accompaniment, make me feel very exposed indeed. Momentarily, I'm transported back to the karaoke bar, when my confidence initially wavered. This time I don't get over it quite so quickly. Having Matt listening to me, I feel like I'm on show. I glance back towards him, and he gives me two huge thumbs up, mouthing 'go for it'.

I continue my way through the first verse, setting no one and nothing alight, but as the band launch into the chorus, the music and emotion finally consume me, allowing me to lose myself in the song. The band are full of approving expressions and encouraging nods as I move through the song's climax to the calmer 'outro'. As they play the closing notes, Matt stands up behind me and whoops and claps, and is quickly joined by all the band members.

'That was incredible.' Sammy hops across to me and gives me his friendly slap on the shoulder. 'You're a natural. Took you a moment to get going, but once you did...' He gives an impressed whistle.

'What he said,' Matt calls out jovially, as he wanders over and gives me a squeezy sideways hug. 'How did it feel, Alex?'

I do a quick self-check. The jangling nerves that consumed me before I started to sing have dissipated completely. I'm now feeling surging adrenaline and an unquellable urge to keep going. I look at Sammy hopefully.

'Can we do another one?'

'That's the spirit.' He gives me another friendly shoulder slap. 'Right, lads. Let's put Alex through her paces.'

'Go for it.' Matt smiles at me and plants a firm kiss on my lips that, in my heightened state, reverberates through me, feeling like a million fireworks have exploded in my body.

I turn back to the microphone, where I'm handed a lyrics sheet. The band kicks into the intro of another

Killers song: 'Somebody Told Me'. As the pounding music fills the room, I can't help but move to the beat of the music, and within moments I'm lost again.

An hour and a half later, after some more challenging and less familiar pieces where I needed guidance from the band, we finish up for the evening.

'That was one of the best nights ever. Thank you so much for organising it.'

I lean over and kiss Matt, who, due to his height, isn't that much shorter than me in his seated position. He puts his arms round my waist, pulls me onto his lap and kisses me deeply. My whole body tingles in response.

'All right, break it up. Nobody wants to see that,' Sammy jokes. 'Especially when they don't have a girl of their own to do it with.'

Matt and I pull apart, laughing, and I feel myself redden.

'Sorry, it must be the music.'

'I'm just joshing.' Sammy gives me a cheeky wink. 'Listen, Alex, that lead vocalist slot is yours if you want it. I know you've said you've a lot on, but mate, you should not be wasting that voice. Right guys?'

There's enthusiastic collective agreement from the rest of the band.

I glance at Matt, who simply shrugs, signalling his agreement with the others. What to do? My heart is screaming 'do it', but my head knows better; one thing too much and all the dominos could topple. I don't understand my condition enough yet to know how it will behave. What I do know is that my stamina isn't what it was.

At the same time, it has been such a buzz being here tonight. I feel so energised. Maybe I'm looking at this all in the wrong way. People who stay focused and determined often fare well. You read inspirational stories like this all the time. I obviously can't beat my MS, but who's to say I can't benefit from this state of mind?

Matt and Sammy are scrutinising my expression, trying to work out what's going through my mind.

'What's the time commitment?' I ask.

'Rehearsals once a week – just like this – and gigs most weekends,' says Sammy.

'Do you have a backup singer? Just in case?'

'I've been doing the singing recently. Nowhere near as good as you, but I'm well enough received. It would be no problem if you couldn't make the odd gig.'

I mull this over for a second. 'OK, how about I join you on a trial basis and we see how it goes?'

'We've got a good one, lads.' Sammy whoops. 'Welcome to the band, Alex.'

There's a collective cheer as the rest of the band members click beer bottles and toast me. I suddenly realise something.

'Wait, what are you guys called? Who am I joining?'

'We, Alex, are Capital Parade.' Sammy puffs his chest up proudly.

'I *love* that. Thank you for having me.'

As Sammy joins the other band members to continue the bottle-clinking, Matt squeezes me round the waist. 'I'm so pleased you're in. For you, because you should be making the most of that voice. But also because I can be your groupie. I can run you to rehearsals if you like.'

I'm simultaneously relieved by this offer and filled with a rising excitement. But it sinks like a lead weight the moment I realise something: have I just inadvertently signed up to a future with Matt? If so, what does that mean for me and Dom? And has this decision to join the band and accept lifts to rehearsals been too premature, given we're only on date three and he doesn't know who I really am?

Chapter 27

Over the next few weeks, I manage to successfully juggle the three main elements of my new life in Birmingham: my revitalised career; my utterly delicious, blossoming romance with Matt, which has now moved through all the bases (and to be clear, I don't mean we've been playing baseball); and weekly rehearsals with one of the city's hottest semi-pro bands. It's a near perfect picture, apart from three other things: my MS, which is like an unwelcome shadow, though I try to ignore it and continue swimming a couple of times a week as a way of managing my fatigue; the fact that I haven't yet told Matt about either my MS or about Dom; and knowing that Dom, back in Glasgow, is waiting for an answer.

On the night of my debut appearance with the band, I'm in the ladies' toilets of a trendy venue off New Street – nerves cutting through me like a street drill – when it all finally catches up with me. My throat starts to tighten, my breathing becoming shallow and strained. My brain simply cannot cope with the emotional complexities of my personal life, alongside this imminently terrifying experience of walking out on stage in front of hundreds of people. Unable to get my breathing under control, I pull my phone out of my handbag and dial Sasha.

'Hi, you.' Her bouncy tone carries down the line like a soothing tonic. 'I thought you'd be on stage by now, taking Birmingham by storm.'

I manage a strangled laugh. 'I'm due on in fifteen minutes… supposed to be warming up but instead I'm hiding in the toilets. I'm totally freaking out, Sash.'

'Oh, honey, you'll be fine. You'll be amazing. I know it must be nerve-racking but—'

'That doesn't even begin to describe it. I don't think there's a word to express how I feel right now. Frightened… terrified… petrified. None of them seem close. And to top it off, my mind has gone into overdrive over all the other stuff I'm trying to work through.'

'You mean the Matt versus Dom showdown.'

'Interesting description. But, yes. That and the fact that Matt still doesn't know about my MS. Or Dom.'

There's a short pause at the end of the phone. 'OK, Lex, I'm going to do two things to help you. The first is tell you to take some slow deep breaths—'

'That's normally my advice to you.'

'Well, are you walking the walk right now?'

'What? I'm just… um… I guess not. Still, I could have thought of that.'

'Yet you didn't.'

'True.'

'I learned from the best, Lex. You. Now, are you ready for my next trick?'

I lean forward against the sink unit, taking slow deep breaths, just as I've counselled Sasha to do so many times in the past. 'Go on.'

'It's very simple. I'm going to give you a massive reassuring hug.'

'Down the phone?' I glance at the illuminated screen in confusion.

As I'm waiting for a response, the door to the ladies' opens and Sasha's voice comes from right behind me.

'You can't hug down a phone, dafty.'

I spin round and see her standing right in front of me, all goofy grin and wild red hair.

'You're here? What the… how…?' I dive into her arms and we squeeze each other tight for a good thirty seconds.

'I thought you could do with the moral support,' says Sasha once we've pulled apart. 'I know Matt's here, but it's still early days for you guys. Not the same as a bestie.'

'Damn right. I can't believe you came all the way down here for this.'

'Well… I can't honestly say it was just for this gig. I was going to tell you when I saw you later − I got the job. Have a couple of apartment viewings booked for tomorrow before I head home.'

My hand shoots to my mouth. 'You're really moving here? Like, *really* really?'

'You never thought I'd do it, did you?'

'I… um… argh, I can't lie to you. I hoped you would. But I figured, you're a nester, you'd eventually decide to stay where you were.'

'No reason to now.' Her lips tremble ever so slightly. 'It was my mum that held me back from doing anything more adventurous. Filling my head with total BS, just so she would have me around to wait on her like a skivvy. Nah-uh. I'm claiming back my life.'

'This is amazing, Sash.' I rub my forehead, still trying to digest this fantastic news, then a thought comes to me. 'Wait, what's going on here? I'm supposed to be the rational, practically minded one who doesn't get in a flap.'

266

'I know, right?' Sasha giggles. 'And I'm normally the irrational, panicky one who's paralysed by indecision over the slightest thing.'

'Has there been some weird kind of spell put on us?'

'Maybe. Or maybe we just all have good and bad moments in life. As I said, I learned from the best.'

'I don't feel like the best right now, Sash.' I switch on the cold tap, plunging my wrists under it once more in a bid to calm my racing pulse. 'I feel like Birmingham's soon-to-be shortest-lived lead vocalist ever. And that's just the problems of the next few hours. Beyond that, with Matt, Dom... I can't even compute it.'

'So, don't. You can't do anything about the guys right now. Just focus on the next few hours and enjoy the experience. The stage fright will pass. Lose yourself in the music and let your brain figure the rest out for you.'

I switch off the tap and look at her, appreciating her in this moment more than I ever have. 'You're so right, Sash. Thank you for turning up when I needed you the most. And now, I'm going to politely ask you to turn round and walk back out the door so I can fit in some last-minute voice warmups. But I can't wait to see you again later.'

'Me neither. Break a leg.' She gives me a final hug, plants a kiss on my cheek and disappears back out of the toilets.

I turn back to the mirror and focus on getting myself calm and into balance. Thank goodness for Sasha turning up like that. She's probably just saved me from a full-on meltdown. Sash and Lex. Propping each other up since ninety-three.

Several minutes later, I'm on stage behind a giant black curtain doing the final sound checks with the band. Sammy helps me set the mic up just as I need it.

'All set, Alex? I know you're nervous. Best advice I can give is don't make eye contact with any of the crowd. Not until you're in your stride.'

'OK, thanks, that's helpful.' I take a deep shaky breath.

'You've got this.' He grabs my shoulder and squeezes it affectionately. 'It's not that different to singing karaoke.'

As he makes his way back across to his position and slings his guitar strap over his shoulder, I suddenly have an idea.

'Sammy, what do you think of redheads?'

'Men or women?'

'Women, obviously. You mentioned the other night you'd like one in your life.'

'I don't really have a type if that's what you're asking. There are some really hot redheads out there. Nicole Kidman and Isla Fisher for a start.'

I flash him a little grin. 'In that case, there's someone I need to introduce you to later.'

Minutes later, the curtain is drawn back, the stage lights flash and we burst to life with our opening track, one of the band's own songs, 'Space Poets'. It's lively, rocky, bursting with energy. The perfect gig opener; and the crowd instantly love it. This is an enormous relief to me as I stand centre stage, belting out the lyrics, fuelled by their support. My nerves are almost immediately extinguished by the sight of so many elated faces bobbing up and down in the darkness, and the face of one person in particular: Matt. He's right at the front, dancing like a maniac, whooping and cheering me on.

The adrenaline courses through me and I lose myself in the song. It feels like no more than a moment before the band are playing the outro and Sammy's addressing the crowd before launching us into another of the band's own pieces. We play one track after the next; we mix in some well-known covers, but I'm surprised to see the crowd are responding more enthusiastically to the band's own tracks. Some are even singing along.

As I bounce lightly on my toes, interacting playfully with my fellow band members and the crowd, I feel a surge of happiness like I've never felt before. It's like a drug, taking me through such a high. I feel invincible. Unstoppable. I'm not the woman with MS, I can conquer the world.

I don't want it to end but it does, to rapturous applause and wolf-whistling. It's a moment like no other, taking that bow and feeling the stamping appreciation reverberate through the venue. Basking in the experience, just as Sasha suggested, the pieces start to fall into place and my brain finally offers me the answer I've been seeking.

–

'OMG, you were amazing!' Sasha launches herself on me when I, Sammy and the other band members emerge from backstage.

'Oof! Thanks, Sash.' I hug her back.

'How did it feel, Lex? You were so natural up there, a pro rock star. Looked like you'd been doing it for ever.'

'It actually felt that way too.' I grin at her, still buzzing from the gig.

Sasha melts into the background as Matt steps forward and pulls me in for a stomach-swirling kiss. 'You were incredible, Alex.'

'I second that.' Sammy appears at our side, undeterred by the fact that we're locked in a passionate embrace. 'Matt, mate, you're a lucky bastard. So many blokes would kill to go out with a hot rock chick.'

As he says these words, a familiar feeling of guilt intrudes on my consciousness and I untangle myself from Matt.

'Not sure how I feel about being called a "chick", Sammy, but I know the intention is good.' I give him a little wink.

'Where are the post-gig drinks tonight?' Matt asks.

'Got us some VIP passes for a place round the corner,' says Sammy.

'I hope you have an extra one.' I grab Sasha by the hand and pull her forward. 'Everyone, this is my best friend, Sasha. She'll being joining us.'

'Ah, this is a surprise,' says Matt. 'Great to meet you, Sasha. I've heard a lot about you.'

'Right back at you.' Sasha grins at him.

Sammy takes in Sasha's tousled red hair and bright blue eyes and lets out a low whistle. 'Dang, she's cute. This why you were asking me about redheads, Alex? All I can say is, I think red Afro hair is the coolest thing around.'

I bite my lip to stifle a laugh as Sasha looks at us, confused.

'He's suggesting he'd like to have babies with you,' I whisper in her ear and she turns scarlet, but at the same time looks elated by this comment.

'Enchanté.' Sammy steps towards Sasha and kisses her hand. 'May I escort you to the next venue?'

'Hello. Of course.' Sasha giggles as he leads her off towards the exit.

'Nice bit of matchmaking.' Matt snakes his arm round my waist.

We follow the rest of the band out of the building and onto New Street, where there are plenty of lively Saturday night revellers in transit, probably moving from one bar to the next. 'You ready for a drink?'

'Definitely. You go ahead. I need to make a quick call.'

'No probs.'

Matt catches up with the others and as soon as he's out of earshot, I look up Dom in my contacts and hit the call button. He answers on the fourth ring.

'Lex, hi. Sorry, give me a moment. I'm just out with the guys.'

I hear garbled voices and distorted music for a few moments until his voice comes back down the line clearly.

'How are you? Everything OK? You're not unwell, are you?'

'No, I'm fine, Dom. I'm just out with Sasha and a few others.'

'Didn't realise Sasha was with you, that's nice. Who are the others?'

I hesitate, unsure what to say.

'I see.' Dom's voice loses a bit of its enthusiasm. 'So that's not fizzled out then. I was hoping you might be calling to say it was all over and you're ready for me to hit the button on moving down.'

'I... erm...' I cringe, annoyed at myself as I realise I'm about to ruin Dom's night out with his friends. 'Actually, maybe it can wait.'

'Hey, only joking, kitten. You know that. It's been so great chatting with you the last couple of weeks. Can't blame a guy for being a bit impatient, eh?'

'No, I guess not.' I kick lightly at a bollard in discomfort, suddenly feeling the chill in the air. 'Look, Dom. I *am* phoning about us, but I'm afraid it's not to tell you what you want to hear.'

'Ah.'

Taking a deep breath, I blurt it all out. 'Dom, I'm so sorry. I really am. It's just… I've found a new life here and it's changed me more than I realised. I'm just not sure that we're right for each other any more.'

'You mean you like this other guy better.'

'What? No. It's not that simple. Tonight, when I was on stage, it just—'

'What do you mean you were "on stage"?'

I give myself a mental kick – I hadn't mentioned the band to Dom before now, due to it being Matt-related. 'I've joined a band, as their lead singer. They're Matt's friends and I had my first gig with them tonight. It was amazing. I felt so alive and it just made me realise that this change I've made in my life has been for a reason.'

'Right.' Dom clears his throat. 'I thought the reason was your MS, Lex.'

'It was. But now, my illness aside, this is the life I should be living.'

'You mean you're on a high after your gig.'

'Well, yes, but that's not all it is.'

There's a short silence at the end of the line. 'Lex, have you really thought this through? Things are going great for you right now. But will that last? Isn't this just another case of denial? How can you expect to sustain that lifestyle?'

I frown at my phone. 'What… what do you mean?'

'I mean, what happens to your place in the band when you relapse? Do they know about your situation? Does Matt even know about it? I'm guessing not. And when he finds out, do you think he's just going to shrug and say it doesn't matter?'

'I… it'll be fine.'

'That's your answer? Have you thought this through or are you just ignoring it? Because you can't, Lex. No matter how much you want to. Joining a band on top of your aspirations at work – it's all admirable. But it would be a lot for a healthy person, never mind someone with your condition.'

I feel myself smart with annoyance. But unfortunately, Dom has sliced open a deep vulnerability, which snuffs out any ability to face up to him.

'Look, Dom, I'm doing the best I can. I can't live a lie just because I'm ill.'

'So, I'd be the lie? Nice, Lex.' Hurt seeps through his words.

'No, I don't mean that, I—'

'It's OK, I get it. I'm not exciting enough for you. I'm offering you a lifetime of love, stability and support, but it's not enough.'

'It's not that—'

'Then *what* is it?'

'It's... you're... you suffocate me, Dom. You want to play the rescuer all the time. You treat me like an invalid. Yes, I'm ill. Yes, my life is a bit more uncertain and I'm vulnerable to flare-ups. But that can't be the focus day in, day out. I'm still me. I do love you, but I can't have a life where I can't breathe because you're just as overbearing as my—'

'Lex, I have a reality check for you. People give a shit. You *are* ill and they just care about you. Deal with it. This guy, the only reason he doesn't see you that way is because *he doesn't know*.'

As Dom's words pour through the earpiece in my phone, I suddenly feel sick. 'You... you don't know that.'

'Well, I'm not the one who has to find out. Good luck, Lex. I hope he's worth it. Maybe my mates are right, I should just appreciate that I've had a lucky escape.'

With that, he cuts the call, leaving me in cold, blunt shock. I stand like a statue for several seconds, unable to fathom what's just happened. Then as I come to, I lean on the bollard in front of me, taking several deep shaky breaths. Once I've composed myself enough to face the others, I turn in the direction of the bar – where I see Matt standing just feet away from me, looking very confused indeed.

Chapter 28

The breath is knocked out of me again as I make eye contact with Matt. I try desperately to read what's going on behind those dark, penetrating eyes. How much did he hear? The end of that phone call gave glaringly obvious clues to the two things I've been hiding, out of fear he would run for his beloved hills. If he did overhear, there's no avoiding the final showdown: right here, right now.

'Hey,' I manage finally.

'Hey.' He mirrors me in his reply but stays where he is.

'Sorry, my call took longer than I expected.'

'That's why I came out.'

'Right.'

'Is everything OK, Alex? I wasn't eavesdropping. I only came out when you hung up but from your reaction, I can tell it wasn't good news.'

Relief floods through me. He didn't overhear. This isn't going to be the conversation I dreaded it might be. But two things are now very clear: he knows something's up; and he does not deserve anything other than the truth. But not right now. This is not the time or the place.

'I, erm… Matt, there is something I need to talk to you about…'

'There's a statement every bloke is keen to hear,' he quips. 'It's you, not me, right?'

I remain rooted to the spot. 'It's nothing like that. There's... a couple of things you should know, before this goes any further. But would you mind if we had this chat tomorrow? It's been an exhausting – but obviously amazing – evening and I feel like we should be with our friends right now.'

He seems to consider this. 'Of course. If that's what you want. Whatever it is though, Alex, I doubt it will change anything for me. You could announce you're an international assassin with alien ancestry and a third leg and I'd still be completely into you.'

I try to smile at his attempt at reassurance. 'Right. Well, that's good to know. Though I'd say the extra leg discovery is unlikely, given our recent slumber parties.'

'That is true.'

A fleeting memory of our first night together in my apartment passes through my mind, sending my hormones into a spin. They're then put firmly back in check as I also remember Matt's previous comment about the kind of future he's looking for: an equally active wife, two-point four children and two dogs – living the outdoor lifestyle, climbing lots of hills together. A future I can never give him. His comment about whatever I have to say not changing anything, while amusing and gallant, will quickly lose its significance once the enormity of what I have to share with him sinks in. As this realisation dawns, a swell of premature loss creeps up on me. I have to fight against the raw emotion so he doesn't pick up on it.

'Let's get back to the others then,' says Matt. 'Whatever this is, we'll tackle it tomorrow, yeah?'

He extends his hand, encouraging me to join him. It's as if the glue that's been rooting me to the spot comes unstuck. I dive into his arms, pulling him into me as tightly as I can, all too aware that it may be one of the last times I get to hold him in this way.

'Hey.' He soothes me, then lifts my chin and kisses me softly. 'I don't know where you're at, but I want you to know I'm falling for you – hard.'

Though I feel exactly the same way, I stay quiet, too scared to expose myself in this way when there's still too much to be revealed. Tomorrow I'll be telling Matt I have a lifelong degenerative disease that means I can never be part of the future he's so passionate about; as well as admitting to the fact I've been torn between him and my ex. Cue another 'lucky escape'. It almost seems inevitable.

–

'What have you two been up to?' Sammy gives Matt a boisterous wink as we enter the VIP area of the bar, hand in hand.

'That would be telling, mate.' Matt gives him a friendly jab in the arm. 'Gin and tonic, Alex?'

'Yes please.' I could certainly do with one after this rollercoaster of a night.

As Matt heads to the bar, I pretend to laugh along with the banter, while my mind is in turmoil over my conversation with Dom. It was never going to be easy. But the way he ended the call shocked me. His friends thought he'd had a lucky escape? I've hung out with them many times, considered them friends of mine too. How could they be so cruel? And why did Dom feel the need to share that? Was he just letting his emotions overwhelm him like before or was he trying to hurt me like I was hurting him? Whatever the reason, it further confirms that I've made the right decision.

I do still love Dom, but not in the way I used to. I've caught myself too many times thinking of him as a security blanket, the guy who'll give me everything and accept my situation – if Matt doesn't. That's not right or fair. I can forgive Dom his outburst, he's confused and he's hurting. But I couldn't forgive myself if I used him as my fallback position. If Matt walks once I've shared everything with him (which I fully expect him to), then I go on alone. I focus on all the good stuff, and if the right man eventually comes along, that's a bonus.

'You OK?' Sasha extricates herself from her flirting with Sammy and lowers her voice as she sits down next to me. 'Want to go to the toilets for a chat?'

'Nah, I'm fine.'

'You sure?'

'I'm sure.' I swallow thickly, then, keeping my voice low, I quickly fill Sasha in on what's happened.

'Oh, Lex. I'm sorry,' says Sasha once I'm done. 'But you've done the right thing. You're *doing* the right thing. It'll all work out, I promise.'

'You can't promise that, Sash.'

'No, I can't. But I get a really good feeling from Matt.'

'I do too. I'm totally falling for him. But no matter how great a person he is, he may not want to take things any further – and that's absolutely his prerogative.'

'I know. I guess…'

'You just want it to work out. As do I.'

'Exactly.' She screws up her nose in frustration at having no control over the situation.

'You two seem to be getting on well.' I nod in the direction of Sammy.

'He's so sweet. I love his hair, it's so funky. He's asked me on a date already.'

'Fast mover.'

'I know. We're going for brunch tomorrow.'

Sasha's eyes are alight with excitement and anticipation. It's so lovely to see after the hard time she's had.

'There you go.' I give her a playful nudge. 'You've not even moved here yet and you've already found yourself a Brummie. Is brunch straight after spending the night together? No walk of shame for you then.'

'Stop it. Don't jinx it, Lex. And we won't be spending the night together. I just met him, like five minutes ago.'

'All right, but I want a full run-down after—'

'What are you two whispering about?' Matt sets my drink down in front of me.

'Oh... um...' Sasha stumbles. 'I was just... suggesting to Lex that she share with you the song she wrote.'

'You've written a song?' Sammy's ears immediately prick up. 'Let's hear it.'

'Yeah, let's hear it,' says Matt.

'Thanks, Sash.' I give her a look that says, 'couldn't you have come up with another excuse', then turn to the guys. 'How about you just read the lyrics yourself?'

I pass them my phone with the notepad app open. They pore over the words in front of them as I sit there cringing and staring daggers at Sasha. She simply shrugs in return.

'Alex, this is really good,' Sammy says eventually. 'It could almost be a charity song, but there's a deeper, more personal message there. What inspired you to write it?'

'Oh... I...' I glance at Sasha, whose face is a picture, having clocked that she's thrown me into dangerous territory. 'Just the way the world is right now. So much bad stuff going on, but also people being so self-involved. You know, obsessed with selfies, glued to their phones, living in a bubble. They don't see the world as it really is. It's sad because if everyone took a moment, it would make such a difference overall – hence the title.'

'"Take a Moment".' Sammy nods thoughtfully. 'I get it. Love it. How does it go?'

They're all looking at me expectantly. My first instinct is to shy away from the attention, then I remember that I'm a lead vocalist now. I need to step up. I take a stomach-expanding breath and tentatively start to sing, in a very light melody.

> *We grow up unassuming, we grow up unaware*
> *We live in a world where too many people, they don't care*
> *Take a look around you, tell me what you see*
> *Illness, conflict, suffering, too much poverty…*

Sammy joins in and I'm amazed by how quickly his ear tunes in to the song. He lets me take the lead where there's a change of direction he can't anticipate, but otherwise it's like we're singing a perfectly rehearsed duet.

> *Then stop, take a moment to reflect, make sure you have it noted*
> *You've made a selfless gesture in a world where self-indulgence is promoted…*

As we sing out the chorus and come to a finish with an enthusiastic high-five, Sasha and Matt break into rapturous applause.

'That was awesome, Alex.' Sammy grins at me broadly.

'It was,' I reply. 'Not really the type of music the band does though.'

'It's not totally on point. But it shows you can write lyrics as well. We'll definitely need to tap into that.'

'Is there any end to your talents?' Matt puts his arm round me and squeezes me affectionately.

I make a show of laughing bashfully, but the washing machine in my stomach is back on spin cycle in pure undiluted anticipation of the conversation I need to have with him the next day.

Chapter 29

I wake early on Sunday, the nervous churning in my stomach having continued right through a restless night. Matt is still asleep, arm draped across me. I lie and watch him drowsily for a few minutes, just taking in his gorgeous features. Even with his incredible dark chocolate eyes hidden by his slumber, he's still so good to look at, and only I get to see him first thing in the morning.

Gently extricating myself from his hold, I get out of bed and pad through to the kitchen to make myself a cup of tea. I illuminate my phone to check the time and it informs me that I have a WhatsApp message from Dom.

> Lex, I'm so sorry for the way I spoke to you last night. I'd had a few too many and it all came as a shock. My friends didn't say that, not ones that I hold in any high regard anyway. Really hoped you would choose me but I respect your decision, even if I don't like it. Dx

A swell of emotion surges within me, along with the familiar feeling of loss that's hung around me like an annoying fly for several months now. Though I'm moving on and it's been the right decision, I'm still not totally over

Dom. His reappearing in my life like this hasn't helped. I swipe at my tearing eyes and quickly tap out a reply.

> No, I'm sorry, Dom. It was insensitive of me to do that when you were out with your friends. I should have waited and called you today. Take care of yourself. You're an amazing guy and you deserve the absolute best. xx

I hit send and place my phone on the counter top. Within moments, it buzzes a reply.

> The absolute best is you. :(Dx

'Oh, please stop it,' I inadvertently murmur out loud.

'Stop what?' Matt's voice comes from behind me.

I quickly lock my phone and turn to greet him. 'Oh, you're awake.'

'I sure am.' He slips his arms round my waist and pulls me to him. 'It's a bit early though, isn't it? How about we go back to bed and have a rerun of last night?'

As he says this, a delicious memory of the night before runs through my mind: Matt's strong arms around me, the feeling of skin on skin. That certainly diverted my attention from the looming conversation of today. But now the sun is up, I just want to get it over with.

'Sounds lovely.' I reach up and kiss him. 'But I need to talk to you… about the stuff I mentioned last night.'

'Right.' He looks wary all of a sudden. 'Can I grab some coffee first?'

'I'll get you it.'

I make our drinks, then bring them across to the coffee table. Matt scootches along the sofa and I settle down beside him.

'Matt, how would you define *us*?' I ask him suddenly.

He raises a quizzical eyebrow. 'I thought you had something to tell me. This sounds more like "the talk".'

'Please humour me. I need to know before I continue.'

'OK… well, I'd say we're seeing each other. It's early days but I'm keen for it to go somewhere. I haven't "staked my claim" yet, if that's what you're asking?'

I swallow nervously. He's astute. Already cottoned on to the idea that there may be another bloke in the mix.

'I… yes, I guess that is what I'm asking. OK, good. Think we're pretty aligned on that.'

He stays quiet, so I continue.

'When I was on the phone last night, it was to my ex-fiancé. He wants to get back together. He came down here a few weeks ago to tell me and I was left with a really difficult decision.'

'Because you'd only just started seeing me, and he's someone you know inside out.' He wrinkles his nose. 'Hmm, wish I hadn't put it quite like that.'

I clear my throat to stifle a giggle. 'Yes, well, that's pretty much the picture and I've been really confused.'

'Why did you break up? You never said before.'

This question cuts through me so sharply I can almost feel the slice. My stomach bubbles with nausea. This is it. I have to tell him about my MS and once I do, I know he'll never look at me the same again. I take a deep breath, feeling a trembling to my core that quickly extends down my arms right to my fingers.

'We… we broke up because… because… we weren't seeing eye to eye and we never addressed the important stuff. Then it all crept up on us before we could deal with it.'

It's out my mouth before I can stop myself. I can almost see my 'untruth' hanging in the air, taunting me for being such a coward. It's not a complete lie: those elements did factor in my break-up with Dom. I've just omitted the catalyst that brought them to light. Now I have one chance to correct myself and tell the full truth.

'It happens.' Matt shrugs, and it's clear he's not going to probe further. He's too respectful for that. 'So, you're either about to tell me that you've chosen to work through these biggies with him, or you've decided to take a chance on a Brummie lad.'

'You're not angry?' I ask, bewildered.

'Why would I be angry? You had a decision to make, you've clearly made it, and now you're about to communicate the outcome. As an engineering professional, I'm quite satisfied with that process. Nice and logical.'

He casually reaches over, picks up his coffee and takes a slug.

'Right.' I rub my forehead absently. 'So, just to check, you're not mad that I was sort of seeing my ex at the same time as you?'

'I don't really see it that way, Alex. I've said that I hope there's a future for us, but I'm also aware that it's early days, so I don't have any right to take issue with it.'

'Does that mean you've been dating other women?'

'No. One at a time is more than enough for me.'

I'm so relieved to hear this, I almost forget I've left out the most important part of the conversation.

'So, are you going to tell me whether I'm in or out?'

'Yes. Sorry, I…' My stomach lurches uncomfortably, as if giving me a telling-off for not being totally honest, but I just can't do it right now. 'It's you, Matt. I want to see where this can go too. I told Dom – my ex – that I didn't want to get back together. He didn't take it so well.'

'I bet he didn't. Look, I'm sorry you had to work your way through that, and I feel bad for your ex, but I'm so glad you've chosen me.'

He reaches for my hand and threads his fingers through mine, his brown eyes clearly conveying the feelings he's described having for me.

'I am too.' I firmly shut out my nagging conscience.

'Does that mean we're a proper couple then?'

'I guess it does.'

'Well, in that case…' Matt leaps to his feet and scoops me up, grinning like a kid who's won the biggest teddy at the fair '…it's definitely time for round two. If that's OK with you?' he adds, and I laugh as he kisses my nose and heads straight for the bedroom.

-

'You didn't tell him?' Sasha squeaks in disbelief. 'But, Lex, why? That was your big opportunity.'

It's three in the afternoon after a lazy morning in bed with Matt. He's now away scaling a 'small' hill (apparently racing against the sunset), while I'm in Grand Central with Sasha hearing about her fruitless apartment viewings. We're also enjoying a late lunch together before she takes the train back to Glasgow.

'I know that, Sash. I missed it. No. I totally avoided it. Couldn't bear for his view of me to change. And it would, there's no "maybe" in that.'

Sasha looks genuinely pained as she grabs at her noodles with her chopsticks, letting out a huff of frustration as all but one slither back onto her plate.

'You want a fork?' I ask.

'No. I'm going to learn. I'm not taking the easy way out of anything any more.'

'That's good, Sash, but you've been at it for ages and you've barely eaten any. If you don't admit defeat, you'll be making a choice between your new approach to life and your train home.'

'OK, fine. But I'm going to practise.'

'You do that.' I hand her a fork from the cutlery holder on our table.

'Anyway, we were talking about you. I know you don't want Matt to see you differently, but you can't hold this back for ever. The longer you leave it, the more you risk the relationship.'

'You think I don't know all this?' I sink the last of my coconut water. 'I was shaking and I went onto autopilot. I literally couldn't tell him. One of the biggest problems between Dom and me was that he mollycoddled me, he couldn't see past my condition. With Dom, I'm the girl with MS; with Matt, I'm *me*.'

'And you worry that it will go that way with Matt when you tell him.'

'That's if he sticks around long enough for me to find out.'

'I do get it, Lex. But you're now in a relationship that's not open and honest. Leave it much longer and you'll *definitely* lose him.'

I sigh heavily. 'I know. OK, let's stop focusing on my mess and talk about your hot date with Sammy this morning. How was it?'

Her expression immediately turns dreamy. 'It was amazing. He's so bouncy and full of life. Such a sweetheart too.'

'It's like you're describing your mirror image.'

'You know, we are kind of similar. Apart from the band thing. I can't believe I went on a date with the lead guitarist in a band.'

'And now you're having lunch with the lead vocalist.'

'*Right?* It's just so cool, this whole band thing. I want to be a proper groupie. *Sooo* can't wait to move down here. Sammy's already offered to help me move.'

'Wow, he *is* a fast mover. Though as he was imagining your children two minutes after I introduced you, not sure why I'm surprised.'

Sasha beams and turns scarlet. It's so good to see her happy.

'Did you kiss?' I ask.

Her expression deepens to a shade of beetroot. 'We did.'

'It's OK. Matt and I kiss too. It's what grown-ups do.'

'Stop it, Lex.'

Chuckling, I say, 'I'm sorry. I'm done. Promise.'

Sasha purses her lips and looks at me as if she wants to say something but is unsure.

'What is it, Sash? You can talk to me about anything, you know that.'

Sasha squirms a little in her seat. 'I was actually just wondering… you know how you suffer from that fatigue and can't do much by way of exercise…'

'Yeah?'

'Well… how do you… you know, do the deed with Matt without your symptoms getting in the way?'

I let out a snorting laugh as I take in Sasha's cringing, mortified-but-not-enough-to-not-ask-the-question face.

'Let's just say that good sex doesn't need to resemble a gyrating Duracell bunny.'

'Right. Good.' Sasha's now so red her face is almost indistinguishable from her hair.

'Shall we go?' I grin.

'Yes, please.'

Chapter 30

The next day, I'm back in the office, dragging myself around due to an unexpected worsening of my fatigue, my head thick and woolly. My walk to work felt more like a climb, despite the gentleness of the gradient, and I'm a bit clammy, even just sitting in the ambient temperature of the boardroom. It's another of my leadership programme events – a group development day with my fellow participants – so I'm determined to ignore my symptoms and make the most of it.

'Morning, all,' Terrence, our programme facilitator, greets us. 'Today we're going to get our first sense of your practical leadership skills. You'll be split into three groups and each team is going to take on a real-life business challenge. You'll work on this throughout the day, then we'll bring you back together later to present your ideas to John Chambers, your company's chief exec.'

'Sounds like *The Apprentice*.' Danielle's eyes light up in enthusiasm, which I notice triggers some eye-rolling around the room.

'It's not quite as glamorous, I'm afraid, but I guess there are some similarities – we do have our own Karren and Claude, so to speak. I'll be introducing you to them shortly, and I'll be observing the third team myself. This is to provide us with a benchmark for your progress, so please behave as you would normally. It's about leaders with a small "l" – which means there's no need to battle to be team leader.'

A murmur goes around the room as we digest this information.

'I cannot *wait* for this,' Danielle declares.

The rest of us simply share a look of 'which poor bastards are going to end up in a team with her'.

'Right, you four will be one team.' Terrence points at members of the group randomly. 'You… one, two, three, four, will be another, which means those of you who are left will form the final team.'

There are subtle gasps of relief as the members of the first two teams gather together. My heart sinks as I realise that as one of the remaining five, I'm in the same team as Danielle.

'Alex, we're in the same team – *again*.' She flashes me her signature fake smile as we take a seat together. 'So glad we're working together on this.'

'Yeah, great.' I mirror her in response.

The other three unlucky members of our group reluctantly drag their chairs across to us.

'Hey,' I greet them sombrely.

'Hey,' they murmur in unison.

'You lot are cheery,' Danielle huffs, glancing around enviously at the other, more enthusiastic and animated, groups.

'Everything all right over here?' Terrence pulls up a chair to join us.

'This lot are a bit lacking in get-go,' Danielle complains. 'I mean, what kind of team name would describe this set-up? The Dullards? Maybe you should disperse them around the teams.'

Myself and the others freeze, and I can tell we're all feeling the same mix of emotions – shock that she'd actually say that out loud, and mild offence at being described as 'dullards'. Unlike Danielle, Terrence seems to have picked up on exactly what's going on.

'Perhaps they just need some creative brainstorming to get them going, Danielle. Best not to judge up front.'

'Huh.' She sits back and folds her arms. 'No way we're going to win this task then.'

Terrence gives her a warm smile. 'It's not a competition. This is simply about getting a measure of your leadership skills as part of a team dynamic. Leadership with a small "l", remember? Think I'll shadow you five today. How about that?'

All we can muster in response are a collection of unenthusiastic shrugs.

'Right, come on then.' He ups his positivity in an attempt to bring us round. 'Alex, Danielle, why don't you be the first to select your team challenge? There are three different scenarios pinned to the whiteboard. Have a read and decide between you which challenge your group will take on today.'

We obediently get to our feet and head to the whiteboard. As we do, Danielle mutters something under her breath. My first instinct is to ignore her, but as we're going to have to work together, whether we like it or not, I decide I need to make some sort of effort.

'You OK?' I ask.

'Oh, it's nothing.'

'You sure? Problem shared and all.'

We start to read through the scenarios on the whiteboard, but Danielle clearly can't help herself.

'I was just thinking…' She lowers her voice. 'This room, it's not very reflective of the society we live in, is it?'

'What do you mean?' I wonder if she's going to come out with something truly insightful for once.

'Look around you. There's almost as many people on this programme from ethnic backgrounds as there are who would tick "White British" on a form.'

'Sorry… what?'

'I'm not being racist or anything. It's just that this whole equality thing seems to be going too far. Take the demographic breakdown of the UK: the majority of people are still white, yet about half this room is not.'

Danielle raises her eyebrows in a gesture of 'just look around and you'll see', and then fixes her attention on the challenges pinned to the board by different coloured magnets.

Her words trickle through my consciousness like bitter, seeping filter coffee. Her comment is completely inappropriate, another clue to her values. She doesn't approve of homelessness, and it now appears she's not a fan of diversity-friendly environments, even when everyone on this programme got onto it through merit alone – other than her.

I begin to wonder if she'd be just as scathing of my disability and the support I've had. I can certainly imagine a similar statement coming out of her mouth. This stabbing realisation, alongside the fact that I'm struggling a bit today, unfortunately propels me to lose my patience with her.

'You do realise, Danielle,' I say quietly, 'that if you have to start a sentence with a disclaimer, it probably means you're behaving exactly the way you claim not to be.'

She stops reading the information and stares at me coldly. 'I didn't mean anything by it, it was just an observation. Jeez, who made you diversity police?'

'We all have a responsibility to live by the values of this company, Danielle. Even more so as potential future leaders here on this programme.'

'Want me to remove that poker from your arse, Alex? Or can you manage yourself? You're already on the programme, no need for your little act any more.'

'Excuse me?' I feel my body flood with angry tension in response to her bitchy remark.

'Oh, don't pull that with me,' she sneers. 'You make me sick with this Mother-Teresa-of-the-project-management-world thing you've got going on. You and Emmanuel: the way you trot around together like some kind of world-saving sisterhood. You've got skeletons the same as everyone else in life. *No one's* perfect.'

'Wow, that's probably the first accurate statement you've made today. You're right, I'm not perfect, but I do try my best – and that involves getting on with people and supporting them, no matter what walk of life they're from.'

She narrows her eyes at me. 'Bullshit. You hated me from the moment you met me. *I'm* from a different walk of life – in case you haven't noticed. It just happens to be a better one than you. That's how life worked out. You can't hold it against me.'

'I don't. But what I *do* hold against you is how you behave because of it and the fact you got "Daddy" to get you a place on this programme.'

I'm shaking inside as I deliver this cutting statement, knowing full well I've let myself down. After months of holding my own with Danielle, I've allowed her to properly get to me, and I feel wretched about it. Especially as I'm here on a programme where I'm supposed to be demonstrating the very best of myself.

'Everything all right, ladies?' Terrence appears beside us before Danielle can spit back a response, but I can see from her face that she's furious.

'Yes, fine. We'll take…' I quickly scan the three challenges and pull one off the whiteboard. '…the culture change one. Seems really interesting: looking at our behaviours and what we stand for as an organisation. Right, Danielle?'

Danielle doesn't miss the underlying message in my choice of task, but all she says in response is 'whatever', then she flounces back across to the group.

'Do I need to be concerned about you two?' Terrence asks me quietly.

'No. It's fine.' I shake my head, the trembling finally starting to settle. 'She got to me there, I won't lie. But I can deal with her.'

'OK, then. I'm aware of the politics here, and I'm also tuned in to how everyone is feeling about it.'

'It just doesn't reflect what this is supposed to be about, and I think that's bothering people.'

'I know. Good thing you're all going to become great leaders who will protect that in the future. Your current CEO won't be around for ever, you know.'

It's a verbal nudge, which makes me chuckle.

'I'm ambitious, Terrence, but CEO is a stretch.'

He looks at me questioningly. 'Why is that? From what I've seen – perhaps minus the last five minutes, but we all have our moments – you're absolutely the kind of leader an organisation like this needs as CEO. Don't let the sexual inequality of our current society stand in the way of that.'

'Oh, don't worry, I'm not.'

I return to my seat, his words echoing in my mind. It's not being a woman that will limit my career. Probably more what physical state I'd be in by the time I got close to an opportunity like that. And whether the likes of Danielle can successfully sabotage my career ambitions long before then.

Chapter 31

On Tuesday morning, my alarm goes off at seven a.m. as usual, but it's far from a normal day. The first thing I notice is a slightly disoriented feeling. Still drowsy from waking, I'm momentarily confused, until I try to sit up and it's like a car has parked on my torso. I gasp and strain but no matter how hard I try to force myself to sit up, my body will not cooperate. Exhausted and out of breath, I let my muscles relax and stare at the ceiling in consternation.

'Shit,' I cry out loud. 'What's going on?'

I lie there for another few moments, trying to tune in to what I'm feeling. I'm very weak and also clammy again, like yesterday. It's like the car didn't just park on top of me; it ran me over first – at high speed. With my attempts to sit up thwarted, I change tactics and attempt to exit the bed sideways. Putting everything I have into it, and using my body weight as a lever, I eventually manage to roll over on my side and slide out of the bed onto my knees. It's as if I've attempted a marathon with zero training. I crouch there, panting heavily, sweat beads gathering on my forehead. My head swims and I have to grab at the bed frame to stop me from toppling over.

'Oh, shit,' I cry again. 'Shit. Shit. *Shit.*'

I reach across and grab my phone from my bedside table. After I've caught my breath again, I google 'MS relapse'. The list of symptoms in the top search result immediately confirms my worst fears. That's what this is. I'm having another relapse. After months of hard work to get back on my feet and having a life again, I'm back to square one.

'*No*,' I wail. 'This is not happening. I've got a project team meeting this morning. I need to be there.'

Clutching the bed frame, I attempt to stand up, but halfway to my feet I'm overbalancing again, my legs buckling from sheer exhaustion. I allow myself to fall forwards onto my bed. Then I use the last of my energy to pull my legs up, so I'm at least lying down again.

Shit, this is bad. What the hell am I going to do? One thing's for sure, I'm not going to work today. I'm not going anywhere at all. I can't even make it to my own kitchen.

As this thought crystallises, I realise that not getting to work should be the least of my worries. How am I going to drink? Eat? Go to the toilet? I'm in serious trouble here – exactly the kind of trouble my mother and sister predicted. I can't call Matt; he doesn't know about any of this and I'd be mortified if he found me in this state. There's no way I'm calling my family and letting them gloat – because that's what they'd focus on, not actually helping me. Sasha's miles away, and anyway has to be at work herself. I realise I have no choice. I'm going to have to call a doctor. But first, there's another call I need to make and I'm completely dreading it.

'Morning, Alex.' I hear Emmanuel's kind and jolly voice in my ear after two rings. 'Everything all right?'

I go to speak but nothing comes out. Shame and mortification settle over me like a thick woollen blanket.

'Alex? Are you all right?' Emmanuel's voice changes to one of concern. 'Talk to me. *Can* you talk to me?'

Tears prick at my eyes as I realise I must say the words out loud. I can't stay mute on a call. Emmanuel will end up calling the emergency services.

'I… I've had a relapse.'

There's a momentary silence as Emmanuel digests this. 'Oh, sweetheart. I'm so sorry. Are you at home?'

'Yes.'

'In bed?'

'Yes.'

'OK, good. That's where you need to stay. How bad is it – on a scale of one to ten?'

I consider playing it down, but where's that going to get me? If this is anything like my last relapse, I'm going to have to fess up pretty quickly. And what scares me is that at this particular moment, it feels a lot worse.

'It's a ten.'

'OK, sweetheart. First thing – I don't want you to worry about work at all. We were prepared for this. We took you on knowing it would happen at some point.'

'But it's not "some point". It's too soon after my last one. I've only been with you a few months. Thought I'd get to a year, maybe even two, before this kind of setback.' I flinch at how pathetic I sound.

'And you may have that period of remission in the future, you know that. But we need to deal with what's happening now. Alex, I know you're on your own down here, so I hope you don't mind if I ask you this: are you able to get out of bed?'

My throat tightens with emotion and the tears finally overflow, tracking their way down my cheeks. 'No.'

'OK, that means you need some help. Do you have anyone you can call? What about your boyfriend, Matt is it?'

Matt's gorgeous face flits through my mind.

'I can call the doctor,' I say in a small voice.

There's a pause. 'He doesn't know, does he?'

'No.'

'OK, I tell you what. I'm going to come to your apartment and be there with you until—'

'Emmanuel, no. You have work to do. I don't want to set you back too.'

I also don't want her to see me like this.

'Alex, *nothing* is more important right now than this. Plus – and I don't want to upset you – I'm going to have to contact your letting agent to ask for a spare key. If you're unable to get out of bed, you're not going to be able to let me or a doctor in.'

This realisation hits me hard. She's right. I've allowed myself to get into a ridiculous situation, all because I was determined to be independent and live my best life. Now I'm experiencing the humiliating result of that decision.

'No, please don't, Emmanuel. I can try again. It may be worse because I've just woken up.'

'Alex, there's nothing to be—'

'Please, Emmanuel. Let me try first.'

There's another short pause. 'All right. But I'm going to stay on the phone. Please don't overdo it and get yourself into a worse situation.'

'I won't.' I put the phone onto loudspeaker and place it beside me. 'Can you hear me?'

'I can hear you.'

'OK, let me try this.'

I repeat my previous movement, straining to roll over and then sort of falling out of the bed. By the time I'm on my knees again, gasping for breath, I know there's no way I can make it to the door, not even by pulling myself across the floor.

'Alex, you sound like you're struggling.' Emmanuel's concerned voice comes through the speakerphone. 'Please stop, and give me your address.'

Admitting defeat, I relay this information to her, then when she's disconnected the call I put my head in my hands in despair. I no longer care whether I can get back into bed or not. After the high of the weekend, my life has just reached its lowest point yet.

–

By lunchtime, I've experienced the humiliation of a woman from my letting agent coming to my apartment to let my boss in, having to use a makeshift bedpan with Emmanuel's help, and then being carted out to a waiting ambulance strapped to a wheelchair. I'm now lying on a hospital trolley in a cubicle of the A&E department of the Queen Elizabeth Hospital Birmingham. Emmanuel has returned to work, but has promised to visit in the evening.

'How are you doing, Alex?' The nurse who's been attending to me whips back the blue and white horizontally striped curtain and enters my cubicle.

'OK, I guess.' I fiddle with my phone absently.

'We're arranging a bed in neurology for you, and you'll be taken for an MRI scan soon.' She prods my ear with a digital thermometer, then reads the output on the device. 'You're still running a fever. I'll give you something shortly to bring your temperature down.'

'Sure.'

She stops and looks at me. 'I know you came in with your manager, but is there anyone else I can contact for you? Parents? Husband-slash-partner? Any other family members?'

'No, thanks. I'm fine.'

'You shouldn't be coping with this alone.'

'I'm fine. Honestly.'

'All right then. I'll leave you in peace.'

She disappears out of the cubicle and I start scrolling absently through Twitter. As I do so, a banner appears at the top of the screen signalling a text message from Matt. I immediately click it open.

> Morning, gorgeous. What are you up to tonight? I know I'll see you tomorrow for band rehearsals, but I'm keen to have you all to myself for an evening. How about I come over with some healthy takeaway food? x

Ordinarily this message would have made my stomach perform a double somersault and fill with happy, fluttery butterflies. Today all I feel is empty loss as my decision to conceal my illness finally catches up with me. The stark realisation that I've been kidding myself is like a sharp kick to the guts. Matt, the band, my big career. I can't sustain any of it. It was all just a fantasy. Emmanuel says my job is safe, but for how long? How can they keep me on if I suffer two relapses a year? And the leadership programme – there's no question; I can't continue with that.

I'm aware that I shouldn't leave Matt hanging but, unable to give him the answer he's looking for, I'm at a loss as to how to respond. I don't want this to be the end, but what choice do I have? He's been open about hoping there's a future for us. But he's also been really clear about the type of future he wants: that rosy picture of the two of us scaling hills together, with our adorable kids and a couple of dogs. An active outdoorsy family. It sounds wonderful, but it's not a future I could ever be part of.

With frustrated tears in my eyes, I quickly tap out a message and hit send.

> I'm afraid I can't do tonight. Think this is all moving too fast and I'm just not ready for it. I'm so sorry, Matt. Please tell Sammy I'm sorry but the band is all too much for me too. xx

I put my phone down beside me face down and close my eyes in a bid to stop the relentless tears. After a few minutes it buzzes, signalling his response. I almost can't bear to read it, but I'm unable to help myself.

> If that's what you want. Comes as a bit of a shock but I have to respect your decision. Shame because I saw such an amazing future for us. x

'I know. But it wasn't real,' I whisper through my tears.

I'm suddenly overcome with grief for everything I lost when I found out I was ill – and everything I've just lost all over again.

Chapter 32

By early evening, I've been moved to the neurology ward. Due to staff shortages, my MRI scan and visit from the consultant have been delayed until the next day. It's a dismal environment: a large shared room that smells of disinfectant, with some very poorly inhabitants (myself included, unfortunately). A repetitive frustrated cry accompanied by loud banging floats along the corridor from one of the other ward rooms: clearly a very distressed patient. As I learned from my first stint in this type of ward, neurological disease is one of the cruellest forms of illness.

I'm surveying my rubbery cheese and tomato omelette disdainfully when Emmanuel walks through the door. I place the heat cover back on my untouched meal and push the tray table as far away as my weak, fatigued body will allow me to.

'Hi, Alex.' She greets me warmly, her face full of sympathy. 'How are you doing now?'

'Basically the same,' I grimace, trying to control the wobble in my voice.

'Have you been seen by a consultant yet?'

'No. Tomorrow afternoon, they said. After I've had my scan in the morning.'

'I see. Well, please let me know how that goes.'

'I will. How was your day? Once you actually got there.'

Emmanuel sits on one of the chairs beside my bed.

'Alex, please don't feel guilty or embarrassed about this morning. A big part of my job is to look after the wellbeing of my team members. You'll learn more about that – and how important it is – on your programme.'

'I won't really though, will I?'

These words are the final nail for me. The emotion I've been trying so hard to suppress spills over in a huge sob, quickly followed by another and another.

'Hey. Come now.' Emmanuel grabs some tissues from the box on my bedside cabinet and hands them to me. 'What's on your mind? You've only been ill for one day and you don't have all the information yet.'

'I've been here before, Emmanuel. It took me two months to get back on my feet then and this feels much worse. Last time, I could at least get out of bed, make it to the toilet myself – it was exhausting, but I could do it. Look at me now. I'm using a bedpan because I can't even do that.'

Relentless tears pour down my cheeks at the injustice of it all.

'I know, Alex. I can see you're really not well. All I'm saying is that we don't have all the answers yet so let's not fill in the blanks ourselves.'

I stare ahead of me miserably. 'Emmanuel, whatever this is, it's been a wake-up call for me. I've taken on too much. Tried to pretend that nothing's wrong and I've been kidding myself.'

'You've had a positive and pragmatic approach to managing your illness, Alex. Making the most of opportunities that have come to you. I don't consider that to be "kidding yourself". Your application through New Horizons was a move that was well thought through and you've been keeping an active lifestyle, which is important for a person with chronic illness. What's the alternative? You lock yourself away from the world?'

'I don't know. But I've pushed myself so hard. I'm ambitious and I knew if I couldn't fulfil that urge, it would make me unhappy.'

'Which proves once again that you've thought all this through.'

'Yes, but why couldn't I be happy just having a good job? Why did I need the leadership programme? And the band? What if adding all of that has caused this? The gig was on Saturday and now look at me. I just need to accept that I can't do everything I want to do.'

Emmanuel takes my hand in hers, which could feel weird with her being my boss, but surprisingly it doesn't.

'Alex, please listen to me. You're panicking and you're jumping to conclusions. You told me just yesterday, after the team event, that the singing was really good for you because it made you so happy and it gave you energy. You felt "almost unstoppable", you said. You were also pleased with how the group task and your presentation to the CEO went – despite the fact you were obviously under par, as I now realise – and you had to deal with Danielle being so difficult. All these things were positives until this happened.'

I know she's right. I've U-turned dramatically since things went south this morning; but I have good reason. There will be no place for me in the band or on the leadership programme if I can't be there to take part. Someone else should have the opportunity. Someone more reliable.

'Have you spoken to Matt yet?' Emmanuel asks.

'We're not together any more.'

'Oh? He hasn't broken up with you because of this, has he?'

'No.' I stare at the floor miserably. 'I was lying to him. He would have walked when he found out anyway.'

'Alex. You have this all worked out in your head. But you're making decisions for other people without letting them make their own choices.'

'Better that than him telling me it's over.' I shrug.

'Look, I understand, I really do. But if this man is half the person you've described to me, he may not react in the way you're assuming.'

'He will, believe me, I've seen it before. Doesn't matter how good a person he is. My ex, Dom, went all weird over it and it finished us. Matt's got the perfect excuse: he can't trust me. He doesn't even have to admit it's because of my MS. Wouldn't blame him one bit.'

Emmanuel exhales heavily. 'All right, this is your choice. But at least think it through. Promise me that.'

'OK, I promise.'

I know full well I'm going to do nothing of the sort. Matt's had a lucky escape, just like Dom. He may not know it right now, but he'll be better off without me.

My phone buzzes beside me on the bed. I pick it up, seeing it's from an unknown number, and read the message on my screen.

Your secret is out. Knew you were a fraud.

'What the…' I stare in horror at the words on the screen.

'Alex? What is it?'

I look at Emmanuel vacantly, then come to. 'It's…an anonymous message. What did you tell the team about me being off today?'

'I told them you were unwell.'

'That's all?'

'Absolutely. Alex, why are you asking this? What does this message say?'

I hand the phone to Emmanuel, now shaking with panic. She reads the message, her face grave.

'Do you have any idea who sent this?'

'I… can hazard a guess. Danielle.'

Emmanuel looks thoughtful, then pulls out her work phone, looks something up and studies the two phones side by side. 'You're right. I have her number in my phone for the business continuity call tree.' She hands my phone back to me.

'But, how does she know? How *can* she know?'

'I can think of only one way. But it may be hard to prove.'

'How?'

'She's got a friend in HR. But by sharing the inform-, ation, her friend would be putting her career at risk. I do wonder if she'd be willing to do that.'

A thought comes to me. 'This friend in HR. Is she tall, slim, blond?'

'That's her. Have you met her?'

'I had an unfortunate run-in with the two of them one day on the canal bridge. She certainly didn't come across well.'

'That may well be the source of the leak then. Alex, leave this with me. This is very serious indeed.'

I'm still shaking, but anger has begun to flare inside me. 'Wait. She hasn't said anything specific. We don't have proof that she knows anything. I'm going to reply and ask what she knows.'

'All right, I'll be back in a few minutes,' Emmanuel informs me, and leaves my side.

I'm physically exhausted and my mind is foggy, but some of my determination has returned. If Danielle has accessed this information through her friend, the pair of them must be stopped before they out me to the whole company. I slowly tap out a message and hit send.

> Who is this? What is it you think you know about me?

I'm distracted waiting for a response from Danielle. If I have her worked out the way I think I do, she won't be able to resist the chance to try to demolish me. A minute or so later, I receive a reply. I'm right.

> That you're a charity case. Got your job through some special scheme. That's why you get special treatment. Now everyone knows you're a fraud.

I've got the evidence I need, but all I can focus on is the last line of the message. Everyone knows? That means it's too late. She's destroyed my reputation. The inner trembling intensifies and I battle the urge to cry at everything falling down around me. I should never have faced up to her yesterday; it made her want revenge: a dangerous thing with a personality like Danielle's.

Emmanuel re-enters the room and her face tells me what she's about to say before she can say a word.

'It's gone public.'

She gives a pained nod. 'I've just spoken with one of my managerial counterparts. It seems a WhatsApp group was set up earlier today from an anonymous number – not Danielle's. It contains information about your medical situation and how you were hired into the organisation.'

I feel like I'm about to pass out. 'Who was it sent to?'

'All of our team – except me – and about twenty other members of staff across the organisation. One of them forwarded it to my colleague out of concern.'

'Shit. *Shit*. This can't be happening. Sorry for swearing.'

'Alex, swear all you like. This is beyond what I ever thought Danielle to be capable of. I will do my very best to make sure she incurs the most serious consequences for this. Did you get a reply to your message?'

I hand her my phone and she reads Danielle's reply.

'But Emmanuel, if this turns into something huge and Danielle is disciplined or even fired, I will get the back-lash. It might be seen as further proof that I get "special treatment". I don't… there's no other option… I'm going to have to leave.'

At these words, Emmanuel looks like she's about to go into orbit. 'Alex, you are going nowhere. This lies firmly at Danielle's door.'

'It doesn't matter. The information is still out there. Now my every move will be scrutinised and questioned. Nothing will ever be seen as a *true* achievement.'

'That's not true, Alex, and I think I can prove it.' She picks up her phone again and unlocks it. 'The person I spoke to sent me some screenshots. She kept them as evidence. Take a look.'

I take the phone from her. A series of screenshots show the original message – which is so cruel it makes me gasp, causing tears to well in my eyes once again – as well as the replies from various people. Every single one is condemning Danielle's message, and expressing full support for me. I read one response after the next, saying how I'm one of the most talented project managers they've come across; how, if that's what I've been up against, I deserve to be where I am more than anyone else; and how I'm a total inspiration. I become so completely overwhelmed by this that the sobs come once more, this time so thick and fast that a passing nurse stops to check I'm all right.

Emmanuel sits with me quietly, allowing me to work through the jumble of emotions I'm feeling, until I'm calm enough to have a coherent conversation again.

'Sorry.' I'm embarrassed as I remember that this is my boss I'm with.

'You have nothing to be sorry for, Alex.' She stays and chats about lighter things for a while longer until it eventually dawns on me that she won't have had anything to eat.

'Emmanuel, it's nearly seven p.m. You'll need to get your dinner. Why don't you head off and I'll call you tomorrow once I've seen the consultant?'

'All right. I am needing to see to a few things. I'm glad you're feeling a bit calmer.' She gets up from her chair. 'I'll come by tomorrow after work again.'

'You don't have to do that.' I feel tremendously guilty that Emmanuel is having to fill the gap that would other- wise be filled by family or close friends.

'Enough. I want to come and see you. And I could get some more things from your apartment – that is, if you're happy for me to do that? We didn't manage to pack much yesterday.'

'Only if it's not too much trouble.'

'It's not at all. I can nip there straight after work before coming here. It's not much of a diversion.'

'OK, sure. I'd really appreciate having my iPad. Maybe some more comfortable clothes. Also, my toiletries bag in the bathroom is the one I use when I swim. It's got everything I need in it.'

'Not a problem. I'll see you tomorrow then. Chin up. This will pass.' She gives my hand a squeeze, before heading out of the ward.

Once she's gone, it's not long before unhelpful thoughts start to plague me. Danielle has really messed things up. Though I seem to have everyone's support, they're all going to see me differently now, probably even treat me differently. While this huge worry is taking up space in my mind, a big bubble of sadness is also competing for space. My career has been compromised, but Matt's gone from my life for good. Memories of our time together flood my mind: our first date; the walk in the woods; all the other amazing meals out and nights in since. The way he kissed me, his touch, those eyes. Now, all gone as if it never happened. It's all too much to bear. I pick up my phone and dial Sasha.

–

I have very little sleep overnight: partly due to the constant noise of the ward and in part because of the vast feeling of emptiness that's been gnawing at me since my break-up with Matt. I'm also very worried about how long it's going to take me to get back on my feet and how I'm going to manage on my own once I'm discharged from hospital.

I'm taken for my MRI scan around nine a.m. and then delivered back to the ward. The exhaustion finally overcomes me, and I sleep into the early afternoon. I'm not long awake and am picking at my lunch when a petite middle-aged woman with long dark hair pulled into a ponytail enters the room.

'Alex? Good afternoon, I'm Dr Kasani. How are you feeling today?'

'Much the same, unfortunately,' I reply.

'Can you tell me what happened yesterday? And a bit more about what symptoms you've been experiencing?'

I give her a comprehensive run-down, which she listens to intently. She's very focused. There's no peripheral chat.

'Do you mind if I do some physical checks?' she asks once I'm done.

'Of course.'

She performs the same tests I experienced while in hospital in Glasgow and several times after that during my outpatient appointments. Some of it is painfully difficult given my current predicament.

'OK, Alex,' she says eventually. 'I think I've put you through enough for now. I have good news for you.'

'Oh?'

'From reviewing your MRI scan and listening to your description of your symptoms, I do not think that this is a relapse.'

'What?' I look at her in confusion. 'If it's not a relapse, what *is* wrong with me? Because this is not normal.'

'You have a viral infection – probably one of the winter bugs that's doing the rounds – which, I believe, has exacerbated your existing symptoms.'

'Are… you sure? I can't get out of bed. I can barely move. And I don't really have a sore throat or anything.'

'I am quite sure. These viruses come in many guises. You are running a fever, so my guess is a flu-like illness. Your MRI scan also shows no change from the last one. All this suggests to me this is not a relapse.'

'So, once the virus runs its course, I'll be OK?'

'I expect you will be back to how you are normally. But it might take a couple of weeks. You must also contact your doctor if you do not recover in this timeframe, but I would be very surprised if this were the case.'

As I take all this in, it's like I've been handed my life back. 'Thank you, Doctor. You've no idea how good this news is.'

'I have delivered this message many times over, so I have a fair idea.' She gives me a warm smile. 'We are going to keep you in for two to three nights to monitor your progress. I would also like you to see our occupational therapy department while you are here. My understanding is that you do not have a care plan in place. Creating one will help you cope better when a similar situation arises in the future.'

'That's fine. One thing I like in life is an effective plan.'

'I will get that organised then and hopefully the unit will see you tomorrow. I will also arrange for you to have the annual flu vaccination to reduce the risk of these events in the future. A serious flu can trigger a relapse, so we wish to avoid that where possible.'

'Sure. Thank you. I think the doctor in Glasgow did mention that but I must have forgotten about it.'

'It is a lot to take in when you are newly diagnosed. Now, please can I ask you to have a think about who might be able to offer you some support? We cannot discharge you until we know you have someone to help you manage, or that you can manage yourself; you are a bit away from that. I will pop by tomorrow to see how you are getting on.'

Dr Kasani lifts the folder at the end of my bed and scribbles down some notes, then gives me a quick nod and moves to the bed two down from mine for her next patient consultation.

I lie back and close my eyes, letting the reality of the situation sink in. It's not a relapse. Hopefully it means I can get back to work in a couple of weeks, rather than a few months as I had first feared. But my positivity is short-lived as the other developments of the last twenty-four hours creep back into my consciousness. With Danielle having stuck the knife in and given it a damn good twist, what kind of work environment will I be going back to? One like it was back in Glasgow? Emmanuel won't remove me from my role, I'm confident about that. But what about everyone else?

And that's just work. I'll no longer have Matt to brighten my evenings and weekends – or the band. Wonderful, gorgeous Matt. With whom I now realise, without doubt, I have fallen completely in love. An empty, sick feeling develops in the pit of my stomach.

To take my mind off my broken heart, I decide to update Emmanuel on my situation. I send her a text instead of calling, just in case she's in the middle of something. She replies quickly.

Sorry, in a meeting but that's great news.
See you in a few hours. E

With that done and nothing else to focus on, I close my eyes once again in the hope that sleep will come and rescue me.

Chapter 33

A couple of hours later, I'm wakened by a bustle of activity, signalling the start of visiting hours. Feeling groggy and not yet switched on, I don't see the person approaching until they're standing right at the foot of my bed. I look up and gasp.

'Matt?'

'Hey there,' he replies softly.

'What are you... how did you...?'

I instinctively swipe at my mouth to make sure I haven't drooled in my sleep, then try to sit up. But I do it too quickly and immediately receive a stark warning from the lead weight that is my body.

'Don't try to get up. I'll come to you.' Matt moves round the bed and takes a seat beside me.

It's so good to see his face, but I'm totally confused as to what's happening.

'How did you know I was here?'

'I went to your apartment after work because I couldn't get my head around why you called things off like that. No real explanation – and by text message. I wanted to hear it face to face but then your boss answered. She told me you were here.'

I swallow nervously. 'Did she tell you *why* I'm here?'

'No. She said that was for you to share. But she did say there was something I needed to hear. Alex, what's going on? Why are you in a neurology ward?'

I blink through stinging, glassy eyes. 'Because… oh, this is so hard…' I take a deep breath and bite the bullet. 'I have MS, Matt. I woke up yesterday really unwell and I thought it was a relapse, but it's a viral infection that's caused my symptoms to flare up.'

'Right. Shit.' Matt hangs his head, taking this in. 'Why didn't you tell me?'

'I wanted to. Actually, that's not true. I *didn't* want to. At first, when we were casually dating, it felt too soon to mention it. We barely knew each other. But when things got more serious between us, I knew I had left it too long. I nearly brought it up when I told you about Dom at the weekend.'

'You said then you had a couple of things you needed to talk to me about. But you only mentioned him.'

'I knew it would change things, probably end our relationship, so I bottled it.'

Matt lifts his gaze to meet mine and my stomach squirms nervously in response. It's almost unbearable. I can't take his pity, his expression of sympathy as he makes his excuses.

'You thought I'd walk away.'

I wring my hands anxiously. 'Yes. But I wouldn't blame you. Who would want to sign up for a lifetime with someone this broken? With all the complications and limitations that it brings. Who wants to commit to that?'

'Maybe *I* do. You never gave me the chance to decide.'

'Matt, please. Don't do that. You know as well as I do how unlikely that is.'

'Why is it so unlikely, Alex? Because that's how things go in your head? People weigh up the logic and arrive at the obvious solution. Is that how you make your own decisions?'

'I...' I look away, unable to respond.

'In deciding how I was going to react, you missed a few important factors. Like the fact that you're different to any woman I've ever met – in such a good way. You're beautiful, inside and out. As clichéd as that sounds, it's true. And I've already fallen totally and completely in love with you.'

My heart starts to pound in my chest as I look back towards him and meet his eye. 'What did you just say?'

'I love you. I know it's fast, but it's true. So, if you want to call things off because you think you're going to be a burden on me, or some nonsense like that, feel free. But know that it will be on you. I'm not walking away.'

I stare at him in astonishment, unable to speak.

'You wrote in your song about a world where there's so much hardship,' Matt continues. 'How you want people to care for others, not just themselves. "*You've made a selfless gesture in a world where self-indulgence is promoted.*" Why talk about wanting change that you yourself won't accept? I want to care for you, Alex. I want to be your rock. Your MS is part of who you are and as much as I hate that this is happening to you, that's not what I'd see every morning when I wake up to you. I'd see an amazing woman who's full of spirit and determination. I'd be proud that you'd chosen me to share your life with and we'd face it together.'

As he finishes his wonderful tirade, tears spill down my cheeks. I'm trying so hard to keep it together but it's just too much.

'Do you really mean that? You're not just feeling sorry for me? Because if you've got any doubt in your mind whatsoever—'

'Seriously? Is what I just said not enough to convince you? What do you want – a proposal?'

'Sorry. *Definitely* not. Way too soon for that.' An involuntary giggle escapes from my mouth.

He's right. So right. I decided how he would react to my situation and in doing so, I overlooked the connection between us, the feelings he has for me. I took the experiences I had with my family and Dom and applied the same formula. But Matt's not them, he's different. He's just played his hand and there was some tough love in there. That's not a guy who's going to mollycoddle me and try to stop me from living my best life.

'So, what happens now?' I ask.

'What happens is this.'

He gets up from his seat, leans in and kisses me, his hand cradling the back of my head as he does. He tastes so delicious, it takes me about thirty seconds to tune in to reality. I pull away from him suddenly.

'Wait, I've got a flu virus. You shouldn't be coming near me. You'll catch it.'

'It's worth the risk.' He starts to lean in again.

'I've also not had a shower for two days. I must be totally disgusting.'

'Have you brushed your teeth today?'

'Yes, the nurses helped me by bringing a basin.'

'That's good enough for me.' He swoops in and kisses me again before I can protest any more.

I loop my weak, exhausted arms round Matt's neck, luxuriating in his closeness, his beard tickling my face. I can't help worrying that I'm dreaming and I'm about to wake up to the depressing reality of a few hours ago. This was an impossible scenario then. But now it's all real.

'Oi, no kissing on the ward,' the nurse who's been looking after me calls as she makes her way past. We pull apart suddenly and she starts to laugh. 'I'm only kidding. What do you think this is – prison? Nice to see you smiling, Alex.'

Matt and I chuckle in embarrassment.

'Feels a bit like being in prison. Though it just got a bit more bearable.' I beam adoringly at Matt, who reflects the same expression right back at me.

'So how long til you're better? When can you get out of here?' Matt asks.

I bite my lip, unsure how to answer that.

'Spit it out, Alex.'

'It'll probably take about two weeks to get back on my feet properly. The doctor said I can go home when I'm able to look after myself or when I have someone to support me.'

He looks thoughtful for a second. 'Right, well that's sorted then. I'm breaking you out of here.'

'I have to stay at least another couple of nights though. To see an occupational therapy specialist tomorrow and for them to monitor me.'

'Fair enough. But as soon as they say you're safe to leave, I'm taking you home.'

'To my home or yours?' I grin at him.

'Where would you like to be?'

'Probably mine. All my stuff is there.'

'Fine by me. I travel light.'

As he says this, another thought pops into my mind and my body chills. 'Matt, you do realise I'll probably never be able to climb your beloved hills with you? I can't give you your dream future. That worries me because it's so important to you.'

He looks at me as if I've lost the plot completely. 'You do know I'm not Bear Grylls, right?'

'Ha ha. Don't take the piss.'

'Alex, I've got lots of people I can climb hills with. That picture of the future was never a deal-breaker. There are other things we can enjoy together. And some of those I *definitely* can't do with those other people – not without ending up with a black eye or in jail.' He gives me a cheeky wink and I try to bat his forearm playfully, but instead end up panting like a tired dog.

'Thank goodness for Emmanuel. If she hadn't stopped by my apartment after work...' I tail off, unwilling to entertain this alternative ending.

'That reminds me, I was to give you this.' Matt points to a plastic bag containing my iPad, clothes and toiletries.

'Thanks. And thanks for... being you.'

'I do my best. So, a couple of days then. And once you're properly better, you can go back to band rehearsals. I hadn't yet passed on your message to Sammy.' He looks pleased to be able to tell me this.

'Oh, Matt, no. I'm going to have to pull out of the band. And the leadership programme at work. I need to start being realistic about what I can cope with. There's being determined, and there's self-destructive stubbornness. If I push myself too hard, I leave myself vulnerable to more infections like this.'

Matt searches my eyes briefly before shrugging. 'That's a shame, Sammy will be gutted. But I understand how you feel.'

'Thanks. Now, is there anywhere you can get me a huge chocolate bar? Now that I've finally woken up from my craziness, I'm really hankering after one.'

–

By Friday afternoon, I'm sitting in a hospital wheelchair with my things balanced on my lap, ready for Matt to transport me to his car. It feels a bit weird and I'm a little self-conscious using it. But the alternative was for Matt to lug me to the car park like a sack of potatoes, which was even less appealing. Plus, using wheelchairs from time to time is something I'm possibly going to have to get used to, so I just need to suck it up.

'That you all sorted and ready to go, Alex?' the shift nurse asks me.

'Yes, not sure why we're still here. Are we going, Matt?' I prompt him impatiently. 'I can't wait to get out of here. No offence, Nurse Colmes.'

'None taken at all.' She smiles at me kindly. 'It's great to see you looking a bit brighter already. Our aim is always to get you home to your loved ones.'

As she says this, Matt and I share a goofy loved-up grin.

'So, are we going?' My gooeyness is short-lived.

'You may be physically done in but your cognitive functions are clearly recovering already.' Matt pats my head affectionately, causing me to scowl like a grumpy bulldog – a playful quirk of our newly blossoming relationship. 'Just two more minutes.'

'Two more minutes for what? We've got everything.'

'Think you're going to have your hands full,' Nurse Colmes says to Matt as she excuses herself.

'Wouldn't have it any other way,' he calls after her. 'Ah, you're here. Great. Thought I was going to have to start feeding this one treats to distract her.'

'Hey! Cheeky.' I look up at him with a put-on pout and then crane my neck round to see who he's talking to. 'Sash? What are you doing here?'

'Hi, Lex.' Sasha walks round to face me and hugs me tightly. 'I left my job early so I'm here to help look after you.'

I automatically grimace at this turn of phrase.

'Sorry, I'm here to hang out with you while you recover,' she corrects herself and I catch Matt giving her an approving wink.

'How did you manage to leave your job early?'

'I had some holiday left over. Was going to have them pay me for it but then I realised I wouldn't have any kind of break or chance to do some proper flat-hunting before starting my new job. When this happened, it seemed the obvious thing to come and support— hang out with you at the same time.'

'Amazing. I'm so happy to see you. Have you got any viewings set up?'

'Yes, Sammy and I are going to see a couple of places over the weekend.'

'You're not moving in together already?'

'No, dafty,' Sasha giggles. 'He's just helping me find a place. He and Matt are also going to hire a van and bring my stuff down from Glasgow to save me the removal costs.'

I beam at Matt. 'That's fantastic. I can't believe you're here. So, you lot have been plotting behind my back then.'

'I'm not sure "plotting" is the right word.' Matt leans over and kisses me. 'We've definitely been up to nice things to make you happy. Right, Sash?'

'Right. Oh, you guys are *sooo* cute together. I'm so glad you're back together.' She suddenly looks all dewy-eyed and emotional.

'Stop it,' I command. 'No more crying. It's banned. I've done enough of that to sink a ship these last few days.'

'But they're happy tears.'

'Don't care. Now can we go? *Please.*'

A chuckling Matt obediently releases the brake on the wheelchair and we set off together. As we head towards the ward exit, I glance into the patient rooms, seeing one poor soul after the next, lying alone, some of them talking to themselves or crying out in frustration or distress, and all I can think is that I hope it's a really long time before I have to be back here again. And how lucky I am that after feeling so lost and alone just days before, I now have the most incredible boyfriend in the world and my best friend taking me home.

Chapter 34

After what feels like endless days cooped up in my apartment (although in reality, it's just two weeks), I'm back on my feet and almost at 'my normal' again. My first day back in the office is a cold, crisp Thursday morning in early December, so I get an additional boost from the twinkly Christmas lights peeking out from residential windows.

As I walk, I can't help smiling to myself. It's not just the freedom and returning sense of independence that's cheering me, I'm also so thankful for having Matt and Sasha in my life. They've rallied around me relentlessly over my recovery period, taking it in 'shifts', and they've been so discreet about it. Matt has played the role of human-sized hot water bottle perfectly, cuddling up to me and keeping me company on the evenings and weekends, while Sasha's been out viewing apartments and having her 'Sammy time'. Sasha has also whiled away the days with me, tempting me with chocolate, chatting dreamily about Sammy, and shouting at the TV during the more tense moments of the box sets we've enjoyed together.

Though I'm generally positive about my return to work, my stomach clenches anxiously as I enter Brindley Place and approach my office building. Despite Emmanuel's reassurances, I'm still feeling apprehensive. It's only been two weeks, but things have changed enormously now that my situation is out in the open. It's possibly not helping that it reminds me of when I went back to my old job in Glasgow.

Before walking inside, I take some slow, deep breaths to calm myself. I try to focus on nothing but my breath billowing out in clouds before me. I'm just going back to work. The office is full of the same great people I worked with before I went off.

When I eventually reach my desk, I'm surprised to find that none of my team are there. I hang my coat over the back of my chair and dump my bag on the floor, about to unpack my stuff, when I notice a yellow Post-it on my computer monitor. Scrawled on it in black ink is the message 'Alex, come straight to the boardroom when you get in'. I frown. Emmanuel didn't mention an early meeting. If I'd known, I'd have come in earlier. I hate turning up late.

Slinging my bag back over my shoulder, I head back down the corridor. However, as I reach the boardroom door, I realise there's no noise coming from inside. Usually when it's occupied, you can hear the murmur of voices. I give a quick knock and open the door, and as I do, there's an eruption from inside.

'WELCOME BACK.'

I almost drop dead from fright. Suddenly there's music and laughter and colour. And a big bright banner sporting the words 'Welcome Home' hanging across the whiteboard at an odd angle. My whole team is there – other than Danielle, I clock – and so are a handful of colleagues from other teams with whom I've developed strong working relationships. To say I'm overwhelmed is an understatement. I stand there open-mouthed as Emmanuel approaches and gives me a hug.

'Welcome back, Alex.'

'Did you arrange this?' I ask her.

'This is the work of the team. I had nothing to do with it. They asked if I thought it would be all right and I said I expected you'd be very touched.'

'I'm definitely touched. No, that's not enough. It makes my previous return to work seem like I had a highly contagious disease and was released from quarantine too early.'

'That's really not how it should be.' Emmanuel tuts. 'Well, hopefully this lot have made up for that.'

'They sure have.'

I greet my teammates individually, as they approach me one by one.

'Great to have you back, Alex.' Dhruv gives me a fist-bump, followed by a sequence of complicated 'handshake' movements I can't follow.

'You know I have coordination issues, right?' I decide it's best to just get things out in the open.

'Was a test.' He gives me a sneaky wink. 'Still not convinced you're not a spy. Reckon you've been off on some kind of secret mission.'

'Right, sure… by the way, Ethan Hunt said to say "hi".'

He looks baffled for a moment, then laughs loudly, extending his thumb and pointing his index finger at me in a you-just-about-had-me-there gesture.

'Nothing wrong with your wits then. Seriously, Alex, mate. So good to see you. Want you to know I've got your back anytime.'

'That's good to know.' I smile at him appreciatively.

'Alex, very good to have you back.' Felix moves forward as Dhruv turns to speak to Emmanuel. 'You have been missed, my friend.'

'Thanks Felix. It would seem so. Tell me, did someone recycle that banner from another event?' I chuckle, pointing towards the whiteboard.

'Why do you ask this?'

'Because it says "welcome home", not "welcome back".'

'I think it's intentional,' Emmanuel calls across, giving me a telling nod.

I look at the banner again and the full meaning of all this hits me. This isn't just any 'welcome back' party, it's a very pointed 'you-belong-here-so-don't-you-ever-think-otherwise-even-if-a-nasty-cow-tries-to-destroy-you' party. My teammates and colleagues have clocked my gaze and gone quiet, waiting for my response. I glance around at them and then a huge grin spreads across my face.

'Aww you guys… come here, all of you.'

Needing no prompting, they swoop in around me and I'm cocooned in my first ever workplace group hug. Just what I needed to settle back in. There's just one thing that's lingering in my mind though.

'Emmanuel, have you got a second?' I ask, once everyone has dispersed and are having their own conversations again.

'Sure, Alex. I think I know what you're going to ask. Let's pop outside.'

We leave the room and nip into an empty meeting room next door. Emmanuel closes the door behind us and turns to me.

'You want to know what happened with Danielle at the disciplinary meeting yesterday.'

'Yes.' I nod. 'This is all so lovely, but I need to be prepared for whatever is to come.'

'She's gone, Alex.'

I gasp in shock. 'She was fired?'

'Not exactly. Although I expect that might have been the outcome if someone else hadn't stepped in.'

'Her dad.'

'It would seem so. The case against her was strong. She was still denying she had anything to do with the WhatsApp message, and we couldn't prove she sent it. But her friend from HR admitted everything. Apparently, she had shared the information with Danielle in confidence after being put under pressure to do so – and she had not expected it to be broadcast the way it was. Once she saw it was out there, she knew she would be fired and said she wasn't going down alone. That information along with the text messages Danielle sent to you was enough for us to treat it as gross misconduct.'

'So what happened?'

'Two hours before the meeting, I received a message from the chief exec's office. Danielle had resigned with immediate effect, and the disciplinary hearing would not go ahead. Also – and I'm afraid this will bother you – Danielle's record was to be wiped of any trace of the pending hearing.'

'What?' I almost can't believe what I'm hearing. 'She doesn't deserve that at all.'

'No, she doesn't. But there's nothing I can do to change it.'

I shake my head at the injustice of it all. Danielle should have answered for what she did and now she gets to walk away unblemished.

'Keep one thought in your mind, Alex.'

'What's that?'

'Her dad won't always be around, or have the influence, to protect her. His friendship with the CEO worked in Danielle's favour and she burned that opportunity. She might not be as protected wherever she goes next.'

'That's true.' I suck in a deep therapeutic breath. 'OK, that's just how it is. The main thing is, she's gone. And so is her little sidekick. I now need to focus on all the wonderful colleagues I have next door.'

'You do.' Emmanuel smiles warmly. 'Shall we go back and join them?'

'Definitely.'

As we get up and leave the room, I switch off the lights and close the door firmly behind me, treating it as a symbolic moment. I'm shutting Danielle and all the trouble she caused inside and it's not coming out again... ever.

Chapter 35

Six weeks later

'Where are we going tonight? Come on, please tell me.' I playfully wrestle with Matt's hand while we're enjoying a Saturday morning lie-in together.

'Are you completely incapable of enjoying the mystery?' He affectionately traps my hand under his and I find myself stuck. 'It's a surprise.'

'I don't do mystery. I do plans. Perfectly executed plans.'

'Then you need to learn to live a little.'

Matt lets go of my hand and kisses my nose. I wrinkle it up to express my disapproval of his statement.

'How about I make you breakfast in bed?' he suggests. 'Then we can snuggle up and enjoy a box set marathon. Save our energy for tonight.'

'Why, what's going to take so much energy?'

'You are relentless, Lex.' Laughing, he untangles himself from me and gets out of bed.

'Some would argue it's one of my best features.'

'Your best feature can also be your worst.'

I stick my tongue out at him as he makes his way through to the kitchen.

'Yoghurt and granola? And a cup of tea?' he calls to me, moments later.

'Perfect. Will it just be you and me? Or are we meeting the others?'

His head appears round the door frame, exasperated grin plastered across his gorgeous face. 'Let it go. Or you'll be enjoying a solo box set marathon today.'

I make a show of huffing loudly. 'Fine.'

He disappears back into the kitchen and I lie back, losing myself in my thoughts. How lucky I've been that everything has fallen back into place. Work has been amazing. I've been treated with nothing but respect – by everyone. And Danielle no longer being there makes it so much better. Every workplace comes with its challenges, but now they're the kind of challenges I expect.

While I never thought I'd be comfortable with people knowing about my MS, it has actually made things easier. I no longer have to lug around my big sack of a secret. I share what I'm comfortable sharing. Make light of it when I bump myself on a table leg or my concentration dips. It's there, but it's not seen as a big deal. I've also carried on with the leadership programme after Emmanuel persuaded me to stick with it – but with no firm obligations in relation to career advancement. She knows how much I thrive on professional development.

Then there's Matt. Incredible, amazing, gorgeous Matt, who at this moment is conjuring up my breakfast and who I know will add a little something extra to it, because that's who he is. He cares for me and he spoils me. But he also challenges me. Dom would have tried, and he would have done so many things right. But ultimately, he wouldn't have been able to relinquish control and let me live my life the way I want and need to. He's a hands-on leader, and he's very good at it. But he's not right for me. He's also not Matt. Incredible, amazing, gorgeous Matt.

'Right, here you are, princess.' Matt appears at the door once again with a tray.

I prop myself up against my pillows, ready to receive it.

'Thank you, gorgeous man.' I look up at him adoringly as he hands me the tray then bends down and kisses me gently.

'Have I told you I love you, Alex Morton?'

I put on a thoughtful face as he nuzzles me with his beard. 'Not sure. Maybe I need to hear it again?'

'I love you,' he whispers in my ear.

I turn my grinning face towards his and kiss him again. 'I love you too. Thank you for being you.'

-

By six p.m., I'm sporting a black sparkly festive minidress, my hair tonged into bouncy ringlets, make-up super-glam to match my outfit.

'How do I look?' I do a little turn on the spot and Matt gives an appreciative whistle.

'Stunningly beautiful. How about me?' He does his own little pose, which makes him look silly, and I start to giggle.

'You're beautiful too.'

'Great. Now let's go or we'll be late.'

'Late for...'

'Would you just let it go? You only have another half an hour til you find out.' He ushers me out of the door and downstairs to a waiting taxi.

We drive through the street-lit roads of Birmingham until the taxi pulls up outside what looks like a huge nightclub.

'We're going clubbing?' I glance at Matt in confusion. 'Is it not a bit early? And why all the secrecy?'

'You'll find out.'

Matt pays the driver, then we step out of the taxi and make our way inside the building. It has some kind of information desk in the foyer, where Matt hands over some tickets and is handed a couple of lanyards in return.

'What are those for?' I ask.

'You'll find out,' he simply repeats, and I have no choice but to pad along quietly beside him.

We walk down a long brightly lit corridor until we reach a door with a security guy standing outside it.

'Hey, mate.' Matt greets him and dangles the lanyards in front of him.

The bouncer opens the door and gestures for us to enter. We then climb a short flight of steps, which I have to take at a slow pace, and find ourselves in a bustle of activity.

'What *is* this, Matt?'

I look around and spot Sasha locked in a passionate embrace with Sammy, as well as the rest of the band members. There are music-related items strewn everywhere: guitar cases, lyric folders, drumsticks, a microphone stand.

'It's a Capital Parade gig?'

'It sure is,' replies Matt. 'Really difficult to secure a gig at this venue apparently. Shows how well the band are doing. There's even backstage passes.' He waggles the lanyards in front of me and I grab one.

'So that's what these are. Fantastic. Gosh, this really is a grander place than the one I sang with the band at... but it still doesn't make sense. Why all the secrecy?'

We're interrupted as Sasha leaps on me with a huge hug and Sammy and the rest of the band gather around us.

'Lex, how amazing is this?' Sasha squeals.

'It's really amazing.'

'Alex, how you doing, mate?' Sammy hugs me, then turns to greet Matt with his usual blokey handshake-cum-hug. 'Have you asked her yet?'

'Has he asked me what? What's going on here?' I probe, then a thought pops into my oversensitised mind and I blurt it out before I can help myself. 'You're not going to *propose*, are you?'

My eyes are wide, unfortunately betraying the slightest hint of panic.

'Steady.' Matt lets out a chuckle, then narrows his eyes at me jokingly. 'Though it's good to know it would be so well received.'

'What? No. I mean, we're only—'

'I'd quit while you're only marginally behind, Alex.' Sammy pats me on the shoulder.

I feel myself redden, then I decide I can't take all the secrecy any more – especially if it's going to land me in trouble.

'OK, fine. But is someone going to tell me what's going on here?'

'Thought I'd leave it to you.' Matt raises an eyebrow at Sammy.

'I got this,' says Sammy, and to my utter befuddlement, he gets down on one knee in front of me. 'Alex, we've only known each other a few months, but I feel like what we have is really special and I can't imagine a future without you in it…'

He pauses dramatically and I glance around at the others, trying to figure out what the hell is going on. All I'm met with is a collection of stifled sniggers.

'Alex…' Sammy continues and my attention snaps back to him. 'We've all missed you so much. Will you be our lead vocalist again?'

I'm so baffled by this peculiar turn of events, I find myself speechless. After letting Sammy's words sink in, framed by an anticipatory silence from my onlookers, I kick into gear.

'I… err… Sammy, that was a lovely "proposal"—'

'For future reference, that's how it's done, mate.' He gives Matt a pointed wink, then focuses his attention back on me. 'I'm sensing a "but" here. Are you really going to reject me, here in front of all these people?'

I look around at the hopeful faces and I can hardly bear to let them down. 'Sammy, what are you doing to me? I'd love nothing more than to be singing with you guys again, but it's not that simple. I'm not reliable—'

'We can work around that.'

'More importantly, I need to look after my health and hold down a job. It's not just about my career, I need to be able to pay my bills too. I'm sorry, it's just not something I can do. I also can't face having to let you down all over again.'

'You don't know that that's going to happen, Lex.' Matt puts a supportive arm round my waist. 'You didn't have a relapse. You had the flu. Everyone gets winter bugs. It just hit you harder.'

'Matt, I love that you're encouraging this, but I just can't.'

Matt looks at Sammy, then at Sasha. 'Are we in agreement that it's time?' They both nod. 'All right. Bring out the secret weapon.'

337

'The secret what?' I'm beginning to think they've lost the plot. Then out from behind one of the changing room doors walks Emmanuel.

'What the...' I gasp. 'Emmanuel, what are you doing here?'

'Hi, Alex. Matt expected you'd have this reaction because of your job. So, I'm here to tell you that you can do this.' She seems quite pleased with her supporting role in this little charade.

'But—'

'No buts, Alex. You love singing with the band, right?'

'I do, but—'

'What did I just say?' She smiles at me. 'When something like that makes you so happy, it's good for your health, not the opposite. Work is important, but so is having a life and living your dreams. It's even more important for you to be able to do that now. You have my full support for this. And if you decide you need to improve the balance in your life, we could talk about reducing your hours. But only if that's something that would work for you.'

'I've never thought about doing something like that.'

'Well, it's open to you if you want to explore it. There are plenty of people with challenging, successful careers who don't work full time.'

I take a moment to think about what Emmanuel's just said. Between this, and Sammy and the band being happy to work around my illness, I have no reason to say no any more.

'OK, I guess I'm in.'

There's a collective whooping cheer.

'So, I'll see you at rehearsals next week to get started again?'

'Actually, we were kind of hoping you would sing with us tonight,' Sammy replies.

'Tonight?'

'Just a few songs you know well. So we can reintroduce you. We've got an hour to practise and warm up before the gig.'

I look from Matt to Sasha, then Emmanuel, and they're all grinning at me encouragingly.

'OK, sure?'

There's another whooping cheer.

'I'm so glad you're going to do it.' Sasha leaps on me with another huge hug.

'Well done,' says Emmanuel. 'Always remember, you have my full support.'

'Thanks, Emmanuel. That means so much,' I reply, then turn to Matt as the others disperse, nervous knots already forming in my stomach, but in a good way. 'I'd better go and rehearse then.'

He slips his arms round my waist and pulls me towards him, planting a sensual kiss on my lips. 'You go. I'll be in the crowd with Sasha and Emmanuel, cheering you on.'

'Make sure I can see you. I'll need your support.'

'You can count on that. Actually, before I go, is it really such a scary thought, me proposing to you?'

'What? No. It's not. It's a wonderful thought that you might do that one day. Not sure I'd want it to be in front of a raft of people though.'

'All right then. Noted.' He plants another kiss on my lips and then heads off to join Sasha and Emmanuel at the bar.

Chapter 36

Just after 8:30 p.m., the curtain lifts and the band springs into action with its signature gig opener. A sea of concert-goers cheer loudly, bouncing on the spot, singing along to the music; a much bigger crowd than the one at the gig I did previously, and just as lively. Sammy takes the lead with the vocals as I wait just out of sight for the reintroduction he's insisting on. It feels a bit odd to be reintroduced when I'd only managed one gig before – he'd be as well introducing me as a brand-new band member – but he wasn't having any of it. I sing along to the music, flexing my nicely warmed-up voice, trying out some new vocal effects while no one can hear me.

As the song comes to an end, I brace myself, nerves jangling – but not to the level of the first time I walked on stage. That was such an amazing and exhilarating experience, it seems to have made a sizeable – and more importantly, lasting – dent in my stage fright.

'GOOD EVENING, BIRMINGHAM,' Sammy hollers into the microphone.

There's a collective roaring cheer from the crowd.

'I said, GOOD EVENING, BIRMINGHAM,' he shouts again, louder this time.

The crowd match his volume increase.

'It's fantastic to see you all here tonight. Before we get going properly, I'd like to reintroduce our newest band member. She's had to take some time away due to illness, but she's back and she's ready to rock your night. She's an inspiration – please give a massive cheer for… *Alex*.'

At Sammy's cue, I walk out onto the stage smiling and waving to the cheering crowd. It's an odd and uncomfortable experience being the centre of attention, quite different to the previous gig. That time, Sammy didn't introduce me, or any of the other band members. I can see he's lifting it up a level, to give us that professional sheen. As he proceeds to give each of other band members a mention, I focus on steadying my nerves, making sure I'm breathing deeply, right into my abdomen.

Then before I know it, we've launched into the second song of the night (another one of the band's own) with me at the helm. It feels electric. As I belt out the lyrics, my nerves melt away like ice thrown into a fire. Becoming lost in the rhythm and the beat from the drums, it's like I've never been away.

I immediately know I've done the right thing rejoining the band. Emmanuel is right. This kind of happiness can only be good for me – the world's healthiest drug. With my nerves fully in check, I begin to scan the audience, making eye contact here and there, smiling and connecting with our fan base.

Doing so, I spot familiar faces – lots of them. My gaze lands firstly on Matt, Sasha and Emmanuel in the front row, dancing around like idiots. Just near them, I spot my team members from work. My eyes lock with Dhruv's. He's bouncing on the spot, grinning and mouthing 'You are insane'. But the biggest shock of all comes when I spot my mother, my sister and John on the far right-hand side. I'm so astonished, I miss a beat and turn to Sammy with an apologetic look. He simply grins back at me, shaking his head in a gesture of 'forget it'. It's clear he's perfectly aware why I've faltered.

As I continue to sing my heart out, I look back towards my family. It's like I've entered some kind of parallel universe. How on earth did they end up here? Carol's doing a good enough job of trying to fit in, and John's clearly enjoying the music, dancing like an embarrassing dad. But my mother looks like she's been brought here with a gun to her back. Her stuffiness gives her the air of a French poodle living among a family of warthogs. Only the crazy mix of feelings I'm experiencing from having spotted the two of them – stunned surprise, delight and a touch of resentment – stops me from bursting into fits of laughter right there on the stage. As I watch them, Carol looks up and gives me an uncertain wave, then nudges my mother, who herself gives an awkward nod, and was that just the hint of a smile?

We continue with a mix of original tracks and covers back to back until Sammy gives me a nod that he's going to say something at the end of the current song. Once I've wrapped up the final lines of 'Sex on Fire', I step back from the microphone to give Sammy centre stage. He stands there, arms stretched high in the air, as the crowd goes wild with applause.

'Isn't she incredible?' he calls into the mic, and raucous cheering reverberates round the auditorium. 'Oh yeah, she's incredible. What Alex doesn't know is that her final track of tonight is one that she herself wrote. It's a bit different to our usual stuff, but we're sure you're going to love it. It's called "Take a Moment" and Alex was inspired to write it when she was battling with her own illness.'

A loud supportive cheer bursts from the crowd as bubbling nerves erupt in my stomach. What's Sammy doing? We haven't even rehearsed it, other than that one night when we sang together in the bar after my first gig – but that doesn't count. Does he even remember how it goes?

'Alex, you're up.' Sammy gives me a little wink as he leaves the mic.

'You sneaky shit,' I say through gritted teeth as I pass him. 'I'd never have agreed to this if you'd mentioned it earlier.'

'Why'd you think I didn't mention it?' He raises an eyebrow and resumes his lead guitarist position. 'We'll follow your lead. You know this well enough. You were seamless when you sang it with me before.'

'You'd better hope so.'

Taking a few calming breaths, I brace myself once again, tapping my feet to the intro of my song, which is actually amazing to hear brought to life properly. Then, like it's automatic, I'm singing the opening verse, my voice filled with energy and emotion as I connect with the words I wrote so passionately all those months ago.

We grow up unassuming, we grow up unaware
We live in a world where too many people, they don't care
Take a look around you, tell me what you see
Illness, conflict, suffering, too much poverty...

The crowd love it. Despite the fact they don't know the song, they dance, cheer and clap along with gusto all the way through. The atmosphere is completely electric. Then during the final chorus, something amazing happens: they've picked up the words and they start to sing along, forming sporadic lines with their arms round

343

each other's shoulders. A gesture of support and solidarity – with each other, and with me – and it's clear they've connected with the message within the song. It's so moving, my voice cracks at a crucial point, but all it creates in response is a huge encouraging cheer. As I move into the climax, it's a feeling I've never felt before and I drink it in, unable to get enough.

> Then stop, take a moment to reflect, make sure you have it noted
> You've made a selfless gesture in a world where self-indulgence is promoted…

As I sing out the repeating chorus, they're all with me: Matt, Sasha, Emmanuel, Dhruv, Felix, the whole team. I sneak a glance across at my sister and my mother, and I'm shocked and delighted to see them dancing, arms round each other's shoulders – and my mother actually looks proud of me. It's the perfect end to a perfect gig. As the song wraps up, the stamping applause feels like it might actually bring the roof down. Then someone's bra flies onto the stage and lands at my feet. Stunned, I pick it up and say into the microphone: 'I'm sorry, I've got a boyfriend,' and the whole places falls about laughing.

–

A short time later the gig ends, with a roof-raising, crashing finale, and when the curtain comes down and the lights come on, the band starts to pack up. I step onto the stage and tap Sammy on the shoulder.

'I want a word with you.'

He turns with a grin. 'Alex, what a performance! "Take a Moment" was spot on, the crowd loved it. Thinking we should make it a regular part of our set.'

'Never mind that. What was that all about, tricking me into singing it? I thought you were going to ease me back into things.'

'Mate, you don't need that kid gloves stuff. You rocked it good and proper.'

'What if I hadn't? I'd have cocked up the whole night for you.'

He shrugs. 'Knew you'd nail it. No question.'

My lips curl up at the edges. 'I kind of did, didn't I? OK, you're forgiven. It was actually the most uplifting moment of my life, hearing it brought to life, getting to share it with all those people. But how? We only sang it that one time in the bar.'

'Suggest you direct that question to Sasha.' He gives me a cheeky wink and then resumes packing away his guitar.

After a quick refresh in the changing rooms, I head to the venue's VIP bar with the other band members. It's a small room with a minuscule bar, but it's nice and cosy.

Sasha, as usual, is first to throw herself on me. 'Lex, you were *amazing*.'

'It was OK then?' I grin at her.

'It wasn't OK. It was phenomenal!'

'Wow, that's the highest of praise.'

'And well deserved.' Matt approaches and wraps his arms round me proudly.

I sigh with pleasure, adrenaline and joy coursing through my veins at how stupendous this night has been. 'Sash, I have a question I've been told you can answer.'

'Uh-oh. Think I know what this is.' She chews her lip guiltily.

'You sure do. So?'

'The night you and Sammy started singing the song in the bar… I might have secretly recorded it on my phone. I wanted to have something to remind us of how great that moment was.'

I chuckle, giving her a playful nudge. 'I suppose that means I have you to thank for the fact I just got to sing it on stage.'

'Not entirely. I was one of the plotters but the whole thing was Matt's idea.'

'That doesn't surprise me for one second. He's so incredible.' I turn and give him cow eyes, which he responds to by dropping a light kiss on my lips. 'Where's Emmanuel?' I ask, looking round the room as we rejoin the others.

'She went to the next bar with your workmates,' replies Matt. 'We'll join them in a bit. She wanted you to have this moment with the people you're closest to.'

'What? She's one of those people. She can't not be now she's helped me use a bedpan.'

The others laugh and I glance across at my mother, sister and John. They're standing in a corner, looking a bit awkward.

'Sash, are you responsible for those three turning up tonight?'

'Nope.' She signals towards Matt with her eyes.

'It was you?' My wide eyes land on Matt. 'But how?'

'He gave them a bollocking when we were up in Glasgow moving my stuff down.' Sasha looks gleeful. 'Made me give him your mum's address, then just rocked up and gave it to them straight. It was magnificent.'

'You did?'

Matt shifts slightly in his stance. 'I'd say Sasha's added some content for dramatic purposes. But yeah, I went and had a word. Couldn't accept the way they had treated you and I told them as much. They do want you in their lives, Lex, they just wanted it on their terms and I made sure they were clear that would never happen. They were difficult at first but they came round.'

'Turns out the coven are actually human after all,' Sasha giggles.

I'm so shocked, I can barely take this in. 'Matt, oh my goodness. I can't believe you did that for me.'

He shrugs. 'I care about you. It needed sorting so I sorted it. But to be clear, I won't be fighting all your battles for you.'

'That's good to know.' I smile, appreciating once more what a good match the two of us are.

'Shall we go and say hi?'

'OK, sure, but just give me a second to message Emmanuel.'

I pull out my phone and tap out a quick WhatsApp message.

> You should be here. You're as big and important a part of my life now as everyone else. Not just my boss. Such a great friend. xx

I see that she reads it straight away and starts typing, so I wait until her message comes through.

I'm honoured that you see me that way. I see you as a great friend too, Alex. Just thought I should stay with the team and make sure they don't get lost. It's like herding cats as you well know. See you shortly. x

I chuckle at her message. I do indeed know what the team can be like. But thankfully it's a bit easier now, sans Danielle. I quickly reply that we won't be long, then turn to Matt.

'Ready?'

'Let's do it.'

Hand in hand, we make our way across to my mother, sister and John.

'Hi, how are you all?' I greet them.

'Hello, love. It's great to see you.' John immediately steps forward and pulls me into a hug that suggests he's really missed me, making me realise how much I've missed him too. 'That was an incredible performance before.'

'Thanks, John. It's great to see you too.'

'This place is sweet, Alex,' remarks Carol, in place of a greeting. 'You've landed on your feet.' She eyes Matt approvingly.

'Hello, Alex.' My mother's voice is more timid than usual, perhaps in fear that she'll get another going-over from Matt. 'That was quite a performance earlier.'

'Did you enjoy it?'

'It's not my kind of music, but you did very well.'

'Gosh, Mother, that's quite the compliment coming from you.'

She purses her lips awkwardly. 'Yes, well. Your Matt has helped me realise that I haven't been as supportive as I could have been.'

That's the understatement of the century, but I decide not to vocalise this observation. I'm actually really pleased to see the two of them, despite the way they've frozen me out all this time. I also don't want to make things uncomfortable for Matt.

'Well, you're here now, that's all that matters.'

I step forward and give them both a heartfelt squeezy hug, which I note is enthusiastically reciprocated. So much so that it creates a swell of emotion inside me and my eyes start to sting. I clear my throat to get myself under control.

'Would you like a drink? A glass of champagne, perhaps?'

'Oh lovely, yes, please,' my mother and Carol reply in robotic unison.

'Great, back in a few moments. Then we can have a proper catch-up. Matt, give me a hand?'

'Of course,' he replies, and we turn and walk to the bar together, talking in hushed tones.

'I honestly can't believe you did that, Matt. And you were also the ringleader in getting all this organised tonight. I really have bagged myself the best bloke in Birmingham. No contest.'

'Just in Birmingham?'

'You know what, you're right. I don't think there's a single man on this planet as incredible as you.'

'Perhaps a step too far?'

'Maybe, but as far as I'm concerned, you're a superhero. My very own Wonderbrummie.'

Matt laughs and puts his arm round me as we wait to be served, then leans over and murmurs in my ear. 'If that's the case, I have a proposition for you. We might not be at the proposal stage yet, but how do you feel about moving in together?'

A huge grin spreads across my face. 'I think that sounds amazing.'

'Think you've just made me the happiest guy in the West Midlands.'

He gives me a delicious, lingering celebratory kiss, which is eventually interrupted by the barman asking if we want drinks. As Matt relays our order, I gaze up at him, unable to believe the turnaround in my life. Just months ago, it felt like it was over. It seemed inconceivable that I could have any kind of fulfilling life, never mind a great career, a lead vocalist spot in a semi-pro band, and an unbelievably amazing boyfriend. Now, even though I know there will be tough times ahead, I also know that with Matt, Sasha, my family and all my new friends by my side – cheering me on, not propping me up – I have plenty more adventures to look forward to.

One more thing before you go...

Take A Moment is a work of fiction. It's also a story close to my heart, because the inspiration for it came from my own life-changing illness.

In 2014, my body failed me in incomprehensible ways: I experienced extended episodes of uncontrollable shaking and tremors, difficulty walking, loss of balance, faltering speech. My vision and hearing were distorted; I lost my ability to concentrate, couldn't find words, could barely eat and I would fall flat on my face several times a day. That was only part of the picture.

After several months, a Neurology Consultant eventually diagnosed me with a condition called Functional Neurological Disorder (FND). Simply put, my nervous system isn't working properly and there's a problem with the messaging between my brain and my body. FND can range from very mild (e.g. weakness in one leg) to severe, with multiple physical, cognitive and sensory symptoms (unfortunately the version I have).

The good news is that it isn't a degenerative condition, though it can be as physically debilitating and life limiting as MS and other neurological diseases. The bad news is that it's a condition for which there is no known cure, and that requires much more research. Some sufferers get better and others don't. Some end up in wheelchairs, on incapacity benefits, unable to work or have any quality of life.

I'm in the middle. I've managed to rehabilitate enough to have a reasonable (but somewhat limited) quality of life, but every day I'm battling varying levels of chronic pain, fatigue, breathlessness and an overreactive central nervous system, among other symptoms. There are still days when I can have difficulty walking or with my balance, but thankfully these are much less frequent.

Despite all this, and with incredible support from the people who love me, I've managed to come through this real-life nightmare fairly unscathed mentally and emotionally. And I've found a positive: my passion for novel writing. I actually started writing my first novel (very slowly!) as part of my rehabilitation, to get my cognitive and physical functions working again. So, as far as I'm concerned, I've been lucky. But I can see how, without the right support networks, it would be easy for someone with a chronic illness to become isolated, unemployed, and if things got really bad, homeless.

When I started writing *Take A Moment*, I didn't intend to write a biography, but I did want to draw on my experience to raise awareness of neurological illness as well as tell a good story. I chose to write about a character with MS so that it wasn't too close and because many of the symptoms I experience overlap. It was important to me to get across what it feels like to have your life suddenly shattered, while at the same time keeping the story light and humorous enough that readers could easily engage with it.

Alex's song within the story – also named *Take a Moment* – is in fact a song I wrote, with help from a brilliant musician called Willie Glass, when I was a good way through my rehabilitation. It's a recognition of the struggles many people experience in life, while others live theirs as if on autopilot. It's a message to be kind, to care and to open our eyes to what's going on around us – and to make a difference where we can.

Since writing the song, it has been my goal to do something with it. As well as giving it a home within my novel, I've used my own money to get it recorded professionally, and the difference I would like to make is to raise some money through music streaming and downloads to support two very important charities: The MS Society and FND Hope.

During the process of receiving my diagnosis, I spent a short time on a neurology ward and I witnessed some of the saddest, most heart wrenching sights I've ever seen. It really is one of the cruellest types of illness a person can experience.

Take a Moment has now been released in the music charts worldwide and is available for download and streaming on all major music platforms. I'd hugely appreciate it if you'd consider downloading it and spreading the word.

You can find out more about my fundraising on my website, *ninakaye.co.uk*.

If you're interested in knowing more about MS and FND and the life-limiting impact they can have, you can read about them on the MS Society and FND Hope pages. www.mssociety.org.uk
https://fndhope.org web

Thank you for everything you do.

Yours
Nina Kaye x

Acknowledgements

Take A Moment is a story especially close to my heart: inspired by my own health challenges and my fight to regain my life after a sudden and debilitating illness with which I still live. These acknowledgements, therefore, go way beyond a thank you for support in writing this novel and getting it out into the world.

First up, my incredible husband, James. You are my Matt. Although we were already together when my health challenges reached a real low point, you never seemed to waver and you picked me up off the floor (both meta-phorically and literally) too many times for me to count. You were by my side every step of the way; you have also offered me steadfast support and encouragement with my writing – and even some brilliant ideas. Thank you.

To my family: my amazing mum and dad, brothers, sisters-in-law and my niece and nephew. You were a huge part of my recovery, and also cheered me on with my writing, so I thank you from the bottom of my heart. A special thanks to my dad as for being my 'unofficial editor' and to my mum and sister-in-law, Geraldine, for reading my early drafts.

A huge thank you to Kate Nash of the Kate Nash Literary Agency for continuing to be a fountain of know-ledge and support, and to Emily Bedford of Canelo for your fantastic editorial support. Also, to the whole team at Canelo for seeing the potential of *Take A Moment* and for doing such a brilliant job of getting it out there.

Then there are three very special ladies, whom I have never met in person, and who have been there with me (virtually) through all the ups and the downs of the last couple of years: Sandy Barker, Fiona Leitch and Andie Newton. I genuinely don't know what I'd do without you. Thank you for everything – and I mean everything!

Another important thank you goes to Karen McCurry BEM, Centre Manager at the Multiple Sclerosis Centre, Mid Argyll, who very kindly read *Take A Moment* and gave me feedback before it went on submission to publishers.

I also want to extend a heartfelt thank you to all my friends and colleagues who have cheered me on with my writing for several years now. You know who you are, and you are wonderful.

And finally, thank you to all the readers of my previous novel, and of *Take A Moment*, for giving a chance to a new writer; and for the lovely reviews that lift me up every single day.